MINDSPEAK

HEATHER SUNSERI

Sun Publishing
VERSAILLES, KENTUCKY

Heather Sunseri/Sun Publishing
PO Box 1264
Versailles, Kentucky 40383
www.heathersunseri.com

Book Layout ©2013 BookDesignTemplates.com

Cover design by Mike Sunseri

Ordering Information:
Quantity sales. Special discounts are available on quantity purchases by corporations, associations, and others. For details, contact the "Special Sales Department" at the address above.

MINDSPEAK/ Heather Sunseri. -- 1st ed.
ISBN 978-0-9887153-3-2

For my mom.
For always believing in me.
For encouraging me to explore the mysteries of life
through books
and by simply living.

ONE

I couldn't believe Coach had called a six a.m. practice. It was the first day of classes for crying out loud. Not to mention the start of my last year at Wellington.

And the last year of drowning in secrets—mine and everyone else's.

I pushed through the locker room door to the swimming pool that Friday. Cool water splattered against my ankles. After breathing in steam and chlorine, I stopped short.

Briana had an arm draped over Coach Williams' shoulder, studying the clipboard in his lap. With a flip of her curly red hair, she threw her head back and belted out a laugh that tangled the tiny hairs on the back of my neck.

My head throbbed too much for a run-in with my arch nemesis. I walked toward the pool and dunked my swim cap in the water.

When I turned back around, Briana was in my face. Well, her breasts were. She was a solid five-foot-ten, while I was more the size of a tall Olympic gymnast. I leaned away. "What do you want, Bree?"

"It's a shame you missed practice yesterday. I shaved more than a second off my fifty-free. If I'm not mistaken, that's good enough to beat you on your best day."

I smiled my best it-would-be-a-shame-if-you-sucked-in-too-much-water-during-practice smile. "Congratulations. I'm super sorry I missed that." To think Briana Howard and I were once friends was mind-boggling.

"Lexi, Briana. In the water. Now," Coach Williams yelled from his office.

"Okay, Coach," I said without removing my eyes from Briana. "You first, Bree." I gestured with my palm facing up toward the pool. I wasn't about to turn my back on the girl who'd practically jerked the ponytail out of my head over some boy last year.

"Gladly." She strutted over to the edge of the pool and completed a perfect swan dive into the middle lane.

I rolled my eyes and joined some sophomores three lanes over. Not nearly far enough away.

I stretched my swim cap over my head and tucked loose strands inside the folds. With my arms spread wide, I fell backwards. The water, cool and refreshing, enveloped me. The whooshing sound shut off all noise—the sounds outside my head anyway. I pushed off the wall and glided arms first.

My workout was the one hour of the day when I could think uninterrupted. For the next sixty or so minutes I would forget evil teen frenemies and dream of the day I would break free of high school. More importantly, the day I would walk away from Wellington Boarding School forever and into college bliss.

As I crawled through the water, I relished the thought of freedom—or the anonymity—that college would bring.

Escaping to a large university meant fleeing from the secrets that haunted me at Wellington. Secrets that, though different for each student, plagued many of the teens who attended the little-known boarding school. Secrets that begged extra security and a gated entrance. Secrets that made me realize that I never *really* knew the people I called my friends at this school. Secrets that had required me to change my name when I was twelve years old.

I hadn't been in the pool very long when a hand pushed softly on my head during a water break. I perched my goggles on top of my cap and looked up at Coach Williams. "What's up, Coach?"

"Dean Fisher needs you." He pointed over his shoulder with his thumb. "Some new kid is starting today. He wants you to play tour guide."

Straining my neck, I peered around Coach. Dean Fisher waved me out of the pool. A boy stood beside him, his back to me. Sandy hair in need of a trim flipped haphazardly above the neck of a black tee.

"Just great," I said under my breath. "Can't you get me out of it? I really need the practice." I couldn't let Bree get further ahead of me. Not to mention that showing some new boy around just wasn't my thing for too many reasons to name.

"Sorry, kid. You'll have to make up the practice later."

Coach Williams offered me a hand and lifted me from the pool with little effort. I tipped back a bottle of water as I padded over to the dean. His three-piece suit and salt-and-pepper hair screamed distinguished.

"Lexi, your stroke's looking strong. You ready for this week's meet?" Expectations were hidden behind the dean's smile.

"I'm trying to be, sir." It would help if I could get my practice in uninterrupted.

His expression faltered briefly before he turned slightly and reached a hand to his guest's elbow. "I want you to meet Jack.

He's joining us for his senior year. Jack, this is our star swimmer, Lexi Matthews."

I turned to the new guy, cringing a little at the title the dean gave me. I was far from a star. Besides, I resented the pressure.

Water dripped off the end of my nose as I once-overed Jack. He was dressed in blue jeans and a black concert T-shirt that did nothing to hide the well-defined muscles underneath.

I offered my hand and my best attempt at a smile. It wasn't his fault my practice had been cut short. "Nice to meet you."

His palm wrapped around my outstretched hand. My eyes drifted up to his, the color of the sky at twilight, in time to see him scan the length of my body. A shadow of darkness grazed over each inch, all the way to my toes. Though my swimsuit covered all the important parts, I was suddenly self-conscious with nowhere to hide as he studied me.

I pulled my hand from his grasp and slid the swim cap off my head, running my fingers through my long hair. I crossed my arms and forced my gaze toward the dean.

"Dean, I would love nothing more than to show Jack around, but I'm afraid I really need the practice today."

"I've already spoken to Mr. Sayre. He said you could have seventh period today to make up the practice. Besides," Dean's grin returned, "Jack is attending Wellington this fall while getting to know those of you hoping to join The Program."

A gasp escaped my mouth. "Sir?"

"Jack has already been a part of The Program for a year. I'm sure he can answer any questions you and the others might have."

Jack was part of The Program as a junior? That made less than zero sense. "I thought The Program was only for Wellington seniors, sir."

"Jack is part of the initial pilot program along with a few others."

"A few others?"

"Your questions will be answered soon enough, Lexi," Dean Fisher said. Discussion over.

I didn't understand the big secret. But that's Wellington. One big secret after another.

It didn't matter. I didn't care about The Program anyway. I already knew the lengths medical researchers went to in order to save one life to the detriment of another thanks to my infamous father. The Program was just another way for Wellington to take parents' money and teach children the controversial lengths doctors go to in order to cure terminal diseases and life-threatening injuries.

The dean and Wellington teachers assured students that acceptance to The Program practically guaranteed seniors acceptance to the pre-med program of their choice. I'd guarantee my acceptance to a top pre-med program another way.

"Why don't you grab a shower? Jack will meet you outside the girls' locker room." The dean started to walk away but turned back. "Oh, and you'll need to get to know Jack and introduce him at Thursday night's dinner."

A smiled played at the corners of Jack's lips. And the way his eyes bore into mine... The look was strange. Unnerving even.

The two men headed for the pool exit. A chill galloped down my spine. Get to know him? "Yes, sir," I said with a casual salute once the dean was out of earshot. I took a deep breath and squeezed the bridge of my nose, hoping to massage away the growing headache.

Dripping and breathing hard, Briana stepped beside me. "Who's the yummy new guy?" Her goggles dangled at her hip. "Please tell me they're not letting you introduce him to our school. You'll run him off just like the last person they allowed you to mentor."

Would I tell Briana that Jack was more than just a new student? Briana would be more than interested in the "yummy new guy" if she knew he was part of The Program. "You mean Anna? The eighth-grader who developed viral pneumonia and had to be hospitalized for six weeks?"

Briana shrugged. "I'm sure you were partly to blame for Anna never returning. You're toxic, Lexi. You'll scare this guy off, too."

She was probably right. I *would* scare this guy off. Most likely by choice.

~~~~

Jack sat on a bench between the sports center and the boy's dormitory. He straightened his legs out in front of him, his Chuck Taylored feet crossed at the ankles, and his arms stretched across the back of the bench. The sun glinted off his hair, the color of wheat just before harvest, and glimmered peacefully over his face.

I looked out across the school's front lawn. A perfect mid-September day in Midland, Kentucky. The leaves on the trees had begun to change a little—a mix of red and gold among
~~~~

mostly green. A good day to walk around campus and introduce fresh eyes to Wellington, I supposed.

I moved into the sun's line, shadowing Jack's face. "You were supposed to wait for me outside the locker room." I regretted my tone immediately.

He opened one eye, but otherwise remained where he was. "Did you have trouble finding me beyond the one door that separated us?"

Sarcasm. I guessed I deserved that. "So, I'm supposed to give you a tour. We should get started."

"Actually..." He bent over and reached for something at his feet. When he rose, he held two mugs from the school's coffee shop. "The nice man at Common Grounds said you appreciated a good Chai, and the dean said you would have questions for me. You know, for my big introduction into the school."

I raised an eyebrow, studying his expression. There was a smugness about him. Reaching for the drink he offered, I wrapped my fingers around the warm cup and lifted the opening to my nose. The sweet scent of Chai perked up my mood just a little. "Thanks. I guess I could sit for a moment."

Dropping my bag at my feet, I sat and balanced a notebook and pen on my lap while I reached into my satchel for my prescription pills. Realizing Jack was staring at me, I shrugged. "Headaches," I answered his silent question, although I wasn't sure why I owed him an explanation.

The smirk that had spread across Jack's face faded. He nodded. "We can do this later."

"No, it's fine." Since "never" was not an option. I lifted my pen, poised to take notes. "So, doctor, I guess?"

Jack choked on his drink. "Excuse me?"

"You're planning to be a doctor, right? Most students are on a professional track of some sort at this school. Mostly by their parents' choice. Since you're already part of The Program, I assume you're on track to become a doctor."

He narrowed his gaze. "I guess. Yeah."

Figures. "Music or visual arts?" Everyone at this school was required to be well-rounded. Academically, athletically, artistically. I enjoyed the visual arts, myself.

"Music?" A grin reached all the way to his eyes this time, and my belly did a little somersault.

I sucked in a deep breath, letting it out slowly, as I struggled with what questions I could possibly ask. This was an impossible task. I was forbidden by Wellington's honor code to pose the questions I wanted. Wellington had a "don't ask, don't tell" policy in order to keep the students of this fine institution safe from outside harm. Nevertheless, I always found myself wanting to know a person's story. Their real story—why they needed Wellington's security, what their greatest fears were, their greatest secrets, what they *really* wanted to be when they grew up and if it matched what their parents wanted for them. "What instrument?"

"Um... Any of them?"

I set my pen down. Jack stared straight ahead, distant, like his mind had wandered. "Any of them?"

After a couple of beats, his eyes found mine again. "Yeah. Guitar, piano, fiddle, harmonica, and some others."

"Harmonica?" I couldn't suppress a smile of my own.

"You're avoiding the questions you really want to ask." He angled his body toward me, his knee brushed against mine.

"Do the students here really not know anything about each other?"

I shrugged. "Some stories surface." Many do, actually. "Some are hard to keep hidden when parents make the news. The son of a famous actor gets photographed while home on Christmas break. A senator is exposed due to some scandal. Rumors fly on a regular basis."

That was putting it nicely. Wellington students snooped constantly. I thought about the day Briana and Kyle saw me eating breakfast with my father at a restaurant in Lexington. One of them recognized him from a recent news article and knew he was in town for some symposium. One meeting with the dean later, Briana and Kyle were sworn to secrecy.

Mostly secrets were kept due to the obscene amount of wealth in a family. Except in my case. My identity was kept secret because of the highly confidential medical research my dad was involved in.

Darkness swarmed in Jack's eyes. "Do you trust your classmates?"

I squirmed uncomfortably. Goosebumps danced down my arms, and I reached to rub them. "I guess." However, *this* guy was starting to give me the creeps.

"Aren't you curious to know who the people around you are?"

Yeah, like right now. Why was he asking these questions? I was sure the dean had told him the rules.

"Or worse, are you ever scared the wrong classmate will find out who *you* really are, who your father is, and what he does for a living? Put your life in danger?"

I jumped to my feet. Blood rushed to my head, throwing me off balance. A throbbing pain pulsated behind my eyeball. "Maybe we *can* do this later?" I rubbed my temple. "After I get rid of this headache." I tried to cover my sudden unease.

Jack stood, his brows squeezed together. "You okay?"

"I'll be fine. Like I said, just a headache." *And you're freaking me out.*

He studied me a moment before he reached his fingers to my temple and brushed them from one side of my head to the other. The gentleness of his touch temporarily distracted me from the creepiness of the moment. The muscles in my legs tightened. I couldn't move.

A cooling sensation spread from the top of my head, across my temple and behind my eyes. Then the pain subsided.

He slowly retracted his hand, dropping it to his side. His eyes never left mine.

Then I asked the forbidden questions. "Why are you at Wellington, Jack? Who are you, really?"

He shrugged. "I'm just Jack. And I was curious."

"Curious? Curious people go to the zoo or the FBI museum, not a high-security boarding school for over-intelligent teenagers."

"Yeah, but I wasn't curious about panda bears or gorillas, I was curious about *you*."

TWO

"You should have seen him. He was so... so..." I stopped pacing and faced Danielle Gray, whose head was upside down in the downward facing dog pose. Her blond ponytail grazed the floor. "Are you even listening to me?"

My roommate and keeper of my darkest secrets dropped to her knees and placed her hands together as if in prayer. Dressed in black yoga pants and a fitted red paisley tank, she took in a deep cleansing breath and let it out slowly. Finally, her eyes popped open revealing her light brown eyes. "Yes, of course I'm listening. He was so... what?"

I gave my head a little shake. "How can you do yoga at a time like this?" I sat on my bed and put my head between my knees. Breathed in... and out...

"Time like what? A time when one of our imaginations is doing double time. Seems to me you could use a little Anjali Mudra." She closed her eyes again. "So? He was so... what?"

"He was so... mysterious," I said, my voice muffled between my legs.

"He sounds hot."

I raised my head. I remembered the coolness of his fingers and how my head stopped aching at his touch. The deep blue color of his eyes. "He was not hot, Dani," I lied, my voice rising, because she was so missing the point. "He was weird... strange... creepy. I think he knows who I am. Worse than that, I think he knows who my father is."

Danielle shook her head. "No way. That's not possible." A wrinkle formed between her eyes. For the first time, concern registered. "What are you going to do? You need to talk to the dean. Get him reassigned. Let someone else show him around."

"On what grounds? Besides, I have to find out what he knows." I stood and began pacing the room again. "And why he's here. He's already part of The Program. Which is weird."

"You mean that new class or whatever for you geeky medical types?" I nodded. "Are you going to tell your dad?"

"And risk being moved to a different school? Not sure yet." I walked to my closet. "Speaking of my dad, I almost forgot. He's in town." I pulled several dresses out, and with the wave of a dramatic hand said, "My father, the renowned Peter Roslin, is speaking at some fancy dinner."

"And you're going?"

I nodded. "Skyped with him earlier. He didn't want me to come, but I argued that only stuffy doctors would be at this dinner. No one who is out to kidnap me for his money or for his top secret medical advancements," I laughed.

"What are you going to do about Mr. Enigmatic?"

I wiggled a couple of dresses in front of Danielle. "I'm going to throw one of these dresses on and go find him before I leave for dinner." Keep your enemies close and all that. "Which one?"

~~~~

Jack was nowhere to be found. He had simply disappeared after only one day of school. It was strange that classes started on a Friday, but it gave students, especially the new ones, a
~~~~

chance to get settled into the dorm before everything kicked into high gear on Monday.

Maybe it was good I didn't find him. Instead I could talk to Dad and see if he thought the new guy's behavior was strange.

Or not. Because if he thought the behavior was risky, he'd move me.

I stared at Dad now, delivering his keynote address to the Association of International Physicians and Research.

All eyes focused on him. All except those belonging to the two men in suits—bodyguards, I guessed—on either side of the stage, protecting him.

Seemed like overkill to me, but what did I know? As long as they didn't keep me from speaking with him after his speech.

The topic of stem cell research and reproductive cloning was morally divisive, but dad had delivered it brilliantly. He had always kept me sheltered from his work. For good reason. He knew I hated the thought of him playing around with human life.

"Embryonic cloning is not out of the realm of possibilities any longer," he said in his speech. "You could already know someone who has benefited from the advances in medicine from stem cell research." While Dad acknowledged the ethical concerns of human cloning, he touted the benefits that the technology would add to the treatment of many fatal and debilitating illnesses. Or the growing of organs for transplants. And advances would continue to be made by the medical community despite critics' best efforts to stall them.

I had my questions and doubts. As did the critics, whose buzzing now spread throughout the room like an out-of-control forest fire.

"There's no way he's doing this research in the U.S., is there?" a man one table over asked his neighbor.

"I heard he's on the verge of cures for some pretty serious diseases, like cancer and Alzheimer's," said another.

Dad backed away from the podium and waved to the banquet hall full of doctors and other brilliant people. The speech was over. Finally, he and I could have that talk he promised when he called yesterday—after I begged him to let me come.

Some of the crowd stood in ovation after the controversial address. The media flashed their cameras and started moving in on the guest of honor.

Which meant it would take eons for him to weave through the crowd and make his way to me. A picture of distinction on the outside—designer suit, crisp white shirt with monogrammed cuff links, no doubt—he stepped down from the stage. He shook the hands of surgeons, patted the backs of pediatricians, and threw quick waves to every gastroenterologist. Politicians could learn something from Dad's gladhanding prowess.

"There you are," Dad said when he spotted me. He grabbed my elbow, and pulling me close, he leaned in and kissed my cheek. The squeeze on my arm didn't hurt, but the tightness of it made me wonder if he had taken his blood pressure medicine. That and his reddened face. He raised a finger to someone to our side, indicating he needed a minute. The bodyguards stood just beyond the crowd around us.

"This was a mistake." He glanced over my shoulder again. "I shouldn't have had you come tonight."

I drew my head back. "Why, Dad? I wanted to see you. I never get to see you."

"I know, honey." He leaned in again and kissed my forehead. "You know I love you, right?"

"Of course." I searched his face. Despite the time we spent apart, we had an unexplainable father-daughter connection.

He smiled at me now, but his eyes continued to dart over my shoulder. "You also know that there are always people in this world who disagree with the research I'm doing."

I nodded. Like me at times. "But you're making a difference, Dad. I know it."

His face relaxed, the lines smoothing out. "Now, how's the application for The Program coming?"

I sighed. "Fine." When he cocked his head, I continued. "I'll get it done." I squeezed my eyes shut, attempting to hide the guilt hidden there. How could I tell him that I didn't want to learn more about all the controversial things he did with human life to advance science and medicine?

"See that you do." His fingers tightened around my arm and he leaned closer to speak directly in my ear. "Now, Sweetie, I need to know what you did with the furniture and personal items that were in our house."

My heartbeat picked up at the urgency of his voice. His mood had completely transformed into something I didn't recognize. "I had everything moved when the original storage place closed, remember? Why? Is something wrong?" My eyes drifted from his severe look to the death grip he had on my elbow.

"I'm sorry." He loosened his hold. His gaze surveyed the crowd before it came back to me. "Can you write down the address for me?"

"I don't know it by heart. I'll have to look it up when I'm back at school. I'll email it to you tomorrow. Why? What are you looking for?"

His face relaxed again. He waved to someone over my shoulder. "Just some old journals. No big deal."

Sure didn't seem like 'no big deal.' Dad dropped his hand to his side, and I rubbed the spot on my arm. People hovered all around us waiting to speak to the guest of honor while the bodyguards lingered close.

Unable to hold the people off any longer, Dad shifted and reached a hand to someone behind me. "Lexi, you know Roger Wellington and his wife, Brenda?"

I turned to find Dad shaking Dr. Wellington's hand. His wife, dressed head-to-toe in Chanel, linked an arm with her husband. The fumes from her perfume reached all the way to the back of my throat. "Of course," I said as I shook hands with the President and founder of Wellington Boarding School. His wife gave me her fingers in the daintiest of shakes.

I made idle chit-chat with the Wellingtons, nodding in all the appropriate places before Dad took over the conversation. His demeanor was light and airy, not like his tone when he'd cut off my blood supply while asking about some junk in storage.

I ran my tongue over my parched lips and turned my head in search of a server who could locate a glass of water or a Diet Coke. From my left, a bald man approached in a slow, purposeful walk. His hands were balled into fists. His eyes were singularly focused on Dad with a look that made me want to hide behind the nearest table.

Dad threw his head back and laughed loudly at something Mrs. Wellington said, oblivious to the man stalking him like a lion about to pounce on prey.

The man stared. Inched closer. Then looked at me. I pushed calm, tranquil thoughts at him. His face softened slightly. Unfortunately, it wouldn't do any good. This man's anger was beyond anything I could calm with my mind. I could feel it.

I took a step closer to Dad.

Just as I reached to grab his elbow, the old man clocked him right in the jaw.

Dad stumbled backward against a server carrying a tray of champagne flutes and then fell to the ground, taking the cocktail server with him.

The bubbly and shattered glass showered him, and the who's who of the Kentucky medical community rushed to help him stand. Three men, including one of the bodyguards who was *supposed* to be protecting him, grabbed his arms and supported his back as they pushed him to his feet. Dad was a large man—six-foot-three, probably two-hundred-fifty pounds. A heart attack waiting to happen, something I had talked to him about over and over.

I jerked my head from Dad to the man with the exceptional left hook. A good-looking man, even with the shaved head. One of the bodyguards had his arms behind his back. Only then did I notice the boy in a black suit beside him with a hand on the boxer's arm. *Jack.*

That explained why I couldn't find him before I left for the dinner.

"Father, was that necessary?" he asked.

Father? Who the hell are you?

Jack's eyes snapped toward mine as if I had spoken my thoughts.

A bodyguard stepped forward. "Dr. Roslin?"

Focusing back on the situation in front of me, I sent out thoughts to the people fussing over my dad to back away. *He's fine. Let him be. Everyone just back away.* I turned my attention back to Dad.

"It's okay." Dad pulled his arm away from the men who brushed beads of champagne from his sleeves. He tugged at the cuffs of his jacket. "I'm fine."

"Dr. Roslin? Would you like for us to remove this gentleman?" the bodyguard asked.

Dad shook his head. "No. That won't be necessary."

Not necessary? Why wasn't he firing those two loser-bodyguards?

I continued to direct my calming thoughts to the many people standing around gawking. *Go on. Go back to your conversations. Drink and be merry.* The crowd dispersed and the party resumed.

"Dad?"

Ignoring me, he reached a hand to his chin and moved his jaw back and forth. "It's nice to see you, John. How long's it been?"

Mrs. Wellington approached me from the side and handed me a cloth napkin. She leaned in and whispered in my ear, "Sweetie, your nose is bleeding."

I gasped. "Oh. Thank you." I took the napkin and blotted at my nose. I should never have tried controlling the thoughts of people around me without tissues handy. *How embarrassing.* To top it off, Jack's probing gaze studied every move I made. *Just perfect.*

The boxer, John, appeared to be calming. "Apparently," he started and shot a quick glance at me, "it's been about sixteen years, Peter."

Sensing that the nosebleed wasn't too bad, I wadded the napkin in my left hand and offered Rocky my other. "Lexi Matthews. Seventeen-years-old, actually. Would you like to tell me why you hit my dad in the middle of this...?" I swirled my hand in the air. "This... party?"

The corners of his lips lifted, a smile that mirrored that of his son's next to him. "John DeWeese," he said. His warm hand enclosed mine and held on a little longer than I was comfortable. "And, well, your dad had that coming." He chuckled.

"John DeWeese," I said, furrowing my brows. "The goat-cloning guy?" Dad's oldest and dearest friend and long-ago lab partner.

"The one and only," Dad responded, still massaging his jaw. "And you must be John, Jr."

Jack stepped forward and shook Dad's hand. "It's Jack, actually." He turned to me and picked up my hand. Shook it. Or held it. I wasn't sure what he did, but I lost time when he touched me and flashed a paralyzing grin in my direction. "It's nice to see you, Lexi," he said as if he hadn't met me just hours before. His smile was so condescending I wanted to scream.

I pulled my hand away and folded both arms across my chest. "So, Dr. DeWeese... It is doctor, isn't it?"

The older DeWeese nodded. Light gleamed from his perfectly bald head.

"Is this how you greet all of your long lost friends? Punch them in the face?"

"Lexi," Dad said, chastising in tone.

"It's okay, Peter. It's a fair question. Like I said—"

"He had it coming," I finished for him. "Right."

"Peter, I think we need to find a place to talk," Dr. DeWeese said. "In private. Unless you want to have this conversation here."

Dad looked at me, his expression screaming an apology, then back at Dr. DeWeese. "No, probably not." He leaned in and kissed my cheek. "I'll make this up to you. I promise."

Of course he would. He always did. With a present of some sort. A random package in the mail containing rich European chocolates or clothing that was useless at a uniform school. "What am I supposed to do?" Was I just supposed to grab a cab? Somehow find my own way back to school? I was probably forty-five minutes away. Besides, I didn't want to go back. I wanted to spend time with Dad. Who knew when I would see him again?

Dad pulled his phone from his pocket and made a quick call. When he replaced the phone, his brown eyes softened. His best feature. So unlike my eyes, the color of an avocado. "There's a car out front to take you back to school. The concierge will show you. I'll call you in the morning."

After a silent exchange between John DeWeese and Jack, Dr. DeWeese and Dad walked away leaving me exposed and vulnerable with Jack still staring at me.

I debated whether to bolt or make nice. I hated looking weak, so I chose the latter. Sort of. "Well, Jack, it was sure interesting to see you and meet your classy father. I can't for the life of me figure out why he and my dad lost touch."

"Look, I don't know why my father threw that punch. I can assure you it's not in his character."

"Uh-huh." I nodded. "Like I was saying, it was nice to see you. I don't even know why I bothered coming tonight." Over Jack's shoulder, I watched Dad's back disappear through a door. "And now... I'm leaving." Why couldn't I just ask him the question that was lighting my insides on fire? Why couldn't I ask him what his intentions really were for attending Wellington? Did he know who I was before he arrived this morning?

Jack stepped forward and grabbed my wrist, stopping my quick exit. "I will tell you this." He stood so close I could see the golden specks in the blue of his irises. His pleasant scent threatened to topple me. "My father cancelled his trip to Scotland when he heard your dad would be the key-note speaker tonight. And I don't think it was to hear the speech."

~~~~

I stood on the curb outside the Hilton Hotel in Lexington, KY waiting for the car that would deliver me back to Wellington.

Men and women circled through the large revolving door leading to the hotel lobby. A man in a navy bellhop suit helped a lady out of a limo. A case hung on her arm, and a white dog poked his head from a small opening.

I smiled as the dog yapped his head off.

The air had turned unusually cool for so early in September. Goosebumps popped up on my arms and spread down to
~~~~

my bare legs. "Where is that car?" I tapped my peep-toe, high-heeled shoe against the sidewalk and pulled at my light sweater, trying to trap in some heat.

Thoughts of Dad being punched in the face competed with the frustration coursing through my blood at not getting to speak with him about Jack.

A body knocked into me, pushing me forward. After I regained my footing, I looked up. A man continued by me, turning as he stepped. A wolfish grin played at his lips. "Sorry, ma'am..." His words cut off when his eyes met mine. What started as a look of apology morphed into one of recognition.

Another touch to my arm sent me spinning and jerking backwards.

"Whoa." Jack raised both hands as if to say, "no foul."

"Oh, it's you." I whipped back around, but the man with the lupine smile disappeared between parked cars.

Jack took a step closer, standing shoulder to shoulder with me and rocking back and forth on his heels. "Yep. Just me. Good ol' Jack."

Out of the corner of my eye, I saw him staring at me.

"What do you want, Jack?" I asked without looking at him.

"Just thought I would wait with you. They're bringing my transportation around."

"That's not what I... never mind. What are our fathers talking about, exactly?"

"Oh, I'm sure they're just catching up on old times."

Jack's sarcasm lit the fuse of a slow-burning firecracker just beneath my skin. "They didn't appear to be on that great of terms." Understatement of the year.

"Oh, you'd be surprised how much love and adoration was behind that punch." Jack moved to stand in front of me. "You okay? You're shaking."

I pulled my sweater even tighter around me. "I'm fine." He started to remove his suit jacket, but I raised my hand to stop him. "Please don't."

"Why? You're freezing." He draped the jacket around me anyway. "Nice dress by the way." His eyes wandered the length of my body, not stopping with the dress that hit a couple of inches above my knees.

I rolled my eyes. "You're such a cliché. I don't need you sacrificing your jacket. Besides..." I paused, recalling the weird conversation we had at school. How much *did* Jack know about me? Did he really transfer to Wellington because he was curious about me? Ridiculous thought. But the look his father gave me before he decked Dad? I shivered.

"Besides what?" he asked.

I gave my head a little shake. "My ride is here."

A bellman opened the door to the backseat of a Lincoln Towncar and stood waiting for me to get in. At the same time, a valet pulled past the town car on a Harley-Davidson motorcycle.

"Mine too," Jack said.

Not such a cliché after all. I started toward the open door.

"Wait," Jack said, a sense of urgency in his command. He stepped close, towering over me. His dark gaze met mine. "Let's go somewhere. Get a coffee or something."

"What? Why?" I glanced at the bellhop holding the car door open for me, his eyes averted elsewhere.

"Because I think you and I probably have a lot to talk about. Things others wouldn't understand."

"I don't think so," I answered quickly, though a small part of me regretted it immediately. It was just that his sudden appearance in my secret life frightened me.

"Well, you'll want to sooner or later." He ran his pointer finger down the bridge of my nose. "How's the nose bleed?"

I leaned my head back, away from his touch. "It's fine. No big deal." I struggled to find a clear voice while he stood so close. Did he know why I got a nose bleed?

He reached his hand further. His fingers feathered my forehead. "And the headache from earlier?"

A nervous knot flipped in the pit of my stomach. I studied his expression—the lift of his brow, the slight curve of his lips. He was right. I had so many questions. Like, how did he know where I went to school if his father and mine hadn't seen each other in years? Why did I feel like we knew each other already when his father looked shocked to see me, a seventeen-year-old? "It's fine, too." What did any of this have to do with The Program?

"Suit yourself. We'll talk another time then. See you around." He backed away slowly before turning and climbing onto his motorcycle. He pushed his helmet down on his head and snapped the strap in place before kick-starting the bike and riding away.

I realized too late that I still had his jacket.

THREE

Briana leaned across a study table and ran a finger down the page of Jack's spiral notebook. She flipped her red curls over her shoulder and giggled at something he said. Her blouse barely covered the precious parts of her ample body thanks to one button too few.

Only Bree could find a way to make school uniforms sexy.

From behind the stacks across the library, I stared, my mouth agape. Anger built just watching that girl throw herself at Jack. Apparently, she'd learned he was in The Program.

When Briana laughed out loud a second time, Mrs. Roberts, the librarian, raised a quick finger to her lips and shushed her. I laughed softly.

"Why are you here, Jack?" I muttered under my breath. Great. Now I was talking to myself.

Jack's eyes lifted. His gaze circled the room until it landed on me. His lips curled just slightly, and he lifted his head in a silent "hello."

Only then did I realize I was still smiling, always glad when Briana was in trouble, even if only a little. I busied myself with sorting books on the pushcart, while still studying Bree and Jack.

Briana followed Jack's line of vision, and after giving me the snake-eye, she shifted to block Jack from my view.

I had led him around every inch of campus that morning, managing only small talk. When he'd tried to discuss the previous Friday night, I'd changed the subject, still hoping to speak with Dad about Jack and his father.

Dad had delivered a controversial speech in the States after a two-year absence the same night his long ago partner and friend decided to deck him. That doctor's son was now at my school asking questions that were off limits. It was all just a little too weird.

I turned up the music on my iPod and finished shelving the cart of books. Then, I found a private study desk in the far back corner of the library. I pulled my laptop out of my bag and after turning it on, began an online search for articles about Friday night's dinner. Reporters were calling my dad an "International Man of Mystery." Puh-lease. I thought that title was reserved for Austin Powers.

A title like that made medical research sound glamorous. Definitely not the case. Doctors and scientists worked long hours, sacrificed time with their families, and gave up any resemblance of a normal life. That's what I knew about Dad's "glamorous" life. Growing up, I hardly saw my father, often only getting leftovers. Friday, I didn't even get that.

Another article discussed the various controversies of embryonic cloning and the many organizations that are currently protesting any use of such technology. The article said, "Geneticist and reproductive specialist, Dr. Peter Roslin, announced in a private meeting before the dinner that he was on the verge of declaring a monumental scientific discovery."

Monumental discovery? "What kind of discovery?" I wondered.

The article went further to speculate that this announcement was the reason the host of Friday night's dinner hired private security for Dr. Roslin during his stay in the United States.

What had my dad discovered that would warrant the hiring of security? I rubbed my fist in circles over my heart, massaging the ever-increasing anxiety there. Was he in danger?

There was no mention in any of the articles of Dr. DeWeese punching Dad in the face.

Next, I clicked on a link within the article that brought up an old feature story about the work Dad did long ago while still in the states.

"Can I join you?" Jack stood above me.

I pulled out my ear buds. "Um, there's no other chair. Sorry." I tried to keep my tone light and breezy when the pounding of my heart was anything but.

He walked away and returned a moment later with a chair. "Thanks for showing me around this morning." He placed the chair beside me and sat backwards, chest against the back, facing me. "It's tough. Starting a new school. Not knowing anyone."

I cocked my head. "Seriously?" I pictured Briana draped across his books and in his face only minutes before.

He smiled. "No." Jack nodded at the computer screen "That's a nice picture, don't you think?"

I glanced at the picture on my computer screen of my father and his. I turned back. "What do you want Jack? Why are you here? And why did your father hit mine last night?"

"Wow." He sucked in a deep breath. "Which one of those would you like for me to answer first?" he asked, teasing. Daring me to choose.

I considered the weight of each question. He stared, his eyes steadfast on mine. Again, his face lengthened. The smug smile that usually brightened his eyes was gone.

"Fine. Why did Dr. DeWeese punch a friend he hadn't seen in years?"

Jack glanced over his shoulder and leaned in closer. I studied the slight stubble on his chin and breathed in a subtle scent of shower gel. "I can't tell you that," he said and leaned back.

"Why not?"

"Because you're not ready."

"What is that supposed to mean?" I asked. My words echoed through the library.

"It means exactly what it sounded like." His voice took on a more serious edge.

Blowing out a breath of air, I stood and began stuffing my laptop into my satchel. My hand shook. He must have noticed because he covered it with his palm, pushing my hand to the desk and stopping me from zipping my bag. His hand was cool over the heat of mine. I lifted my head and met his gaze. "You knew me before you arrived at this school. How?"

"I overheard part of a conversation my father had."

"With whom?"

Again, Jack smiled, cocking his head.

"Fine. Whatever. Don't tell me. Look, Jack. I don't know what kind of game you're playing but I'm not interested. Stay away from me. Got it?"

Before he could answer, or I gave into the urge to slap the grin off his face, I left him and took off for the pool. I had missed enough practices and needed to clear my head before dinner. Besides, it was just easier to run from life's distractions. From Jack.

~~~~

I folded my clothes into my gym bag and started to close the locker door, but my phone sounded. Instead of ignoring it like I should have, I dug deep into the side pocket and pulled the phone out. A text.

"Lexi, honey, please send the address of the storage place to this number. Thanks. Love, your father."

I didn't recognize the phone number. It wasn't the number I had for Dad, and he didn't sign texts with "your father." Daddy, maybe. Or just Dad. As if that wasn't weird enough, I had already emailed him the information he wanted.

What was so important in that storage anyway? As far as I knew, he hadn't touched anything in that storage in more than five years. Why now? Some old journals? I let the phone slide back down in the pocket and slammed the locker door.

The warm steam of the heated water and the strong smell of chlorine accosted me when I stepped onto the pool deck into a puddle of water. I left my goggles and cap sitting on the edge of the gutter and dove through the water like a bullet. The only thing better than early morning team practices was having the entire pool to myself. I pretended to swim in the ocean. The open water. Free. Without limits. For more than an hour.

Although my mind wanted to get stuck on such things as absentee fathers, mysterious quests for some old journals, and Jack, I pushed hard against them. I imagined winning the high
~~~~

school swim championships, being accepted to a college where I could become whatever I was meant to be, and life after college as a doctor. I dreamed of freedom away from this school. I dreamed of spending time with Dad.

After pushing my workout to the limits, I stood under the hot shower and attempted to further drown the tension in my shoulders. The heat of the shower soothed my tired muscles, but something about the text I'd received earlier bugged me.

After the shower, I slipped into some sweats, brushed the tangles from my hair and tied it up in a knot on top of my head. The locker room was quiet except for the constant drip echoing in the showers. I wriggled my headphones into my ears. The soft strains of Yo-Yo Ma played, a soothing sound after a hard workout.

I wrapped my damp towel around my neck and lifted my bag. My sliders flopped against my heels as I walked toward the exit, my mind already shifting to the trigonometry test I had yet to study for that day.

Suddenly, a loud bang interrupted the soft music and my distant thoughts. I spun toward the sound. A shadow moved along the far wall near the door between the locker room and the pool.

I pulled a headphone from my ear and listened. I heard only the drip of a leaky faucet, so I shook off any paranoia. The sound must have been a locker closing. Another swimmer getting in an evening swim.

Shrugging, I started toward the exit again. The lights went out. I couldn't see my hand in front of my face. My body froze, muscles tightened. Swallowing hard, I removed my ear buds and stuffed them in the pocket of my hoodie. "Hello?"

Nothing. The door to the pool area creaked opened and closed. The only light shone from an exit sign above the door to the hallway.

I stood, unmoving. Listening for footsteps. Anything. Maybe a custodian who didn't realize someone was in here. I took another step.

The crashing of lockers cracked the silence, like a sudden clap of thunder in the dead of night. I flinched. My heart raced as if I had just finished a fifty-yard sprint. Paralyzing fear never won races. With my eyes finally adjusted to the dim light, I ran.

I swung open the door and almost pulled it from its hinges. I flew into the hallway, plowing into someone walking by. The person grabbed my arms and attempted to stop my forward motion, but it was too late. I knocked into the figure so hard that we both tumbled to the ground, tapping heads along the way.

I reached out a hand to break the fall and my arm got trapped beneath both bodies.

"Ow," I moaned. "I'm so sorry." I raised my head and met stormy blue eyes. "Jack?" Of all the people... A lightning bolt of pain shot through my arm, and my head ached.

"What is wrong with you?" Irritation wove through each word. He lifted his head, our faces only inches apart. The annoyance slowly faded, replaced by a bemused smile.

I breathed hard. Rolling off, I held my arm close to my body. "Ow," I groaned again. The pain was enough to make me lightheaded. Had I just broken my wrist? Heat spread upwards to my cheeks.

Jack pushed himself up and then lifted me easily. "Why are you in such a hurry?" he asked.

"Someone was in there." I inhaled and let the breath out slowly. Embarrassed, I pretended to cross my arms, while in actuality, I cushioned my arm against my ribs. I didn't want Jack to know I might have just broken it.

Concern blanketed Jack's face. "What do you mean? In there?" He thumbed toward the locker room. "Who?"

"If I knew, do you really think I would have bulldozed you?"

"Well, let's just have a look, shall we?" His voice was calm. He pushed through the door to the girls' locker room.

I followed close behind him. A cold sweat broke out across my forehead and down my arms.

He flipped on the lights. "Is anyone in here?" We searched around every corner until we reached the opposite side of the showers and through the door to the pool.

"No one's here." He turned his eyes on me. "Why don't you tell me exactly what happened?"

By then, my heart had slowed. Whoever had been in the locker room was long gone. Then it dawned on me. "I'm such an idiot." I laughed. "Great. That's just perfect."

"What's perfect?" he asked. A line formed between his eyes.

Briana. Exactly the sort of thing she would do. Put me on edge; try to knock me off my game. "Nothing. I'm sorry. Someone was just playing a bad joke on me. And I think I know exactly who."

"Who?" he asked, not convinced.

I shook my head. "Not your problem. Really. I think someone was just trying to scare me. Do you mind if we just forget this?"

He seemed to let it go. We walked back the same way we came. "You missed dinner," he said when we reached the door to the hallway again.

"I'll live." I hated my aloof tone. But what? He was tracking my eating habits now?

I entered the hallway, followed by Jack.

"Well, well, well. What do we have here?" Kyle Jones, captain of the swim team, stopped in the middle of the hallway. A smirk spread across his face.

"Hi," I said, cringing. Though Kyle was a friend, he was also friends with Briana, and I didn't really need anyone knowing I had paranoid fears of that girl. "Have you met Jack?"

"I don't believe so. Hey, man. You're the new guy, right? How's it going?" Kyle shook Jack's hand.

"Great. Nice to meet you." Jack stuffed both hands in the front pockets of his khakis.

"Kyle is on the swim team with me." As I'm sure Jack could tell by the Wellington Swim Team sweatshirt he had on. "And my really good friend."

Kyle nodded, his dark brown hair hung in a messy shag around his face. His grin and the way he folded his arms across his chest told me he couldn't wait to get me alone and ask me what was going on between me and the new guy.

"Lexi was assigned to be my tour guide." Jack gave me a sideways glance, answering the question I suspected Kyle had. His eyes drifted down to my arm that I still held close to my body. I squirmed under his scrutiny.

"And she was showing you the girls' locker room?" Kyle asked.

Fire crept up my neck and exploded across my cheeks. "You know me. I like to be thorough." I flashed an unspoken "thank you" to Jack for not telling Kyle what had happened. I didn't need Kyle joining the growing list of members in the Lexi's a Freak Club. Jack was already president. That was enough.

"Well, I've got a trig test to study for," Kyle said. "I'll catch you two later."

I gave him a low wave with my good hand as he passed us and continued toward the boy's dorms.

Alone again, Jack brushed his fingers along my hurt arm. "You okay?"

"Yeah, I'm fine." I tried to keep my tone even. The truth was my arm radiated fire. "Thanks for not revealing to Kyle that I'm an idiot."

"What? Because someone purposely tried to scare you while you were alone in a locker room? That makes you an idiot?"

"And they were quite successful. I feel stupid, that's all." I looked down at my pink toenails peeking out from my sliders. When I lifted my head, Jack's eyes burned into mine.

"How's your arm?"

I squeezed my eyes tight. Caught. I tried to move my fingers, but pain stopped me. "Broken?" I sighed. "Which is just perfect. How am I supposed to swim with a broken arm?"

"Your face is pale." He reached his fingers to my face. "You're clammy. And you have a knot on your forehead where our heads hit."

Thank you for that thorough examination.

He reached for my other arm. “Let’s go.” He glanced down the hallway in both directions before leading me back into the girls’ locker room. His eyes were wide, crazed.

“What are you doing? Where are we going?”

He said nothing as he led me around the corner close to the bathroom stalls and I let him. This guy, who showed up yesterday, was going to murder me right here inside this locker room, and no one was going to find my body until morning. By then, he’d be long gone.

I wasn’t usually one for melodrama, but...

Jack faced me. “I’m sorry. You’re not ready for this, but you’ve left me no choice.”

“Not ready for what?” My chest rose and fell.

“Sit.” Jack walked over to the sinks and splashed water on his face. He stared at himself in the mirror like he was mentally preparing for something.

“Excuse me?” I examined the tile floor. A used Band-aid littered a nearby corner. “I’m not sitting on this disgusting floor.”

He closed the distance between us. His fingers wrapped around my good arm. “Sit.”

I should fight him. Kick him in the shin. Punch him in the face. Something. Instead, I leaned against the wall, and holding my elbow, he guided me down the wall.

He knelt on one knee in front of me. “You’re going to have to trust me.”

“Trust you?” My breathing sped up. I searched his eyes and found a warmth there that I struggled to believe. “I barely know you.” I wanted to trust him, but fear wrapped itself around my heart and squeezed. My arm throbbed.

"I know." His voice was calm. "This isn't ideal circumstances, for sure." There was zero humor to his voice. I sensed something, though. Regret, maybe.

"What are you going to do to me?" A tear escaped down my cheek, and he wiped it away with his thumb. His touch felt gentle.

"I want you to take a deep breath when I say 'now.' You are going to feel intense pain at first, but then it will be gone. Try not to scream. Okay?"

I shook my head. *Try not to scream?* "No, it's not okay. Don't—" I wanted to scoot away from him. Run. But he didn't give me time to think.

"Now! Deep breath."

I did as I was told and sucked in the deepest breath. My eyes locked onto his as I held it.

Jack wrapped both of his hands around my broken wrist. Pain exploded through my arm. I was paralyzed by the fire beneath his palms.

He closed his eyes. Tears escaped mine. My mouth went dry.

Almost as suddenly as the blast had shot through my arm, the ache dulled. Jack let go of my arm. I released my breath. I was close to passing out from the lightheadedness and pain. Jack's hand supported the side of my head, lowering me to the cold floor.

He stood and darted to a bathroom stall. I wasn't sure, but it sounded like he threw up. He returned to the sink. I heard running water. My vision was fuzzy.

Next, I felt the coolness of his fingers linger around my forehead. I tried to focus on his eyes, but couldn't.

"You're going to be fine." One arm slid under my legs, the other hugged my back, and he lifted. He bent his head into my neck, his breath next to my ear. "I'm sorry."

FOUR

I woke in a haze. An orange glow shone through the blinds of a window to my left. I smelled a strange mix of alcohol and Clorox. When I moved, my head hurt a little.

"Hey, hon," a female voice to my right said. "I'm Barb, the nurse. How you feelin'?"

A lady dressed in white scrubs decorated with different colored band-aids fiddled with a stethoscope hanging around her neck. Her platinum blond hair was tucked into a short ponytail.

"What happened?" I inspected the length of my body, still clothed in my navy sweats and hooded sweatshirt.

"You bumped your head. You've suffered a slight concussion, I think." She lifted my arm and slid a blood pressure cuff over it.

"How long have I been out?" I asked as she pumped.

"Oh, not long at all. Thirty minutes, maybe." She set the sleeve aside and shone a light just above my eyes. "Follow my finger."

I did as instructed.

"Nice knot, though."

I lifted my fingers and brushed the spot on my forehead. *Jack.* My eyes darted around the room. Then at my arm. I wiggled my fingers and then swallowed hard. "The guy who brought me in?"

She placed the stethoscope over my heart and listened. "He said he would check in on you later." She smiled. "Handsome young man. He seemed very worried about you. Attentive. You've got yourself a keeper there."

Yes, handsome. And frightening. I massaged my arm. No pain whatsoever. My arm had been broken. I was sure of it. I had practically passed out from the pain.

Had he healed it? Was that humanly possible? He had said I wasn't ready. Ready for what, exactly? Had he healed me with his mind?

If that was the case, my mindspeaking ability seemed trivial in comparison.

I threw my head back against the pillow, wincing from the headache as I did. "Can I go? Are you keeping me for any reason?" I had to find Jack. He couldn't just leave me after doing whatever it was he did.

"You suffered a concussion. You'll need to sleep here overnight."

Oh, no I won't. "Barb, is it?" When she nodded, I reached for some tissues beside me and began building my case. *Look, Barb. It's only a slight concussion. My roommate can watch me overnight and make sure no worrisome symptoms pop up. You will allow me to go. Make notes in my file that I appeared to have no long-lasting symptoms.*

Barb began scribbling in my medical file, then smiled. "You're all set."

"Great." I swung my legs around and planted my feet firmly on the ground. Barb backed away forcing me to rely on my own balancing ability.

Placing my full weight on my feet, I stood, swaying slightly. I steadied myself with one hand and wiped my bleeding nose with the other. "I feel fine," I lied. I wiggled the fingers on my right hand in front of my face. More fine than I should feel.

I slid into my sliders and reached for my bag at the end of the bed. "Thanks, Barb."

"You'll call if you feel light headed again?"

Maybe. "You'll be the first."

I walked slowly, stretching my hands out for balance. The minute I was at the door, I pushed through with caution and dug for my phone. The sun was fully set on the horizon, leaving just a faint glow in the west. Students congregated outside the library, across from the infirmary. Some girls screamed. I jerked toward the sound. Just some students horsing around, but the quick motion made me dizzy.

I dialed the only number I had for my father and reached his voice mail. "Dad. You have to call me. Something strange happened tonight. I really need to talk to you." *Not to be confused with every other night that I need to talk to you.* "You never called me after the dinner, and... Just call me. Okay? I... I love you."

I shut off the call and slid the phone in my pocket. Where in the world would I find Jack this time of night? Did I even want to find Jack?

~~~~

"But, Lexi," Danielle said. "Bree worked the dinner shift tonight. She was in charge of scraping." Danielle smiled at that. It always gave us satisfaction to see Princess Briana Howard scrunch up her nose at the smells while scraping half-eaten
~~~~

Salisbury steak and applesauce off the dinner trays into an over-sized trash can.

"Are you sure? She was there the whole time?" That blows that theory all to pieces. Who would want to scare me like that if not Briana?

"Yeah." Danielle straightened her legs out in front of her on the floor and leaned her chest forward, reaching her hands to curl her fingers around her feet. "Now, tell me again how you ended up in the infirmary?"

I leaned back against my headboard, staring at a pile of books in front of me. "I told you. I ran from the locker room, straight into Jack. We bumped heads. And I ended up with a slight concussion." I wished that was the whole story. I rubbed my right arm where my wrist had been broken. I was sure of it. Now, it was like nothing had happened. No pain. No bruising.

Panic bubbled up in my chest again remembering how Jack had touched my arm. Healed the broken bone. A chill ran down my spine. When I'd gone looking for him, no one knew where he was. Not his roommate. Not Briana. Like she'd tell me if she did know. Not many knew who Jack was yet. Obviously, I didn't know who he was.

"No, I mean the part about you falling on top of him. Tell me that part again. I like that part." She lifted her head. A side braid snaked around her neck and hung past her shoulder. A playful grin spread across her face. "What?" she asked when I cocked my head. "You could use a little sexy in your life. Did you get a load of his abs?"

"There's absolutely nothing romantic going on between me and Jack. Besides, he's already been admitted to The Program and is applying for pre-med." I bent my head into the hood of my sweatshirt. The smell of his shower gel lingered there from where he carried me to the infirmary. I still remembered the warmth of his breath on my neck.

When I woke up in an infirmary bed, he was gone, but his scent was there, and the lightheadedness from his touch to my arm hung on like a good flu.

"Oh, that's right." Danielle rolled her eyes. "You don't date doctor-types."

"Or Wellington guys." I picked up my trig book and draped it across my lap. I had to put the past twenty-four hours and Jack out of my head and study. How did I ever expect to be accepted to a pre-med program if I didn't keep my grades up? Just because I had no intention of applying to The Program didn't mean I didn't want to go to medical school. "Wait a minute. When did you see his abs?"

She shrugged. "A group of us played lacrosse out on the front lawn this afternoon. He may have removed his shirt for part of it. Man-oh-man." Her legs now spread wide, she used ballet arms to stretch a hand to the opposite foot. "He's not my type, of course, but definitely something new and improved to look at around here."

"What do you mean not your type? What's not to like? Sandy blond hair. Blue eyes with the depth of the ocean." I fluttered my eyelashes, lifted my hand and fanned my face. "Swoon."

Danielle reached up on her bed and threw a pillow at me. "I knew it! And here I thought you weren't interested."

"Easy," I yelled. "The head."

"Oh. Sorry."

"Anyway, I'm not interested, but I'm not blind, Danielle." I flipped the page of my book. "Remind me again. Why am I taking this class?" I tried to change the subject.

"The same reason you take all the advanced classes. So you can be a famous doctor like your father some day. You and Jack were cut from similar molds, apparently." She pushed herself up to her feet, straightened her legs, and leaned her chest against her knees.

"Oh, yeah." I shook my head as her words sunk in. I didn't want to be famous, but I did want to become a doctor. A pediatrician, maybe. So I had to do well on this test and every other if I was going to get accepted to a top pre-med program early. "I just hope Dad understands when I don't turn in my application to The Program."

"I guess I'm lucky. My parents couldn't care less what I do with my life after high school."

I frowned at Danielle. "Have you talked to them recently?

She shook her head.

My phone alerted me to a new text.

"Lexi, love, I need that address."

I dialed the number where the text came from. It wasn't even a real phone number. Just a free texting service.

"Something wrong?" Danielle had finished her stretching and was opening her own books in the middle of her bed.

I stared at my phone. "I don't think so." Except, I was certain that these texts were not originating from Dad. He never called me "Love."

Something strange was going on. I couldn't find Dad. I couldn't find Jack. I needed answers.

FIVE

Jack successfully avoided me the whole next day. And the day after that. He was supposed to be in most of my classes, but it was as if he never existed. Never transferred to Wellington.

By Thursday afternoon, I had worked up quite an attitude. I was nearly late to trigonometry, sneaking in just as the bell rang.

There, in the back of the room sitting next to Briana, was Jack. He laughed at something the prima donna said. When he met my glare, the corners of his lips tightened into a straight line.

One smoldering look from him ignited electric shocks in the synapses of my nervous system and traveled from the center of my brain to the pit of my stomach, then on to the tip of my big toe.

What was he doing to me?

I dropped my bag to the floor beside my chair, and sat heavily just as Mr. Crain handed me my test. A big fat "C" was scribbled in red at the top. That wasn't going to help my cause to get accepted to a top college or make my father proud.

Trying to calm myself, I stuffed the test in my bag. As I did, I checked my phone again, hoping for a message or something from Dad. And not another text from an unknown number.

I hadn't heard from either since the night I hit my head and broke my arm.

I tried to sneak another look behind me. When I turned my head, my eyes met Jack's, staring straight at me.

Briana reached a hand and brushed her fingers along Jack's arm. After a whisper, a giggle, and a hair flip, he turned his attention back toward her.

I concentrated my thoughts at her hard. *Scoot away from him, Bree. You don't even like that idiotic loser. Plus, he thinks you're pathetic. Do you really want to be associated with a jerk like him?*

Briana immediately scooted her chair a couple of inches away from Jack. Her hair fell forward, shielding her face. She situated her body to face toward the windows and away from Jack.

He raised an eyebrow at her sudden movement and then redirected his gaze at me, catching me in a grin.

I felt the blood leak from my nose. I whipped around and dug a tissue from my bag.

I had so many questions for Jack. I didn't need Bree hanging all over him in the meantime.

Had I imagined my broken arm? And the fact that his touch healed it?

What about the headache the first day we met?

An hour passed. Class was nearly over. Fortunately, the bleeding stopped. But my notebook page in front of me was blank. I had managed to blow off the entire class.

Suddenly, the idea of confronting Jack overwhelmed me. My hands began to sweat. Maybe Jack was right. Maybe I wasn't ready for whatever it was he could tell me.

The bell rang, and I panicked. Overcome with nausea and intense fear, I darted from my seat and out the door.

Not quick enough.

Jack's fingers slid around my elbow as I rounded the corner. "We need to talk." His voice was low, steady as he followed close.

I stopped. Even I could sense the rapid rise and fall of my chest. "Why?"

"Are you serious?"

I pulled my arm from him. "Why now?" I lowered my voice, looking around to see if anyone was listening. No one was. My fear slowly began to morph into something different. A tight ball of fire churned in my stomach. Heat traveled up the back of my neck. "I mean, I plow you over, we hit heads, I break my arm, and magically my arm is all better? Then, you just disappear for like three days. So, why now?" I hated how much I sounded like a whiny four-year-old.

He gestured with a hand for me to walk. "Let's go. I'll buy you a Coke or something." He placed his hand in the small of my back and we wove our way through classmates congregating in the hallway. Their faces were happy and light, unaffected by the way Jack led me away from them. To others looking on, we probably seemed like a couple.

Heat from his palm seeped through my thin blouse. His calmness compared to the anxiety bubbling in my chest made me want to scream, but I buried it.

"What would you like?" he asked when we arrived at the campus store.

I examined my choices. "A green tea?"

He waited patiently behind a couple of our younger girls, who cupped their hands over their mouths, giggling. Eventually, he grabbed a cold green tea and a Mountain Dew from the display case, paid for both and led me back outside.

We walked without speaking. For someone new to Wellington, he knew exactly where he was going. I followed him to the bleachers overlooking the multi-purpose ball field where the boys' lacrosse team was practicing.

"How'd you do on the trig test?" he asked as we climbed to the top and sat. He handed me the tea.

I cocked my head. "Is that why you bought me a drink and dragged me all the way out here? To talk about the trig test?"

A crease formed between his eyes. "I just wondered if you were able to study for it after what happened the other night." He frowned, sucking in a deep breath. "You need the grades to get accepted to The Program."

"Ah, yes. The Program."

Jack's eyes narrowed. "Why did you leave the infirmary so soon? You really should have stayed until the doctor said it was safe for you to leave. Concussions can be very serious."

I nodded, then looked away toward the Kentucky farmland that stretched behind the small stadium. He was right, of course, the concussion could have been serious, but as it turned out, it wasn't. A slight breeze blew a wisp of hair across my face. I pushed it back behind my ear, and when I got up my nerve, I faced Jack. "What *was* that? Did I imagine my broken arm?" I couldn't suppress the shakiness in my voice. Did I really want to know?

He kept his gaze on me, never breaking eye contact. "You didn't imagine it. Your arm was broken. In two places."

I sucked in a deep breath and whispered, "How'd you do that?"

"The short and easy answer is I don't really know."

"You don't know?" *That's just perfect.*

As if he could hear my exasperation, his tone became defensive. "How do you alter people's feelings?"

A blush crept onto my cheeks, and I turned away. "I don't know what you're talking about."

"Oh, sure you do. At the dinner the other night. My father. You tried to calm him before he hit your dad... And what? You thought I wouldn't notice Briana's sudden coolness toward me. You jealous, Lexi?"

I snapped my head toward him. "I most certainly am not."

The corners of his lips lifted. "Then why go to the trouble of giving yourself a nosebleed? That's what happens, right? When you think too hard at someone else."

I broke eye contact again. "You know how crazy that sounds, right?"

"Crazier than fixing broken bones?"

"Which makes you violently ill." It was not a question. I thought of him racing to the toilet in the girls' locker room. "For three days?" He nodded. My heart sunk just a little. He'd made himself sick and revealed a huge secret over my broken arm?

"It was a pretty bad break," he said, his voice regretful.

I doubled over and gasped for a breath as if I had been hit in the stomach with a soccer ball. This was all too much. I'd spent my whole life hiding my ability, pretending it wasn't happening at first. Then I found a way to kind of enjoy it and use it to my advantage. However, healing a broken bone is a far cry from altering someone's thoughts. "You're not answering the question." I reached a hand to massage the spot over my heart. "How is it possible that you fixed my arm?"

"Are you ready to hear this?"

"Do I have a choice?" How could I possibly know if I was ready? "Who are you, Jack?" I spoke softly, almost a whisper. I should have asked, *what are you*? What was I, for that matter? Except that sounded too much like I thought we were aliens or something.

"You know who I am. I'm the son of your dad's ex-lab partner."

"From eighteen years ago. What does that have to do with me now?"

Jack scooted closer to me and leaned in like he had a secret to tell. He rested his elbows on his knees and dangled the Mountain Dew can in front of him. "Do you know much about the history of your father's research?"

"The history of it? Like the fact that he and your father cloned some goat more than twenty years ago, the goat died, and the lab and all evidence of the research burned to the ground?" That was all in the papers. "Or, Jack, are you talking about the time he spent after that attempting early retirement? When that didn't work, he returned to the lab to study stem cells, which turned out not to be good enough for my mom. So, she left soon after I was born, and Dad took off for Europe or somewhere while my grandmother raised me? To which part of this history are you referring?" I hated myself for letting my emotional family scars creep into the conversation.

Jack's mouth opened like he was about to speak, then closed. His stare made me shift where I sat. Finally, he said, "I'm speaking of the embryonic cloning part of the history."

"The stem-cell research?"

"That's part of it."

"Are you trying to tell me that their research has something to do with the fact that you have healing powers?" I shook my head in disbelief.

"And you, apparently, have some sort of ability to control people's minds."

I stood up and continued to rub my chest, trying to ward off an impending panic attack. "Do you hear yourself? This is nuts."

Jack wrapped his fingers around my hand and pulled gently, urging me to sit back down. "Crazy, maybe. Not unbelievable. Hasn't part of you wondered if there were others out there who wouldn't find your ability unusual?"

I looked up at the sky, then down at him. His eyes were as warm as I had seen them since meeting him. "No, I haven't," I lied. I was fine believing no others existed like me, and even more fine that no one knew about my ability. Some might call that naïve. I liked to think of it as safe.

"Please sit down. I need to tell you more."

I didn't know how much more I could take. I sat and pulled my hand away.

"Did you know your father stayed with us after the dinner the other night?"

"How did that happen? Did your father extend the invitation before or after he clocked him?" Of course I didn't know my father had stayed with them. My father hadn't bothered to call me.

"After, I presume."

I studied Jack's profile. He watched the guys scrimmaging on the lacrosse field. His lips did not twitch. No hint of a smile at my sarcasm. Neither the sweetness, nor the coolness of the tea helped the dryness in my mouth.

Jack lifted a leg behind the bleacher and faced me, inching uncomfortably close. "Our fathers' research went way beyond the cloning of a goat. They were on to something really big many years ago."

"What do you mean by 'big'?"

"Cure-for-terminal-disease-big."

"Yeah?" I said. "I thought curing diseases was the whole idea of medical research."

"Yes, but our fathers worked for a lab that didn't mind how controversial their methods were."

"What are you saying? Did they break laws?" My heart tightened into a ball of rubber bands. Any minute one would snap from too much tension. Was my father in trouble?

"Do you know if your father keeps journals of his research?"

I narrowed my gaze. "Why do you ask that?" I thought about Dad's request for the storage address.

"My father has always claimed that journals of the research surrounding the cloned goat were lost in a lab fire soon after the experiment failed. But I wondered if maybe your father kept some."

I swallowed hard. Was Jack asking about the same journals my father hoped to get out of our storage?

"Your hands are shaking." He reached a hand and grabbed both of mine. My nerve endings fired up like a blowtorch.

I started to pull away, but his fingers closed over mine. "I know you don't trust me. But I'm here to help."

"Help me how? I don't need help. Why should I trust you, Jack? I don't even know you."

"Your dad's in trouble, Lexi."

My eyes drifted from where his thumb rubbed my hand to his eyes. "What kind of trouble?" My voice barely climbed above a whisper.

"Father didn't arrive home with your dad the other night until two a.m. They looked tired, disheveled. I had fallen asleep playing Xbox, and I heard them come in. It was no accident that your dad was back in Kentucky. He wanted to meet with my father. Your dad called mine a week ago to let him know he'd be in town. That's when my dad cancelled his trip."

"But you still haven't told me what kind of trouble my father's in."

"Jack, there you are," Briana's voice broke through the quiet conversation Jack and I were having.

I winced. Jack muttered something under his breath I couldn't make out. Briana climbed her way up the bleacher steps, her smile as big and lipstick red as a painted clown's face. Okay, maybe not that big, but...

I pulled my hands away and folded my arms across my chest.

Jack stood. "Hi, Bree," he said with a pleasant tone. Very different-sounding from the conversation we'd been having.

"I've been looking everywhere for you," she said.

"And lookie here. You found him." I screwed the cap on my iced tea bottle, stood and swung my bag over my shoulder.

Jack's eyes pleaded with mine. Our conversation wasn't over. What was I supposed to do? Bree wasn't there to see me. Besides, I wanted to make a phone call. I needed to hear Dad's voice, his explanations. I had to ask him about these journals. About Jack.

"I'll catch you later?" Jack asked, his tone desperate.

Bree stepped up beside Jack and leaned into him. "She won't have time. She needs more practice and rest for the swim meet Saturday, don't you, dear?"

"Absolutely. Otherwise I might be forced to grab onto another swimmer in order to stay afloat. I would hate to accidentally drown someone."

The coldness of Bree's glare froze my spine vertebrae by vertebrae as I turned my back to them and stepped down the bleachers.

~~~~

I ended the call after leaving another voicemail for Dad and headed toward the library. I'd check my email again. Maybe Dad had replied to the message I sent him with the storage address.

The library was quiet. I ducked my head and refused to look over at the circulation desk. I didn't need or want to get stuck in a conversation of idle chit-chat with whoever was working today.

I took the stairs to the upper level two at a time and went straight to the computer lab. I had left my laptop in my dorm room that morning. Since Wellington didn't have Wi-Fi in the dorms the computer lab was quite convenient. The lab was empty except for one team of computer geniuses in the back. Probably only one was working the computer lab, and the others showed up for moral support or something.
~~~~

I logged onto my email account. No message from Dad. I had a message from Danielle with a link to a big sale at Anthropologie. Plus, another message from an address I didn't recognize.

The subject line read: *Sarah Alexandra Roslin...* Someone knew my real name.

My pointer hovered over the email. My hand shook. Finally, I opened it and continued reading.

Hi, Lexi.

As you can see, I know the name you're hiding under and the email address you use. How long do you think it will take me to learn your whereabouts?

The little hairs on the back of my neck stood at attention. My eyes darted around the room as if the person who wrote the email was hiding under the desk across from me.

Someone had found me. How? More importantly, why?

The only other female in the room climbed into the lap of one of the boys and proceeded to type on the computer in front of them. "Here, let me," she said and started typing furiously. They all laughed.

I forced my attention back to the computer and the email that had my leg bobbing up and down.

Don't worry. Your physical location isn't important, yet. What is important if you want your father to remain out of prison (or worse) with his reputation intact is the location of the journals your father kept of his research when he worked for Wellington Labs. Locate them ASAP and I won't expose you for the lab rat you are or your father for working with an International Intelligence Agency director on a secret medical and scientific program. Do you know what your Dad did to you before you were born, Sarah? I'll be in touch.

Otherwise, the attached document and others get sent to WikiLeaks.

I double clicked the attachment. A PDF of an email popped up on the screen, dated June 5, 1995.

The email was from S. Whitmeyer to Ruth.Daniel@InternationalIntelligence.com. And cc: P. Roslin and J. DeWeese.

Dear Dr. Daniel:

Embyros altered – A SUCCESS! Success rate 2%. Embryos lost – 351. Will be in touch.

SW

Wellington Labs, Inc.

The words blurred on the screen. *Embryos altered*? I rubbed circles over my heart. What did that mean? Like designer babies? The computer geeks' muffled conversation sounded like it was traveling through a tunnel. The room began to spin, and the walls started to close in.

"Think, Lexi. Think." I drilled two fingers into my temple and replayed the conversation with Jack. "Eighteen years ago," I whispered. Dad's lab burned down eighteen years ago. He and Jack's father stopped working together eighteen years ago. John DeWeese hadn't seen my father in eighteen years—since before I was born.

International Intelligence Agency? Dad had received threats before. I'd heard him talk about it. Still, this email was different. Not only did this email suggest that Dad was involved in something with Jack's father and the IIA, it suggested that I was a "lab rat." What did that mean?

Furthermore, Dad had cut ties with Dr. DeWeese. Why?

Did Dad trust Dr. DeWeese now? Could I trust Jack?

I pulled out my phone and dialed Dad's number. Straight to voicemail. I hung up.

I took deep breaths. In and out. "Dad, what did you do?" Why was someone targeting me? I'd never even seen the journals. I raised my head. My eyes circled the room for the millionth time that evening.

Reaching for the mouse, I printed both emails and then logged out of my account.

After I grabbed the paper off the printer, I lifted my bag over my shoulder and slipped out of the room.

I was going to be late to dinner, and tonight was the night I would introduce the enigmatic Jack DeWeese to Wellington.

SIX

I followed behind Kyle in the dinner line. After every inch forward, I glanced at the phone positioned carefully on my tray.

I couldn't get the email out of my mind. I was starting to worry that something had happened to Dad. Why else wouldn't he have called me?

"Oh, Miss Sanders, you are the sweetest lady at this school," Kyle said when one of the ladies served him way more than his share of spaghetti noodles and sauce. Then Mrs. Flowers gave him extra bread.

I rolled my eyes. "You're going to sink to the bottom of the swimming pool."

"Are you kidding? Pasta creates energy. I'm going to win big in every race on Saturday."

"Arrogant, much?" I glanced backwards again.

"Why are you so jumpy? You keep looking over your shoulder and at your phone. Who are you expecting a call from?" Kyle asked, impatient.

"No one," I said and picked up my tray. "You lead, but if you sit anywhere near Bree, I won't give you my dessert."

Kyle chuckled. "Something new happen between the two of you?"

"Nothing out of the ordinary."

The cafeteria bustled at full speed. Kyle led the way. I didn't bother to pay attention to which table he set his tray until it was too late. He was settling in across from Jack. I either followed suit, or appeared rude and drew unnecessary attention to Jack and me. It wasn't like I could ask Jack right in front of Kyle over spaghetti and garlic bread, *Hey, by the way, were our embryos altered before we were even placed in our mothers' wombs? Were we like designer babies or something? Did your mom prefer to only have blue-eyed babies with a predisposition to a perfectly-sculpted pectoral region?*

What did I care about appearances? "I'll catch you later, Kyle," I said, not giving him time to react, and continued on to a table by the window in the back. I still had to prepare some sort of introduction for Jack anyway.

Maybe I could fake a stomach bug. At that moment, I wasn't sure how far an upset stomach was from the truth. When the smell of garlic and oregano hit my nose again, I pushed the plate of spaghetti away, then looked down at my phone. "Call, Dad." Too bad my mind tricks didn't work from far distances.

Deciding there was no way I was escaping Jack's big introduction, I grabbed the folded emails and a pen from my bag. One page of the printed emails was mostly blank paper. I tucked the actual emails under my phone and began making notes on the other piece of paper.

"Why hello, Miss Matthews."

Jack stood beside the table. Close. I followed the line of his hips up past the tight curves of his chest, hidden only slightly by the navy polo, until I landed on those blue eyes I was beginning to suspect were created custom. He pulled out a chair beside me and sat down.

I tucked my hands under the table and began massaging my pressure points. I wasn't sure I wanted to talk to Jack again until I spoke with Dad. Although, if Dad kept avoiding me, I'd have no choice. "Where's Bree tonight?"

"I wouldn't know." He paused a couple of beats, opened his mouth to speak, closed it, and then opened it again. "There's nothing going on between Bree and me."

"Does she know that?" I asked, fighting back a smirk. I'm not sure why I cared. "It would seem you and she have gotten pretty tight since you arrived here."

Maybe I could get Bree to introduce Jack.

"I'm not at this school to meet girls. Just to get to know one." The corners of his lips tipped up as he reached for the garlic bread on my plate. "You going to eat this?"

I shook my head, and swallowed the urge to throw up on Jack. Was he flirting with me? Then, before I could stop myself, I did throw up… words. "Did our fathers alter our embryos before we were conceived? Are we what they call designer babies?" It sounded stupid saying it out loud now. And arrogant to think we were born to parents who cared about our eye color, or how tall we would grow to be.

Jack shot a quick glance over each shoulder, then took a bite of garlic bread. A line formed between his eyes. My words hung in the air like the elephant in the room that they represented—the secret kept from poor, little, weak Lexi her whole life. "Not exactly," he finally said.

"Then what? Shit, Jack." I placed my face in my hands. I couldn't suppress the quiver from my voice. "Did Dad think I was too weak to handle the truth?"

He tossed the rest of the bread back on the plate. "Look, I'm sorry. I want to tell you everything. The thing is, I simply don't know it all. I'm trying to piece it together myself." He took a heavy breath in and let it out slowly while staring out the window.

"What are you not telling me?"

"Oh, there's a ton I'm not telling you. So much of it doesn't make sense. And when I realized you were speaking to those peoples' minds and then to Briana's earlier, I knew."

"You knew what?"

"That we were alike. We both were keeping a secret so big."

"But you knew me before you even arrived."

Jack ran a hand through his hair. Silence followed.

"Jack. Tell me. Are we some sort of scientific experiment?" Of course we were. I was such an idiot. When he didn't answer, I lifted my head and glanced again at my phone and the piece of paper underneath.

"Couldn't get a hold of him?"

I shook my head. Then, without thinking anymore about it, I reached and yanked the printed email from under my phone and handed it to Jack before I changed my mind.

He unfolded the piece of paper and started reading. Meanwhile, Dean Fisher stood on the stage at the front of the dining hall and asked for all those who were making introductions of new students to make their way to the podium.

I started to stand, but Jack grabbed my arm. His eyes wide with fear. "Where did this come from?"

I pointed to the email address at the top of the page. "That's all I know." I pulled my arm from his grasp. "I have to go. Everyone is staring."

"Lexi," he said. My gaze met his. "Try to act normal. You don't know who knows what around here."

Right... Normal.

I made my way to the front of the dining hall, wringing my hands as I skirted around tables. It was Thursday night. Many of the teachers stayed and ate at the staff table near the front, as they often did when introductions were made.

Danielle waved. "Where've you been?" she mouthed as I passed by her.

I shrugged and forced a smile.

Next to her, Bree pretended to scratch her temple with a completely inappropriate finger.

Most of the introductions were from the newest seventh grade class entering Wellington. There were only a few from each of the classes after that and just one senior—Jack.

I stepped up to the podium, reminding myself that these intros were supposed to be light and fun. My legs felt barely strong enough to hold me. Swallowing the lump in the back of my throat, I said, "I'm here to introduce Jack DeWeese, who joins our senior class. He's standing there, in the back of the room." I pointed to Jack. He waved. "He's another one of those ridiculously smart kids." I rolled my eyes. "You know the type... The kind that breaks any possibility of a curve on the tests. He's aiming to get accepted to a pre-med program on early admission. So, if you're looking for him this semester, you'll find him in the library."

I paused, while several students laughed. Jack made a circular motion with his hand that said, "Wrap it up."

I leaned closer to the mike. "For all you gals out there, I'm sorry to say, Jack's already spoken for. He left his girlfriend of two years back at his last school. So he gave me permission to tell you, hands off the goods."

A low rumble of chuckles erupted as I stepped down from the stage. Bree stared at her plate of half-eaten spaghetti, her face the color of her remaining peas. I wove in and around tables to join Jack in the back. When I reached him, he handed me my bag and my phone and gestured toward the door.

His hand pushed into the small of my back as we walked. He leaned in, his mouth close to my ear. "FYI, I was home-schooled until now." When I stiffened, he said, "There are no other girls. Only you."

~~~~

"Where are we going?"

"Somewhere we can talk uninterrupted."

The lit windows from the dining hall got smaller and smaller the further away from the main school buildings we got. I had to take three steps for every two of Jack's just to keep up. We approached Wellington's horse stables, on the very back of the property.

"You don't think the horses will interrupt us?" I flashed an uneasy smile as Jack led me away from the main campus buildings.

His words echoed in my ears. *Only you.* What did that mean? I was the only girl he was currently stalking. The only girl who might find the journals that proved we were freaks.

The stables were typically off-limits unless you boarded a horse there. I did not own a horse, so I rarely ventured into the barns. It wasn't that I disliked them. However, they did smell at times. Like now. I breathed in the stench of hay and horse manure.
~~~~

Darkness settled into the shadows of the barn the closer we got. An autumn breeze sent goose bumps down my arm. Leaves swirled in a tornado pattern in front of us.

Gravel crunched beneath my feet with each step. At the same time, my heart sped up at the uneasy silence that churned in the air, void of students hustling about this far away from the main campus. I could hear my breaths as I marched into a situation I couldn't control. "Jack, please wait." I stopped and placed a hand on the side of the large black barn and pressed the other into my queasy stomach. I bent over at the waist and sucked in several quick breaths.

"Are you hyperventilating?

I flipped my hair out of my face. "Probably." I dug my palm into my chest. "I need you to just tell me. What am I? Did my dad do something to us?"

He took a step closer. "Lexi, I don't know exactly. I'm still trying to figure all this out, too. Why do you think your dad hasn't called you back?"

"I don't know." I studied Jack's face. "But I'm scared, Jack. Something frightened him the night of the dinner. And now..." my voice cracked. "...I'm getting threatening emails." My eyes pleaded with his. "Just tell me. Is it what this email says? Was I altered as an embryo? Did our fathers figure out how to play with human genes? To change them? Are my eyes freakin' green because Dad wanted green eyes?" That sounded ridiculous when I said it out loud. I was losing it.

"Not exactly. At least that's not how I think it happened." Jack reached out a hand to me.

I studied it with a raised eyebrow.

"What? You scared of my hand, now?" he asked.

"Terrified."

"Grab my hand. I've got something to show you."

I slid my hand into his. His grasp was firm, but warm and comforting in a way. I followed him around the sidewalk to the barn entrance.

"Hey, Barry." Jack nodded at a man in jeans and a baseball cap. "Everything okay?"

The man looked up from the pile of leather bridles and the like at his feet. "Oh, hi, Jack. Come to see your pony?"

"Yeah. How's she doing?"

"Oh, she's good. Settlin' in real nice." The man lifted the bridles and began hanging them on hooks. "You guys can't stay too long, okay? I'm headed out. The night watchman will make his rounds later."

Jack's hand tightened around mine and tugged gently. The heat of his touch reached all the way to my core. He led me through the barn to the last stall where a sliding door with a cut out window hung. Inside, a large chestnut horse stood, munching on straw and a bucket of feed. When she heard us, she stepped in our direction.

"She's beautiful." I let go of Jack's hand and reached to rub her nose. She bobbed her head up and down, and I laughed.

It felt good to laugh. Release a little of the stress, even if only for a moment.

I turned my head toward Jack. His smile sent a flush across my face.

"Meet Cherriana. Arrived today," he said while reaching a hand to her nose the same way I had and touching his pinky finger to my thumb. "The first-ever cloned quarter horse."

I pulled my hand away. My head spun in Jack's direction. "Cloned?" Again with the rapidly pumping heart. I looked back. Barry was exiting the barn at the other end. Did he know? Was this even a secret?

He nodded. "Exact replica of another horse and born twenty-six years after the original."

"How old is she?"

"She's twenty."

"They did it," I whispered as I stroked her mane. "They cloned a mammal that lived. Why was this never reported?"

"Father's story is that the labs couldn't handle any more bad publicity after the goat. When they did decide to go public, the fire destroyed all of their records, and... I don't know. I think something spooked them. He doesn't talk much about it anymore."

"And our fathers don't talk to each other," I whispered.

"Exactly. Why do you think that is?"

"I don't know. What does your dad say about... your ability?" I dared a sideways glance at him.

"Not much."

At that, I faced him. "What? Jack, you mend bones by a simple touch. You and your parents don't discuss this?"

He shook his head. His face was serious. "There's nothing simple about it."

"No, I guess not. But it would seem you would question your parents more."

"It's something I've always done, since I was little. Besides, my relationship with my parents is complicated. They've always had these really high expectations for me. Pushed me to do and learn so much more than normal teens."

"But Jack," I sucked in a breath, "you can heal bones. You have any idea how huge that is? People would—" Darkness settled in over my thoughts.

"Pay good money to have that ability? Or knowledge that someone else did?" Jack rested his arm on the stall door, his hand rubbing the underside of Cherriana's head like he would a Golden Retriever's. "Did you ever tell anyone? That you could put thoughts into people's minds?"

"Are you kidding? I barely have friends now."

"What about your dad?"

"No." Occasionally though, I wondered if he somehow knew. I studied Jack's profile and the way he looked at his horse. I continued. "By the time I realized I was actually mind-speaking, I was smart enough to know that I would be perceived as crazy if anyone knew. Besides, it's not like I can do it very often. Sometimes the nosebleeds are pretty bad. And the headaches..."

"Tell me about it." He smiled. "Mending a bird's damaged wing when I was five was nothing. I threw up for a full twenty-four hours after I fixed your arm the other day." Jack brushed a hand down the front of Cherriana's nose.

"Sorry I made you sick."

He shrugged like it was nothing. Bending down, he grabbed a cup of grain and poured it into the horse's feeding bin. Her reddish-brown mane and ears twitched while she ate.

I lowered my hands to my side. I wished Jack didn't make me nervous. It was like watching someone play with the pin of a grenade. I never knew when he might explode with more information I couldn't handle. "These things we can do aren't normal," I said.

"What *is* normal?" He stared at me now, testing me. I backed away a step. "Landing men on the moon? Creating a nuclear bomb that could take out an entire country? Giving someone an artificial heart? Scientific experiments and advancements are just that—making the abnormal... normal.

"And what about living a life of secrets? Is normal having your name changed and being hidden away in a school in the middle of nowhere, Kentucky? Why *did* you change your name?" Jack's rant was razor-sharp.

"My dad thought it was necessary. I do what he tells me." Most of the time anyway. I backed away from Jack a little more. "Why did you come to Wellington? Why now?"

"Would you believe I needed the advanced classes they offer here?"

I gave my head a little shake. "I know what classes are required to be accepted to The Program. You've already taken everything you need to graduate high school, be enrolled into The Program *and* be accepted to college."

Jack draped both arms over the stall door and appeared to ponder my words. Or maybe analyze what to tell me next.

"Did your parents make you come here for the year?" I asked, because that would totally make sense. I get parents who micromanage the lives of their children like puppets.

"No. My father offered it as an option, and after my mom strongly opposed the idea, I knew I had to come."

Interesting. So, he respects his dad, but not his mom? "What did you expect to find here?"

"Other than you? I don't know. I didn't think really. I just hoped you might have some answers to questions I don't even know how to ask."

I heard the frustration in his voice. I stayed silent, hoping he would continue.

"And I know Father thinks your dad kept journals," Jack continued. "He wants them. And part of me wants to find them before anyone else does."

"Did he ask my dad for them?" Just as I started to relax around Jack, my danger radar vibrated again. Why was everyone interested in these journals?

"Yes, your dad denied having them."

I took another step back. "What makes you think I know anything more?"

"I know you do, Lexi." He shuffled closer. "You told me your father mentioned the journals the night of the dinner. And I read that email. Someone else knows your father is hiding these journals. They obviously have some important information if this many people are after them."

"Why would I give them to you?" I stared at Jack, searched the darkness of his eyes for a sign. A sign that would tell me to run from the mysterious guy in front of me, or a sign to trust him. Even if only a little.

"I just want information, Lexi. Don't you? Don't you find it strange to meet me? Someone who shares a past that was hidden from you? And some sort of unnatural ability?"

I didn't know what I wanted. I needed to think. I needed to breathe. I needed to get away from Jack.

The thumping started slow and began to build inside my chest like an earthquake—pressure of an impending volcanic eruption. My stomach churned like water inside a hot spring.

I moved past him and walked out the rear of the barn. "I can't breathe," I whispered mostly to myself. I knew what was happening, and there was no way to stop it. I hated that Jack would witness it. My hand covered my mouth, and I ran. Away from Jack. Away from the situation.

Where I was going, I had no idea. But I had to get away from Jack. I didn't feel safe, and I couldn't get in a breath.

My thoughts raced. My father had tucked me away. To hide me? Or to protect me? I'd always thought it was the latter. Now, I had no idea, because suddenly all my walls of safety crumbled around me with each revelation Jack spoke.

Things I'd never questioned before poked at my brain.

Nothing made sense.

I ran along the path behind the barn until it led into a treed area along the rear of the property. The sounds of Jack's footsteps were close behind me.

I, of course, ran out of breath and had to stop. The leaves of the trees that now towered above me rustled in the wind. My chest ached from breathing in the cool night air.

"Damn, you can run fast." Jack bent over at the waist, catching his breath. "Do you have panic attacks often?"

I ignored his stupid question. "We're lab rats," I breathed. My eyes blurred, staring at the dirt in front of me. "That's what the person said in the email. He called me a lab rat." My voice took on an uncontrollable edge.

"Lexi, don't panic. Look at me."

I lifted my eyes. My chest rose and fell; my breath labored in heavy gasps. "That's what we would be." I shook my head. "If someone finds out we're here... That we have these talents." I locked eyes with Jack. "You knew I was here before the dinner. If you found me, who's to say someone else couldn't? Someone already discovered my email address. Now, more people know about these journals. And Dad seems to be missing."

"Calm down. Please. I promise I'm here to help."

I raised my chest and went at him. "Why did you come? Are you leading them to me?" Whoever "them" was. I pushed at his chest, but without much effort. I was too tired from running. He stumbled backwards, his brows scrunched up, and caught my hand in his when I made contact.

I jerked it away and leaned against a tree. Tears stung my cheeks.

He stepped closer to me. With a gentle touch, he wiped my tears away with his thumb. "I'm not leading anyone to you. I didn't come to Wellington to scare you. Or hurt you in any way."

"Why *did* you come, then?" My voice was barely audible. I was naked, exposed. Danger lurked behind every falling leaf.

"I think you know there is so much more to this story. Your dad's journals would be a good start toward helping us learn exactly who we are."

"I don't have the journals." Although, if they were in the storage unit, I'd find them. I ducked away from Jack and walked a few steps.

"We also need to figure out who emailed you. And why."

"I told you. I don't have any idea who could have sent that email. I didn't think anyone even knew who I was." Or cared, until Jack arrived.

My eyes darted from tree to tree. My mind raced, filing and categorizing the fears and dangers swirling around me. None of which were present before Jack arrived.

I'd always thought I'd been hidden at Wellington for my protection because of who Dad was. Now? I was starting to wonder if I was hidden because of *what I was*.

With my back turned, I sucked in a deep breath. I'd find the journals. And I'd find them without Jack.

SEVEN

Please, Dani." I pleaded with Danielle outside the yoga room. I sounded whiny, which I hated.

Her yoga mat hung on her back. She crossed her arms and tapped her foot. "Can't we go after yoga? I really need to de-stress from that stupid European History test."

"There won't be time." I closed my eyes and squeezed the bridge of my nose. "Look, something really strange is going on. I need your help."

"You need me to drive you."

I batted my eyelashes. "I want your company."

"This is about Mr. Hot Abs, isn't it? Does he really have a girlfriend?"

I had forgotten that tidbit I had made up and told the school when I introduced Jack the previous night.

Danielle chewed on her cuticle as if nothing was urgent. When I didn't answer her question, she said, "I bet it's not serious. I've seen the way he looks at you. It's kind of creepy, and hot, actually."

"Danielle! Focus."

She craned her head to see into the yoga room. Soft music played. The smell of incense wafted all the way out to the hallway. The class was starting. She turned back around. "Oh, alright. But you owe me."

"Awesome. I'll even carry your yoga mat." I lifted her carrying case off her shoulder.

I pushed the door open, held it for her, then twirled around and ran smack dab into Jack. Why was he always everywhere I was?

"Hello, ladies." He had already changed from the school uniform into an old gray shirt and sweat shorts. And by old gray shirt, I meant shirt that did nothing to hide the rock-hard curve of his pectoral muscles.

I shifted under his probing stare.

Danielle sidled up beside me and threw an arm around my shoulders, an eyebrow raised in my direction. "Hi, Jack. What ya doin'? Come to see Lexi, did ya?"

I glared at her so hard she withdrew her arm and formed her lips into an O. Her eyes widened as she tried to hide her smile.

"Where're you girls off to?" His finger grazed the mat on my back. "Doing a little yoga, Lexi?" A sly grin pulled on his lips.

Before I could answer, Danielle said, "Lexi here, has talked me into taking her to the..."

"Store... Supplies..." I closed my eyes and took a breath. "We need supplies for a... project."

"Yes. The store." Danielle agreed.

"Yeah. And we better hurry." I linked my arm with Danielle's and pushed her forward.

"That's right. Need to get those supplies." Danielle waved to Jack over her shoulder. Under her breath, she said to me, "You're such a pathetic liar."

~~~~
~~~~

The U-Store was deserted. The sun hung low in the sky, casting deep shadows on the buildings and making it appear darker than it really was. A late summer breeze stirred up dust from the gravel.

I directed Danielle to drive past the office to the third row and make a left. "Right here. Unit 391." We climbed out of Danielle's vintage 1990 BMW that was in major need of a paint job. Danielle coughed dramatically from the stirring of gravel as she shuffled around the car. Her coughs echoed off the sides of the identical buildings all in a row.

Armed with a flashlight and a storage box that I'd bummed off the school secretary, I handed the box to Danielle. "Here, help me." I dug for the key in my pocket.

"Why are you running so hard from Jack?"

"I'm not running from him," I said like it was the most absurd thing ever.

"You always run. The minute someone looks your way, you do something to push them in the opposite direction." She balanced the box on her hip while I bent down to unlock the garage-like door. "I don't know what you're going to do this time, little Lexi. I've got a feeling about this one. I don't think he'll back away as easily as the others have."

"Jack is not at this school to fall in love, Dani, any more than I am."

"Who said anything about love? I didn't say the l-word. Did you say the l-word? Oh...I do believe you did."

I puffed hair out of my eyes and glared at her. "Doesn't it scare you that he already knew who I was when he arrived?"

"Your father and his are friends. I think you're looking for trouble where there is none. As usual."

"Let's just find these journals my dad mentioned." I pushed the door up overhead.

"What's in these journals, anyway?"

I grabbed the box from Danielle. "I don't know." I only knew what I hoped would be in the journals. Truth. "But my dad made them sound pretty important. And Jack knew about them, so—" I lost all train of thought when I faced the storage unit.

Danielle and I just stood there for a moment. I stared at the ten by twenty-five foot space. My mouth fell open. The contents of the drawers were emptied out on top of the desk and on the couch beside it. Tables were turned on their side.

"What a mess," Danielle finally said. "I've never thought of you as a slob before, but..."

I cocked my head sideways at her. "I didn't do this." But who did? My dad? He's the only one I emailed the new address to. Had to be. He must have been in quite a hurry.

I entered and sat the box on top of the desk. "Well, let's find these journals and get out of here." Danielle pushed up her sleeves. "It's starting to get dark, and the deserted feel of this place is starting to freak me out."

I eyed Danielle for a minute. She had an intense fear of the dark, and I didn't want her phobia to kick in while we were here. Though the sun was setting, there was still enough light to work by.

I surveyed the room. Something told me the journals were no longer here, but sheesh. Dad didn't have to destroy the place.

Since we were there, I decided we might as well have a look. Where to begin...

All I had done when the other storage place closed was have a moving company move everything from one location to another. I hadn't unpacked any boxes or cataloged the content.

Nevertheless, as I climbed over furniture and studied the content, I knew one thing for sure—someone had removed some of the stuff. Then they'd made a mess of the rest.

The boxes were labeled: dishes, kitchenware, towels, bedding, Christmas decorations, books, photographs. I opened several of the boxes, including the one labeled books. None of the boxes included journals. I found a set of bookshelves in the back. Empty.

Danielle looked through drawers of furniture, every once in a while looking up to ask, "Anything?"

I shook my head.

The room grew darker. I was in the very back of the unit with a flashlight, while Danielle worked by the remaining light from outside.

Finally, I stopped, wiped the perspiration from my forehead, and decided the journals weren't there. "Let's just go." I turned off the flashlight, relying on the minimal light coming from outside, and tucked it in the waistband of my jeans. "I'll just have to keep calling my dad until I reach him."

I started working my way back toward the front. Danielle faced me.

I climbed over dressers and tables, moved around stacks of chairs.

A loud banging noise came from just outside the storage unit.

I jerked my head up.

"What the..." Danielle whipped around.

The garage door slid down and the room grew dark.

"Shit. What was that?" I asked. I couldn't see my own hand in front of my face.

"The door just closed." She sounded panicked.

"Obviously, Dani. But how?"

The room was dead quiet. I reached for my flashlight, but before I had a chance to turn it on...

"Lexi!" Danielle screamed.

"What's wrong?"

Silence.

I turned the flashlight around, feeling for the on/off switch. "Dani, answer me." My breath caught in my throat. "Dani."

Nothing.

Finally, I found the flashlight switch and flipped it on. The fluorescent light lit up the place, and I shone it toward Dani. She stood frozen and wide-eyed.

I scrambled around the furniture and boxes separating us.

When I reached her, I ran my hand down her arm. "Dani, sweetie."

Her body shook. Her eyes had glazed over with fear.

"Hold this." I pressed the flashlight to her hand and closed her fingers around it. "I'm going to open the door, okay." I darted toward the door, knocking my hip into the corner of a desk as I did. "Ow." My hand flew to the spot of the pain.

I bent down and lifted the door open. What light remained illuminated the front of the room. A car's tires screeched and scuffled in the gravel at the end of a row of units.

When I reached Danielle again, I put my arm around her and thought hard. *Push away the fear, Dani. You are bigger than this phobia of the dark. You can squash it.*

I led her outside into the fresh air. She sucked in a deep breath and pushed it out slowly. Twice. Any minute she would drop into a dolphin pose.

"Better?" I asked.

She nodded. "Better." She sucked in another cleansing breath. "Oh, honey, your nose is bleeding."

I touched the skin under my nose. "Oh, it's no big deal." I ran to the passenger side of the car and dug a tissue out of my bag. When I returned, I said, "I'm sorry about that. I don't know what happened."

"All I know is when that door closed, I had visions of Anthony Hopkins eating my tongue. You know, like in *Silence of the Lambs*." She tilted her head side to side. "And it didn't help that I'm already terrified of the dark. But inside a storage unit of all places. You know what was weird?"

I shook my head while continuing to squeeze the bridge of my nose.

"I was terrified when that door fell, but the most amazing peace came over me when you put your arm around me." She kicked against the gravel in front of her. "You have such a knack for soothing people, Lexi. You're going to make a great doctor some day."

"Oh, stop it. I'm just sorry I dragged you all the way out here."

"Did you know there are people actually scared of things that are yellow?"

When I raised a skeptical eyebrow, she said, "I swear. It's called Xanthophobia."

I gave her a sideways hug again and leaned my head against hers. "I love you, Dani." She was perfect evidence of how serious phobias could be.

"Love you, too. We're family, you know?"

I did.

She stood, allowing all fear to drop away from her face. "Anyway... Can we get out of here?"

"Absolutely." Especially since what I was looking for wasn't here.

~~~~

I entered the student center at a little before nine p.m. Curfew on a Friday night was ten, and I had to take it seriously if I didn't want to get kicked off the swim team.

The scent of coffee pulled hard at me from Common Grounds, but a good night's sleep was more important the night before a big meet.

I cut through the crowd in the basement game room. That's where I found Jack draped over a pool table shooting eight ball. Briana leaned against a stick in the corner. She was so busy watching him that she didn't see my approach.

"Hi, Briana. Who's winning?" I crossed my arms and watched Jack sink a striped ball in the corner pocket. He glanced over his shoulder when I spoke.

"Why are you always hanging around, Lexi? You're starting to look desperate and pathetic. Can't you just face it? Jack's not interested in you."
~~~~

My heart sped up, and I told myself it was because I fought the urge to start a catfight with Briana, not because her words sliced deep. "Funny. I was thinking the same thing about you."

Briana threw her stick down and took two steps toward me. She had six inches and at least a full cup-size on me.

I also told myself that it didn't bother me that I had found Jack down here playing pool with Briana. Of course, that was a lie. I stood as tall and strong as someone my height could stand against Briana. The fury in her eyes should have scared me.

"Whoa." Jack stepped between us, his back to Briana, but his face to me. His smirk reached all the way up to his eyes.

I stepped over to a table and began pulling at napkins inside a metal dispenser, preparing for a full-on nosebleed. Jack cocked his head in an is-that-necessary sort of way. He handed his stick to one of the other guys. "Sorry, Bree. Raincheck?" he said more than asked. The disappointment on her face reminded me of those commercials—priceless.

Jack glided toward me, grabbed my hand, and led me from the basement. "Aren't you a little small to be picking fights?"

We exited the building. It was a pleasant night with a perfect breeze—not too cool, not too warm. I looked sideways at him. "Sorry to break up your game."

"No, you aren't."

I grinned. Okay, fine. I wasn't. But why was she always around?

"Where did you go earlier?" he asked.

"What do you mean?"

"Oh, please. You think I bought all that crap about you needing supplies from the store?"

Still holding my hand, he pulled me toward the multi-purpose field again. Only this time it was dark.

He dropped my hand, and I watched him walk out onto the field.

"People will see us out there."

"So." His lips twitched. "I would think you would like that. Out in the open where I can't hurt you. Not without witnesses anyway."

"Ha. Ha."

"I'm not trying to be funny, Lexi." He stopped and faced me. "You think I can't sense your fear of me? It's one thing that you don't trust me, but I honestly think you're scared to be alone with me." He walked close, standing almost a foot taller than me. He lifted his hand and brushed hair off my forehead. "I am not here to hurt you," he whispered. "Quite the opposite, really."

A chill danced down my spine. His touch lingered long after he pulled his fingers away.

He took a few steps backwards and then lifted his head to urge me to follow. I did. As nervous as I was around him, I was even more curious to know him. To know who he really was and why he was at Wellington. I was drawn to him in a way I didn't understand—beyond wanting more information about our fathers.

When we reached the middle of the field, I turned in a circle amazed at how vulnerable I was out in the open. As if Jack would see inside me and see everything—my flaws, my scars, my hopes, my fears, everything that made up the true me.

He sat down on the grass, stretching his legs in front of him and leaning back on his elbows. "So, why did you interrupt my game? To tell me what you bought at the store?"

I wrung my hands, then crossed my arms. How could he always be so relaxed when I had so many questions? "No. But I also didn't interrupt just to break up whatever it is you have going on with Briana." Finally, I sat down and crossed my legs. "Just want to make sure we have that clear."

He scooted closer and leaned his head toward mine. I felt the tickle of his breath against my cheek. For a brief moment, I thought he might kiss me. "I'm glad you cleared that up." He retreated, and his smug grin returned.

That arrogance lit the fire inside my veins that threatened every time I neared Jack DeWeese.

"Why did I think I could have a conversation with you? Everything's a joke to you." I moved to stand, but his fingers quickly laced around my forearm.

"Don't go."

"Why not, Jack? You think this is a game. You're right, I am scared of you. I don't know what you're trying to accomplish by being here. Or what you're hiding. I'm just... I'm scared."

"I'm sorry." He loosened his grasp on my arm and rubbed his thumb across my skin, sending electric pulses along my arm. Some level of sincerity warmed the eyes that made my heart skip beats.

What was he doing to me? I couldn't think around him. One minute I wanted to run and the next I wanted to melt beneath his touch.

I needed Jack, though. His father was the only one to have had contact with Dad since the dinner, and I desperately wanted to talk to him—to give Dad the chance to explain to me what or who I was. To ask him if he took the journals from storage.

"I had Danielle take me to my family's storage unit to find Dad's journals."

Jack's eyes widened. "And?"

"And nothing. They weren't there."

He seemed to let out a large breath when I spoke. Why did that relieve him?

"What would I have found, Jack? Do you know?"

"How am I supposed to know what's in the journals?"

"I think you're lying." I glanced at my watch. Five minutes until curfew. "But I don't have time or even the energy to argue with you tonight."

"Lexi. I don't know what we're going to find in those journals. I hope we find the truth to all of our questions." His voice was different. There was no hint of humor when he spoke now. "I just wish..."

"What? You wish what?"

"I just wish you wouldn't try to find the answers alone."

"I wasn't alone. Danielle was with me."

"And you're going to share with Danielle whatever you find? What if our fathers broke the law? What if the law is after them, or even some bad people who want this information?"

"Bad people? Do you hear yourself?" I couldn't hide my astonishment. "You make it sound like a James Bond movie."

"No, Lexi. I wish this was fiction—the make-believe world of spies and crimes solved by cool gadgets. It's not. This is real life. And you're going to have to trust me at some point if you want to get to the truth."

"Why should I trust you?" Why was I even sitting here with him?

"Because as long as your father is ignoring your calls, I'm all you've got. We obviously have a lot in common. And a lot to hide."

I cringed. "That's not fair."

"No. It's not. None of this is fair, but neither of us knows enough. I have as much to lose as you do if the truth is discovered. I just wish you wouldn't shut me out."

"Why haven't you confronted your father about all this?"

"It's complicated." His eyes iced over. I had hit a touchy spot. "And you're about to break curfew." He stood, and grabbing both of my hands, he lifted me to my feet.

I pulled away, but not before breathing in the clean scent of shower gel that was quickly becoming so familiar to me. "I'm trying to understand all this. I really need to talk to my dad. Do you think your father knows where he is?"

"Let's find out. Tomorrow, we'll ask him."

"I have a swim meet."

"After that. We'll go to my house. It's a date." Another smile played with the edges of Jack's lips. He'd gone an entire fifteen minutes without toying with me.

"It is not a date. But I'd appreciate the chance to talk to your father."

He tilted his head side to side. "Whatever."

I walked a few steps away from him toward the girl's dorm.

"Lexi?"

I turned.

"I would really appreciate you not shutting me out if you decide to go in search of these journals again. You need me whether you want to admit it yet or not. That email mentioning the IIA? That was a warning."

The IIA should have been all the warning I needed to beg Dad to change my name again and transfer me to another school. "I'll think about it."

"I'm scared for you, Lexi."

I turned and walked away. *I'm scared for me, too.*

EIGHT

The Imperial March—Darth Vader's theme song—woke me at seven a.m. the next morning. "Dad!" I gasped. I threw the covers back and leaned over the side of the bed. I patted around my books stacked on the floor for my phone, which must have fallen off the bed during the night.

I had begged my phone to ring all week. And now? Could I talk to Dad? Tell him I knew the truth? What truth was that, really?

A cold sweat broke out across my forehead.

"Dad!" My voice came out barely above a whisper when I finally answered.

"Lexi, honey?" He sounded rushed. Like he was walking outside.

"Dad, where've you been? I've been so worried."

"I had to leave town, but I'm back in Kentucky."

I massaged my eyelids, willing them to fully open now that the initial shock of the phone ringing had subsided. "Some really weird things are happening."

"Are you okay?"

Was I okay? I didn't know. "Yeah, but dad, somebody threatened me in an email and wants to know where your journals are. Sent me a strange lab memo as well." Danielle's blond hair fanned across her pillow. Her chest rose and fell in a slow even tempo. I hoped she was still sleeping. She typically slept through most of my craziness. Though, I wasn't usually this insane. "And I went to the storage place. It was a mess."

"Look, honey, I'm in town. I'm coming to see you this morning." His tone was hurried, kind of like a doctor at an appointment. Like if you didn't get everything in that you needed to say, he'd be gone, and you'd still have this place you thought might be a tumor.

"I have a swim meet at nine," I blurted out.

"Good. Great. I haven't seen you swim in a long time." Though rushed, he sounded upbeat and actually excited to see me, his only child, in action at school.

For a brief moment, I felt normal. "Dad, you can't do that. I thought you told me no one could know that you were my father." It was a very brief moment in Normalville.

"Don't worry about that. I'll take care of it. Lexi, honey, did you mention anything about the journals to anyone else?"

"Jack DeWeese is here. I mentioned them to him. But no one else." I closed my eyes tight. Waited for a response.

"That's good."

Good. He said good. I opened my eyes and sat straighter. "So, I can trust Jack and his father, Dad?"

"I... I think so. We'll talk soon."

My shoulders relaxed. Soon. We'd talk. Dad loved me. He would answer my questions. Everything would be fine.

"Lexi, I want you to keep your eyes open. Look out for anything strange."

Strange? Did he not hear what I just told him?

"And don't mention the journals to anyone else until we've talked, okay? I'm leaving the airport. I'll be there to see you swim."

"Okay."

I dressed quickly, making sure to pack extra goggles. I didn't want anything to ruin this morning.

For some odd reason, I wasn't angry. I'd always known something was *off* about me. Weird. Strange. Unusual. But I was still me. And my dad loved me.

And he was coming to see me swim. We would get to have that talk. And he would fix whatever this threat was.

~~~~

What did Dad mean when he said he thought I could trust Jack and Dr. DeWeese? Did he mean, "Yeah, sure. Of course we can trust them." Or did he mean, "I *think* we can trust them, but I don't know."

Doubt crept in by the time I reached the pool deck.

With headphones in my ears, I stretched in the back corner of the pool area with the rest of my team. "Chasing Cars" by Snow Patrol played. I purposely positioned myself away from Bree. The last thing I needed was a super dose of that piece of evil.

The other team, our archrival from Frankfort, Kentucky, climbed up on starting blocks and began warming up in one-half of the pool. Spectators filed into the bleachers on the other side of the pool. I kept one eye on the door for Dad.

Jack walked in with other students. His eyes found mine immediately. He offered a wave, a silent hello. He looked at ease in jeans and an untucked black t-shirt. It was Saturday, so students were dressed in casual street clothes.

I shot him a low wave.
~~~~

When the coach gave the signal, I stowed my iPod away and removed my sweats for warm-ups. Bent over at the waist, I dug through my bag for my goggles. Someone knocked into me, pushing me against the wall. "What the...?" I whipped around and faced Bree.

"I don't know what game you're playing." Bree pointed a finger into my chest. "Stay away from Jack."

"What are you, eight? You going to call 'dibs' next?"

"Just stay away from him, Lexi."

"Or what, Bree? You're going to beat me in the big race today?" I asked in a mopey toddler voice.

She stepped closer. Looked down on me. "I'm going to do that anyway."

Just to prove a point, I smiled, angled my body around her, and waved. She followed my line of vision. Jack just shook his head.

Coach Williams approached. "You girls ready?"

"Sure am," I said. "Good luck today, Bree." I smiled.

She glared.

I searched the stands. Still no dad.

Jack shrugged and mouthed the words, "Who are you looking for?"

"My dad," I mouthed back.

His face registered surprise.

"In the water, Matthews." Coach stood on the deck. He blew his whistle to start his swimmers off the starting blocks.

The team and I swam a few hundred meters, and when I was done with the warm-up, I resumed my search for Dad. It was no use. I checked my phone. Nothing.

When I was called for a race, I swam. And won.

Then came the race that Bree had looked forward to beating me in all week. The 100-meter freestyle. Eight swimmers stood behind the starting blocks waiting for the command. I glanced over at the door. And to Jack, who mirrored my concern.

"Swimmers up," the race starter called. He announced the event, the heat number, the length of the race and the stroke.

I climbed up on the block and sucked in a deep breath. I adjusted my goggles. Shaking my arms, I tried with everything I had to rid my body of the built-up tension that pooled at the base of my neck and spread down my arms.

I closed my eyes briefly, pushing all other thoughts from my head other than a picture of myself winning this race. I pictured my father walking in at the last second before the starter sounded the horn to start the race, and he would see me swim.

"Take your mark."

I put one foot forward and bent over at the waist. My hands curled around the edge of the starting block.

The horn blew. I pushed hard with my legs and stretched my arms out in front of me.

The race was over in fifty-nine seconds. My hands touched the wall second. I lost.

After I ripped my goggles and swim cap from my head, I dipped under the water to smooth my hair back. Coach Williams pulled me out of the pool and gave me a pat on the shoulder. Two lanes over, my arch nemesis on my own team smiled at me and slapped her hand down on the water in an "I did it" sort of way.

I leaned my head back against my neck. Defeated. The taste of chlorine seeped through my lips and onto my tongue.

Still breathing hard, I turned just in time to see Jack looking over his shoulder at me as he followed his father and Dean Fisher out the door. I still did not see Dad anywhere. At least he didn't come all the way here and see me lose.

"What's Dr. DeWeese doing here?" I said under my breath. While the rest of the team chatted about our team victory, I headed to the locker room. I raced through my shower and, ten minutes later, headed for the exit.

When I opened the door, Jack waited against the opposite wall in the hallway. His arms were folded across his black T-shirt. He bent one knee, resting his foot against the wall. When our eyes met, he pushed away from the wall. He seemed to hesitate as he stepped.

"Is my dad here?" There was no mistaking the excitement in my voice.

"No." He stuffed his hands in the front pockets of his jeans.

"I don't understand. He called this morning. He was on his way from the airport."

"Come on." He lifted his head in the direction of the door. "My father is in the dean's office. They want to talk to you." He grabbed my elbow. We started down the hallway.

The feeling started slow—the building of panic. In my stomach. My chest. I stopped abruptly and pulled my arm away. "Something's happened. What?"

He looked past me, over my shoulder.

"Look at me," I said. The furrow of his brow shadowed his intense blue eyes. "I'm not taking another step until you tell me what's wrong. I'm tired of all these secrets."

"I'm sorry."

"You're sorry about what?"

Jack's silence was deafening.

"Jack... You're sorry about what?" My voice grew louder and insistent.

"The police are here, too. It's your father."

"What about my father? Is he in jail?" Had he really been in trouble, like Jack said? "Where is he?"

"Let's go to the dean's office. They'll explain everything."

"Jack." I gritted my teeth. My hands shook. "Tell me," I pleaded, my voice lower and more in control. I could handle whatever this was. "Is he in trouble?"

He tilted his head. "There's been an explosion. Your father..."

"What about my father?" I asked, shaking my head.

"Your father's car..."

My lower lip quivered. I swallowed hard against the lump in my throat. "No, you're wrong. There's been a mistake."

"I'm sorry, Lexi." He reached his arm around my shoulders and pulled me close.

"It can't be," I said against his chest. "He was on his way to see me." We would finally get to talk. He was going to watch my swim meet.

Other swimmers were exiting the locker rooms now. Maybe they had been already, but I hadn't noticed.

Bree pranced out the door and right over to me. "Isn't this just perfect?"

Jack dropped one arm to his side, and kept one hand on my arm. I turned to Bree. Her perfect red curls framed her face and a smirk as big as a Kentucky racetrack screamed victory.

"I told you to stay away from him," she whispered through gritted teeth.

I thought hard at Briana. *Go ahead. Get angry with me.*

"Back off, Briana," Jack said. "This isn't the time."

A spot of blood dripped from my nose. *Want to hit me? Do it. Cause a scene.*

"You're a freak, Lexi. Your stupid nose is bleeding, and I haven't even touched you."

"Lexi?" Jack's voice edged over Briana's. "Lexi, stop whatever it is you're doing."

Come on Bree. Come at me. You want to hit me so bad. You know Jack DeWeese isn't interested in you. It makes you so mad, doesn't it? Throw the first punch. Or better yet, throw a weak, girly slap.

Bree came at me fast and with hate in her eyes. She lifted an open hand and aimed it straight for my face. A crowd had formed and witnessed Bree taking the first swipe.

Of course, I was prepared. I caught her wrist and shoved it away. I raised both hands and placed them on her chest, and I pushed with every ounce of rage in me. I shoved her against the wall, and she fell to the ground.

"What is the matter with you?" she screamed. "You think I won't tell the dean?"

"What are you going to tell him? That you took a swing at me, and I defended myself? Be my guest." I gestured to all the witnesses.

Everyone gawked at us. Even Jack was surprised. I saw the pity in his eyes, and I felt sick. So, I ran. I ran as fast as I could. I turned the corner and continued until I reached the main doors out of the school. I didn't need anyone's pity.

Once outside, I saw a few small gatherings of families in the parking lot. Parents and siblings who'd come to watch their children swim or just to visit that sunny Saturday morning.

To my right was the school's bus. The driver stood by a tree waiting for students to finish loading.

After wiping any evidence of tears or blood from my face, I approached him slowly, giving myself time to regain composure.

"Good morning, Miss Matthews. Good meet today? The chlorine did a number on those green eyes of yours."

I glanced toward the door. No one had followed me so far. "Hi, Mr. Jenkins," I said. "Where are you headed this morning?"

"I'm taking a group into the city. Dropping off at the public library on Martin Luther King."

"Can you drop me at the nursing home on your way? I'm supposed to work today."

"Sure, honey. Get in."

The dean and Dr. DeWeese exited the building, along with a couple of police officers. Jack followed right behind them, searching for me.

I climbed the steps onto the bus and found an empty seat in the back. Sitting, I brought my knees to my chin. The hood of my sweatshirt shielded my head and face. The bus lurched forward and headed for Wellington's gates. I tilted my head to the side and stared out the window. That's when the tears came.

My body shook.

My father was dead. I had no one.

No one except the grandmother who'd raised me.

NINE

I shuffled into the nursing home in Midland, Kentucky, my grandmother's home for the past six years. My hair hung past my shoulders in damp, brunette waves. Dried tears stung my face. I immediately smelled the scent of Pine Sol mixed with floral arrangements and urine.

Most people who knew me thought I only visited the facility as a volunteer. Few knew that Gram was my only family left in the world.

"Oh, dear, you've been crying," Gram said when she saw me. She was seventy-six years old, and suffered from the late stages of Alzheimer's. Her silver hair was combed, pushed behind her ears in a neat bob.

I knelt beside her wheelchair. She reached a shaky hand to my cheek, and I leaned into her gentle touch. Her palm was cool and soft against my face. The smell of her hand lotion competed with the flameless candle on the vanity across the room, a Christmas present I'd given her last year.

"Oh, Gram," I sobbed.

"Do we know each other?" she asked.

I squeezed my eyes tight. Tears leaked out, streaming along already well-worn paths. When I reopened them, Gram stared out the window where a couple of cardinals dangled on a branch of a magnolia tree.

This was not the woman who'd fed and cared for me until I was eleven. The one who drove me to swim practice five days a week, delivered me to and from school until I was in the sixth grade, and made sure I had a place to call home.

No, this was just a shell of that woman, overtaken by a disgusting disease. I saw glimpses of her from time to time, but she was missing the spark she got in her eye every time I came home with an A in math or won the swim races she knew I worked so hard for. When I was happy, she was ecstatic. When I was sad, she was devastated. She even threatened to beat up the first boy to break my heart when I was eleven.

I smiled at the memory.

"What am I going to do, Gram?" I whispered as I curled up in a chair across from her and laid my head against the back. And sobbed harder. My head ached. I couldn't take in a breath.

Car explosion? Did someone actually murder my dad? Who would want to kill him? I couldn't wrap my brain around the enormity of it all. Everything was coming at me so fast.

My grandmother pointed at the red and brown birds and smiled.

I cried until I had no tears left.

I wasn't even sure how much time passed. A lot, because the lighting in the room had changed. The sun hung lower in the sky and cast an orange glow through the mini blinds.

I must have fallen asleep. When I assessed my cramped body, a blanket was draped over me, and my neck ached.

A nurse entered and placed a vase of flowers on Gram's bedside table. I stood and picked up the blanket that fell to the floor.

"Hi, honey. You okay? Can I get you something?"

I shook my head. "Can you tell me what time it is?"

"Close to eight."

I was going to be in huge trouble at school. "Where'd the flowers come from?" I asked, assuming another resident had received more than her share.

"A handsome young man brought them in." She chomped on a piece of gum like her life depended on it. "Oh, and there was a note." She reached into the pocket of her multi-colored nursing jacket and pulled out a small envelope.

"Thanks," I said, taking it from her. "Would it be a problem if I stayed here tonight?"

The young woman bit her bottom lip. "I guess it would be alright."

I glanced toward the brown leather chair and then rubbed at the knot forever wedged between my neck and shoulder.

"That chair actually scoots and unfolds into a horizontal surface," she said. "I'll get you another blanket."

"Really? It's no problem, is it? Because if it is, I can..."

"Sweetie, it's no problem. But... don't you have some place you need to be?"

Eyes that I thought had run dry produced yet another tear. "No," I managed.

Without further questions, she left.

I pulled a note card from the envelope and leaned in to smell the bouquet of white stargazer lilies and roses.

I am so sorry about your dad, Lexi. My father and I want to help. I know you feel afraid and alone, but you're not. I'm in the front lobby when you're ready. ~Jack

Jack? How did he know where to find me? How did he fit into all of this?

Well, he was in the front lobby if I wanted to find out. I scratched my bottom lip with the corner of the card.

Bending over, I kissed my sleeping grandmother on the cheek. "I love you, Gram," I whispered. "I'm gonna find out who did this. I promise."

The bright fluorescents in the hallway blinded me temporarily. I passed the common area where some men played checkers. One of them threw a checker at Alex Trebek, apparently not liking the answer to Jeopardy's Daily Double.

Across the room, a familiar-looking man snagged my attention. I stopped and backed up against the wall. I inched forward slowly and peered around the corner. He spoon-fed Mrs. Whitmeyer Jell-O. I'd seen him recently. But where? His wolfish grin sent chills down my spine.

"What are you doing?"

I jerked backwards and flattened my back and head against the wall at the sound of Jack's voice in my ear. "Geez, Jack, you scared me."

"Well? What are you doing sneaking around? Spying on old people is kinda rude."

"I wasn't sneaking. I just thought I saw someone who looked familiar."

"Oh, yeah? Who?" He craned his neck to peer around the corner.

I grabbed a handful of his shirt and pulled him back. A little closer to me than I intended. "Don't." His fresh, clean smell practically sent me asking for a wheelchair of my own.

"You're serious, aren't you? Who's over there?"

"It's no one. Just a friend of my grandmother's. He's got a crush on her, and I'm not up to his questions." I shook my head and tried to laugh.

"How about I give you a ride? You look exhausted."

"Really? I thought I was looking pretty good. I probably need a little make-up or something, but all-in-all..." I was positive I looked hideous. Red, puffy eyes. Zero make-up. My hair a mess from lack of effort after the swim meet. I didn't care.

His expression darkened, and he frowned. Except, it was more than sadness. Fear, maybe. "I am really sorry about your dad."

Nodding and swallowing against the forever-present lump in my throat, I pointed my eyes to the ceiling hoping to ward off the unwanted tears.

"Let me give you a ride."

"I appreciate it, but I'm going to sleep here tonight. I want to be close to my Gram."

"You can't sleep here, Lexi." His words sounded like an order.

"Yes, I can, Jack." I matched his authoritative tone. Who did this guy think he was? "I've already arranged it. Why are you here anyway? I don't need you hovering all over me or your protection. Go home, Jack." Nothing had been normal since he showed up at my school.

"Hear me out." He pulled me down the hallway to the front waiting area. He sat down and waited for me to do the same. When he leaned forward, our knees touched. "I can't imagine what you're going through."

My lip quivered.

"But I want to help you. My father and I want to help you."

I searched his eyes and sucked in a deep breath. His father wanted to help me? They didn't even know me. I shifted so that our knees no longer bumped. "Why did someone kill my dad? I know controversy followed him everywhere he went, but murder? They blew him up, Jack." Tears streamed down the sides of my cheeks. I swiped at them.

Jack pulled me into a hug. "I don't know why," he said. His hand pressed the back of my head into his chest as he smoothed out my hair.

As much as I didn't want to admit it, I liked it there in his arms. It was the safest I had felt in days.

~~~~

While Jack pulled his car around, I said good-bye to Gram. I held her hand up to my cheek and remembered a time when her stern words of reason were all I needed to face my fears and any obstacle in my path.

"I love you Gram," I whispered in her ear. "I'll be back soon, okay."

She continued to sleep. I sent warm thoughts to her. *Remember my love, Gram. Always.* I never knew if she heard them or not.

I raised my backpack over my shoulder and turned. The man with the canine grin blocked the doorway.

"Hi, Lexi." He cocked his head with curiosity.

He wore dress slacks and a light-colored plaid button down. Thin, wire-frame glasses made him look smart and professional, but his expression sent a chill down my arms.

I took a step backwards. "Who are you?"

"Someone who means you no harm."

Then why was I scared? "Oh, yeah? Then you won't mind backing out of the room and speaking to me out in the hallway."
~~~~

His mouth twitched. "I can't do that. This is a private message." He stepped closer to me, forcing me further into the room.

I calculated the number of steps to the door, then studied his face again. He was definitely familiar. Then I remembered. The dinner. After Dad's speech. Outside, as I had waited for the car. He'd bumped into me. Coincidence? "I saw you at the dinner."

He cocked his head again. "Your father and I go way back."

Gram was asleep in her bed. The hallway buzzed with activity. What could he possibly do to me here in this nursing home? There were probably five nurses at the station around the corner. "I could scream."

"You could. But there's no need. I mean you no harm."

Tell that to the organ about to leap from my chest.

He took another step and reached for the door behind him.

No, don't close it. My heart sprinted. I held a hand out in front of me. "Just stop right there. Don't come closer or I will yell my freaking head off." I glanced around the room for a weapon. "How do you know my father?" I asked, present tense, as if he wasn't blown to bits earlier today.

"Your father knew my sister." He inched closer. "I'm sorry about his death."

"His death? You mean his murder?"

"Yes. It's all over the news."

"Who are you?"

"I'm just someone who wants the truth exposed."

"The truth? And what truth would that be?"

"The truth of who... what you are."

I heard Jack's voice in the hallway, apparently speaking to one of the nurses.

"Jack," I yelled, but more softly than I intended. I darted forward, knocking into the wall of a man blocking the doorway.

He grabbed me and turned me around. My back pushed up against his chest. He held me there. "Listen to me, little girl," he whispered. "I am not going to hurt you. But you have no idea what or who you're dealing with. I didn't kill your father. I'm sorry he's dead, actually. But I will make your life a living hell if you don't find his journals."

"I don't have the journals."

"You'll find them. And they'll answer all of your wildest questions." He squeezed me tighter. "Oh, and one more thing," he whispered. "Be careful who you trust. Jack DeWeese isn't being... What's the word? Forthcoming. If he found you, who's to say someone else won't?"

I clawed and pushed at his arm. Finally, he shoved me forward. By the time I regained my footing, he was gone.

TEN

Shit!

I slid my satchel over my shoulder and ran from the room. There was no sign of Wolfman in the hallway. Only Jack, waiting by the exit.

I massaged my chest over my wildly-thumping heart. Who was that? It didn't take a nuclear engineer to know that Jack wasn't telling me everything. That wasn't news.

I sauntered toward him. Giving me a smile of pity, he lifted my bag off my shoulder. He pushed the door open and led me to his car—not the motorcycle, thankfully—waiting out front.

He glanced toward my profile as he drove in silence. I assumed we were headed in the direction of school until I was sure we weren't.

Wolfman's words scrolled through my head. I wanted to tell Jack about the man at the nursing home, but something stopped me.

I probably should have been nervous to be alone with Jack, but what did I care? I had no one. No one who cared about me. No one to answer to. As far as one of life's low-points, this was it.

He and his father had been notified of my father's death before I was. I was definitely curious about that.

"Thanks for the flowers," I said, breaking the thirty-minute silence. "That meant a lot. My Gram loves lilies and roses."

Jack pulled the car up to a large iron gate. Where was he taking me? He reached up and pushed a button on his visor.

The gate opened. We wove along a tree-lined drive. A horse farm, by the looks of it. I barely made out a couple of horses in the dark behind a black plank fence.

We pulled up in front of a large brick house. No, not large. Enormous. Path lights glowed along a walkway leading to the front door and another leading around to the side of the house. Though summer was practically over, flowers still decorated window boxes and flanked either side of the grand, wooden doorway under a small covered entrance.

"Where are we?"

"Home."

"Your house?"

He nodded.

"Why did you bring me here?"

"You need some sleep. We thought you would rest better away from school." There was that authoritative tone again.

"We?"

"Mom, Dad and me."

"I'm guessing someone from school must be looking for me." At least part of me hoped so.

"They know you're here."

I met his gaze. "I don't understand."

The whites of his eyes glowed in the dark. He reached a hand and tucked my hair behind my ear. "You're safe here. Father says that the police and FBI are working on who wanted your father dead."

Jack helped me out of the car and led the way to the front door.

Once inside, he lit a gas fireplace. "How about some hot tea?"

"Okay." I watched him leave the room. He seemed nervous. Quiet. Distant.

Lately, every time someone claimed they meant me no harm, or that I was safe, my bubble of security seemed to deflate slightly.

I ran my hand along the straight line of the white sofa. Glanced at pictures as I circled the room until I landed on one picture in particular.

"Father told me that was taken a year before I was born."

I traced the outline of my dad's shape. He stood next to Dr. DeWeese, who had a full head of wheat-colored hair at the time. "You look so much like him in this picture," I observed.

Jack took the picture from my hand and replaced it with a cup of hot tea.

I took a sip. Soothing chamomile. The hot flavor of honey slid down my throat. "Thank you."

"You're welcome. Anita helped me with it." He stuffed his hands in his front pockets. "She also prepared a room for you."

"Anita?"

"Housekeeper. And my nanny of sorts." Something akin to sadness flashed in his eyes.

"Ahhh." I swallowed another sip, pondering the questions ping-ponging through my head.

A door closing echoed in the foyer just beyond the living room. We both turned toward the sound. Dr. DeWeese and a woman entered the room.

"Oh, you poor dear. John and I have been so worried about you." The woman glided toward us. She was dressed in an expensive-looking suit of reds and oranges. Bleached-blond hair rested perfectly on her shoulders. Chunky gold jewelry decorated her neck and ears. She stuck her lip out in a strange pout before her arms stretched wide and pulled me into a tight embrace. "I'm so sorry. Peter was a brilliant man. We loved him dearly." She pushed me back, holding me at arms' length. "How are you holding up?"

The way-too-long hug and hairspray that would kill fleas suffocated me. Without answering, I backed away.

"Mom," Jack said, moving closer and shaking his head. "Lexi, this is Cathy DeWeese. My mother." Jack rolled his eyes and shrugged at the same time, making me feel less guilty about the first-impression I was forming of the woman who gave him life.

"Nice to meet you, ma'am." My voice was suddenly shy.

"None of this 'ma'am' stuff. We are going to be great friends. Call me Cathy."

"How are you, Lexi?" Dr. DeWeese asked. A look of pity dragged his lips downward.

"Confused. Sad. Pissed off." Yeah, that about summed it up.

"We are too," he said. "You can stay here as long as you need. And come back as often as you like."

I furrowed my brow and looked from Dr. DeWeese to Jack. "I really appreciate that, Dr. DeWeese, but..."

Mrs. DeWeese eyed her husband. "Ahh, honey, she doesn't know—"

"Mom." Jack shook his head, stopping whatever she was about to say.

"I don't know what?" I asked.

Silence. The three of them traded glances with enough pity to swallow me whole.

It was Dr. DeWeese who stepped forward and placed a gentle hand on my elbow. "Let's sit, Lexi."

I obeyed, although I was pretty sure I would erupt in a childish fit any second if these people didn't stop tip-toeing around my feelings.

"Your father visited me a week ago."

"Yes." I already knew that.

"He was afraid something might happen to him. He left instructions in case anything did."

"What do you mean by instructions?" Had he thought someone would try to kill him?

"Where you are concerned. He wanted to make sure someone looked after your interests."

My interests? John, Jack and Cathy all stared at me. I stretched and recurled my fingers into fists, rubbing them back and forth along my thighs.

"Your father didn't want to leave you abandoned," Dr. DeWeese continued.

Yeah, well, that's how it goes sometimes. The threat of tears stung. "I'm not abandoned. I have my grandmother. And I'm practically eighteen."

Dr. DeWeese cleared his throat. "He left clear written documentation of what to do with you if he were to..."

"Die," I finished for him. "What to do with me, you say. You mean where to stick me? Where to tuck away the orphan child?"

"Oh, dear, what he's trying to say is..." Cathy took a step closer.

I leapt to my feet and backed away from all three of them. "Just spit it out, will you? Who's in charge of me now?"

Dr. DeWeese stood. Looked me straight in the eye. "I am. It's only to help you finish your last year of school, get into The Program, and then college. I only want to help you, Lexi, to reach your dreams the way your father would want."

I nodded, pursing my lips. School. The Program. College. With Dad gone, who now decided what I would study?

"You'll be a part of our family," Cathy said as if I'd just won the lottery.

I angled my head toward her. Then to Jack, who stood motionless and silent. His eyes locked with mine.

"I'd like to go to bed now," I whispered. It was all I could manage at this point.

~~~~

I woke in a dark room. My body was tangled in a sheet and drenched in sweat. I pulled free from the covers, sat straight up in bed, and clutched my chest.

An image from my dream of Jack and me running down a long, white hallway, holding hands, was vivid. I could still feel the tightness of his fingers around my right hand and the fear of whatever it was we ran from. The glimmer in his eye when he looked at me in the dream tugged on my heart, leaving me short of breath.

"What the hell was that?" I whispered in the still of night. *And where am I?*

After inspecting the entire room with my eyes, I remembered I was in one of the DeWeese's guest rooms. Then the full weight of reality sliced through my chest.

Dad was dead.
~~~~

Dr. DeWeese was my new legal guardian.

Jack was in the next room over.

I buried my head in my hands. I had so many questions, and no one to trust with them.

What did it all mean? I massaged my forehead with the heel of my palm, trying to wipe away the images of Jack from my dreams.

Deciding I was wide-awake and starving, I pulled my sweatpants on to accompany the cami I had been sleeping in—the same clothes I had arrived in, minus the sweatshirt—and went in search of a kitchen. That couldn't be too hard to find, could it?

I padded lightly down the stairs. My hand grazed the banister as I stepped.

Moonlight shone through large windows along the backside of the house. The DeWeeses lived on a horse farm, from what I could tell when I arrived, and behind the house was nothing but darkness this time of night.

I skirted around some chairs in what appeared to be a sitting area of some sort. The house was eerily quiet. When I arrived at another open doorway, I had found the kitchen, lit only by a small dome light over the stove.

As I entered, the kitchen tile felt cold on my feet. The large windows continued in the kitchen. Next to them, a door. To the back patio, maybe? Craving fresh air, I walked to it.

My fingers wrapped around the doorknob.

"I wouldn't do that if I were you."

I whipped around. My hand flew to my chest. "Shit, Jack. You scared me," I spit through clenched teeth. How did I not see him when I entered the kitchen? *Why does he always seem to be sneaking up on me?*

"I wasn't the one sneaking around in the middle of the night." He sat on top of the kitchen island on the other side of the room. His legs dangled off the edge. A smug smile tugged at the corners of his lips. "You making a break for it? You might want to rethink leaving through that door." He sounded like he was kidding, but it had to look like I was sneaking out, for sure.

I stood there a few seconds analyzing him and his words. I'd had enough of others deciding what was best for me. I turned, grabbed hold of the doorknob, and yanked.

Suddenly, a deafening whirring noise sounded. I pressed my hands to both ears. *Crap*. Of course the DeWeeses had an alarm.

Jack pushed off the counter and jogged to the panel beside the door so he could shut off the stupid alarm. He then stepped past me, raising a single finger to his lips, and backed out of the room.

He crossed the sitting area in record speed. Quick footsteps thumped overhead.

When he got to the stairwell, he said, "Dad?"

"What set off the alarm?" Dr. DeWeese asked from upstairs.

"It was just me. Sorry. I was trying to set a spider free and forgot about the alarm."

I heard some huffs and puffs, followed by heavy footsteps and the closing of a door.

Jack returned. "I told you not to open it." He chastised me with humor in his eyes.

"You could have said why." I crossed my arms, realizing only then that I was wearing a skimpy cami and sweat pants. It wasn't like I had a chance to pack a bag for this unplanned sleepover.

Jack's face softened. "Couldn't sleep?"

I shook my head. Jack's eyes shimmered in the dim light. I turned and walked toward the back windows again. "Did you shut off the alarm? Can I go outside?"

"Yeah, but it's pretty cool out tonight. Here."

Jack lifted his sweatshirt over his head. Thankfully, he had a t-shirt on underneath.

"Thanks." I slipped it on. As I did, Jack's familiar scent wrapped around me as the fabric brushed against my face.

"Do you want to be alone?" Jack asked. "I could come with you."

Part of me wanted to run away from this house, from the DeWeeses. From Jack. But another part of me, and maybe an even bigger part, wanted to know Jack better—to let him in.

Dad had obviously shut Dr. DeWeese out of his life all those years ago for a reason. Now, I would never know his reason for getting back in touch.

Anyway, why would that preclude me from allowing Mr. Tall, Dark and Handsome into my lonely life? He raised an eyebrow while I deliberated. Confusion balled up in my stomach. I barely distinguished between it and hunger.

"I appreciate that..." The sleeves of the sweatshirt fell past my hands. I looked up into Jack's dark, serious eyes. "I think I'd like to be alone if that's okay."

He nodded. Some level of understanding registered on his face. "How about I find some turkey for a sandwich while you're out?"

I nodded. He seemed to know exactly what I needed at the time I needed it. "I would really like that."

Outside, I walked along a plank fence separating me from horse pastures. My eyes adjusted to the light of the moon, and I could see outlines and shadows of trees and the plank fence in the distance.

The last few conversations Dad and I shared replayed over and over in my head. They were the last words he would ever say to me.

Why would someone kill him? Did it have something to do with his recent research?

A strange clicking sound disturbed my thoughts. I searched through two rows of fences where I could just make out a dark figure that appeared very much like a human form. An orange light around the figure's head burned brighter. A cigarette.

I inched up to the fence line and tried to focus through the planks. Was this figure watching me? Or was it a stranger out for a midnight stroll, like me? Did someone live close to the DeWeeses? Or on their farm?

I stepped further along the fence line. When I looked toward the figure, he walked in the same direction as I, a field apart. I sped up.

The figure stopped. A small light of fire fell to the ground in an arch. Then he appeared to get taller as he climbed the fence and leapt to the ground on the other side and ran toward me.

I gasped and turned toward the house. I was much further away than I'd realized. I could only make out a small patio light in the distance. I glanced over my shoulder. The figure gained on me. I sped up.

When I reached the end of the fence line, I cut hard to the left toward the house and hit a wall. I looked up into Jack's face. "Someone's chasing me." I spoke through heavy pants.

His head jerked up, looking in the direction I had just come from. "What? Who?" He pushed me to the side and stood in front of me.

"Do you really think I know who?" I stood behind Jack and peered over his shoulder. Nothing. "I swear he was right behind me!"

"He?"

"He. She. I don't know. *It* ran like a damn gazelle."

He grabbed both sides of my cheeks. His palms lit my face on fire. "Tell me exactly what you saw."

"I don't know. I was just walking along the fence, when I heard a clicking sound, a lighter, I think. Across the field, someone stood there, smoking and watching me. When I started to move away, he moved toward me. When I ran, he ran."

Jack dropped his hands. He looked again in the direction from where I had come. I had no idea if he thought I was insane or if he thought like I did—someone was watching me.

ELEVEN

Dr. and Mrs. DeWeese worked the crowd. I sipped my punch while trying to be one with the floor-to-ceiling draperies at the back windows.

Growing up, I always did as I was told. "Be a good girl and let Daddy work," Dad would say. Or "Be a good girl for your Gram while I'm away."

So, when Cathy DeWeese informed me she would handle the arrangements for a wake in honor of my dad, I nodded and said, "Yes, ma'am."

My soul ached as I scanned the DeWeeses' living room. It was packed full of doctors (some I recognized from the recent dinner, some I didn't), Wellington teachers, and friends of the DeWeeses' who Cathy claimed loved my father.

I was skeptical.

When Dad had insisted I attend Wellington under a new name at age eleven, I'd assumed it was to soothe his fears that I would be killed, kidnapped or tortured for the top secret work he did. Never in all the years that Dad warned me of the dangerous nature of his research did I consider that *I* had been one of his projects.

That my name was changed to protect my identity, not his.

Nor had I considered that his life was in danger.

Now, he was dead.

And my identity? Not so secret these days.

The Program—a program Dad insisted I be a part of this year? Would it teach me about this controversial research? Would it give me clues as to why my dad is now dead?

I watched the faces of the adults scattered about the room. Were these people really Dad's friends? I only considered a small handful to be my friends—the very few classmates who even knew who my father was, including Briana.

At least Dr. DeWeese and Dean Fisher agreed to do it away from school. The fewer students who knew who I was—or who Dad was—at this point, the better. I hadn't even told Danielle, my best friend, about the email I'd received. Most people knew nothing more than what was reported in the papers—Famous Geneticist Killed in Strange Car Explosion.

Wellington's teachers gathered in a small group in one corner of the room. Guests approached me, taking my hand in theirs. They offered their condolences and wished me well. Dr. DeWeese and his wife stood behind me at times like monkeys on my back.

I smiled and said "Thank you." Like a good little girl. When what I really wanted was to go for a swim. Or go back to the nursing home where Gram lived. I wanted to escape this thing that had become my life.

Jack stood with Danielle and Kyle. They drank punch and spoke in whispers. I only imagined they were discussing me and what I must be going through—attention I didn't welcome.

I was just thankful Danielle knew me well enough to pack me a bag of clothes, otherwise I would have been standing there in my swim team sweats. Or worse, forced to borrow something from my new guardian, who wore bright canary-yellow tonight. She claimed black was "cliché."

Danielle brought my favorite black skirt, gray silk blouse, and a pair of heels that I wanted to throw across the room. But why take out my grief on a lovely pair of peep-toes?

I shook my head, remembering how Cathy DeWeese had buzzed around the house all day like she was planning a huge party.

Briana approached me slowly from the left as Mrs. Crain, my biology teacher, walked away. She wrung her hands in front of her and appeared to struggle to make eye contact. When she finally did, I noticed her mascara smeared under her eye as if she had been crying.

"I'm sorry for your loss, Lexi," she said. It sounded rehearsed, but her eyes were sincere.

"Thank you." I had uttered those words two-hundred-thirty-four times that evening by my estimate.

She bowed her head toward the floor. Then suddenly she threw her arms around me. "I'm so sorry for everything."

I patted her back lightly and then gently pushed her away, holding onto her shoulders. "It's okay, Bree. It's still me."

A tear escaped her eye, and she sniffled. "I just don't know what I would do without my parents. I mean," she touched a tissue to her nose, "my parents pretty much suck as far as handing out any kind of love, but I at least have somewhere to go for holidays."

"Thank you for that, Bree."

She nodded and walked away without another word.

Danielle raised an eyebrow in a silent question from across the room. I answered with wide eyes and the release of a long breath. I was definitely done with this memorial service. I didn't understand why Mrs. DeWeese insisted on having one.

She'd said it was so I could find closure. Except these people didn't know my father. Not really. I wasn't going to find closure in a room of strangers.

As I tried to make my way to the door, I was stopped by another hand to the elbow.

"Lexi, we are so sorry."

"Dr. and Mrs. Wellington." The president of Wellington Boarding School and his wife were dressed in conservative dark clothing. I allowed Mrs. Wellington to take my hand in hers. Her skin was cool. "We're sorry to see you under these circumstances," she said.

"Thank you." Two-hundred-thirty-six. "That's very kind of you."

Dr.Wellington placed a business card in my hand. "If you need anything, anything at all, you'll call us."

"I will." I smiled weakly. "Thank you." I lost count.

Jack stepped beside me and touched my arm. "Good evening. Dr. and Mrs. Wellington. It's nice to see you both. I need to steal Lexi away for a minute."

"Of course. Again, we're sorry for your loss, dear. Your father did amazing work. He'll be missed."

Jack led me toward the kitchen. Anita, the DeWeese's housekeeper, took a tray of mini quiches from the oven and slipped me a sympathetic look. I only met her briefly over bacon that morning, but I already liked her.

Jack and I continued out the back door and walked around the DeWeeses' swimming pool. I sat on a wrought iron bench and bent over at the waist, breathing hard. "Thank you for getting me out of there."

Jack sat beside me. His leg pushed against mine. "I'm so sorry you had to go through that."

"I can't breathe," I whispered, burying my face into my hands.

He rubbed my back, up and down. His hand burned like a hot iron through my silk blouse. "It's going to be okay."

I rocked back and forth, holding my stomach. "No, it's not. How can you even say that? Nothing is ever going to be okay."

My dad is dead. I never even knew my mom. My grandmother doesn't recognize me. I'm a freaking science experiment. I don't even recognize myself when I look in the mirror.

Nothing was okay. And I was definitely losing it.

"It might be a while before it feels okay, but you will find peace again. I will help you figure this out."

I stopped rocking. Jack's hand rested on my neck. His forefinger rubbed a spot just behind my ear. Everything that had happened the past week made me not want to trust this golden-haired, blue-eyed boy who showed up out of the blue one fall morning.

But breathing in his scent and sitting with him by the light of the swimming pool, I wanted him to help me—help me process the death of my father, help me find these journals my father must have kept, and help me find purpose in this crazy life I was being forced to face alone.

"You're not alone, Lexi."

"What, are you a mind-reader, too?" I searched his eyes.

He tilted his head, and his lips twitched. "My mother and father don't know you, but they want to. And they want to help."

I stood and walked over to a fountain, part of the DeWeese's extensive landscaping around the pool. Jack followed, standing directly behind me. I closed my eyes and remembered a time when I would throw a penny into every fountain I came across, wishing with every ounce of being for my father to come home from some European country. I dreamt of a time when life was simpler. I prayed for that now.

"So, are we like brother and sister now?" I asked. An exasperated chuckle escaped at the ridiculousness of the question. "Now that your parents are my legal guardians, that is?"

His hands were suddenly on my arms. He spun me around and held me firmly in front of him. I drew my head backwards just slightly, stunned by the abrupt movement.

His furrowed brows further darkened the intense look in his eyes. "I still have a lot of questions about us. How were we created? Who all knows about it? What does this guardianship mean for you or for my family? But hear me now." He stopped talking and leaned closer.

I didn't dare take my eyes off his. Their intense blue met my green. I sucked in a breath and held it while I studied the soft lines of his face. His warm breath feathered against my skin. Just when I thought he was going to say something else, he closed the remaining gap and pressed his lips to mine.

My eyes flew open. My hands lifted and grabbed his waist, clenching the fabric of his shirt. Every instinct told me to push him away. Instead, I closed my eyes and eased into the kiss.

A desire I had tried to suppress erupted in the pit of my stomach and spread until it reached my face. My lips molded against his, opening slightly and letting him in.

He released me, remaining close. His eyes stayed locked on mine. "Let's get one thing straight," he said against my lips. "We are not brother and sister. Got that?"

I nodded, breathing hard.

His face softened. A gasp escaped through his parted lips, and he backed away. "I'm sorry." He ran a hand through his hair. "I don't know what's wrong with me. Well..." He narrowed his eyes. "I do know, but this wasn't the right timing."

"It wasn't?" I asked all shy-like and feeling a little disappointed at the sound of regret in his voice.

"I didn't mean to take advantage of you. You know..." He waved a hand in the air. "With the circumstances and all."

I wrung my hands, and backed up. "Well, I'm glad you did."

"You are?" His brow shot up.

"For the briefest of moments, I forgot how devastated I was. I forgot how worried I was about my future. That I didn't have a home any longer. That there was no one left on this earth who gave a damn about me or what happened to me." And I forgot that I always did the right thing, like a good little girl.

I looked away. The pool water lapped at the edges of the steps.

He slid his hand under my chin and directed my face back toward him. "Well, then, I'm glad I could help, I guess." A sly grin eased across his face, and up to his eyes. "I do believe you're blushing, Miss Always-In-Control."

"I doubt that. I don't blush."

"Uh-huh." His chest lifted and lowered in a sigh. He brushed the back of his hand against my cheek. "Your friends and I planned a little surprise-something in the barn. I'm supposed to take you there... When you're ready, that is."

"What about the wake going on inside?"

He leaned in and brushed his lips with mine again. "My parents will understand that you simply got tired from too much attention."

Sounded reasonable. Of course, Jack could probably have talked me into mucking stalls at that particular moment.

~~~~

Early the next morning, I lay back against the pillow in the DeWeese guest room. The house was still dark and quiet, but my eyes were opened wide, staring at the ceiling.

The "small something" in the barn had been nice. Danielle, Kyle, Briana, and Jack attempted to take my mind off Dad's brutal murder with boarding school gossip and small talk.

I squeezed the bridge of my nose and thought about the exact thing I couldn't talk about with my friends the night before—why was Dad murdered? Was I somehow in danger now?

I rolled over and stared out a window to the fields behind the house. The sun was just beginning to peek over the horizon. When my mind wandered to the kiss—the soft, soothing touch of Jack's lips on mine—I threw back the covers and got up. What was I thinking?

Fifteen minutes later, dressed in jeans, a black sweater and bare feet, I crept my way downstairs and around the unfamiliar house. I heard muffled voices and my name as I stepped down a hallway in their direction. A light shone from a cracked-open door.

I eased forward. My hand brushed against the wall.
~~~~

"I don't care, John. I don't want Jack anywhere near her. You're not seeing this clearly." It was Cathy, Jack's mom, and her voice was steeped in anger. Completely opposite from the bubbly voice that greeted me the night we met.

"Be reasonable, Cathy," John said. "He's safe at Wellington. And he can watch for anything out of the ordinary."

"You mean he can watch after her."

"Yes. I promised Peter."

"You promised Peter," she repeated. "That's rich, John. You're not doing this for Peter," Cathy said through what sounded like gritted teeth. "You're doing this for *her*."

A loud sound like the slamming of a book from inside the room made me jump. Was I the "her" she referred to?

"Don't you dare bring *her* into this," John said. "You knew what marrying me meant. Don't stand there and pretend to be the hurt housewife."

"Why not? She has everything to do with this. When was the last time anyone heard from her? How do you know she's not responsible for bringing Peter back to the states? Or for killing him?" Cathy let out an exasperated laugh that had nothing but fury behind it.

"You know damn well she would never have killed Peter." John's voice grew softer for every octave Cathy raised hers.

Who was Cathy talking about? I directed my thoughts at her. Ordered her to tell me more.

Get mad, Cathy. Who are you talking about? The warm trickle of blood tickled my upper lip, but I didn't care. *Tell John why Jack shouldn't be near Lexi. It has everything to do with "her," doesn't it? Tell John who you're talking about.*

"Have you given consideration as to why Peter was killed?" Cathy's voice had quieted, but the intensity was still there. "Don't you think it's strange that you received a threat the same week Peter showed up on our doorstep?"

Dr. DeWeese was threatened? *It's because of "her," isn't it, Cathy?*

"I've thought of nothing else," John said so softly I had to strain my ears. "We have to find those journals. Everything's going to be fine once we do."

"Are you hearing yourself? Nothing is going to be fine. You have to tell Jack. You have to tell him, and then you're going to have to tell Lexi about Sandra."

"Don't you dare speak her name." John's voice was quick and furious. "Don't say it again."

"Why, John? Are you going to hurt me?" Cathy's voice was again strained. Was Dr. DeWeese hurting her? "Don't you see? This is Sandra all over again."

"What has gotten into you? This is not like you."

A silence passed. I said her name over and over inside my mind. *Sandra. Sandra. Sandra.*

"I think that's enough of the dramatics for today," John said.

"You're right." Cathy sounded stunned that she had said way more than she meant. "I still don't want Jack near Lexi. Not yet. It's not safe."

"Leave it alone for now. It's not like we can forbid him. He's already eighteen, and fully capable of running if he thinks it necessary. Let's see what comes out in the papers in the next few days and what the investigators find."

"How did Jack figure out who she was anyway?" For the first time since I met Cathy, she sounded tired.

Now, for the first time since meeting the DeWeeses, I wanted to find the journals before anyone else did.

~~~~

Anita was arranging pastries and bagels on a platter when I stormed into the kitchen. "Lexi, everything okay?"

I stopped suddenly, and swiped a tissue under my nose one final time insuring my nosebleed had stopped. Jack sipped coffee at the breakfast table by the windows on the other side of the room. *Did everyone rise early in this house?*

Jack smirked for some reason, then narrowed his eyes.

What? I squeezed my nose again with the tissue. The bleeding had stopped.

"Would you like some breakfast, Lexi?" Jack asked.

"I could make you an omelet," Anita offered. "Or some tea?" A silent message passed between Anita and Jack.

I surveyed the counter. "Um... tea would be great. Thank you." Unusually bashful, I approached Jack slowly and slid into a chair across from him.

"Everything okay?" he asked.

My eyes wandered toward Anita, who steeped a tea bag into a cup and then back to Jack. "Fine, why?" Could I talk to Jack in front of Anita? Should I ask him why Cathy hates me? Or about Sandra?

Suddenly, Jack knocked over a glass of orange juice. It formed a river that ran right into my lap.

I pushed away from the table. Anita came running with a clean towel. "No use crying over spilled orange juice," she said.
~~~~

An uncomfortable chuckle escaped my mouth as I continued to wipe my jeans. “Maybe I should ask *you* if *you're* okay,” I said to Jack.

“I'm fine,” he said, his voice suddenly edgy.

Anita wiped the table, lifting plates and silverware. “Can I get you more juice?” she asked Jack.

He shook his head. He shifted his dark eyes on me. “What's with the nosebleed so early in the morning?” He poured himself another cup of coffee from a carafe. His tone sounded angry, which confused me.

I was unsure whether to tell him what I had just overheard. His mood seemed strange, like it had changed since I stormed into the kitchen. “It's just a nosebleed. I'm fine.” After a final wipe of my jeans, I tossed the towel on the counter. “I'm going to go change. When do you want to go back to school?”

“You want to go back today?” he asked.

“Why wouldn't I?”

“I just thought you would want some time.” He sat his coffee down. “Sit for a second.” He pushed the chair out with his foot.

Anita left the room. I pressed my hand against my nervous stomach, but then took a seat.

“The dean said to take a couple of days.”

“I don't want a couple of days.” I glanced over my shoulder to verify we were alone. “I appreciate what you did for me last night...” A shoulder to cry on. A consoling kiss. A get-together in the barn.

Jack slid his hand under mine and rubbed my fingers with his thumb. “But...?”

"But I need to get back to school. I have things I need to take care of."

"Like what? What can't wait?" His eyes drilled into mine.

I shifted in my chair. "Stuff." Lots of it.

"What kind of stuff?"

"I don't answer to you, Jack." Retracting my hand, I sucked in a deep breath and blew it out, exasperated.

He stared at me. "No, you don't. But I thought we were... friends."

I stood. "I don't mean to hurt you, Jack, but I've known you all of a week." He winced at my words. I pushed two fingers into my temple and rubbed. "And a lot has happened since then."

"What is that supposed to mean?"

I rolled my eyes to the ceiling. When I met his eyes again, he couldn't have appeared more hurt. I fought through the lump in my throat. "I'm confused, Jack." I didn't know what else to say. "I just need to go back to school."

With that, I turned and shot out of the room, thankful not to run into Cathy.

TWELVE

The rest of the day was business as usual—swim practice, a full day of classes, work in the library, avoiding all grief and any thoughts of the chilly ride back to school. Jack hadn't spoken to me since he dropped me off at the girls' dorm that morning.

That was fine with me, or at least that was the lie I was telling myself.

Yeah, business as usual until I turned the corner out of the dinner line to face a group of seniors arguing over tacos. Kyle gripped a handful of the shirt of Wellington's best soccer player. Tom's face was as red as the bowl of salsa on the table in front of him, and Kyle dared him to repeat whatever it was he had said.

"Hey, what's going on?" I yelled, sidling up beside them. Kyle did not relax his grip. The creepiest of smirks spread across Tom's face.

Danielle pushed back from the table, grabbed her tray and approached me. "Come on. It's just a stupid fight. Let's go sit outside."

"She's going to hear it eventually," Tom said.

"Shut up, man," another guy at the table said. "Show some class."

Kyle pulled Tom closer then shoved him backward, letting go. "You're such a jerk."

Tom fell backwards over the chair, landing on the floor. Mr. Keiser, the physics teacher, came running over. "What is going on here?"

Danielle tugged on my arm. "Come on. Let's get out of here."

We passed by the food line just as Jack came around the corner. He lifted his chin in a silent hello. He seemed to assess the situation behind me. Danielle pulled me on.

We carried our trays outside to the picnic tables behind the cafeteria. It was a nice night. A comfortable breeze rustled the plastic peeking beneath the trash can lid. Two other groups of classmates surrounded tables at the other end of the patio extending the length of the dining hall.

"Want to tell me what that was about?" I asked, sprinkling toppings inside my chicken soft taco.

She just stared at me. Her cheeks drooped.

"What? About my dad? The tabloids? I already know what the trash media is saying, Danielle."

"You're not upset?" she asked, playing with the corner of her napkin. "You know... that they know who your dad was?"

"It was just a matter of time before our wonderful classmates figured things out and formed opinions. I can't stop that. My dad was who he was." My voice cracked. I couldn't blame them for forming opinions. Not even I was immune to disagreeing with Dad. "I don't want to talk about any of that tonight, okay?" I had cried enough.

She smiled. "Sounds good to me." She pushed my tray closer. "Now eat."

"Yes, mom." I dolloped sour cream across my taco.

I didn't want to talk about what the tabloids were saying because I was frightened they were right. What if my dad had been producing cloned human beings for years? I already knew he supported the altering of embryos' DNA. What if he was producing deformed and diseased monsters he would later have to destroy? What if I was one of those monsters?

I shuddered at the thought of an innocent child being born with no arms, or only one eye. Or what if the baby appeared normal only to be plagued with illness his entire life—a faulty heart or kidneys that didn't work? How could my dad do something so controlling and thoughtless? So completely god-like, but without love or compassion for life?

Then there was Jack and me. I still wasn't sure what we were. How had our minds been tweaked? Did that mean my dad had created me without love?

If Dad did what the tabloids were saying, would that make him a monster? I shuddered. I had to find whatever proof was out there before that proof fell into the wrong hands. I had to know. Although I was fairly sure I didn't want anyone else to know the truth.

"So, roomie," Danielle started, interrupting my thoughts. "Tell me what's going on with you and Mr. Six-Pack-Abs." She swirled a tortilla chip in the air, dripping salsa on the table.

I spooned a rather large bite of guacamole in my mouth. "Nuuuhhing," I mumbled, and green goo must have shown through my teeth, because Danielle scrunched up her nose and turned away laughing.

"Euwww," she said. "You're so gross. But effective in changing the subject."

I laughed. And it felt good. Grief followed me around all weekend. This was the first meal I actually felt like eating without throwing up.

"Don't look now," Danielle said, bowing her head in my direction. "Mr. Hot Abs at twelve o'clock." Her lips twitched into a sly smile. Her eyes roamed past me over my shoulder. "Holy cow." Danielle shot up like she had just spilled her drink. "What happened to you?"

I rotated in my seat and lost my appetite again when I saw blood streaming down Jack's face. I knew the mark of a fist when I saw one.

~~~~

I dabbed gauze against a cut dangerously close to Jack's left eye. We sat in chairs outside Coach Williams' office by the swimming pool. The reflections of the water danced in his eyes.

He smelled so good, even over the strong scent of chlorine, as I leaned into him and studied the injury. *Think of something to say,* I told myself. *Anything.* "You need ice." I bowed my head and rummaged through the first-aid kit.

Jack smiled. He watched my every move. His head dipped when mine did. His eyes were directed at mine whenever I risked a look at him. He wanted to kiss me, and I wasn't completely sure I didn't want him to. Why did I feel like he saw straight through me? Reading my mind even?

"You gonna fight every one of my fights, bro?" I asked. He winced. Whether it was from the pain when I applied antibiotic ointment or from the title I gave him, I couldn't be sure.
~~~~

He glared at me with his one good eye. "I'm warning you, Lexi. Don't call me that."

I reached across him and grabbed a couple of butterfly bandages from the first aid kit.

Just as I chalked the uncomfortable tingle in my belly up to the two bites I'd managed to swallow of refried beans, Jack grabbed my arm and stopped me from pulling backwards. I concentrated on his good eye, which was a vivid blue tonight.

"You know you won't be able to fight what's going on here forever." With his other hand, he pointed back and forth between us.

I thought my heart might implode. "And exactly what do we have going on here, Jack?" My words came out a little snippier than I had planned. "You are the son of my new legal guardian. You've sworn to watch over me while investigators do their thing. I've known you all of three minutes." I sucked in a deep breath. "And someone killed my father. This isn't Romeo and Juliet." Although his mother did say she didn't want Jack anywhere near me.

I heard the crack in my voice when I mentioned Dad. I had fought back tears all day. I wasn't about to let them flow now. Not in front of Jack.

He released his hold on my arm. A look of hurt passed over his face. "I get it, Lexi. But you're not alone."

Oh, yeah? Then why do I feel that way?

He slid a finger under my chin and lifted. "You're not alone." He said each word slowly.

I nodded while he held my face directed toward his. "So, why can't you heal this spot over your eye? I'm afraid you might need stitches."

"Everyone saw me get hit. I wouldn't be able to explain the miraculous healing." He let go of my chin, his fingers lightly brushing my skin longer than necessary.

"Ahh."

"Besides, I was sick for three days after I healed your arm. There are consequences to these powers we have. You of all people should know that."

I thought about my nosebleeds. They'd gotten worse lately. I smoothed the butterfly bandages over Jack's cut, allowing my fingers to linger along his temple. Or had I been speaking to the minds of others more, therefore making my nosebleeds more frequent? My pills were supposed to help that.

"Shit! My pills."

"What?" Jack's eyes opened wider. "What pills?"

"I take pills for my headaches and nosebleeds. They're supposed to prevent them. Or at least minimize them."

I shifted in my chair and pulled my bag into my lap. I dug past books and notebooks until I wrapped my fingers around the small pill bottle.

Just when I flipped the cap off, Jack grabbed the bottle from my hand.

"Hey," I reached for his arm, but he stood and walked toward the pool. "What are you doing?"

He turned the pill bottle upside down and emptied the entire bottle of pills into the pool. "When was the last time you took one of those pills?" he asked.

"I can't believe you just did that."

"When, Lexi?"

"I don't know. I... I guess..." I studied his face. His expression was serious. "The day you arrived at Wellington. We were sitting on that bench, and you had bought me a Chai tea. I totally forgot about them with everything going on."

"Are your headaches more frequent without them?"

It was like he was testing me, and it was starting to piss me off.

"Answer me. Are the headaches and nosebleeds worse since you stopped taking the pills?"

"No," I said. The nosebleeds were more frequent because I had been bending people's minds more. My headaches had been the same. "Why did you throw them in the pool?"

"They'll dissolve. I don't want you taking those."

"Why do you care?"

He narrowed his gaze.

"I meant, how do you know that those pills weren't helping my headaches?"

"Because I was taking those pills. Started them when I entered The Program. I could barely heal a paper cut while on those pills."

~~~~

A loud bang startled me awake. I sat up in bed and took in my surroundings. Only I wasn't in my dorm room. I was back in Gram's house—the house I grew up in.

I climbed out of bed and ran from the room, down the stairs and outside. My grandmother stood on the porch holding a shotgun.

"Gram?"

She turned to me. Her face softened. She reached a hand and smoothed my hair out behind me. "It's okay, dear, go back to bed. You're safe."
~~~~

"Gram, what are you doing with that gun?"

"I'll always protect you, Sarah Alexandra." Suddenly, Gram's body shifted and morphed into a dark figure. The figure bent over and picked up something from the table. When it stood, it held a cigarette that flared.

It laughed as it flicked the lighter open and closed.

Then it turned and aimed the shotgun directly at my head. Before it could fire the gun, another sound rang through my thoughts.

An alarm. Someone grabbed my arms and shook my body. "Wake up, Lexi."

I opened my eyes. I was lying flat on my back. Jack stared down at me. Danielle stood behind him with a strange deer-in-the-headlights look. I glanced from Danielle, back to Jack. "What are you doing?" I sat up and took in my surroundings. I was outside.

His lips twitched. "What am *I* doing?" There was uneasy laughter behind his words.

"Sweetie, the fire alarm is going off." Danielle stepped around Jack. "It woke me up, but you were already gone. Jack and I found you asleep on this bench."

How had I gotten here? I ran my fingers along the wood of the bench outside the library. "Is the alarm going off in both dorms?"

"What? No," Danielle said.

"Then why are you out here?" I studied Jack's expression.

He shifted uncomfortably, ran a hand through his hair. Girls gathered outside the dorm behind him. A fire engine blared in the distance. "Danielle, do you mind finding out if there really is a fire? Lexi is shaking she's so cold."

The pajama shorts and tank top I wore barely covered me. Goosebumps spread up and down my arms and legs. Jack removed his light fleece jacket and wrapped it around me, leaving himself dressed only in pajama bottoms that hung low on his hips, his bare chest exposed. I gasped at the sight and prayed he didn't notice.

He knelt in front of me, resting his elbows on his knees. "If you're going to sleepwalk, could you please sleep in more clothes? For your sake and mine." A mischievous grin spread across his face, and I must have blushed. "Want to tell me what's going on? Do you usually wander in your sleep? Is this something I need to start worrying about?"

Is that what I had done? Walked in my sleep? I'd never done that before. "What are you doing out here?" I asked

"I heard the alarm. I was concerned." His tone was defensive.

"About what?"

"About you. And for good reason. How did you get out here?"

I leaned over at the waist and buried my face in my hands. How *did* I get to this bench? The image of my grandmother saying my full name had been so real. Had she actually done that? I didn't remember her ever holding a gun. And she didn't smoke. The figure had morphed into someone else. And the memory of the gun pointed directly at my face made me shiver. I lifted my head and our eyes met. "Something strange is going on, Jack."

"What do you mean?" His voice rattled with nervousness.

I rubbed my hands back and forth over my face. "It's like someone is getting inside my head." First the figure with a cigarette at Jack's farm that turned out to be my imagination, maybe. Now this strange nightmare.

Jack sucked in a quick breath. A line formed between his brows.

I could almost see his mind wandering elsewhere. "Why do you think our fathers hid so much from us? I mean, if we're in danger now, wouldn't it be logical to tell us everything?"

"You would think. I'm sure my father thinks he's protecting us."

"You've gotta give me more, Jack." I reached out and touched his hand. "Please."

He parted his fingers and allowed mine to slip in between his. "I don't know what I can tell you." He lifted his eyes, his face wrinkled in discomfort. From the touch maybe. Or the line of questioning. "From what mom told me, the lab burned down, your father left town, and my dad picked up the pieces of his life and started over doing stem cell research for another lab."

"How did you find me at Wellington? What made you even look for me?"

Releasing my fingers, he pushed off his knees and sat on the bench beside me. His knee knocked against mine. The constant touch threw me slightly off balance. "I told you. I overheard a conversation."

I reached out and directed his face back toward me. "Between who?"

"Between my dad and the private investigator he hired to find you."

THIRTEEN

"He did what?" I jumped up. "Why would he hire a private investigator? That's crazy. And why didn't you tell me this?"

"He and your dad were best friends." Jack's voice was soft, calm. "And one day after the lab burned, your dad disappeared. Do you have any idea how that must have felt for him?"

My eyes traveled to the group of girls huddled outside the dorm—to Danielle, my best friend since practically the day I'd arrived at Wellington. I used to tell her everything. Lately, I struggled to trust anyone. "I can only guess."

"Your dad also hid your existence from my father."

"Why didn't he just search for Dad? Seems like that would have been easier."

"Your dad didn't want to be found. I think Father tried early on, but then just let it go."

"What changed?"

"He saw your picture in the paper. You had won a swim meet or something."

"That was a mistake," I whispered, then gave in and sat beside him again.

"What?"

"That picture was a mistake. A picture of me was never supposed to make it to the paper. But someone from outside the school snapped it last year after State Swim."

"Well, he saw it. It was buried in the back of the sports section on a weekday. That's when all hell seemed to break loose around my house. After listening to my parents argue for several weeks, I asked him about it. When he blew me off, I started snooping and listening. I did my own sort of investigation. Before I knew it, Father moved us to Lexington, close enough to Wellington, and I joined The Program."

"That doesn't explain anything, Jack." I shook my head, fighting through a haze of confusion. "This all has to do with The Program, doesn't it?" I squeezed my eyes shut. "It's more than just a fast track to a top pre-med program."

"Yes. Those pills you were taking? They were designed to block the part of your brain that was altered. The Program is designed to teach you how to use it."

"But I'm able to speak to people's minds."

Jack rubbed the back of his neck. "I think your mind was altered to do more."

"Are you kidding? Like what?" It wasn't excitement in my voice. More like dread.

"I don't know yet. I'm learning as quickly as I can at the Program." His eyes found mine again. "But if those pills weren't able to block your abilities fully, I can only imagine it's something big."

"You've been attending Program classes since you've been here? When?"

"In the mornings. Early. Same time you're at swim."

I had no idea. "Here or do you leave each morning?"

"Here. I skype with someone who is teaching me about the research and other controversial stuff our fathers have always been involved in. It's fascinating, really."

"Just you?"

"I'm the only one at Wellington, so far."

"This is crazy, Jack." He reached and pulled my hand closer to him, and I let him cradle it between his and rub. "Why only you so far? And why are the dean and others so hell-bent on me joining?"

"Not sure why I was the first at Wellington. Maybe it has to do with being further in my studies?"

I angled my body more toward him, leaving my hand in his.

"I've been homeschooled all of my life. Mom, my father, Anita, online college courses... they've all had a hand in making me who I am. I'm trained in advanced biology, molecular physics, and all forms of genetics. Though I don't have the degree or the experience, I'm practically a doctor, Lexi."

I leaned back, my eyes wide.

He continued. "Then, of course, there's The Program." He paused. Contemplated. "Your dad's name came up all the time in my studies. Even more frequently once I was enrolled in The Program. I knew he was my father's lab partner once upon a time. When I learned he had a daughter near my age... I knew I had to find you." His eyes bored into mine.

I hadn't even noticed the blaring fire truck siren until it had been shut off. Now, the only noise was from the chatter of girls a hundred yards away and my heart pulsing blood through my head as I processed Jack's words. "Why?"

"Why what?"

"Why did you want to find me? I just think there has to be more. Seems to me you took a big risk by finding me. I mean, what if the wrong people learn what you can do? Can you imagine what that would mean?"

"It was a risk I was willing to take. I had to know if you had some sort of ability like I did."

"I bet you were gravely disappointed when you discovered my ability stretched only as far as subtle mind manipulation." Basically, I knew how to get my own way. Very impressive to Jack, I was sure.

Jack cocked his head. "Disappointed is nowhere on the list of emotions I've felt since I met you. As far as your ability, we don't even know what you're capable of yet. You've only tapped into a small facet of what your mind was modified to do."

What other facet could there possibly be? "I bet your mom was not excited about this." *In fact, I know she wasn't.*

"Uh... no. That's an understatement."

"Why does she hate me?" I glanced toward the swarm of girls who were re-entering the dorm.

"She doesn't hate you. It's just... complicated with her."

"Because of Sandra?"

He narrowed his eyes. "You know about Sandra?"

"Not really. Heard her name mentioned."

"Where?" he asked.

"The other morning at your house. Your mom mentioned her. I don't think she likes her."

Jack cocked his head, considering.

"Who is she?" I asked.

Danielle wove through student traffic toward us. "Lexi, they've given the okay for us to go back in."

Jack bowed his head in frustration at the sound of Danielle's voice.

I cringed at the interruption. "You go ahead. I'll be right there."

Danielle gave me the thumbs up. "Okay, but don't do anything I wouldn't do." She skipped off toward the dorm.

Heat rose to my cheeks with Danielle's words.

A grin crept across Jack's face. He brushed his fingers down my face. "Blushing again?"

I slapped his hand away. "Cut it out. No." I shed his fleece jacket and handed it back to him. "I'm just hot, that's all. Here." *Cover up, for crying out loud.*

Amusement stretched across his cheeks. "Let's talk about this later." He took the fleece and slid his arms in it.

"No, please." I pleaded, "I have to know, Jack. Who is Sandra?" Sandra was key in all of this. I was sure of it.

He sucked in a deep breath, while rubbing a thumb back and forth across my cheek. "I think I've told you enough for one night. You need sleep." He dropped his hand to his side. "But I'll make a deal with you."

"No. No deals. I want to know right now."

His lips twitched. He rubbed both of my arms, generating heat over the goose bumps that formed there. "Patience, Padawan. Friday night, you and me. A date."

I raised a single brow. "Uh... That's your deal? A date?" This was ridiculous. Was my life a game to him? "I don't date doctor types. Or Wellington boys. Everybody knows that."

"Make an exception." His expression turned more serious. "Cause that's the deal. Take it or leave it."

"Why do you want to take me on a date? I'm not even that fun."

"It's like I told you that first day we met. I'm curious about you." He glanced over his shoulder. The last of the girls entered the dorm. The fire truck was pulling away. "And I like the feel of your lips." To prove his point he ran a finger across my slightly parted lips, and I stopped breathing. "So, you go on a date with me, then I'll tell you what I know about Sandra Whitmeyer."

~~~~

I shoved reference books onto the library shelf. Danielle did yoga inches away from me. I pushed the cart forward, knocking Dani's toes.

"Hey, watch it." She backed up, barely breaking from her graceful pose.

I smirked but continued shelving books.

Sandra Whitmeyer. Did Jack say the last name on purpose, knowing I might recognize the name? Or was that a slip? Whitmeyer was the name of one of Gram's neighbors in the nursing home. The same lady Wolfman spoke to before he practically attacked me the night Dad was killed. Except her name was not Sandra. It was Ilene or something.

Maybe I *would* have to go out on that date.

"If I wasn't seeing it for myself, I wouldn't believe it," Danielle said while hooking her right foot around her left knee and raising her prayer hands over her head. She'd been going on and on about something while I was lost in thought.

Rolling my eyes at her flexibility, I slid a book about Buddhism onto the shelf and pushed the cart further down the row. This time, away from Danielle's ranting.

"I mean, come on. Really?" Danielle released her pose and followed before she bent over at the waist and continued stretching while I worked. "You're at least considering going on a date with him, right? You should ask him, if he hasn't asked you. You two look perfect together."
~~~~

Of course we look perfect, we were engineered to look perfect. But together? "Don't you ever get tired of yoga?" I asked.

"You know, you should consider yoga. It would help your swimming." She closed her eyes and gave her head a quick shake. "Don't change the subject."

"What *is* the subject?" I asked. I made room for a rather large book, *History of Middle East Religions*.

"You and Mr. Hot Stuff over there."

I craned my neck around the shelf. Jack typed on a laptop, occasionally checking a notebook beside him. The cut above his eye was healing. The swelling had gone down, but some bruising remained on his perfect face.

I squeezed my eyes tight. These thoughts were clouding my judgment. Could I really go out on a date with him?

"Hello? Lex. Yoohoo! It's me. Your best friend. What were you two talking about last night all cozy and close on that bench?"

I shifted back, keeping the shelf between Jack and me. "Nothing."

She straightened. "Come on. I mean you barely had any clothes on when we found you, and when he took off his fleece..." Danielle fanned herself.

I evil-eyed her, knowing that same heat traveled through me.

"What? Has he even asked you out yet?" She gnawed on a cuticle waiting on my answer. "He did, didn't he? That's why your face is all wrinkled up."

"I have a paper to finish. But yes, he asked me out." I waved a hand in the air as I spoke, and then I pushed the empty cart back toward the circulation desk, leaving Danielle standing in the middle of the religious book section looking like she might faint at the idea of me going out with a guy.

I told myself that the only reason I was even considering going out on a date with Jack was to get more info about the mysterious Sandra and more information about who I was. Not because I couldn't forget the softness of his lips. Or the warmth of his breath on my neck.

After returning the empty cart, I stretched my book satchel across my chest and stared across the library tables at Jack. I'd need to give him an answer about the date eventually. I sucked in a deep breath and let it out slowly before I began the trek over to him.

I slid my bag on the table and sat across from him. His sandy blond hair stood up in the front and some on the sides, like he had been running his hands through it. He didn't even look up at me when I let out a dramatic sigh.

Frowning, I pulled a notebook out of my bag and opened it to the essay I'd been trying unsuccessfully to draft. The deadline to apply to colleges for early admission was still three weeks away, the same time frame for applying to The Program. This essay was only meant for college admissions.

Pen in hand, I wrote, glancing over at Jack every few minutes. He typed, ignoring me. What was his deal?

Briana entered the library and upon spotting Jack, marched right over and sat in the chair beside him. "You ready?"

"Yeah, in just a sec."

It was like I was invisible. And that ridiculous perfume Briana wore made me want to throw up.

"Oh, hi, Lexi," she said. "Missed you at practice this morning." A smirk toyed with the corners of her lips.

"Oh, yeah?" I asked with the same excitement I showed someone waxing my eyebrows. After being out half the night, I'd decided to skip practice and make it up later in the day.

"I don't want to beat you just because you can't seem to fit your team commitments into your busy schedule."

Jack closed his laptop, then stowed it and his books into his backpack. Finally, he looked across the table at me with no readable expression. I, of course, put on my best happy face before glancing down at my notebook.

Did I dare ask where they were going?

"Lexi." Kyle poked his head through the library door. "Dean Fisher wants to see you in his office. You have a visitor."

Jack's brows slammed together in an unspoken question. Perfect. *Now* he was concerned. A minute ago, I didn't even exist.

I gathered my things, and with a melodramatic flip of my hair over my shoulder, I glided out of the library without another glance toward Briana or Jack.

~~~~

"Your father gave me this the last time I saw him."

I took the box from the woman sitting across from me. She crossed her long legs, adjusting her pencil thin skirt to cover just below her knee. Then she uncrossed them and went the opposite way. *Fidgety.*

"And why did my dad give this package to you?"

"I'm not sure, really. He said he had planned on giving it to you in person, but he asked if I would hold on to it. 'Just in
~~~~

case' he said..." Her voice cracked. She covered her mouth with her manicured fingers.

"Ms. Daniels—"

"Call me Marci."

"Marci, what exactly was your relationship with my father?" This was more than just a business relationship.

She swallowed hard, attempting to regain her composure, I guessed. "We were working on something together."

The cardboard box in front of me was opened, but the contents were covered in white tissue paper. "What?"

She scrunched up her face like she hadn't heard my question or didn't understand it.

"You say you were working on something. What? You don't look like a doctor or a research person." I glanced down at her spiky heels, her long, wavy hair, and her perfectly painted lips.

"You're perceptive." She smiled. Relaxed a little, maybe. "I'm a reporter."

"And you were doing a news story on my father?"

"A series of articles," she said, "about his work. Your father was on the verge of rocking the world-wide medical community with some amazing research. He was a brilliant man, Lexi."

That he was. I thought about the mysterious email I received before my father's death. And the attached email sent to the IIA all those years ago. "Have you spoken to the police or FBI about this series of articles?"

"Yes. I have been asked to delay printing them, but I'm under no obligation."

"Free speech and all?"

She nodded and reached a finger to swipe the moisture under her eyes. "Except that they're starting to throw around laws and big words with regard to national security, so who knows if the articles will ever see the light of day." She paused, twirling a sapphire ring round and round on her finger. "Lexi, I admired your father very much. He and I grew... close over the last year."

Close, huh?

"The last time I interviewed him, he spoke of you. Said you were planning to attend medical school. He was very proud of you."

Proud of me because I was going to attend medical school, or just proud of me? I wondered.

"What are the articles about?" I asked. "Exactly?"

Her expression went blank. Her eyes wandered out the conference room window to the front lawn. I followed her line of vision. Students busied themselves with various activities—lacrosse, reading, a yoga class. Sometimes, students at Wellington appeared to have normal lives. On the outside, they laughed, excelled in school, and participated in sports, but on the inside? They missed their parents, wished to live in a suburban house, or attend a normal high school, one in which they could come and go as they pleased.

"Lexi, I'm afraid for you because of who your father was and for me because of what he shared with me. I've been getting threatening messages at work. I think the less you know at this point, the better."

"Why is it adults think they are protecting children by keeping them in the dark? When really the risk and the danger only multiplies the more the lies and the secrets build."

"I know honey, but—"

"And before you know it, the deceit has increased in size and pressure and... boom!" I slammed my fist down on the table. Marci jumped. "An explosion of monstrous and fatal proportions. But that is a recurring theme these days—keeping things from poor little Lexi."

"Lexi, I'm sorry." She grabbed my hand. The gesture was maternal, but she appeared barely old enough to be my big sister. "I'm sorry about your father. I know that he loved you." She paused. Retracted her hand. "I promise I'll come back and tell you what's in the articles before they go to print. I can do that. I owe Peter that."

I pinched the bridge of my nose, a little sorry for my outburst. "Thank you for bringing this to me. I'm surprised Dean Fisher let you."

Marci squirmed under my scrutiny. "I didn't tell anyone about this box. I promised your dad I wouldn't."

She stood to leave, but turned when she reached the door. "Hang on to this," she said, handing me a business card. "If you need anything or ever want to talk, please call me. My cell number and my personal email address are written on the back."

After a brief pause, she added, "Be careful, okay. Your father felt you were protected within the walls of this school, but evil often finds a way."

FOURTEEN

A hard swim did not erase Marci Daniels' words from my mind. She had worn her fear on the sleeves of her Dolce & Gabanna silk suit. And that fear was contagious.

I made my way through the line for dinner, faking a huge smile at Mrs. Sanders—The Best Food Services Technician Ever—for my dinner-to-go container. At the dessert table, I was tempted by the rich smell of warm chocolate-chocolate chip cookies, but grabbed a banana instead. My stomach protested with a large growl.

The intention was to grab food and escape to my room, probably not something Dean Fisher or Ms. Jones approved of, but I had attended boarding school long enough to know how to work around the system.

Students talked and laughed louder than usual tonight. Or maybe my headache made it seem that way. Kyle sat with members of the swim team. Danielle had squeezed into the middle of the group, kind of like a mascot.

My eyes scanned the length of the table, my hair still dripping down the front of my sweatshirt from the swim. Brianna sat across from Jack at the other end. They both had notebooks out, and Bree waved her hands in the air as she spoke.

Why did he spend so much time with her? I just didn't get it.

Jack looked up from their conversation and turned his head toward me, his face expressionless. I hadn't thought of him as moody before, but the cold shoulder in the library, and now...

I tucked my banana inside the side pocket of my satchel and headed for the door.

Some doctor-wannabe was the last thing I needed in my life. And I had no desire to compete further with a nosy redhead.

Ten minutes later, I slammed the door to my dorm room and sat criss-crossed on my bed, wishing I had grabbed the chocolate chip cookies.

On the floor beside my bed was the box delivered by Marci Daniels, reporter-extraordinaire. Thanks to Coach Williams, I hadn't had even a single moment to open it before the makeup practice.

I placed the cardboard box in front of me and began pulling at the tissue paper. Inside was another box. A trinket box. Very similar to other jewelry boxes and puzzle boxes my father had sent me throughout my life.

I traced the edges and grooves of the box with my fingers. A starfish. Made of smooth wood. Cherry maybe. Or mahogany. I lifted a small lid that covered one portion of the box. Inside was a silver necklace. A starfish charm and a key were attached. The metal hung from my fingers as I admired the details of the starfish—made of sterling silver with the front painted a deep green.

Tucked further in the box, I found a small note in Dad's handwriting.

I hope to explain everything to you someday, but just in case I don't get that chance, I want you to know you have all the tools necessary to discover the truth. Love, Dad.

Just in case… Been hearing that a lot lately.

I stared at Dad's words and at the necklace draped across my fingers. Tears stung my cheeks. Dad once called me "his little sailfish," which I balked at. He told me the sailfish was the fastest fish in the ocean, like me in the pool. "Who wants to be known as that ugly fish?" I had asked him. "Surely, you can think of something cuter than a sailfish." I smiled at the memory.

After that, he determined that since I was his star, he would instead call me his little starfish.

Deciding my room was entirely too stuffy, I grabbed my dinner and my banana and headed to the roof.

Settled into a dark corner on top of the girls' dorm, I opened my dinner. The chicken was cold, the broccoli mushy. I peeled the skin of the banana while I lay back and stared at the stars. A cool breeze blew wisps off my forehead.

The door that led to the roof creaked behind me. I stretched my neck in an attempt to see who approached. All I saw was a couple holding hands and walking in the opposite direction.

Having wrapped the necklace multiple times around my wrist, I dangled my arm above my head, admiring how the silver of the starfish caught the reflection of the moonlight.

"Nice bracelet."

I sat up. My hand covered my heart. *Jack*. "Why do you keep doing that? You're like stealth or something."

He smiled, sitting down beside me. I refused to look at him and instead threw my banana peel into my dinner box and shoved it to the side. The things I felt when he was near confused me, and the time he spent with Briana pissed me off.

"Sorry I scared you," he said.

"What do you want, Jack?"

"Do I have to want something?"

"Yes. You're not even allowed up here after nine, which is in..." I looked at my watch.

"An hour," he finished for me. "Who was your visitor today?"

"Why is that any of your business?"

He took a deep breath, letting it out slowly.

I returned to my lateral position, staring up at the stars. When Jack didn't speak, I said, "How'd you even find me?"

"Apparently, your roommate knows you pretty well. And, I think she likes me." I could hear the amusement in his voice.

"That's just your over-inflated ego talking. My roommate is way too trusting." Something she and I would talk about.

"She's concerned about you." He poked at my bent elbow, my arm tucked under my head like a pillow. "You going to tell me who visited, or do I need to call my father? He would probably be interested in knowing you had a visitor."

"What makes you think he doesn't already know?" Of course I assumed Dr. DeWeese had no idea.

"Why the big secret?"

I sat up and faced him. "I don't question who you spend your time with, therefore you have no right to question me."

When the corners of his mouth twitched, the temperature of my blood slowly began to rise.

"Ahh." He lifted his chin. "That's how we're going to play it? You're jealous, so you're going to keep things from me."

I stood, grabbed the box of food I'd barely touched and carried it to the trashcan by the door. Jack's stare followed me, his smile never fading.

I stomped back. "I am not jealous, Jack." At least I was trying not to look at it like jealousy. "I'm just not playing whatever game this is you're playing. I don't have to tell you anything."

He stood, his eyes grabbing mine with their intensity. "I already told you there is nothing going on between Briana and me."

"It doesn't matter. This has nothing to do with jealousy. You can see whomever you wish. There's nothing going on between you and me, either."

He stepped closer. So close I could've counted his eyelashes. "If you believe that, then you really are naïve."

By the way he said naïve, it sounded like he really meant "emotionally stunted." My eyes angled toward his lips. The memory of the kiss by the pool sent prickles galloping down my spine.

The sound of laughter erupted behind us. I turned and watched the couple who had come up on the roof just before Jack got there. They left, and Jack and I were alone.

When I faced him again, his face was still close. His eyes drilled into mine. I wiped the sweat from my palms onto my pants. I had so many questions. I didn't know where to begin. If he didn't make me so angry...

"You're going to have to learn to trust me, Lexi."

"Based on what?" I asked quickly. "How you freely give up information that might shed some light on this huge mystery I call my life?"

"I have no idea how," he said. His shoulders relaxed. "There are things I want to tell you, but I'm just now learning many of the details of a past we seem to share."

"You say you're 'just now learning.' You mean through The Program?" Why did my skin crawl every time the subject of The Program came up?

He nodded. "You're not the only one who has been kept in the dark."

"But you know more than you're telling me."

He did not argue with that.

"Do you know who Sandra is?" I asked.

He ran a hand through his hair. "Yes and no. I mean, I thought I did. She's a geneticist like our fathers. But you said my mother mentioned her, and that struck me as odd. So, I asked her about it." He shifted uncomfortably.

"And?"

"And... My parents are hiding information from me about her. I'm working on finding out more."

I studied his expression. "I'll tell you what." I stepped even closer to him in some small burst of confidence. "I'll go on that date with you if..." I had to know who this Sandra-woman was. "...If you'll agree to find more information about Sandra."

A triumphant smile played with his lips. "Great. I'll take what I can get. And I'll see what more I can dig up. So, you and me. Friday night."

"Fine. Maybe through the course of an evening, we'll find an ounce of trust for each other." I wanted to trust him with every part of my being, and I wanted him to trust me with the information he clung to so tightly. I stared into his deep blues. Then, I shrugged in an attempt to keep my strength and independence. "Or maybe we won't. But if we don't find a way to trust each other? It's over. We go our separate ways, and you leave me alone."

His smile faded.

I kind of regretted my words knowing how hard it would be for me to fully trust this son of a geneticist Dad had hardly spoken of over the past seventeen years. Could I really walk away from Jack?

Nevertheless, I needed to distance myself from him and The Program if I thought for one second the people behind The Program meant me harm. I would not be controlled by whoever was behind this so-called program. I was just tired from all the secrets surrounding my life.

~~~~

I moved my queen diagonally three spaces. My eyes circled the room and landed on Ms. Whitmeyer. Hugging a book, she stared out the window from her wheelchair.

"Check mate."

I turned back to the game in front of me. "Mr. Batman." His real name. "Did you cheat again while I wasn't looking?"

"Now, Lexi, you know I don't cheat. If you'd been paying attention you wouldn't have made such a silly mistake when you moved that queen."

I puffed hair out of my eyes in amused exasperation. "Mr. Batman, you flirt with all the ladies here, right?"

"Only the single ones, Lexi. I'm a gentleman. I have my standards."

"Well, do you have the scoop on Ms. Whitmeyer?" I lifted my head in the direction of the woman I saw Wolfman speaking to the day my father died. She turned the page of the paperback lying across her lap.
~~~~

Mr. Batman cocked his head sideways at me, his bushy gray eyebrows twitching. Just when I thought he was going to scold me for asking him to gossip, he said, "What kind of question is that? Of course I do."

Exhaling, I smiled and when he motioned me closer with his finger, I leaned in.

"She's a fake." He flashed his perfect dentures.

I leaned back, lifted one foot up onto the chair, and hugged my knee. "Mr. Batman. You're a nut. What do you mean, 'she's a fake'?"

"I am a nut." He smiled. "But I'm completely serious about this. I heard her tell the cops last week that she hadn't seen her son in years. He was here that day. Trouble. That son of hers."

"The cops were here? To talk to Ms. Whitmeyer? Why?"

"No idea."

I had an idea. And it had to do with Dad. And Sandra Whitmeyer. "Does she suffer dementia?"

"I've talked to her. She loves that son of hers, and when she suffered a minor stroke, she started having these seizures, and he couldn't take care of her anymore. That's why she's here." He shook his head. "It's a shame, really. But as sure as I'm sitting here, she has her full wits about her."

Ms. Whitmeyer flipped another page of her book. As she did, she lifted her head. When our eyes met, a confused expression passed over her face. Her lips parted slightly, like she wanted to say something.

"Lexi," Mr. Batman said. "Why do you spend so much time here? Why aren't you off dating and doing whatever you teenagers do these days?"

"You know the answer to that." I forced my lips to curve upward. "None of my friends know how to play chess." He and I laughed, and Mr. Batman pushed himself up with his walker. He placed a gentle hand on my shoulder, pausing a moment before he shuffled off for an afternoon nap.

I pushed away from the table and walked over to Ms. Whitmeyer. A couple of ladies to my right sat on a sofa together reading Cosmo—How to Pleasure Your Man in Bed—giggling like teenagers.

I glanced down at Ms. Whitmeyer's floral robe and powder blue slippers. She smelled of peppermint and Vaseline lotion. "Hi, Ms. Whitmeyer. How are you today?"

Her face scrunched up, but she managed a smile. "I thought that was you," she said.

"My name is Lexi."

"What? Oh... I... I must be confused." She twisted in her wheelchair. Her eyes widened, and her face paled as if the nurses had announced no more Jell-O would ever be served. The book that had been draped across her lap slid off into the floor.

I knelt in front of her, and after picking up the book, I replaced it across her lap. "Are you okay, Ms. Whitmeyer? Can I get you something?"

"No, thank you, dear." She reached a shaky hand and grabbed mine. "Forgive me. For a minute there I thought you were someone else. You have the most beautiful green eyes, just like hers."

"Thank you, ma'am, but... like whose?"

"Oh, never mind, child."

I let it go for now. "Has your son been to visit you?" That sounded smoother in my head.

"Oh, yes." She smiled. "He was here last week. He comes at least once a week. Have you met my Seth?"

"Yes, ma'am. I believe I have had the pleasure." A real charmer, that Seth. "Actually, I'd like to talk to him. Do you know how I can get a hold of him?"

"Oh... dear... I have his number somewhere." She started twisting and turning again. "But he'll come this Thursday. He always comes right after his shift, at six p.m."

A nurse approached and placed her hands on the back of the wheelchair. "It's time for Mrs. Whitmeyer's bath."

"Oh, okay." I nodded. "It was nice to talk to you."

"It was lovely to speak to you, dear."

The nurse wheeled Mrs. Whitmeyer away. She glanced over her shoulder at me twice before disappearing around the corner. "Exactly who are you, Seth?" I whispered to myself. "And how are you and your mom related to Sandra?"

~~~~

I spread newspaper clippings and magazine articles about my father's and Dr. DeWeese's research across a blanket on the floor of Gram's room. No mention of a Sandra Whitmeyer in the articles I had.

How much did Jack really know? I rubbed my eyes with the heels of my palms. I could go out on this date with him. What price was I willing to pay for the truths I suspected he was keeping from me? My heart? There was no denying that he reached parts of me I wanted to protect.
~~~~

Gram knitted a scarf or shawl or something in her chair and hummed a familiar tune from my childhood. Afternoon sun filtered through the blinds, and the aroma from the lilies that Jack sent masked the faint smell of antibacterial cleaner that pervaded the nursing home hallways and rooms.

I sorted the articles by subject, but then decided chronological worked better. Stories of when Dad had won an award for identifying a specific gene believed to be at the root of many cancers. Articles about the goat cloning. And about the failure. Another when he turned down a huge grant to take stem-cell research to the next level in the United States because of "philosophical differences."

From time to time, I glanced up and admired my grandmother's work. "Gram, that blanket you're knitting is beautiful."

"Thank you, dear," she said. "It's for my new granddaughter."

I smiled and patted her hand. I was her only granddaughter. "I bet Peter and your daughter are so thrilled."

Even though Gram didn't recognize me as her granddaughter, sitting with her comforted me.

"Oh, they are. She's their first child. And she's so beautiful." Her face lit up, but then drooped, more serious.

"Gram, you okay?"

She gave her head an absent shake. "Oh, yes, dear. I'm just a little worried about my daughter. Pregnancy has been difficult on her."

"Would you like to talk about it?"

"Oh, no. We'll just leave such matters for God to handle." Just like that, she went back to knitting. I was used to those kinds of conversations. One minute we're discussing something, then... nothing. She was always leaving the serious matters to her God in heaven.

It was that simple for her. I stared at the twinkle that was back in her eyes as she hummed.

Mom left Dad and me soon after I was born. Sometimes, I think it was harder on Gram than my dad or me. I'd always dreamed of knowing my mother, but since I had zero recollection of her and no one ever rushed to defend her abrupt exit from my life, it was easier to hate her for leaving.

But not Gram. She surrendered such things. I reached to touch Gram's hand and thought of Mom. Did Mom know what Dad did? Did she know I was the result of a mad scientist playing God? That my genetic makeup was altered in some way? Was that why she left?

Maybe that explained why I looked nothing like the rest of my family.

"You're supposed to be at the University library."

I whirled around. "You scared the crap out of me, Jack."

"Oh, yeah? Well, you're lucky I didn't get the dean, my father *and* the police involved in a search for you. My dad already wants to have your off-campus privileges revoked."

"He can't do that." I reached out both hands and shoved the papers and newspaper clippings into an unorganized mess, stuffing them into the folder they came in.

"He can. And he will." He squatted in front of Gram. "How are you today, Mrs. Matthews?"

"Why, I'm fine, young man. Thank you."

I stood, still turning and tucking the articles that didn't fit neatly inside the folder.

Jack's knees popped and cracked as he stood. His smile mocked and infuriated me. "Gram already loves me." He winked at me.

"Well, she's way too trusting."

My grandmother's hand grazed my arm. "He's a handsome young man, isn't he?"

Flames crept up my neck and spread across my cheeks. "Yes, Gram, but it's what's inside here that counts." I pointed to my heart. "That's what you always taught me, right?" Gram looked confused. Jack chuckled. "This is starting to feel a lot like stalking, Jack. Why did you come here?"

"To save you from being confined to campus weekend after weekend."

Because that would suck, for sure. Dean Fisher had canceled all off-campus travel before when a student was in danger. Like the time Rachel Denton was held at gunpoint outside the local coffee shop and ordered into a car. Had she not screamed and gotten the attention of a bank security guard, she would have been kidnapped. Wellington students were rewarded with six weeks of campus lock down after that. We weren't allowed to go anywhere until the FBI discovered who the kidnappers were.

"And we have a date."

I hadn't forgotten. I slid the folder of articles into my book satchel. "Was that tonight?" I batted my eyelashes. I wanted to know about Sandra Whitmeyer more than ever.

He cocked his head. "Why can't you just accept that there are people who want to help you? Besides, a date with me beats going back to school."

He had a point. "Oh, I don't know, Jack. Maybe it's because the people trying to 'help' me barged into my life a couple of weeks ago. All starting with your father punching Dad in the face." I swallowed hard. "And now my father is..." My voice dropped off. I looked over at Gram. She didn't even know Dad was dead. I didn't want to chance upsetting her on the rare occasion she caught back up to normal time.

Jack moved closer and reached a hand to my arm.

"Don't." I stepped back.

He followed. "Don't what?" He pushed a strand of hair behind my ear. "It's okay to be angry. To be upset. Have you even allowed yourself to mourn your father?"

Don't cry. Don't cry. Don't cry. I crossed my arms, hugging myself tightly. "How can I mourn him, when I don't even know who he was to me anymore?"

"What do you mean? He was still your father."

"He messed with my genetic make-up. He created a freak." I pulled in a deep, cleansing breath. "I've got to figure things out for myself. I realize I barely had contact with Dad before his death, but I always knew he was there. Somewhere. Now?" I glanced down at Gram, who had nodded off. "I've got nobody. If I'm going to navigate through this life... If I'm going to figure out my big purpose, I've got to figure some things out about who I am. Where I came from."

"Those are some really big questions."

"Don't you dare make fun of me." I heard the hitch in my tone, and I internally berated myself for it.

"I'm not making fun." His tone warmed. "I promise I will never make fun of this situation. I get it. I'm the only person in your life who gets it."

My hands shook. He was right, but I wasn't ready to surrender fully to him or anyone. "So much of what's going on is coming at me so fast, and my questions are piling up unanswered."

He took another step and grasped my shaky hand in his. "I'm not going to let you do this alone." He lifted a bag in front of him with his other hand. I hadn't even noticed him carrying it.

"That's mine."

"Yes. Your roommate understands the importance of proper clothes for a first date. And judging by your jeans and sweatshirt, you were either trying to get out of the date, or you have so little experience you thought *this* was appropriate." He pushed the bag gently into my chest. "Now, go change." When I rolled my eyes, he leaned in close and whispered, "Look at it this way. You might actually enjoy our date."

FIFTEEN

"You still haven't told me where we're going."

Jack glanced sideways. "You're pathetic. You have zero patience."

I squinted, studying his profile. He was getting great joy out of keeping me in the dark about his agenda.

It was a warm, fall evening. The sun sat low in the sky when Jack pulled into a small parking lot on University of Kentucky's campus. He rolled down the windows and a pleasant breeze blew the scent of seafood through the car.

"Sit tight," Jack said as he turned the key and shut the car off.

"Where are you going?"

"Patience. Sheesh."

I leaned my head back against the headrest. Sunglasses shaded my eyes and hopefully hid the fact that I rolled them way back in my head at his order for patience. "Fine."

He got out and closed the door, eyeing me one last time before he pushed off and jogged toward the building and around the corner.

A group of college kids passed by. They argued about being late for dinner and therefore late for the band they wanted to hear after. One of the boys slid an arm around a girl's shoulder. "You know we're late because you insisted on changing a fourth time."

The girl laughed and shrugged. "Couldn't be helped."

A straggler ran to catch up to the group.

I heard it before I saw it. The screeching of tires. People yelling. "Jerk. Watch it. You almost killed us."

I looked over my shoulder. A black Suburban with tinted windows slammed to a halt in the middle of the parking lot to allow the group to cross. Behind the wheel, a man shook his head and raised a fist.

Fortunately, no blood was spilled.

Jack was gone five minutes, and when he returned, he carried a large white bag, which he set in the back seat.

He started up the car, and we drove off again. The wind blew wildly through my long hair, and the sun shone through my window. The heat against my cheeks was therapeutic.

I gave up asking where we were going, but it wasn't long before Jack slowed again and pulled into another parking lot. The University of Kentucky Arboretum.

A black Suburban slowed as we turned, but continued past and turned at the next intersection. I started to tell Jack, but his touch to my arm distracted me.

"Let me just say this." He rubbed his thumb along the skin of my arm. "I know you're having a tough time trusting me, or anyone for that matter. Can tonight just be about having a little fun away from school? You know... normal."

Normal fun, huh? His look was intense, but warm. Inviting. Someone I wished I could be close friends with. I glanced down the road again. No Suburban.

It *was* America. It wasn't like big black trucks were unusual.

I met his eyes again. It would be nice to have a typical date like any normal teenager. "I'll try?"

"That's all I can ask."

Once out of the car, Jack grabbed my hand and led me across the street and through the entrance of the UK Arboretum. With an easy wave over his head to a woman at the information desk, he pulled me right past the visitor center. Employees of the arboretum sprayed water hoses on various plants as we passed. A lady said hello to Jack by name. He smiled easily at her, waving.

I lifted a brow. "Come here often?" I asked.

He stopped and turned to me. "Close your eyes."

"What? Why?"

"You really do have trust issues, don't you? Close your eyes."

I stared at him a few seconds longer before I complied, closing my eyes one at a time.

Jack squeezed my hand. My stomach tightened, a feeling not unlike one I've felt before an important race. I allowed him to lead. He directed me when I needed to step up or down. We turned several times, walking on pavement, gravel, and then grass. Then we stopped. "Keep them closed," he warned, but he let go of my hand, and I crossed my arms across my chest and breathed in the flower-perfumed air.

A couple of high-pitched birds chirped to my right. In front of me, I heard the sound of fabric being shaken, like a sheet being tossed over a bed.

I squinched up my face, wanting desperately to open my eyes. "Okay, I'm ready to see again. You're kind of freaking me out."

"Okay, two more steps," he whispered in my ear. I jumped at the closeness of his voice. His hand slid into mine and tugged gently.

I walked two steps.

"Open," he said, his tone soft.

I turned in a circle. The sun had faded. A couple of candles, sitting in hurricane vases, sat on two corners of a blanket. Everywhere I looked, high and low, roses bloomed. Pinks, whites, yellows, purples, reds—and all different shades in between.

"Where are we?" I asked.

"This is the Garden of Old Roses," he said.

I turned another complete circle. "It's beautiful."

Jack removed food containers from a bag, and I stayed cemented to the spot where he left me. I didn't think it was hunger making my insides twist into a fit of nerves.

"Come on. Let's eat." His expression faltered. He jumped up and crossed to me. "Don't do that." He pointed at my face.

"Don't do what?" I asked.

"You look scared to death. Stop it. This," he said, waving a hand toward the quilt, lit candles, and food, "is nothing but a distraction. I just thought it would be nice to let you know you don't have to grieve, discover your past, or decide your future tonight. And you definitely don't have to do it alone."

He could have just told me that. I crossed my hands over my stomach. This was way too much. I didn't know if it was because the grief of losing my dad was so fresh or the fact that I didn't know who or what I was, but maybe a date was too much too soon.

"Alright, that didn't sound right." He inhaled, letting it out slowly. "This is just dinner. A break from school, college applications and murder investigations. We don't even have to call it a date."

I frowned at the words "murder investigation," but quickly pushed the thought away. "Just dinner."

"That's right."

"So, you're just showing me a little brotherly support?" I could work with that.

"Don't push it, Matthews."

I smiled and relaxed my hands to my side. He reached for one and pulled me over to the blanket. He opened containers of food, handed me a salad and a fork.

Chomping down on a pecan from my salad, I eyed Jack, who lay across the quilt, propped up on his elbow. "Why here?" I asked.

"Why the Garden of Old Roses?" he asked. He picked at a leaf that blew onto the quilt and tossed it off.

"Why the arboretum? You're obviously known here. Is this where you bring all the ladies?" *Please say no.*

A smile crept across his face. I hated, *or loved,* the way it reached all the way to his blue eyes.

"No." He let out a breathy chuckle. "You're the first. I volunteer here. Part of the Cathy DeWeese home schooling curriculum last year." He rolled his eyes. "I don't know. I guess I've always loved learning about plants and trees. Doing what it takes to make the rare ones grow—to nurture life."

When I popped a cherry tomato in my mouth, he resumed. "Take the Children's Gardens, for example. Providing an environment for small children to learn the importance of life and taking care of our land."

Jack's words continued to spill out. He sat up and moved his hands as he spoke. A heaviness swarmed inside my chest as I examined the curves and lines of his face.

I didn't even notice when silence fell around us. I was so lost in the sound of his voice and the rose-scented air. My eyes drifted to his lips. He hadn't tried to kiss me again since that night by the pool. Would he tonight?

Jack cocked his head. "I would love to hear what you're thinking right now." He smiled.

Every muscle from my cheeks to my toes stiffened. I must have turned fifty shades of red before giving my head a shake to free the cobwebs. "Sorry. I'm just amazed at your level of excitement. You ever think about becoming a botanist?"

Jack moved the food containers that sat between us off to the side and inched closer to me. "Yeah, actually. But then I realized I can love all this," he waved a hand through the air, "and still become a doctor."

He lay on his side again and reached a hand to one of mine.

"Right." I studied the look in his eyes—a look that went way beyond that of a concerned brother. Or even a friend. He tugged on my hand, and next thing I knew I was stretched out beside him, facing him on the blanket.

"Is this okay?" he asked, our faces inches apart. His breath warmed my face.

My stomach clenched. I nodded. He leaned in slowly and touched his lips to mine, soft at first. When he pressed harder, an electric sensation shot straight through my chest to my stomach.

His hand rested on the curve of my waist, his fingers exploring just at the hem of my shirt as he continued to kiss me.

Slowly his hand moved to the small of my back and he brought me closer to him. I snaked my hand around his neck and slid my fingers into his hair. My lips parted slightly, enough to allow him complete access.

Moments later, he pulled his head back just slightly and rested his forehead against mine. "I've wanted to do that every day since the night by my parents' pool."

I breathed hard. I didn't know what to say. Luckily, I didn't have to say anything because my phone rang.

I sat up and pulled my phone out of my purse. "I don't recognize the number."

"Answer it," Jack said, and I shrugged.

"Hello?"

"Did you have a nice visit with my mom today?"

"Who is this?" *Seth.* The frightened tone in my voice had Jack sitting up and on full alert.

"Who is it?" He stuck out his hand for the phone.

The voice on the other end of the phone said, "I'm just a concerned friend, Sarah. Someone who doesn't want you to end up like your father. Have you found the journals?"

My hand shook. I dropped the phone on the blanket in front of me.

Jack picked up the phone. "Who is this?" He shook his head. "They hung up. What did they say?"

"He called me Sarah. Told me he didn't want to see me end up like my father." My voice came out shaky. "How did I get thrown in the middle of all this? I don't understand any of it."

Jack grabbed my hand. "Come here." He pulled me into his chest and hugged me there, smoothing my hair behind me. "Who calls you Sarah?"

"Dad and Gram are the only two who have ever called me that. I've been Lexi since I entered kindergarten. And Lexi Matthews since I started at Wellington."

"It's going to be okay. No one is going to hurt you."

"Can I get that in writing?" I laughed uneasily.

He bent his neck, buried his face in my hair. "I promise to do everything I can to keep you safe."

"I know who it was that called."

Jack pushed me back a little. "Who?"

I scooted further away from him so I could breathe and think. Did I really want to tell him about Seth Whitmeyer when Jack had been so reluctant to tell me about Sandra? I thought of Seth's warning the day my father died—the warning that Jack was not who I thought he was, not someone I could trust.

"Who was it, Lexi?" His tone had an edge to it.

"I'll make a deal with you."

"I guess I deserve that."

"I'll tell you how I know that Seth Whitmeyer was on the other end of that phone call, if you tell me now what you know about Sandra."

SIXTEEN

How can you know about Seth Whitmeyer, and not know about Sandra?"

My expression must have faltered, because Jack was quick to continue.

"Oh, I get it. You don't really know who Seth is either." He pushed himself up off the blanket. He began putting things away inside a basket and folding the blanket. "No deal." He stopped what he was doing and walked over to me. He reached out with both hands and pushed hair behind my ears. "We're going to have this date. You're going to forget about the Whitmeyers, death, The Program, and those missing journals. If only for an evening. We'll deal with the Whitmeyers later."

"This is still all a game to you, isn't it? This is my life, Jack."

A severe look passed briefly through his eyes. "Not a game. Very serious, but I've been living with some of this medical craziness a little longer than you, and I refuse to stop enjoying life while hoping all the secrets work themselves out. Because, let me be the first to tell you, as soon as one secret is revealed in our world, another secret peeks out from around the next dark corner." Jack stood close. His breath touched my lips. "I would never choose this life for you. But no matter what we learn through all of this, you are a human being with a purpose. I told you I would find more information about Sandra. And I did. But now that I know more..."

I intertwined my fingers with his. "You don't like what you discovered."

Jack squeezed his eyes closed. When he reopened them, I recognized a certain fear in them. "Yes. I uncovered something. And no, I didn't like it. But telling you about Sandra is telling you everything. Once you know, you will have a choice to make. And one of the choices available to you will be whether to walk away."

"Walk away?"

"And I wouldn't blame you. I want to on a regular basis. If you decide you want no part of this life, I will help you. Encourage you to do it, actually. New name, passport, money, everything you would need to start fresh somewhere else."

His words were a punch to my gut. "What are you talking about? You're scaring me." How could I possibly walk away from everything familiar to me? From Wellington. My friends. From Gram. I turned away from him, suddenly overcome with emotion.

"I'm sorry. It can't be helped." He stood behind me, his chest to my back. His arms circled around me and held me close. "I know you are strong enough to handle this. You have to be."

So much of what was happening started the day Jack entered my life. What if walking away from him would bring sanity and safety back? But what if walking away meant I never solved the mystery of who killed Dad or who was after his journals? What if it meant saying good-bye to Jack forever? Possibly the only person in this world who had the potential to understand me and my ability?

I twisted in his arms and faced him again. I peered into his intense eyes, each one a Category Three hurricane. "Would you do that? Let me just walk away?" Was I hoping he would?

The sadness that swirled in his eyes made my insides constrict.

He brushed the back of his hand down my cheek. "You said you hoped we could find a level of trust for each other while on this date. Do you trust me?"

I continued to study the intense look in his eyes. I knew I could demand that he tell me what he had learned right then, and he would. "I trust you."

He brushed his lips across mine, and then hugged me tightly. "I'll tell you everything I can, but I was hoping to make one more stop on our date first." He pulled back. A smile had replaced his serious look.

"Okay." I tried to smile in return.

~~~~

"You brought me to a bar? Am I even allowed in here?"

"Yes. But you're not allowed to drink alcohol." He shot me a sideways grin as he held the door open, allowing me to pass in front of him.

The lighting was dim, so I looked around just inside the door until my eyes adjusted. A band warmed up on a stage at the other side of a large room.

Jack's warm fingers wrapped around my hand. He wove through the crowd and led me over to a table of people.

"Jack, hey!" a guy yelled as we approached. Dark brown, unkempt hair flanked his forehead, tattoos decorated his left arm.

"Hey, Jonas," Jack said.

A tall African-American girl with long, chemically-straightened hair squeezed behind us and slid into the booth.
~~~~

Dark eyeliner outlined her eyes, and a thick streak of glittery purple decorated her lids.

"Guys, this is Lexi. Lexi, meet Jonas, Georgia and over there is Fred."

Fred must have borrowed eyeliner from Georgia. His deep set, darkly decorated eyes matched his black hair, and both contrasted starkly with his fair skin. Underneath the makeup existed what I was sure was a good-looking guy near the same age as Jack and me.

I waved or nodded at each of them. "Nice to meet you."

Georgia gave me the once over all the way down my skinny jeans to my sandals before scooting over and making room for me.

I sat. Jack leaned in to my ear. "Want a bottle of water?"

I nodded and he took off through the crowd, leaving me alone with my three new "friends."

"So, Lexi, is it?" Tattooed Jonas asked. He twirled an unlit cigarette between his fingers like a baton. When I nodded, he said, "How'd you meet Jack?"

"School."

"And he *invited* you to come here tonight?" Guyliner Fred squinted across the table, skeptical.

I shifted in my seat, not answering his question. Didn't feel the need to. I craned my neck in search for Jack. Why were we at this bar?

Jack returned. Handed me the water. "You guys ready?" he asked Fred and Jonas. Then, to me he said, "Sit tight here, with Georgia."

"Where are you going?"

"I'll be back," he said, uneasy.

It was unusual to see him in a rare moment of insecurity. It confused me.

He trailed off behind the other two, disappearing through the crowd that gathered around the stage.

Georgia's eyes were practically bugged out, a huge smile plastered across her face. "You have no idea why he brought you here, do you?"

I gave my head a little shake. Georgia chuckled under her breath. Was I even sure I was safe here? I snaked my neck to look for Jack.

"You're in for a treat then. You two dating?"

"No," I answered too quickly in an "as if" sort of tone. Were we dating? Maybe we were. Did one date or a few kisses constitute dating?

"Does he know that?" She laughed, showing me her perfectly straight teeth. Her facial features were unusual, exotic even. Beautiful.

I unscrewed the cap on my water and took three really big swallows.

Georgia scooted closer and leaned into me. "It's okay. He's easy to like."

Crap. What was I doing here? This was crazy. I needed information. I wanted questions answered. That's it. That's all I was doing. *I give Jack his date; he gives me answers.* I swallowed another drink of water, attempting to wash down the lies I was still telling myself.

The sounds of guitars plugging into amplifiers interrupted the arguments going on inside my head for escaping the bar and leaving Jack to his night of bar hopping.

"Good evening. How is everyone tonight?" A voice I recognized came across the microphone. The crowd that had gathered in front of the stage cheered. "This first song is new. Hope you like it."

The music started up, and Jack immediately started singing.

"Might want to close your mouth," Georgia said next to me.

I did, but I almost had to use my hand to keep it closed.

"He's in a band?" I said, mostly to myself.

"A truly incredible band," Georgia laughed. "And you didn't know?" She had to yell to be heard.

I shook my head. "He never said anything."

Georgia scooted away from me, and I sat back, listening. The music was loud, the lyrics deep. Jack's voice was soft, soothing. Clear. Unbelievable. It sounded like a combination of Coldplay and The Fray, both bands I loved.

As his words touched my ears and the sound of his voice filled my head, feelings I didn't recognize warmed the blood coursing through my veins. Eventually, that warmth surrounded my heart and squeezed.

When the set was over, I downed my water. An excitement filled the faces of the people who had moments before stood up next to the stage, but now made their way to the bar for refreshments.

Jack hopped off the stage, shook the hands of a few people and fist-bumped others as he made his way toward our table. The smile on his face looked genuine, relaxed. Not at all nervous or fearful the way he appeared when he told me he would help me walk away from our lives. At that moment, I didn't think I'd ever be able to turn my back on him. I squirmed, unsure of what to say.

He scooted into the booth, forcing me to move over. My stomach churned and my heart shrunk into a tiny ball of rubber bands. I stared at the condensation running down the new bottle of water in front of me.

"Great set," Georgia said.

"Thanks." For the first time ever, Jack sounded bashful.

Jonas and Fred arrived with waters for everyone.

"Man, did you see the cleavage on that chick right in front of you?" Fred asked Jack. He laughed. "Her eyes didn't leave you, dude."

"Lexi, you like the sound?" Jonas asked, a cigarette tucked behind his ear.

I jerked my head to attention and nodded, speechless.

Jack smiled, embarrassed, but said nothing. He glanced my way.

I didn't know what to say. Did I tell him that I loved the music? That his voice was beautiful? That this was the best date anyone had ever taken me on? "I have to pee," I said, pushing against him.

He stood and gave me a hand up. When I tried to turn, he grasped my hand tighter. "You okay?"

No, I most certainly am not okay. Something is terribly wrong. I think it has everything to do with falling for you. I couldn't breathe. "I'm fine. I'll be right back."

His grin grew. He knew he was getting to me. I was so unbelievably transparent. Or maybe he read my mind. I didn't know what was happening any more.

I tried to pull my hand away from him, but he held tighter and leaned in to my ear. "Don't take long. I have another set coming up." His arrogance was back.

I wriggled my fingers from his grasp. I couldn't get to the bathroom fast enough. When I got there, I went immediately to the mirror and stared at myself. My dark brunette hair hung half-way down my chest, framing my face—a face that was suddenly pale. "What the hell was that?" I asked my reflection. My green eyes stared back with utter confusion. I'd never acted like such an idiot in front of a guy before.

A young girl leaned into the mirror beside me. She lined her lips and spread lip-gloss. Her eyes focused on me through the mirror. "Aren't they incredible?"

I swallowed. What the hell was wrong with me? "Uh-huh." I turned away and went to a stall, closing the door.

I had to go back out there and face him. And say what? *Sorry, I'm an idiot.* Or how about, *you're hot and your beautiful voice really captured my heart, but...* Shit. Shit. Shit.

I could go with the truth. *If I had been born in another life, under normal circumstances, it would be easy to fall head over heels for you. Maybe in that life, you and I wouldn't have secrets. My father would be alive, and nobody would care about some set of journals or the fact that we were part of some science experiment.*

I stepped out of the bathroom and immediately locked eyes with Jack. He leaned against the bar, smiling and waiting. His confidence suffocated me. I made my way over to him, only being shoved once by the crowd.

Just talk to him, I told myself. *He's human. Just because he was perfect at everything didn't make him an alien. Just because he was smooth and articulate didn't suddenly make you an unintelligent being.*

"Hey," I said. So far, so good.

"I'm sorry. I should have told you."

By my reaction, you'd think he had just confided his darkest secrets. What was happening to me? It wasn't like he owed me any sort of explanation, but what I was feeling was a shock. He had told me he could play lots of instruments. This was just a single date. A silly bar band. I took a deep, cleansing breath. Not sure what to say, I decided on, "You sounded really good."

"Thanks." He looked past me and held up a palm, saying *five minutes*. "We're scheduled for one more set, but if you want to go, we can."

I searched his face. He would just leave his band hanging if I wanted to leave right now? "No, of course not. I have nowhere to be." At least, nowhere I'd rather be at this particular moment.

"You can hang out here, or you can sit with Georgia." A playful grin crept onto his face. "Or you can come down front and protect me from Miss Cleavage."

"I think you can handle her. I'll hang out here."

I climbed onto a bar stool, and Jack leaned in and kissed me on my forehead, lingering a bit, before disappearing through the crowd.

The girl who had reglossed her lips in the bathroom winked at me. *Strange*. She flirted with a couple of guys several bar stools over.

I redirected my attention to the stage where Jack plugged a cord into his guitar. He hadn't played during the first set, only sung. Something about the way he slid his hand along the strings made me blush remembering the way his hands touched me while we lay on the blanket at the arboretum.

"Excuse me." The girl with the lips from the bathroom touched my arm. "My friend over here would like to buy you a drink."

The guy she pointed to lifted a cup as if to say, "Hello." Good-looking, clean-cut, not completely out-of-place in this bar.

"Tell him thank you, but no thanks. I'm here with someone." Okay that sounded weird. But I was here *with* Jack, and if it kept strangers from picking me up, well, a girl had to do what a girl had to do.

Lips turned and walked away.

I watched the second set, gaining a new level of admiration for Jack. I wrestled with one thought, though. What could he possibly tell me about Sandra Whitmeyer that would make me walk away?

I also struggled with how on earth Jack kept up with a band all the way over here near the university while attempting to secure a spot with a top-notch college? *Over-achiever,* I decided.

"Can I get you something?" a voice behind me asked.

"A water, please," I told the bartender.

Jack held his guitar in front of him and leaned into the mic. "This last one is one of our originals, but still my favorite. It's called 'Choices.'"

He swung his guitar behind his back and bowed his head away from the microphone. When he lifted his head again, he leaned in close to the mic stand and sang a cappella before the rest of the band joined in with instruments.

As he sang, he scanned the audience until his eyes landed on me. I couldn't suppress a smile. I was paralyzed by the intense look that passed between us. His deep blue eyes reached all the way into the depths of my soul as if the crowd between us had suddenly disappeared and we were alone in this bar.

I was a goner.

"Hey," a voice to my left startled me out of my daydream. "You'll break my heart if you don't let me buy you one drink." Friend of Lips' sidled up beside me with the cheesiest of all cheesy lines. "Hi, I'm Rick."

"Like I told your friend, I'm with someone. But thanks anyway." I forced a smile, willing this guy to move along with my mind and praying I could suppress the nosebleed.

I tried to grab my bottle of water, but this loser blocked my path. "If you were with me, I wouldn't have left you alone this long."

Did he not realize the person I was with sang in the band? Idiot. "That's sweet. And flattering, however—"

"Hey, asshole, leave her alone." A boy playfully slapped Rick on the back of the head. Lips snuggled into his side. They were laughing, and I was sure they meant no harm. But crap... I missed the end of Jack's song.

Rick shrugged his friends off. "I can't talk you into one drink?"

"I have one already." I reached around him, and he helped me out by grabbing the water I was reaching for and removed the lid for me. "Thanks." I tipped back the drink.

"If you're here with someone, where is he? I would never leave someone as pretty as you all alone." He leaned in. "You know, my friends and I are on our way to another bar. You want to join us?"

I nervously downed more of the water. Then I squared my shoulders and faced the jerk. "No. I do not want to go anywhere with you or your friends. Thanks, anyway."

I felt the warmth of another body behind me. The muscles in my back tightened. Slowly, I turned my head, and Jack was there, his hand planted firmly on the small of my back. I relaxed a little. "Everything okay?" He reached for my bottle of water, taking it from my hand and studying the contents.

I looked at Rick, hoping he got the hint. I truly didn't want a bloody nose because of this loser who refused to take "No" for an answer.

"Let's go," Jack said as he took my hand.

He held up the water bottle in front of his eyes again. We passed through a crowd of people. Several called out things like, "You rocked it, dude," and "Awesome set, Jack."

"It was a nice sound," I said, my words slurred. I squeezed Jack's hand and pulled him to a stop. He turned and studied me. His face went in and out of focus. "I feel funny."

"Shit. I knew something was off. They put something in your drink."

"What? Noooo. Why woulthd thomeone do that?" I stumbled toward Jack. He caught me against his chest. "You're stho beauteeful," I said. "You know that?"

"Can you walk?" he asked close to my ear. Was that fear in his voice?

I wanted him to kiss me. The smell of his shower gel, and his firm hold on me invited me in. He slid an arm around my back and supported me while urging me forward. We passed the stage and entered a hallway. When I stumbled again, he scooped me up into his arms and cradled me into his chest.

"This was not at all how I wanted this evening to go," he grumbled.

What? Me in your arms? My head dangled backwards. A giggle escaped.

Jack kicked open a back door and exited the bar. We passed a dumpster and the stench of the garbage had me turning my head into his chest, breathing hard through my mouth. "Ugh. That's awwwful." My syllables continued to slur. I lifted my head just as we rounded a corner.

When we reached Jack's car, he said, "I'm going to set you on your feet. Can you stand?"

"Mmm-hmm." I stood for a second before I threw my arms around his neck. "I don't feel so good, Jack."

I heard the sound of voices and the shuffle of feet on gravel behind me. I tried to turn. Jack struggled with his keys, but was able to get the passenger door open. He helped me in the seat. "You're going to be okay. Sit. Stay." He held out a hand in front of him.

"I'm not a dog," I slurred and rolled my eyes.

Behind Jack, a couple of figures came in and out of view. One of them looked like Seth Whitmeyer. "Seth?" I asked.

Jack turned. "Why did you have to come after her like this? I'm working on finding the stupid journals. You overstepped this time."

He knew Seth?

"I didn't do that to her." Seth sounded surprised. "I have no intention of hurting Sarah. We're not the only ones looking for those journals, and you know it, Jack. You were an idiot to think you wouldn't lead danger to her."

"Leave her alone, Seth. I need more time."

I closed my eyes. I wanted to sleep. My head felt detached from my body.

"Be reasonable," Seth pleaded with Jack. I was so confused, and their voices were so loud. "You can't protect her. We can. You need to bring her in."

When I opened my eyes, I tried to focus on Jack and the outline of the design on the back of his concert T-shirt, which was difficult because it was swirling and pulsing.

He ran a hand through his hair, and I imagined doing the same.

"She's not ready," he said. He shut my door and darted toward Seth. I rubbed my eyes. Tried to focus. What had they drugged me with? Did Seth do this to me? Did Jack put me in danger?

What did he mean by "she's not ready"?

No. I shook my head. Jack wouldn't put me in danger. My head felt fuzzy.

Bright lights bounced off the windshield and lit up Seth and Jack. Both men turned toward headlights from a large SUV. The vehicle sped toward them. Seth and Jack separated.

Jack slid across the hood of the car and climbed behind the wheel, slamming the door. "Lexi, put your seatbelt on." His voice was panicked.

Everything was happening in slow motion. I fought the urge to vomit. I fumbled for my seatbelt as Jack whipped toward the parking lot exit. He turned onto one road, and then another.

Then he floored it.

~~~~
~~~~

Something slammed into the car. I lurched toward the front dashboard. "What the..." I was sure I would throw up. The sound of metal on metal and the impact made my heart skip several beats.

"Hold on," Jack said. Like I had a choice. He struggled to keep the steering wheel steady.

"Who is that? Whatta they want?" I sounded like I was speaking through a tube.

Jack didn't answer.

I wrapped my hand around the handle above my head. The vehicle slammed into us again. My entire body stiffened, bracing for further impact.

Jack sped up, taking corners quickly.

As he took the next turn, I looked out the window at the black suburban following us. "It's the same car."

"What?" Jack said.

"Saw it earlier. At the restaurant. And again at the pretty flower place."

"And you said nothing?"

Uh-oh. He was mad. "Lotsa black SUVs around here."

The truck slammed into us again. My head pitched forward. Jack's knuckles whitened as his grip tightened around the steering wheel.

He sped up, slowing down only for sharp curves. Then we were on a long stretch. We picked up speed. I could see what looked like a curve up ahead. The road looked like it would end, but Jack continued to increase our momentum.

"Hang on," he said.

At the last second possible, he applied pressure to the brakes and took a hard right. I sucked in a deep breath and held it. The tires skidded. We straightened.

My world continued to spin, my vision fuzzy.

"Shit!" Jack watched with horror in his rearview mirror.

I managed to turn in my seat just in time to see two lights getting closer. Brighter. Fuzzier.

The truck hit us. My body lurched forward. The seatbelt tightened across my chest.

"Jack, why're they doing this?" Nothing made sense. I focused on the double yellow lines stretching out in front of us.

The vehicle came alongside and swerved into us. Jack held on and steadied the car.

When the SUV hit us in the side again, Jack lost control. Our car lurched sideways into a field and through a fence before it began to turn on its side. Metal buckled. We flipped once. Twice. Glass shattered.

Finally, we stopped. I hung upside down. The car balanced on its roof. I heard a deep moaning sound that I think came from my own throat. I tried to glance over at Jack, but couldn't.

A sharp pain erupted behind my right eye, and then nothing.

SEVENTEEN

I smelled gasoline, laced with cigarette smoke. Though my mind struggled to process what had just happened, I knew one thing for sure: those two scents didn't go together.

I rolled my head side to side. When my eyes fluttered open, a faceless figure came into focus. The cigarette in his mouth flared as he inhaled, and when he laughed, I gagged, then rolled over into a coughing fit.

What was he doing? Couldn't he smell the gasoline?

Why wasn't he helping us? We had to get outta there. "Jack!"

A hand squeezed my hand. "Shh. I'm right here. Can you hear me?"

"We have to get out of the car, Jack. He shouldn't be smoking. I smell gasoline." I reached a hand to my temple. My fingers met the soft feel of cotton and plastic. I winced, and as I scrunched up my face, my head and face hurt more.

"Lexi, can you hear me? We're not in the car. We got out of the car. We're fine."

I groaned and tried to move my other arm, but met resistance and more tenderness in my shoulder.

My eyes fluttered, letting small amounts of light in. Another figure came into focus slowly. This time, he had a face. And no cigarette.

"Jack?" His forehead was wrinkled with concern. Worry swam in his eyes.

"Yeah. It's me." A lazy curve spread across his lips. He sat on the bed beside me.

I studied his face. "You're okay?" My voice was panicked. I lifted my head, not without pain, and looked around. The guest room at Jack's house. No one else was there. No one smoking.

He nodded. "Just a few scratches." He followed my anxious gaze.

Finding no one in the room with us, and with the smell of cigarette smoke gone, I relaxed back against the pillow. "How long have I been out?"

He looked at his watch. "About twelve hours."

"Am I okay?" I wiggled my toes and fingers. Assessed my pain. My head throbbed.

His face softened as he took my hand and smiled. "You're going to be fine."

"Going to be?"

"A few more scratches than me, but you'll recover quickly. I'll help." He bowed his head and tapped his forehead with our linked hands.

"What's wrong, then?" Besides the fact that some scary guys had tried to send us to our graves way earlier than I planned.

He lifted his head. "I'm so sorry, Lexi. I tried to protect you. I never should have taken you to that bar. I just thought—"

"This was not your fault," I said, willing myself to remain calm. Still, something else played in the back of my mind. "Something tells me I wouldn't be lying here if it hadn't been for your expert driving." I tried to smile. It hurt.

He nodded, swallowing hard.

"Do we know who ran us off the road?" I asked.

"No." Jack sucked in a deep breath. "Dad's investigators found traces of Rohypnol in your water. Fortunately, you hadn't drunk much."

I gave my head a shake. "I don't understand."

"Also known as the date rape drug."

"Why would someone want to drug me with that?"

"The drug isn't only used for assault. It's simply a strong sedative that can be hypnotic and cause a person temporary amnesia. What I don't understand is why someone would spike your drink with such a drug if their intent was to kill you. Or me for that matter."

Suddenly, I felt like an elephant was sitting on my chest. A tear leaked down the side of my face and into my hair.

Jack cupped my cheek and rubbed the tear with this thumb.

"Why is someone trying to kill one of us, Jack?" Or both of us.

"I'm not sure. It could have something to do with our fathers' research, but I just don't know."

"How did I get here?" I glanced down at the t-shirt and girly boxers I wore. Panic crept into my voice and my head. "And into these clothes?"

Jack's lips twitched. His fingers feathered along my arm. "I carried you to bed."

My eyes widened.

"Anita changed you into more comfortable clothes."

My body relaxed, and Jack's smile grew. Given the situation, Jack seeing too much of me should have been the least of my concerns, but...

The touch of his fingers against my skin made my heart rate speed up, but not in a good way and I wasn't sure why. I was forgetting something. Something that happened prior to landing upside down in Jack's car. "My head really hurts."

His fingers drifted up my arm and tiptoed along my brow line. A cold sensation spread along my face and forehead, dissipating the pain with each press of his finger.

I breathed in and out while I searched his face. I wanted to ask him how he took my pain away, but the words got stuck in my throat. Something else teetered at the edge of my brain as his eyes examined each millimeter of my hairline.

I thought about the previous night—the romantic dinner, the sound of his voice over the microphone on stage, and the kissing. With each pleasant memory, my breathing became shallower. I squirmed under his gaze.

The natural light in the room flickered as clouds passed in front of the sun on the other side of sheer curtains. As the room darkened, so did my memories.

The girl with the lips. Rick. The bottle of water that made me feel drunk.

Jack led me from the bar. Carried me. I could still remember the stench of the dumpsters. He set me gently in the passenger seat of his car.

Seth Whitmeyer. He was there. Outside. Behind the bar.

Jack's eyes narrowed.

I pushed his hand away and sat up. "Seth Whitmeyer was there." I rubbed my temple with my fingers. The pain was gone. "You knew him."

Jack did not look surprised by my realization. "Yeah, not exactly how I wanted our date to go," he said.

The flip-flopping emotions battling inside my head made me dizzy. I slid out of the bed, whipped around to face Jack, and stumbled.

"Whoa." He stood and circled around the bed to where I was standing. "Take it easy."

His concern melted the ice wall I was erecting, yet I wanted to hit him. "Where are my clothes?" I looked around the room.

"Anita put them in the closet." Jack held out a hand in front of me. "Stay. I'll get them." He crossed to the closet and returned with the bag Danielle had packed for me. "Why don't you lie back down? We have nowhere to be today." His voice was calm, but his face screamed concern.

"I don't want to lie back down." My words spilled out in a panic. I was definitely losing it. "Those people drugged me last night." Memories were pouring into my head like a torrential rain. "Someone tried to kill us, Jack. Seth Whitmeyer was there. Did he try to kill us?" I raised my hands and shoved him.

He caught both of my wrists and pulled me towards him as he stumbled backwards from my push. His eyes closed briefly. "No. Seth doesn't want us dead."

"But you do know him."

He nodded.

"What is this? Who wants me dead?" Was it the same people who killed Dad? "What does Seth want from me?" Panic attack in full swing, I dug frantically through the bag until I pulled out a pair of jeans, a t-shirt, and a hoodie. "You've been after the journals all along. You and..." I gazed up at him, my breathing labored. "Seth? You're working with him?"

"What? No. Well... Yes. But there's so much more to it than that." Jack guarded his words closely.

Did Jack want my dad's journals so badly he was willing to let someone hurt me? Did he take me to that bar so that someone could drug me? Kidnap me? Kill me?

Suddenly, as if reading my thoughts, he placed a hand over mine as I fidgeted with my clothes. "Stop this. No one is going to get close enough again to drug, kidnap or kill you. I promise. It wasn't Seth who drugged you. You have to believe me. And I had nothing to do with what happened last night." He dipped his head, forcing me to look at him. "I won't let anyone hurt you."

My eyes widened, horrified. Had he just read my mind? I hadn't spoken those questions out loud. I clutched the clothes to my chest, trying to hide the fact that I was shaking all over. Dark realization set in.

I think I'd known it all along. I tried to shake the cobwebs from my head.

I stared hard into Jack's eyes. *How am I supposed to believe you? How can I trust you when you are hiding so much from me? Every bad thing that has happened, happened since I met you. Since the day you showed up at Wellington.*

He took a step toward me. Jack's lips stretched into a tight line. His eyes locked onto mine—stormy blue to what had to be freaked-out green. "The secrets end today."

Then the unthinkable happened. I heard his voice inside my head. His lips didn't move. No sound came from his mouth. *I am not going to let anything bad happen to you. After today, I will hide nothing from you. The bad things that are happening were set in motion way before I showed up at Wellington.*

I stumbled backwards, dropping my clothes to the floor. My hand flew over my mouth. I didn't dare avert my gaze from his panicked face. A mirror to mine, I was sure. *You can hear me.*

I can. And you can hear me.

"I'm going to throw up." I darted to the bathroom and slammed the door.

EIGHTEEN

"Moment of truth, Matthews."

The girl who stared back at me in the mirror looked nothing like me. Her hair hung in tousled strands. Blood smeared across her forehead. Heavy, dark circles under partially swollen eyelids.

I reached a hand and lightly pressed on my shoulder. Pain erupted. Although the shoulder was only slightly swollen, red skin assured me that I was bruised. And if the pain was any indication...

I spread my fingers wide, pressing my palms into the vanity, and leaned in closer to the mirror. Studied my reflection. Green eyes. Brown, stringy hair.

Jack had read my thoughts. How long had he done this? Had he read *all* of my thoughts?

I buried my face into my palms. "Dad! What did you do?" A sob escaped my mouth. I was a freak. And the guy I was falling for... had fallen for... could see straight into my mind and know my every secret thought. For a normal teenager, life didn't get much worse.

I lifted my head again. I was anything but normal. My dad was gone. My grandmother didn't know me. I had no one.

"You have Jack," I whispered. I just had to trust. Could I put my faith into someone who was obviously hiding so much from me, but who had constantly saved me the past few weeks?

What about the journals? Was he after those? At my expense?

~~~~

The guest room was empty when I exited the bathroom. A note waited for me on the bed.

I went horseback riding. Take the time you need, then come find me. Please. I promise I will explain everything I can. -Jack

The DeWeese's house was quiet. Too quiet. The sound of my rapid breathing and my deteriorating nerves followed me down the front staircase and through the house.

I stepped outside on the back patio and walked toward the fence that lined an open field behind the house. It was a cloudy, fall day, the air crisp and cool as it whispered across my skin. I breathed in the scent of impending rain, confirmed by the dark clouds in the distance.

Dressed in jeans and a baseball cap, Jack sat atop a large gray horse that galloped along the fence line. My hands shook. I stuffed them inside the pocket of my hoodie.

Reaching the fence, I climbed up, swung my legs over and sat on the top plank while I watched Jack ride. He was beautiful, so in control on top of the large animal. Part of me wanted to retreat and not hear the truths I needed him to reveal, but that was just my fear of the unknown.

Jack spotted me. He tugged on the reins and turned the horse toward me. My heart beat wildly. He trotted up next to me. His beautiful gray horse nodded in my direction. I ran my hand down his snout.
~~~~

He held out his hand and spoke in a soft, but confident voice, "Get on."

I shook my head.

He grabbed my hand. "Come on. I won't let you fall."

My stomach twisted. I stared into his deep blue eyes, the color of the approaching storm cloud.

Here it was. Decision time. Trust Jack? Or flee?

When he tugged again, I lifted one leg and slid into the saddle in front of him while trying not to aggravate my injured shoulder. His arms circled around me, holding the reins. His chest pressed into my back. His legs squeezed against mine, sending electric shocks through my body.

He made a clicking sound with his mouth and pulled on the reins, steering the horse away from the fence. We trotted toward the trees that lined the back of the property.

A cool breeze blew hair off my face. As we entered the wooded area, Jack instructed the horse to slow. The daylight dimmed by the shade of the large oaks. Shadows danced around the roots at the base of the trees. Leaves swirled in the autumn breeze. He rested his hands in front of me, and his biceps squeezed against my arms. I said nothing. I tried to think nothing, fearing he'd hear my thoughts.

Jack leaned his head into the crook of my neck. I felt his warm breath against my skin. My body tensed, and then he whispered, "I meant what I said. I won't let you fall." I don't think he meant it in the physical sense. He lifted a hand and pulled my hair away from my face. "And I won't allow anyone to hurt you." His voice sounded weird, hoarse.

I closed my eyes, concentrating on the warmth of his body close to mine. "I think I know that." I reopened my eyes and turned my head so that I could see him. The features of his face softened when our eyes met.

He ran his thumb along my cheekbone. I leaned into his touch. I wanted to freeze this moment, to forget about the secrets kept from me my whole life. I wanted only to remember that last night, for a short time, I was a normal teenager out on a date. In this dream scenario, on top of this giant animal, I wanted to pretend that Jack was mine. That we were just out for a romantic ride through the woods.

"You are so beautiful," he said. He leaned closer, kissed my lips. "And I *am* yours."

My body tensed. His fingers tickled the skin around my face and lingered along my neck as his words confirmed that my mind wasn't safe.

"Have you always been able to hear my thoughts?" *Because I haven't always thought the nicest things.*

He smiled and nodded. "Most of them."

I cringed. "Do you hear other peoples' thoughts? Other girls'?"

Jack laughed. "No."

I faced forward while touching the dry skin beneath my nose. "My nose doesn't bleed when I direct thoughts at you?" *Maybe because they're actually my private thoughts that come naturally.*

"Probably."

"Which is completely, one-hundred percent scary. I'm not sure I can control those thoughts."

"You don't have to. You don't need to be afraid of me, Lexi. But—"

Tell that to the circus elephants in my stomach.

He chuckled softly. "I will teach you control."

"Control?"

"Your thoughts. I can teach you to keep your thoughts from me. To allow me to hear only the thoughts you want me to hear."

That's a relief.

"And your other... abilities. You'll learn to control those as well."

"I don't have other abilities."

"You just haven't discovered them yet."

~~~~

A strong storm blew in that afternoon. Horizontal rain pelted the windows along the back of the house, including those in Dr. DeWeese's study.

Jack led me to the sofa and gestured for me to sit. No words had passed between us since we left the barn, but if I was able to read his face and he my thoughts, I knew one thing for sure—we were both scared.

"Where are your parents?"

"Traveling." He continued over to his father's desk where he sat and unlocked a desk drawer.

"Traveling where?" Was he purposely being vague? What happened to no secrets?

"Sicily." A dark look passed over his face.

"That's where my father was living. They're searching for the journals," I said, somewhat betrayed.

Thunder clapped and lightning flashed in dramatic bursts, lighting up the room. I flinched.
~~~~

Jack pulled out a black box from a bottom drawer and placed it in front of him. He opened it carefully, dug through the contents and pulled an item out before closing the box again.

The lighting in the office was dim. He crossed the room and sat beside me.

"This... is Sandra." He handed me a photograph.

Tearing my eyes from his, I looked down at the woman in the picture. I reached a shaky hand and traced the outline of the woman's face, her smile, the curves of her body. Jack's expression was as serious as I had ever seen it. "Sandra?"

He nodded.

Short and slender, she stood between Dad and Dr. DeWeese. The two men had an arm around her. She grabbed at her long brown hair blowing in a breeze. All three smiled. They were laughing. Sandra's green eyes stared straight at the camera.

I didn't understand. "It's me." A voice in my head screamed, *This is a picture of me. I look exactly like her. She looks like me.*

Jack winced as if I had actually yelled.

Sandra stood at the same height as me, coming to just under Dad's chin. Her eyebrows curved the same way mine did when she smiled. Her nose was slightly crooked. I traced the straight line of mine—the only visible difference. "I don't believe it." Jack remained a statue beside me. "What does this mean?" My eyes returned to the photograph—a picture worth way more than a thousand words.

Some of them not nice words.

"So... what?" I asked, searching his eyes for answers he wasn't being terribly forthcoming with. Except I didn't need them; I knew. Maybe I had always known. It was easy to ignore all the signs, tucked away in a boarding school. Different name. A father who lived in some Mediterranean country doing who-knows-what with embryonic stem cells. A mother who fled shortly after I was born. I wasn't really hers. "I was cloned?" Tears welled against the edge of my bottom eyelid. *I'm Frankenstein's monster.*

"No." Jack sandwiched my face with his hands. His palms hot against my cheeks. "No! You are not a monster. We... are not monsters."

We? I looked back at the picture. John DeWeese. With hair. *He is you.* A slightly older Jack, but not by much. Dr. DeWeese in his late-twenties, early-thirties.

"How long have you known?" My voice cracked.

"About being cloned from my father? A while."

"Why didn't you tell me?"

He cocked his head. "How do you tell a seventeen-year-old girl that you care for deeply and who strongly opposes how our fathers played with human life that, 'Oh, by the way, I'm a clone of my own father?'"

"How long have you known I was cloned from Sandra?"

"I suspected the day you overheard my parents arguing about Sandra."

"You heard my thoughts. That day in the kitchen when you spilled your orange juice."

He nodded.

"How long have you known I was cloned?"

"I only confirmed you were like me, genetically manipulated in some way, the day I heard your first thought. But cloned? Not very long."

"But you didn't tell me at first." I couldn't hide the hurt.

"Again, how was I going to tell a girl searching for her own unique identity that she is the result of a genetic experiment? I hoped your father would tell you. And fill in some of the blanks."

I sucked in a breath.

"And I believe he was coming to do exactly that." Jack squeezed my hand.

I pulled my hand away, stood and marched over to the window. Rain pummeled the glass. Lightning strobed. I wrapped my arms around my waist, and my body shook. Like the droplets of water streaming down the windowpanes, tears poured down my cheeks.

I'd known what my father was capable of all of my life. He claimed that the technology for cloning humans was out there. I'd always assumed that "out there" meant scientists were capable, but would never resort to such monstrosities.

I sensed Jack's presence right behind me before I felt his hands on my arms.

I whipped around and backed up from him.

"Lexi..." He wrinkled his brows.

"I feel betrayed," I whispered.

"I know. Please don't hate me. I couldn't stand it if you hated me."

You? I don't hate you. You didn't do this.

He moved a strand of hair off my forehead and tucked it behind my ear. He leaned in and kissed my forehead.

My knees buckled. Jack caught me in his arms and lowered me gently to the floor. He sat in front of me, pulled me into his lap, and rocked. I succumbed to numb shock.

NINETEEN

A residual clap of thunder shook the house. It had been thunderstorm after thunderstorm all afternoon. The electricity flickered a few times before it went out completely. My nerves were shot.

Tucked into the corner of the DeWeese's living room sofa, I drew my knees in and hugged them. My body trembled—I wasn't sure if it was from the slight chill in the air, the loud severe storms that caused the house to be dark and without a security system, or the worried look Jack wore.

He stoked the fire. I eyed his every move. Studied his facial expressions. His command of the house. His maturity. His actions were not that of a high-school senior, yet the smooth skin around his eyes screamed youth.

Finally, he sunk down onto the opposite side of the couch and faced me.

"You thought I would run when I learned the truth of where I came from," I said. Running would be the easy way. Right then, running did have its appeal. But someone had killed my father and tried to kill me. I had to know who.

A shadow crossed his eyes. "I wish telling you that you were a clone was why I thought you would run."

I stared at him. My eyelids felt slightly swollen.

"I don't want to tell you any of it, though. Not now."

"What do you mean?"

"I planned to. When I discovered that the daughter of the famous Dr. Peter Roslin was at Wellington. I planned to tell you everything I knew. Mom forbade me from going to Wellington. But I was already eighteen. I told her I'd run if she tried to stop me."

"What stopped you from telling me?"

He ran a hand through his hair. "I'm so thankful I already know how to control the thoughts you can hear from me." His lips lifted in an uneasy smile.

I relaxed the hold I had on my knees and moved closer to him, stopping in the middle of the couch to keep from touching him. I was not going to touch him. It was bad enough he could hear most of my thoughts. "I thought you said 'no more secrets'."

He sighed, the muscles around his eyes tight. "I did say that." He placed both hands on his knees. His fingers spread wide. "Okay. Here it goes."

He stood and walked over to the fire, placing his palms against the mantle above it. Again, his nervousness struck me as odd. He was holding something back. Information that might send me running, according to him. He seemed... what? Afraid?

"Who would have thought this would be the toughest part to tell you."

"Right now, Jack, I'm so freaked. Start with anything." I stood and wrung my hands. The muscles in my shoulder ached; my entire body was sore from the previous night's car crash. I rubbed my temples while I waited for him to speak.

He faced me. "I wanted to heal your injuries completely last night. But I didn't want to be too sick to protect you from whoever came at us if they struck again. And I didn't want to be too sick to answer your questions about Seth. The thought of you leaving me and not looking back..." He took a few steps forward. "I can make the headache go away." He ran his fingers lightly across my forehead and over my eyelids, where the pain was the strongest.

I grabbed both his hands with mine and lowered them, holding them between us. "You're changing the subject. Just tell me."

Okay, here it goes. "You were created for me. To complement my abilities. And vice versa."

An involuntary gasp escaped through my lips. I dropped his hands. "Come again."

"Sandra was crazy obsessed with cloning humans and enhancing the brain's genetic makeup. So, first, she created human embryos—one from my father's DNA and then one from her own."

I swayed slightly.

"Come. Sit down." Jack grabbed my hand and led me back to the sofa.

When I found the courage, I lifted my eyes and met his. The wind and the rain calmed outside. Any trace of sunlight was MIA and the house was dark. The light from the fire and the candles produced a soft glow on his face, but his eyes carried the storms of the day.

"You said Sandra was a geneticist."

"And a neurologist. They say she was fascinated with the human mind and how doctors might battle injuries and diseases of the brain in the future."

I peered into Jack's eyes. There was more. So much more. I could almost see the inner workings of his own brain twisting and turning each piece of this puzzle—our lives. Did he start with the straight edges, the easier stuff and the foundation for the rest of the hard-to-fit pieces? Or did he just jump into the middle and piece it all together for me from the inside out?

Did he even have all the pieces?

"Let me get this straight. Sandra cloned your father and then herself. Your father agreed to this?"

"Yes and no." Jack held my hand and absentmindedly drew circles on my palm. "Father agreed to test Sandra's claim that she could clone an adult human and enhance the genetic makeup of the brain without compromising the embryo."

"And?"

"According to my father, the embryos were never supposed to become more than that. They were supposed to be destroyed and never implanted. They were never supposed to become human babies."

"But they did. Become human babies. The embryos became you and me." *She created two freaks.*

Jack's expression darkened. He reached his other hand and lifted my chin. "Stop it with the freak talk. I am no freak, and you, my dear, are most certainly no freak."

"Why are you telling me all this now? Why not tell me when you fixed my arm? Or when I asked you if we were designer babies." That thought made want to laugh. As if my parents had wished for me to have green eyes and strong arms and legs for swimming. "Or when my dad was killed? Why didn't you tell me then?"

"I hoped your dad would tell you initially. And then..."

"...he died," I finished for him.

"And I'm only now putting a lot of this together. I knew about myself, but I just started asking more questions about you and your abilities recently."

"Asking questions?" My eyes darted back and forth, searching his. Then, the realization hit me. "The Program."

"The Program is designed to reveal the research our fathers, Sandra and others have been involved in. Information is being filtered to me slowly. Too slowly. When your father was killed... the thought that you were in danger... possibly because of what we are?" He sucked in a deep breath, letting it out slowly. "That's what haunts me now."

"You could have told me some of this sooner."

"Aren't my reasons obvious?"

"Not to me." I searched his eyes. Something besides fear and nervousness was there. I tried to remove my hand from his.

He held tighter, looking deep into my core. "I'm in love with you, Lexi. And I will do anything to protect you from the absurd cards we've been dealt."

This time I pulled my hand away and stood. I walked toward the fireplace and stared straight into the burning flames. *I guess I can't possibly hide what I feel from you, can I?*

Jack's arms circled me and drew my back against his chest. *I know you love me. But, man, you've done a pretty amazing job of fighting it.*

I chuckled, a little from embarrassment. "I'm sorry. These feelings are new to me. And I'm so scared."

Say it now.

"I love you, Jack," I whispered, my voice hoarse.

He turned me around. His eyes searched mine, then drifted to my lips. His hands held my face as he leaned in and kissed me.

I threw my hands around his neck, and I kissed him back like my life depended on it. I ran my hands through his hair, and he mine. We continued like that until neither of us could breathe.

When we came up for air, Jack hugged me tightly, burying his face into the crook of my neck. "I've been so scared to tell you everything."

"I still have so many questions."

"So do I. But we don't have to solve the entire mystery tonight."

"What was my father's part in all this?"

"I don't know," Jack whispered. "I've told you most of what I know."

"But—"

Jack placed a finger on my lips. "Shhh. We both have a lot to learn. And we will."

"But Jack, why is someone trying to kill us? Are we in danger here?"

"We are safe here. This farm is wired with an electric fence, which is thankfully on a generator. Father placed security at every entrance after your father was killed. No one is going to get to you here."

My body tensed. "What about school? Who else knows that we are cloned humans? Are we going to be turned into governmental lab rats?" I suddenly felt so exposed. No wonder my dad hid me away at a boarding school and changed my name. Why didn't he just tell me? Did he think I'd fall apart? Like I was obviously doing. My thoughts and questions raced too quickly for anyone to keep up. Even Jack.

"Stop. Okay?" He kissed my forehead. "Let's take a break."

"A break?"

"You play pool?"

"Pool?" The suggestion caught me off guard. "As in white ball, black ball, lots of colors, and a stick?"

"Yeah. Pool."

How can he possibly be thinking about playing a game? "Really? You want to play pool. Now?"

"I've been dealing with this a lot longer than you. I know. I get it. You're wigged out. I'm pissed that someone caused me to wreck my car last night. I have found that I can't stop trying to mix in a little bit of real. Games. Fun. You know? We have to continue living like the humans we are or we will start feeling like..."

"Freaks?"

Jack shook his head in disapproval. "Pool is a great way to learn control, too. I might be able to show you how to control the thoughts I hear."

I arched an eyebrow. "So, pool?"

"Yeah. Do you play?"

"A little, I guess." I looked away and tried to think of anything but pool. Or how good at pool I was thanks to Kyle. Or about flipping cars, a hurt shoulder, or bloody noses.

"Oh, my. We have a lot of work to do. I had you pegged as a control nut." Jack tapped a finger to my temple. "But your mind is wide open. Even when you try your hardest... maybe especially then... I hear everything."

I blushed, thinking about the not so flattering things I thought about Jack when he first arrived at Wellington, and then at the more than flattering thoughts I had later. My face must have turned crimson.

"I heard loud and clear that you think you play pool pretty well, but that your shoulder might be too hurt."

"Is that all you heard?"

"I'm a gentleman, Lexi."

"What does that mean?"

"It means exactly what I told you earlier. You don't have to hide your thoughts with me." He stepped closer, stared down on me. "Pool or not? Can you handle it?" He grazed his fingers over my shoulder.

I stuck my lips out in a pout. "I can play. I'll live with the pain."

"Good. Because we need to start working on getting you to control your thoughts and mind altering abilities as soon as possible."

~~~~

"Concentrate, Lexi."

"Stop yelling at me." *I'll show you concentration when I concentrate on aiming my knee right where it will—*

Try it. I dare you.

Jack's eyes were hot on mine, daring me to knee him. Something told me I might be the one that ended up on the ground with a new injury if I tried.

You'd be right. Besides, that's another lesson altogether. Now, concentrate.
~~~~

I stuck out my lower lip and blew a strand of hair out of my eyes. "Fine."

I gathered the pool balls and racked them for a new game, then walked over and twisted the square of chalk on the end of my pool stick, giving it a quick blow after.

Candles lit the room. Large, small, some in glass hurricanes.

Jack sat on the edge of a barstool and leaned into his stick. A candle flickered on the table behind him, casting a soft glow upon his face. His eyes followed my every move.

He was in love with me. Even though I couldn't suppress what I was feeling for him, I had to find a way to keep him from knowing my every thought. A girl's gotta have her secrets.

I lined up the white ball and prepared to break while simultaneously concentrating on building a barrier around the inner workings of my brain—coating each thought, each worry, every question I still had with a protective shield.

As I focused on those thoughts and questions, something strange began to happen. Instead of closing my mind off, it opened up. I sensed Jack's presence. I didn't hear his thoughts, but I smelled the scent of his shower gel. Felt the caress of his breath against the back of my neck. His mind knocked against that imaginary coat of armor I constructed.

I shot the cue ball and missed the triangle of colorful balls completely. I whipped around. Jack still sat on the same barstool ten feet away.

His lips curled into a smile. "Very good. You felt me tapping into your thoughts." He stood and approached the table, proceeding to replace the white ball and break. He stepped close to me. This time, his breath *was* on my cheek as he said, "I'll take the solids."

Slowly, a crack formed. Then just like that, all of my thoughts and worries spilled out.

Jack frowned. "That's enough for tonight. Let go, Lexi. It will come. At least now you know what it feels like when I enter your mind. Right?"

I nodded. It was an invasion. Like someone broke into my locked chamber of secrets and stole my... everything, really.

Jack sunk three more solids before he missed. He walked over to me, and grabbing my hand, he lifted it and kissed each knuckle. "Your turn."

I placed my hand on his chest and pushed him aside. How was I supposed to keep him out of my head when he flaunted those well-sculpted pectoral muscles around and kissed me at every turn?

He backed up, chuckling under his breath.

"Something amusing you?"

Most definitely.

I missed again. I was starting to see this game for what it was—an exercise in concentrating amidst heavy distractions. If I were truly going to keep Jack out of my head, I had to learn to control my mind subconsciously.

"Who exactly is Seth?" I asked while I waited for my turn.

Jack shot, sinking the red solid. "Seth is Sandra's twin brother."

Twin? And I'm a clone of Sandra, so therefore... I gave my head a little shake. "He warned me away from you."

"Oh yeah? When?"

"At the nursing home after Dad died. He told me you weren't who you claimed to be."

"He was testing you."

"Testing me? How?"

"He wanted to know if you would run. He was testing your strength."

"Did he have something to do with the cloning?"

"No." Jack leaned against the pool table. His eyes focused on some spot behind me for a moment before finding my eyes again. I attempted to erect the barrier around my mind again, and believed it was working. Jack continued, "Seth found me when we arrived in Kentucky. He convinced my mother and father that he could take my medical training further. For some reason, they trusted him. Of course, my father knew him, but I didn't know that at the time."

"Since they trusted him, and because of your thirst for knowledge, you what? Let him take your home schooling further?"

A line formed between Jack's eyes. "Something like that."

Something about Jack's body language told me I needed to tread lightly where Seth was concerned.

I tried, but failed to suppress a yawn.

"You're tired." He took my stick from me and placed it on the rack against the wall. He returned and boxed me in against the pool table, placing a hand on either side of my hips. "Bedtime." He reached a hand and trailed a finger down my cheek, across my lower lip, and down my throat. He leaned in and pressed his lips to mine. The touch was firm; his lips were warm. He slid his fingers through the belt loops of my jeans. His hips pressed into mine.

My head went all woozy, and I couldn't process a single thought. Even if only temporary, I forgot everything related to the cloning, genetic manipulation, and murder. My hand snaked around his neck and I threaded my fingers into his hair.

The connection between us deepened, and I found myself wanting more. So much more.

But the timing was all wrong.

He pulled back. His forehead leaned against mine. We were both short of breath, and I wasn't sure I wanted to stop.

"I'll walk you to your room. I want to try something."

I raised an eyebrow.

"Stop it. Nothing like that. I'm shocked at how your mind works, Miss Matthews." He fake-gasped. "I had no idea the places you would allow your thoughts to roam." He shook his head.

"What did you have in mind?" I was sure my cheeks darkened three shades.

"I want to try to heal your shoulder and see if I can control the nausea after."

I suppressed a look of disappointment. I did need my shoulder in order to swim. And I didn't want our relationship to go further than it already had. Not now. Not yet. Our complicated existence was based on questionable morals as it was.

But the way he looked at me right now. I'd let him do anything. Well, almost anything.

I felt Jack's mind push against mine. A slight nudge. I had done it. I had blocked him out.

I looked up at him and smiled. I was very satisfied with myself. I'd won a small victory.

"Very good." *But now, I really want to know what you just blocked from me.*

~~~~

I woke with a start to the smell of cigarette smoke.

I sat up and rubbed my eyes. A trail of smoke hovered by the open door to the DeWeeses' guest room like a thick fog.

Jack didn't smoke, and no one else should be here. I threw the covers back, and after slipping out of bed, I padded toward the door. The fog slowly drifted out. I ran my fingers along the door, brushing the doorknob. I was certain I had closed the door before I crawled in bed.

The smoke tickled my nose. I followed it down the stairs, through the house and out the back door.

Strange. The alarm didn't sound. Then I remembered the electricity had been out.

I stepped lightly across the patio and down the steps toward the pool. A figure lounged in a chair facing the deep end of the pool. He lifted his hand and took a drag of his cigarette.

"Who are you?" My voice came out hoarse.

"You know who I am, Lexi."

I tilted my head. His voice did sound familiar. His. A boy.

"How about a swim?" He gestured with his hand toward the pool. It was lit up by a large light at the deep end.

Without thinking, I walked over to the edge of the pool. Instinct told me I should check the water temperature, but as I started to dip a toe in, the voice behind me said, "Go on. Jump in. You're an excellent swimmer, Lexi." My name rolled off the edge of his tongue.
~~~~

I shrugged. Why not? I *was* an excellent swimmer.

I bent my knees and jumped, swan diving into the deep end of the pool.

The freezing temperature of the water hit my skin like a billion tiny needles.

I opened my eyes and looked around. It was dark. Someone had turned off the light. I couldn't breathe.

Against all instincts, I sucked in a breath. Instead of air, I inhaled water. My lungs burned from the icy temperature of the liquid that slid down my throat. I twisted and turned, thrashing in the water. My limbs refused to work the way I knew they were capable. I labored for another breath.

Finally, I stilled. I was surrounded by darkness and calm. My body was numb, and I was no longer able to take a breath.

TWENTY

I gagged. I coughed. Water spewed from my mouth. I threw up. A voice I recognized but couldn't quite place said in a soothing tone, "That's it. Get it out."

I sucked in a long, labored breath. The back of my throat burned like I'd swallowed thumbtacks.

Why was I wet?

I coughed again and continued to fight for air.

The ground around me was hard. I shivered in the breeze. Finally, I opened my eyes to the face of Seth Whitmeyer.

My body tensed. I looked side to side for Jack. How did I get here? Why was I outside?

"Sarah, can you hear me?"

I stared at Seth. My eyes must have been huge. "Please don't hurt me," I whispered.

"Hurt you?" He pulled the sweater over his head and laid it over my chest close to my neck. "I'm not here to hurt you, Sarah. But why on earth did you dive into that pool?"

Why did he insist on calling me by my real name? I turned my head toward the pool. Confused, I looked to the opposite side at the lounge chairs. "Someone was here. A man. With a cigarette."

"No one else is here." I moved to sit up. Seth supported my back. "Let's get you inside and into some warm clothes."

As Seth helped me toward the back door, I glanced over my shoulder toward the chairs again. Jack really hadn't told me much about Seth yet. Other than Seth had taught him things about our fathers' research. Still I feared him. Seeing him now, I realized we looked similar. Did my DNA make me his sister? "Why are you here? I thought the farm was secure."

"It is secure. I've been here all night. In the guest house mainly."

I stopped and pulled away from him, barely able to stand on my own two feet. "Where's Jack?"

"He wasn't feeling well. He's sleeping off the earlier medical treatment he provided your shoulder."

My heart sunk. So it didn't work. Healing me made him sick.

"Inside, Lexi." He gestured toward the door. "You and I have a lot to talk about. But first... warm clothes."

~~~~

Shouting erupted from the direction of the kitchen as I descended the stairs. A hot shower and some warm clothes felt nice, but I still shivered from the sound of the Smoking Man telling me to take a swim.

Was Smoking Man inside my head? How did he convince me to jump in that pool?

"Why haven't you told her?" Seth sounded irate.

"I told her a lot, Seth. It was overwhelming for her."

"Bullshit, Jack. She shares the same blood, the same heart, and practically the same mind as my sister. She can handle the truth. You should have taken her directly to The Program. I'd have met you there."
~~~~

Silence. The Program? Why would I go there? What had Jack not told me? Was he no longer sick? He was ill for days after mending my broken arm.

We're in the kitchen, Lexi. Eavesdropping is not very lady-like.

Crap! Would I ever be able to keep him out of my head?

I passed in front of the living room windows as I stepped lightly toward the kitchen. The sun was just beginning to rise over a distant hill behind the farm.

I pushed open the swinging door and faced the harsh lights of the kitchen, the electricity having recovered from the storms. Anita busied herself by the sink. Jack leaned up against the island holding a coffee mug.

"You okay?" I asked Jack as calmly as I could before I addressed my confusion regarding Seth Whitmeyer.

He nodded. *It wasn't as bad this time.*

Seth sat at the kitchen table by the windows. Completely relaxed, he poured cream into a mug, picked up a spoon, and stirred. He looked at home, like he'd sat in that very spot a thousand times.

He did not look like a man who had just saved a teen-aged girl from the bottom of a swimming pool.

Why is Seth Whitmeyer here?

He pushed off the island and stepped toward me.

"Want some tea or coffee, sweetie?" Anita asked from behind him.

"I would love some tea. Thank you." My eyes fixed on Jack's. He ignored my unspoken question.

"How are you feeling?" Jack brushed his fingers against my hairline and down my temple with his free hand.

Answer me.

Jack smiled. *You first.*

I'm fine. Why is Seth Whitmeyer here? He pulled me out of a freaking pool, Jack.

"Lexi, come sit." Seth kicked out a chair from the table for me.

I walked cautiously toward Seth. Placed my hands on the table in front of him, my fingers spread wide. "When we first met, you told me Jack wasn't who he said he was. What did you mean?"

One side of Seth's mouth quirked into a crooked smile. "Exactly that. Do you remember what you knew about him then?"

I tilted my head to the side. "I guess."

"Does what I said then mesh with what he told you yesterday?"

I squinted my eyes. "But you meant to scare me."

"Did it? Scare you, that is?" He raised both eyebrows. "Not like your recent early-morning swim, I'm sure."

Anita approached the table. "Here's your tea, sweetie." She smiled. I had yet to figure out Anita's role, other than to take care of the DeWeeses. And of Jack.

I walked around the table and sat in a chair across from Seth, rather than the one directly beside him. Very mature.

Jack sat beside me. He reached across and took my hand in his. "What were you doing out by the pool?"

I shrugged. "I don't know. I... don't remember." *Sleepwalking, I guess?*

You practically drowned.

"Is this the first time this has happened?" Seth asked, looking from me to Jack. "The sleepwalking?"

Jack shook his head. "No." He gave my hand a squeeze. "It happened a couple of times before, that I know of."

Am I supposed to trust this yahoo?

"Yes." *You can trust him. Mostly.*

"What?" Seth asked, confused by our mostly silent exchange.

Unable to sit still, I pulled my hand away from Jack's. "Look, Seth. I see that Jack trusts you. But—"

"You don't."

"No. I don't." I crossed my arms. "Why would I? My father was blown up in a car, and next thing I know you corner me in my grandmother's nursing home room and threaten me."

"He did what?"

"I didn't threaten her." He exhaled dramatically. "This isn't child's play. We have work to do, and we're getting nowhere rehashing old news."

"Lexi, Seth would like for us both to go straight to The Program from here."

"What do you mean? The Program is an actual place? I thought you attended The Program through some online portal."

"I do but it's also a place. Near University of Kentucky's campus. A secured facility that is run by Seth."

I squeezed my eyes closed. *The Program is Seth's way of furthering your homeschooling?*

Yes.

"I'm not going to The Program. I never had any intention of applying to The Program. You know that."

"What? Why not?" Seth asked. "Did your dad know this?"

"No. Never got the chance to tell him."

"You know he would not approve, right?"

"Do I know that?" Who was this guy? "Dad never even mentioned you to me. Or your sister for that matter." I practically spit out the word sister. "So, for argument's sake, we'll just assume that I no longer know or care what my dad would think of my intentions." Dad had often threatened to move me at the slightest hint of trouble in the past.

"You were meant for The Program, Lexi. You'd be safe there. Friday night and this morning prove that you and Jack are not safe. We can protect you inside The Program."

Stop saying you can keep me safe. "What do you mean I was meant for The Program?"

Jack ran his hands through his hair.

"You and Jack were genetically engineered for a specific purpose eighteen years ago. If the wrong people were to find either of you, I'm afraid they would destroy you. Or worse, use you for their own purpose."

"Destroy. You mean kill?"

He nodded. Jack's face paled.

"What about you? You think we should hide inside The Program?" I asked Jack, knowing I had no intention of getting anywhere near a secure facility run by Seth Whitmeyer. When he didn't respond, I asked, "What do your parents say? John is my guardian, after all."

Seth's lips curved into a smirk. "You're so much like her."

"I assume by *her* you mean your sister? Where is Sandra?" A shudder moved through me at the thought of facing the woman who'd cloned me. The woman whose DNA I possessed.

"She is nothing like her," Jack whispered. He suddenly stood and faced me. "Yes, unfortunately, I think we should be at The Program. My parents will agree."

"What about Wellington? We can't just leave. The Dean will have everyone from the local police to Homeland Security looking for us." I was being a bit dramatic.

"Not if my father signs the necessary forms," Jack answered.

"You can't be serious." *I'm not going into The Program.*

"I'm dead serious." Jack stuffed his hands into the front pockets of his jeans. "You jumped into a freezing pool. That wouldn't happen inside the Program." *We have to figure out who's inside your head, and you need to learn how to shut them out.*

But Jack, it would mean learning from and agreeing with what these scientists did to create us. It would mean giving up control.

Learning from, yes. We need to know what we were created to do. We—you and I—can choose what we do with that knowledge.

"Why wouldn't we be safe at Wellington?" I stepped closer to Jack and tugged on one of his arms. As I did, I concentrated on building a barrier around my thoughts. This conversation was not going my way, and if I had to run from them both, I would. "You can teach me."

"No." Seth's voice shot up an octave. "You're both coming to The Program. That's final. Now, go pack your things."

I backed away from both of them with a mental shield in place.

What are you thinking? Jack's thoughts were panicked.

It was working, but I didn't know how to block him and direct a thought at him at the same time. I had so much to learn, and for the first time in my life I had someone who could teach me. But at what cost?

Then something occurred to me. I wondered how much Seth knew about me. Had Jack explained my ability or my nose bleeds to Seth?

I reached down and grabbed my teacup sitting on a napkin. While trying to keep Jack blocked, I thought, *What about the journals, Seth? Shouldn't Jack and I make one last attempt to find them? Especially knowing what I know now?*

This would tell me if Seth knew about my ability to plant "original" thoughts inside his head.

"I'll go pack my things." I walked slowly toward the island on the other side of the kitchen and set my cup down. A trickle of blood formed at the opening of my nose. I blotted it with the napkin.

From behind me, Seth said, "You know, maybe you and Lexi should make one last attempt to find Peter's journals."

I stilled.

Turn around, Jack thought.

You left me no choice. I turned and tried to hide the fear I was sure haunted my eyes now.

You have any idea what someone like Seth might do if he discovered you could alter his mind?

"How do you know I'm even looking for Dad's journals?" I asked Seth, ignoring Jack.

"Oh, Lexi. You have proven to be quite resourceful. Don't play games with me. Your father came back to Kentucky to get his journals, and I think you know exactly where they are." He took a sip of his coffee. It amazed me how relaxed he stayed. "As a matter of fact, I think you know way more about all of this than you've let on."

I wiped my nose again. "What makes you think I know anything? I didn't know anything about some stupid journals before Dad came to town."

"But you knew about the clonings."

I gasped. "God, no." I glared at Jack and back at Seth. "This might be some big game to the two of you..." How could anyone even suggest that I knew I was a monster before yesterday? "This is my life you're so eager to play with. Everyone has always been so crazy quick to map out my life's plan for me. And before yesterday, I had no idea how far some people had gone to do it."

Anita reentered the room. She was always so quiet. Seth and Jack both remained silent. Anita and Jack traded a worried glance. I made a mental note to ask Jack later what that was all about.

"Are we done here?"

Seth threw his hands up. "Do you think you can find the journals? Do you have any idea where they might be at this point?"

I had no idea where my father hid those journals. I wasn't about to let Seth know that though. They were in the car with Dad for all I knew. "Sure, I have a few more ideas."

"Fine, then. Both of you, return to Wellington, but keep your eyes open."

"And Jack," Seth continued, "I don't have to tell you how dangerous it is to let her out of your sight for very long."

TWENTY-ONE

I blew through the door to my dorm room early that afternoon, like an EF4 tornado. I marched in with my bag, knocking a book off my desk, but leaving the stack of papers beside it untouched.

The nerve of those two thinking they could force me into some top-secret program for the study of Edward Scissorhands-like medical atrocities. I grew up surrounded by Dad's strange notion that he could cure all the diseases of the world with his crazy experimental research.

Well, I would have no part of it. And they couldn't force me.

"What happened to you? You look awful."

I spun around. I hadn't even noticed Danielle when I stormed in. She glanced up from the open laptop on her bed where she sat in a half lotus—a Yoga position that would kill my knees.

"Thanks." I puffed a lazy strand of hair off my face as I struggled to bend down and pick up the fallen book.

"Seriously, what happened?" She closed the laptop and swung her legs off the bed and onto the floor. "Did you get into a fight?"

I dug through my bag and pulled out my cell phone, then walked to my desk and pulled out the starfish trinket box that Dad had sent me. In it, I had stored the card from Marci Daniels, the journalist who delivered the box.

"What?" I asked as if it was the stupidest question ever. "No. I didn't get into a fight."

I typed a text message to Marci in my phone. "*Hi, Marci. Need to see u. Can u come to me? Hard 4 me to leave school. ~Lexi.*"

As soon as I had texted Marci, I fired off one more text to her. "*P.S. What do u know about Sandra Whitmeyer and John DeWeese?*"

I stared at the phone, willing Marci to text me back instantly. Even I realized how ridiculous it was to expect that. The phrase *a watched pot never boils* came to mind.

Danielle began tapping her bare foot on the floor. I raised my eyes and found her arms folded tightly across her chest.

"I'm sorry. No, I didn't get into a fight. Jack and I were in an accident."

"What? Lexi, why didn't you call me? Are you okay? Is Jack okay?"

"We're both pretty sore, but I think I got the worst of it. Which is pretty good, considering we're both alive and walking around." I tried to laugh.

"Well, thank God." Danielle stood and hugged me. "I don't know what I'd do if anything happened to you."

"I feel the same way. Thanks, Dani." I hugged her back.

My phone buzzed with an incoming text. From Jack. "*Get 2 room OK? Take pain pill and get sleep. Meet for dinner?*"

Mmm. Cafeteria food. How could I turn that down? I was not taking one of those painkillers. They made me completely loopy and overly tired. With everything going on, I wanted my full wits about me.

I shrugged at Danielle after reading the text. "Jack."

"Ahhh. I can't believe we've been here six years, and this is the first guy you've dated."

"We're not dating," I protested. Not really. It was one date. I quickly fired off a text to him. *"Sure. C u l8r."* Who was I kidding? I was in love.

"Yeah, right," she said as she began packing up her books. "Keep telling yourself that." She swung her backpack over her shoulder. "Hey, I've got a study group to get to. You need anything before I go?"

"No, thanks. I've got some studying to do myself."

Danielle left. Just as the door clicked closed, my phone buzzed again.

"Be there in one hour. ~Marci."

~~~~

"What do *you* know about Sandra Whitmeyer?" Marci answered my question with a question. *Journalists.*

"Not much, really," I said. "Only that she worked with my Dad and Dr. DeWeese once upon a time."

Marci twisted and wrung her hands in her lap. We sat on a bench outside a classroom building. It wasn't a popular spot on Sunday afternoons.

From her sneakers and jeans all the way to the conservative auburn ponytail, Marci looked different than in the snazzy business suit and three-inch heels she'd worn the day I met her. No amount of make-up could cover the darkness now living under her eyes.

"Well... I have some articles that were written about her twenty or so years ago. Some feature her research and some
~~~~

societal stuff. Your father didn't speak very… um… favorably of her."

"Any pictures?" Did Marci know I was the spitting image of Sandra Whitmeyer from the time those articles were probably published?

"If there were pictures, I didn't notice them."

"Strange that Sandra's name didn't sound familiar to me when I first heard it. I'm sure she would have been mentioned in the scores of articles I've read regarding my dad's old research." Noticing Marci shift where she sat, I reached over and placed my hand on her fidgety hands. "Are you okay?"

"Yes. This has all been a little too much." A couple of girls jogged behind us, and Marci jerked toward the scuffle of feet. "My editor wants to go ahead and publish the articles. But the FBI has threatened to squash the articles forever… a matter of homeland security." Marci wrung her hands in front of her.

"Homeland security?"

She nodded. "The government can stop anything from going to press. We can yell 'freedom of speech' and 'First Amendment rights' all we want, but if the government deems it a matter of national security, our lips are sealed."

"Can you tell me what the articles are about, now?"

The sadness, or maybe it was fear, that swam in Marci's dark, brown eyes gave her a more youthful appearance, and made me want to comfort this woman who, I suspected, had loved my father for more than the scoop he provided.

"Before I tell you, you should know why I've fought my editor to keep these articles unpublished since your father's death."

"Okay."

"Your father made me promise him one thing before I moved forward." She stood and walked a few steps before turning and facing me. "I promised your father time to move you somewhere secure. He thought you were safe at Wellington while the public was in the dark about his research. But he also thought these articles might put you both in danger. He was already receiving threats."

"And now you think I'm in danger?"

"I think anyone who knows what I'm about to tell you, or *could* know about it, is in danger." She sat again.

Was this about Jack and me? Did she know that we were genetically-altered, cloned humans? Was Dad on his way to move me the morning he was killed? "Just tell me," I whispered.

"Lexi, your father was working for the FBI when he was killed. He had compiled information about a governmental program that was cloning human beings that were genetically altered to be healing machines."

She could have punched me in the stomach and not have knocked the air out of me as quickly as those words did. Healing machines? "What are you talking about? How many human clones are we talking?"

"He didn't know." She buried her face into her hands. "Or he was killed before he told me."

"Why didn't he tell me?" My voice was barely coherent.

"Lexi. He wanted to tell you. He planned to take you away with him."

That was becoming obvious to me.

"Do you know why Dr. DeWeese went to Sicily?"

I shook my head.

"I suspect that, because your father gave them full guardianship over you, they went to collect his belongings."

I'd never known exactly where my father lived. "You think his journals are there," I whispered. What gave Dr. DeWeese the right to collect *my* father's things?

"I think his latest journals *could* be there, but..." Marci glanced over her shoulder and then scanned the area around us, stopping on the school's gate in the distance where a couple of men stood.

"But?" I prompted.

"Your father's too smart to have left his journals where they would be easily discovered."

"If Dr. DeWeese thinks these journals are in Sicily, and if you and your editor already know what this 'discovery' is, then why is someone trying to kill *me*?"

"What do you mean?"

I shared the details of the wreck with Marci. Worry and fear weighed the bags under her eyes down even further.

"Are you safe here?" she asked.

"I think so. But I need your help."

"With what? I'll do anything I can."

"I want to know exactly where Sandra Whitmeyer is. Do you have contacts that can find her? Her current address. What she's doing now."

"Have you asked John DeWeese? Seems like he would know. Or is it too awkward?"

I arched a brow. "Why do you say that?"

"They were supposed to be married before she broke it off. I just assumed he probably kept up with her whereabouts." When my eyes just about popped out of my head, she continued. "I assumed you knew. I didn't realize the importance of that. Their engagement announcement made the society pages." She reached down and began sifting through what looked like a satchel of file folders. "Now that you mention it, I think there might have been a picture."

~~~~

I know you're up here.

I pulled my knees in and scooted further into the darkness. Hiding from Jack was the mature way to go. The roof of the girls' dorm used to be the place I could escape at nights. To figure things out. Lose myself in the stars above. Be closer to heaven and God, maybe.

God. I chuckled. Oh, how he must have cringed when Jack and I were created. No wonder we were almost killed Friday night. We were an abomination.

Lexi, I know you're upset.

Upset? No, upset was way too kind a word. I fought hard to close off my mind and keep him out of it. Jack probably thought I was being quite the drama queen. It wasn't that I was hiding. I was assessing. Searching for some sort of survivor instinct deep within me.

His footsteps grew closer. The stars above me twinkled, reminding me of a time when my grandmother used to sing to me and whisper nursery rhymes as I fell asleep.

Amazing how complicated life can get. I fingered the starfish and the key hanging around my neck.

Please stop this, Lexi. His foot shuffled as he made a turn. He stood close. *Look, I'm sorry. I should have told you.*
~~~~

Go away, Jack. I've reached my allotment for insane stories today. My entire life was engineered eighteen years ago. Right down to whom I was supposed to love. And you knew. I know you did.

"At least you're talking to me now," he said softly, almost a whisper.

I don't want to talk to you right now. Don't you get it? I peeked around the corner of the wall I hid behind.

He turned his head left, then right, and then at me.

I leaned my head against the wall. Did he see me? This really was juvenile.

"You would only have heard my actual words if you were near," he said, leaning against the brick and towering over me.

I tilted my head up. He peered down at me with a smile.

"What do you want? Is it too much to ask for time to deal with all this... all this... life-controlling junk?"

He stepped away from the wall, and I thought he was going to leave. My heart practically stopped. It was what I wanted, right?

Instead of leaving, he walked around and sat beside me. His shoulder against mine. His knees bent in front of him like mine and flush with my legs. Only his were longer.

"You're right. I've had longer to deal with a lot of this junk. I wish I could give you that same gift."

I risked a look at him. I hadn't thought of that. He must have been surprised when he learned what his father had done all those years ago.

"The simple truth is we are what we are." Jack grazed the back of his hand against my knee. "And because of that, someone wants one or both of us dead."

The lump in my throat prevented me from speaking.

"The other simple truth is..." He slipped his fingers under mine, and cradled my hand in his lap. "In one weekend, someone tried to drug you, kill us in a car accident, and drown you in my swimming pool. I don't know if it was the same person every time, or what..." Jack leaned his head against our tangled hands. "I won't let anything happen to you."

"I don't think you can make that promise anymore."

"That's why I think you should run."

"What?" I angled my body towards his.

"I'll help you. I know someone I can trust who can get you a passport under a different name. Cash. Whatever. We'll map out a plan—"

"Are you kidding me?"

He shook his head, with a look of defeat. "It's your only option."

I pressed my finger to his lips. "No."

"You have to." His lips were soft, warm. He spoke through my fingers.

"I'm not running."

"Lexi, please," he pleaded.

"My grandmother would be left all by herself. I would have no one. There is so much I still don't understand about who I am. Why my father was killed. I'm not going to live a lie. I... We were created for some purpose I don't understand. I'm not going to turn my back on whatever that purpose is. Not yet, anyway. Not before I at least understand it."

Jack leaned his forehead against mine. Took in a deep breath. "Okay."

"Okay?"

"I didn't think you would agree, but I had to try." Something in his voice told me this wasn't the last time we'd discuss this. "But you're going to have to get used to seeing me a lot more. I'm not letting you out of my sight."

I smiled. "I think the dean might have a problem with you moving in with Dani and me."

"I don't care. I'll pull the 'she's my sister' card."

I stifled a laugh.

"Okay, not that. I'll think of something."

We sat there for several minutes. Jack played with my hair that hung against my cheek and down past my shoulder. His eyes drifted down to my lips. I leaned closer giving him full permission.

He leaned in and pressed his lips gently to mine. They were soft and carried a faint taste of mint. He tugged on my arm and guided me closer. Next thing I knew, I was sitting in his lap, cradled against him. His lips were hot on mine.

And I knew.

I knew I'd never run. I wouldn't turn my back on my newfound identity, even if it went against everything I believed in. Because turning my back on the monster that I was would be shutting out the beautiful creature who held me now.

TWENTY-TWO

"Listen up." Coach Williams paced in front of the team after morning practice. "Dean Fisher has halted all off-campus travel. No one is to leave Wellington without express permission from a parent or guardian."

Coach's eyes traveled over my teammates' faces but stopped on mine. I shifted and crossed my arms. Water dripped off the end of my nose. I was the reason my classmates and I had been confined to campus until further notice.

"And furthermore, if I find out any of my swimmers sneak out and break this curfew in any way, in addition to the dean's punishment, you will not swim in the state qualifying meet in two weeks."

Why was he staring me down as he said that? I glanced around the deck to see if my teammates noticed the guilt written all over my face.

Kyle stood across from me smirking. "Whatever," he mouthed at me.

When Coach had completed his lecture and stare down, the swimmers scattered toward the showers and Coach to his office. I marched straight over to Kyle. "What's up?" I asked, attempting a level of indifference.

"I refuse to be held prisoner. You and I are practically eighteen, we've raised ourselves as child geniuses, and yet we're held here like we're in some sort of juvenile detention."

"Aren't you being a bit melodramatic?" I chuckled. "It might be for our own safety." That part was definitely true. In my case anyway. "Can you get a waiver that lets you off campus?"

"My uncle will sign one. But where am I going to go if no one can go with me?"

My lips pressed into a thin line. There wasn't even a remote chance I would get off-campus privileges. Not even with Jack.

"If I can get permission, I'll go off campus with you. Where would you want to go?"

A smile played at the corners of Kyle's mouth. "A movie? We deserve time away from here."

Not quite what I had in mind. "Okay. Will you take me by the nursing home, too?" I hadn't seen my grandmother in almost a week. With the recent attempts on my life, I was craving a little family time.

He smiled. A hint of something I didn't understand hid just below the surface of his grin. "Sure."

"Okay. Well, I'll let you know."

I left Kyle and padded off toward the shower.

While the hot water rained down over my tired muscles, I plotted how I would convince the dean to give me permission to leave campus. Why have the ability to mindspeak if I couldn't use it to my advantage?

Jack kept telling me that our abilities were bound by control. If we controlled our mind, we'd reach the potential of what we were engineered to do. It still didn't make sense to me, but two weeks ago I would never have believed my geneticist dad had raised a cloned human as his daughter.

For now, I'd practice my ability. I'd start with gaining off-campus privileges while blocking Jack from knowing anything about it.

~~~~

To beat the boredom the students all swore they'd die from if the dean confined them to campus for long, the school organized an outdoor movie showing on the multipurpose field for the next night.

The school even allowed vendors in to sell kettle corn, hot dogs, deep-fried Oreos and pickles. Only in Kentucky could you get that gourmet cuisine.

Danielle and I surveyed the food choices.

She crinkled her nose. "Are they kidding with this stuff? My arteries are constricting just smelling the grease coming from the fried Snickers stand."

I laughed. "Yeah, they think we're at risk leaving Wellington, but they'll feed us heart attack on a stick for dinner."

Where've you been? Jack's voice prodded my mind.

Jack. I did a three-sixty searching for him among the sea of students who had already turned out for the movie. Even in my head, his voice had a way of sending a shiver down my spine. I hoped he couldn't sense that.

I'd worked hard to keep him blocked out the past few days. Mainly I was practicing for times when I needed to keep him out of my head. I couldn't have him hearing my every thought. Not to mention Jack was convinced someone had discovered how to get inside my head and make me "sleepwalk" right into
~~~~

dangerous situations, starting with the night the fire alarm was set off in the dorm.

I wondered if it went back further than that, like the night Dad died, and someone chased me at Jack's farm but then disappeared. Maybe I didn't have to be fully asleep, just vulnerable.

"Who're you looking for?" Dani had pulled a snack-pack of rice cakes from her backpack.

"Jack. Pretty sure he's already here."

Cold.

I turned my head to the right. Everything was a game to him.

Colder.

"Wish you could see the goofy grin on your face." Dani laughed. "Don't think for a second you're deserting me. I don't mind being a third wheel."

I put my arm around her and steered her around in the opposite direction from where I was looking. "I would never desert you. You're no third wheel."

Oooh. Warm.

Warmer.

I spotted him on the other side of a soccer goal carrying a blanket. I tried to suppress the glow that spread across my face.

Dani rolled her eyes.

"Oh, stop. You're the one who wished for this," I whispered.

"I know, but..." She elbowed me playfully. "You know I'm kidding. I've just never seen you fall for anyone."

"I know." It frightened me.

When we reached Jack, he leaned down and whispered in my ear. "Would you like to go to the movies?"

I pulled back and lifted a brow.

He shrugged. *After last weekend, I hoped to make this an official date. To make up for that disaster.*

So much happened that night and in the days after. Jack's face turned serious, and I realized I hadn't answered the question.

I nodded. *Of course.*

He smiled.

"Oh, my-gee-whiz." Witnessing our unspoken exchange, Dani threw her hands in the air. "I'm going to find Kyle and Bree." And she skipped off.

"Was it something I said?" Jack laughed. He reached down and grabbed my hand and led me through parts of the crowd and over to a quiet spot on the edge.

"Can we see from here?"

"Oh. You want to see the movie?" he asked.

I punched him in the arm, and he feigned like it hurt.

He spread the blanket. "Yes, you'll be able to see the movie." *I'll be watching you and trying to figure out what you're thinking. Don't think I haven't noticed how you've intentionally shut me out.*

I batted my eyelashes at him.

"Hi, you two," Briana said as Kyle fell beside me on the blanket.

Why is she always around?

Be nice. "Hey guys," Jack said. "Danielle's looking for you."

"We just saw her." Kyle pointed his finger out into the crowd. "She was with you." He redirected his finger at me. "I thought it was you, anyway."

"What do you mean?" I asked.

"She was talking to someone who I thought was you." He shrugged. "Must have been wrong."

"How long ago?" *My eyes met Jack's. You don't think... Sandra...*

No. No way. Jack sounded sure.

"A couple minutes. Enough time for us to make a small circle, then spot the two of you."

My heart raced faster than it did after a fifty-yard sprint. *You said no one knew where she was. She has to look like an old lady compared to me, right?*

Don't panic, Lex. In one smooth motion, Jack jumped to his feet. "I'll find her." He kept his tone light. *Stay here. Okay?*

I'll go with you.

Stay, he ordered. He headed off into the crowd, back toward the vendors.

I refused to be treated like some dog he could order around. "You two mind watching our spot?"

Bree and Kyle exchanged looks and after a shrug, Kyle said, "You mean lounge on this blanket and watch the movie? Sure."

I moved in the opposite direction from Jack, careful to keep my thoughts to myself. Everything seemed normal. Kids from seventh grade through twelfth settled in, waiting for the movie to start. The sun had disappeared and darkness fell over the campus.

I heard a girl squeal over my right shoulder. I whipped around to see a sophomore lacrosse player carrying a freshman girl like a sack of potatoes. She was playfully beating his backside.

I tried to relax, but the weight of a thousand bricks pushed hard on my chest. *Where are you, Dani?*

Lexi! You didn't stay put, did you? Jack asked. *Why don't you ever listen?*

I just don't. Find her?

No.

"Hi, Lexi."

I knew that voice behind me. I immediately closed off my mind to Jack. "Seth. What are you doing here?"

"Looking for someone," he said.

"Oh, yeah? At Wellington? Seems strange." My eyes darted left, then right, still searching for Danielle. And now for Jack. How did Seth get through the Wellington gates?

"Yeah, maybe you can help me." He held something in his hand. A picture of some sort. "Does this remind you of anyone?"

He flipped the picture around, but it was too dark. "I can't really see it."

"Let's move into the light." Seth's fingers circled around my forearm, and he led me away from the crowd and behind one of the vendors. Lights were strung overhead. Warning bells blared inside my head.

I examined the picture. It couldn't be. Well, it kind of looked like Briana, but not totally. The hair wasn't right. The girl in the picture had straight, jet black hair, whereas Briana's was red and curly. The girl in the picture had a large gap between her two front teeth. Briana's teeth were perfectly straight and bleached super white.

The girl in the picture was definitely not Bree. Nevertheless, the resemblance was staggering.

"You recognize this person?" Seth's voice was calm, yet his eyes darted in several directions in the span of a second.

"No." I handed the picture back to him. "Good to see you Seth, but Jack will be missing me. I need to get back to my friends."

"Not so fast." He reached out and grabbed my arm again, stopping my forward motion.

"I think you do recognize the girl in this picture."

"Why would I tell you if I did?"

He smiled. "I'm not your enemy, Lexi."

"Oh, yeah?" I was not convinced. "What do you want from me, Seth?"

"Shouldn't you really be asking, 'What does Jack want from you?'" His smirk slid through my veins like a venomous snake.

Okay, I'll bite. "What does Jack want from me?" Besides hopefully, my adoration, and something beyond sisterly fondness. My lips quirked at that last thought.

"Why don't you take a ride with me?"

"What? You're crazy. I'm not going anywhere with you." I tucked my shaking hands into my armpits and looked over his shoulder. "Besides, we're on lockdown." Which is why I was shocked Seth was allowed in.

"You will if you want to know what you were engineered to do. And why Jack spent a year spying on you inside this school."

TWENTY-THREE

Seth left me in a sea of scents from funnel cake to cotton candy, right after I promised to meet him in the parking lot at ten p.m. He promised he could show me what I was designed to do. Not even Jack could do that.

Now, how would I break away from Jack without him knowing where I was going? I smoothed my hands over my jeans before I circled to the front of the vendors to look for him.

Where the hell are you? Jack growled inside my head.

I found him standing beside the blanket. Dani sat in the lotus between Bree and Kyle, who tipped back a bottle of water. I let out a relieved breath.

"Where were you?" he practically barked.

I ran my fingers across his lips and then manually tipped the corners upward. "Turn that frown upside down," I said. "I'm fine." Except now I wondered why he'd spied on me for an entire year before he enrolled in Wellington. That would have to wait. First, I'd let Seth show me what my father had kept from me about my genetic design.

He cupped my cheek. "You scared me."

I'm sorry. I just couldn't stand the thought of something happening to Dani. Did you see anything strange?

He shook his head. *I'm pretty sure it was nothing. Kyle had probably seen you and just misjudged how much time had passed.* He grabbed my hand and pulled me closer. *You owe me a date.*

We both looked down at his blanket at the same time. Three bodies took up the entire blanket.

Wanna make out under the bleachers? Jack wiggled an eyebrow at me.

Heat crept up my back and flushed my cheeks. Squeezing his hand, I led him over to the bleachers. "Not under. That sounds… I don't know. Sleazy or something."

He leaned close to my ear. "I like it when you blush."

"I don't blush."

"Oh, you do, Miss Matthews. And it's beautiful."

My heart sang at his words. I was a giddy teenager celebrating her first teen crush.

We sat just as the opening credits started for *Harry Potter: Chamber of Secrets*. Safe choice given the age range of the students.

Jack leaned back against the bench behind us, and I snuggled into his arm. As he watched the start of the movie, I studied his profile—the crookedness of his nose, like it had been broken before, his eyes so dark they appeared black here in the darkness, and the small amount of stubble to his face after a long day.

He turned and caught me staring at him. His eyes warmed when they met mine. Our relationship had definitely taken a sharp turn somewhere along the path into something different. Something overwhelming.

He leaned in and kissed me, pressing hard. His hand slipped behind my neck. His fingers laced through my hair. When he pulled away, he said, "You learned to control your thoughts rather quickly."

"Hmm." *I figured I had to.*

"I wish you didn't hide so many of your thoughts from me. I enjoyed having you inside my head. Even when you were moody."

"Moody?" I slapped at his arm. He caught my hand and squeezed it, pulling me closer.

We sat there in silence and watched the movie. From time to time, I glanced at him. As I stared at this beautiful boy beside me brushing his fingers up and down my arm, I knew there were many things that could separate us.

I leaned my head against his shoulder.

He turned his head and kissed my hair. *I might not be able to hear your thoughts right now, but I sense your fear of something. I'm not going anywhere. I'll always be here to protect you.*

But what if *I* was going somewhere? I only hoped he wouldn't be too mad.

~~~~

Seth and I entered the nursing home after ten p.m. Strangely, the nurses outside my grandmother's room only waved at Seth and me, barely lifting their heads from their gossip session and late-night chocolate binge.

"They're used to me coming in at strange hours to sit by my mom's bed," he said in answer to my unspoken curiosity.

They weren't used to seeing *me* here this late. I was still in shock that I had just snuck out of Wellington in the back of Seth Whitmeyer's SUV. Jack was going to be irate.

"Why do you come so late?"
~~~~

He pushed open Gram's door, and allowed me to pass through first. I had yet to think of him as a gentleman. He had saved my life last week, though.

"I'm a doctor. I work long hours."

My grandmother slept soundly on her back. Her face looked relaxed and peaceful.

"Sit," Seth ordered.

I evil-eyed him, then scooted the chair closer to Gram's bed and sat. "Hi, Gram," I whispered so as not to wake her.

"Now, I don't know what we're going to discover. Or why you've never experienced something before now."

"What do you mean?"

"Well, your abilities should have been apparent before now. Jack knew he could heal a bird's broken wing when he was five."

I thought about the little white pills that I hadn't taken since the day Jack arrived at Wellington—the same pills Jack tossed into the swimming pool. "Maybe I don't have these abilities you think I have."

"For Jack's sake, I hope you're wrong."

"Why for Jack's sake?" My stomach tightened. Guilt churned there. I had lied to Jack—told him I was too tired to stay out when Dean Fisher granted an extended curfew.

Two kids in love are never too tired to be together. Jack didn't question me, though.

"Jack has a lot riding on what we hope you can do. We'll get to that. Now, I want you to concentrate on your grandmother."

I stared at Gram's beautiful face. The woman who raised me had been confined mostly to a hospital room for the past six years.

"She was diagnosed with Alzheimer's seven or eight years ago, right?"

I nodded.

"Do you understand how Alzheimer's works?"

I nodded again. I understood my grandmother gradually began to forget where she left her glasses, and eventually where she left me. And then who I even was.

I'd done a paper on Alzheimer's when I was in Advanced Human Anatomy so I knew what happened to the brain of someone with the disease. The cerebral cortex shrunk. The ventricles enlarged. Among other things.

"I want you to think about what the brain is supposed to look like. I know you know the brain well, Lexi, from the classes you've taken."

He was right. Was my life an open book to him?

"Now, touch her head. Press your fingers gently into her temple. Or her forehead. We might have to try different things."

My arms, legs, back tensed. I had touched Gram a hundred times. Somehow this was different.

My fingers hovered just above her hairline. Shaking. "I'm scared," I whispered.

Seth, surprisingly, said nothing as I dug deep inside my gut and searched my heart for the courage. Suddenly the love I felt for Gram took over. The shakiness in my fingers subsided. I stood straighter. I stared down at my sleeping grandmother and gently placed my hand on her head.

The coarseness of her silver hair tickled my fingertips at first. I pressed harder and concentrated, pulling up an image of the brain.

The picture of a normal brain inside my head morphed and twisted into a different picture. The cerebral cortex—the squiggly tube on the outside of the brain—contracted. As did the hippocampus. The ventricles grew to more than twice their normal size.

Suddenly, I was looking at the brain of someone with advanced Alzheimer's.

I pulled my hand away with such force that I stumbled against the chair, missing the seat altogether, and fell to the ground, hitting my head against the bathroom door behind me.

"Whoa." Seth stepped to my aid. "You okay?" He knelt beside me.

I rubbed the spot where I knocked my head. "Oh, my." I stared up at the bed where Gram lay. "I saw *her* brain." I couldn't keep the astonishment out of my voice. "I saw what was wrong with her brain, didn't I?" I turned my gaze to Seth.

He nodded, smiling, proud of himself. Or something.

I pushed myself up. "What does this mean?"

"It means, I think, if you wanted to, you could heal your grandmother's brain. Rid her brain of the Alzheimer's."

"What?" I pulled my arm away from him, and pushed with my feet in a crab walk until I was as far away from him as I could get. Backed into the corner of the room. "Heal her brain of Alzheimer's?" But there is no cure for Alzheimer's.

I braced the arm of the chair and pulled myself up. The room spun, and not from the knock to my head. Bile rose to my throat. Suddenly, my senses were heightened. I saw Gram's hand lotion and imagined the smell as if it were right under my nose. A car alarm blared outside the window on the other side of the room, like a distress signal inside my head.

"If you wanted to. Yes, you could heal her."

If I wanted to...

Yes. I wanted to. Why wouldn't I heal the only family member I had left of a horrible disease? "What makes you think I could heal her? Just because I could see the problem?"

"Because that's what you were created to do." Seth backed up and leaned against Gram's dresser. "And everything else that my sister claimed has turned out to be true."

"I'm like Jack?" I asked.

"No. Not exactly. Your ability is different from Jack's. You were created to complement him."

A different reality began to seep into my thoughts. My eyes sprung open. "I'll get really sick if I do this, won't I?" Like Jack.

"Probably. There seem to be consequences to the powers you have." Seth cupped his chin with his hand. "But we have no idea. And you're not equipped to heal your grandmother at this point."

"What do you mean? You just said—"

"Well, it's one thing for Jack to see a break in a bone. It's like sewing up a cut. There's a separation of skin, and that separation needs to come back together. Same with a bone. But with a disease that has affected so many other parts of the body..."

"Where do you begin?" I finished for him. I turned my eyes back to Gram.

Besides, what would Gram be coming back to? A deteriorated body? Her daughter was still long-gone. The loss of her son-in-law? Six years of her life gone. Confusion.

Me. She would come back to me. I could take care of her. She'd have a granddaughter who loved her. "The Program..." I searched Seth's face. "You could teach me what I need to know, right?"

"More or less. It's a matter of practice and trial and error."

Trial and error? How could I even consider this? This was exactly why Dad's research was so controversial. The errors. At what cost were doctors, researchers, scientists willing to extend the lives of others? There was still no guarantee of forever.

I glanced again at my sleeping grandmother. A tear fell down my face. Oh, what I would give to hear my name on her lips again. To see recognition in her eyes.

"Does Jack know about this—my ability?"

"That you were engineered to diagnose and heal matters of the brain?" Seth crossed his arms and one leg. Relaxed compared to the nervous energy pulsating through my veins. "Yes."

I squeezed the bridge of my nose. Why didn't he tell me? He had to know I'd want to do what I could for Gram. "You said Jack spied on me for a year. Why did he do that? Why not just come find me?"

"Jack has told you how John DeWeese discovered a picture of you in the newspaper, right?"

I nodded.

"Well, Jack knew very little at that time about what the two of you could do. But when his dad moved him across the country to be closer to Wellington, he knew it had everything to do with you."

"So he spied on me." That didn't explain anything.

"Before moving, all Jack knew is that he had the strange ability to heal some injuries, but not others. When he found out the daughter of his father's ex-lab partner was at a boarding school known for producing the best pre-med students, he wanted to know if you knew more than he did. So he watched you every chance he got."

"And The Program was formed."

"That's right. He's been slowly learning everything he could about your fathers' research. And what you might be able to do."

"But that doesn't explain why he didn't just confront me. Ask me if I was like him."

"And what would that have sounded like?" Seth smiled.

Like Jack was crazy. I got it.

"You said he had a lot riding on my ability. What did you mean by that?"

"You'll need to ask him that."

"I'm asking you. You brought me here, broke me out of Wellington tonight. I'm assuming to convince me that The Program is something I need—to learn more about my powers. Because if you brought me here to convince me to heal my seventy-six-year-old grandmother of one disease—to play God—only to break her heart that she missed the past six years of her life—"

"No, Lexi. I didn't bring you here to heal your grandmother, necessarily. Unless that was something you wanted to do. You need additional training first." This man was a walking contradiction. "You are very important to the research my sister, your father, Jack's father, and others started twenty years ago."

"Why am I so important to Jack?"

"I told you what I promised. Now, tell me who this resembles and I'll tell you why you're so important to Jack now." He held up the picture that looked too much like Briana Howard.

I stared at the picture again. A cocktail of feelings erupted inside me. Anger at the girl who tormented me at every turn but protective at the same time of my classmate who might well have as many family issues and secrets as I do. And devastated that someone else I knew just might be the result of mad scientists.

Bree was lucky Seth didn't spot her earlier that night.

In the end, girl power and lack of trust for Seth won out. "No deal. I want you to take me back to school."

I'd figure out why Jack "needed" me another way.

TWENTY-FOUR

I heard the screaming from down the hall. "Dani," I whispered.

I ran. Out of breath, I tried to get the key in the lock. Dropped the keys.

Finally on the other side of the door, I darted to Danielle's bedside and gently shook her shoulders. "Dani. Wake up. You're having a nightmare."

Her eyes sprung open. Sweat poured down her forehead into her hair. "Lexi?"

"Yeah. It's me. You were having a nightmare." I reached behind me and grabbed a T-shirt off the floor. I blotted at the moisture across her forehead.

She laid her forearm across her eyes. "Oh, Lexi," she panted. "I was so scared."

I crossed to the bathroom that separated our room from our neighbors' and wet a washcloth.

Pressing the cool cloth to her forehead, I asked, "Wanna tell me about it?"

"I couldn't find you. I was searching and searching through the halls. It was so dark. And I was terrified." Dani took the cloth from me and placed it behind her neck.

I brushed strands of wet hair off her face and tucked it behind her ears.

She closed her eyes. "What a weird dream. The other person running with me was the strangest part."

"Who was it?"

"I don't know, but he kept telling me that I needed to find you. That you were in trouble." Dani breathed hard.

My back tightened. "I'm not in trouble. I'm right here, and I'm just fine." Was it possible for Dani to have the same faceless man in her dreams?

"It was dark. You know how I feel about the dark." Her body shuddered.

"I do." I continued brushing my fingers along her hairline.

"But as afraid as I was of the dark and that I couldn't find you, I don't think the guy in my dream meant me harm."

What a strange night. The image of Gram's brain popped into my head, and then I wondered what a phobia would look like inside a brain. I pressed my fingers to Dani's forehead and imagined her brain.

It looked nothing like Gram's; it was more... normal, I guessed. I lifted my hand and wiggled my fingers.

What did I think I was going to do? Heal her phobia forever?

With Gram's brain, I knew what to look for. I had seen pictures of a brain afflicted with Alzheimer's. Was I really capable of healing her? Was I meant to? It just seemed wrong. But wasn't that what doctors did every single day with medicine and surgery?

Was this different?

Most definitely.

"I'm glad you're here," Danielle whispered. She grabbed my arm, then turned over, hugging my arm like a teddy bear.

"Go to sleep," I whispered.

I stayed like that until she drifted off—kneeling by her bed with my arm tucked inside hers. I was alone with my frantic thoughts. Was Smoking Man in her dreams? Looking for me? Did he want to finish the job he'd started inside the DeWeese's swimming pool?

A chill moved through me. Later, I slipped my arm out of her hold and pushed away from her bed. I crawled into mine fully clothed. The events of the night haunted me, and with Smoking Man now looking for me in my roommate's nightmares, I was terrified to fall asleep.

You up? Could Jack even hear me this far away? He'd heard me the night of the fire alarm. Had that been Smoking Man? I had smelled smoke that night.

What's wrong? You alright?

What if I told him I wasn't? Would he come rescue me? Probably. *Yeah. Just having trouble sleeping.*

Can I help?

I don't know. Can you?

That depends. What are you wearing?

Just like that, a smile spread across my face. *Stop it.*

You started it.

Will you sing to me until I fall asleep? I asked.

Yes. Will you tell me what's wrong, first?

Tomorrow.

His perfect, soothing tone lulled me into sweet dreams.

~~~~

"You did what?" Jack barked into his cell phone. I winced. He had to be talking to Seth.

Shrugging at Dani, I spooned a bite of Cap'n Crunch into my mouth.
~~~~

"How do you stay so fit and healthy?" Danielle asked. Her nose twitched in disgust. "That's gotta be the worst thing you could eat first thing in the morning."

"It's got berries," I mumbled through a mouthful of cereal.

Kyle arrived and sat his tray down by Dani. Two donuts and a pile of bacon covered his plate.

Dani and I traded glances. A smile reached all the way to her eyes. No permanent damage done from last night's adventure through dark dreams.

"No. She didn't tell me." Jack turned his head toward me. His face glowed with seven shades of crimson.

I shrunk where I sat. *Must be Seth.*

Yes, Seth. His brow drooped over his eyes. "Hold on." Leaving a plate of eggs and toast, Jack scooted from the table and slid out of his chair, accidentally knocking my arm.

He exited a door behind me. Shifting in my seat, I watched him through the cafeteria window. He ran a hand through his hair.

Don't freak out.

His eyes found mine through the glass.

Oh, how I wished I could read lips because he had definitely closed off his thoughts.

I directed my attention back to my high-sugar nourishment. I hadn't done anything wrong. Jack should have told me everything. I deserved to know how those nutball scientists altered my mind.

"Hey, Lexi," Kyle said. "Wanna go see your grandmother today?"

"You guys can't leave campus," Danielle said, waving a spoonful of oatmeal in the air. "Lockdown, remember?"

I wrinkled up my face at the reminder. "Yeah. I just need to clear it with my new guardian." Or bend someone's mind in my favor.

"You need to clear what with your new guardian?" I jumped at the sound of Jack's voice behind me. He placed his hand on my shoulders and rubbed. *We need to talk.*

Briana rounded the corner with a tray of food. She sat beside Kyle. "What happened to you last night, Lexi? You missed a fun pool tournament."

"Oh, yeah?"

"Yeah. Jack and I make an awesome team." She winked at Jack behind me.

I tilted my head backwards, peering at him. He shrugged.

Was Briana cloned like Jack and me? Could she read my mind and I didn't know about it? *Hey, Bree. Keep your stupid paws off my man. Can you hear me? Do you know you're a cloned freak?*

Nothing. Except Jack's fingers digging into my shoulders.

"Ouch." I wiggled under his grasp.

"Sorry." *We really need to talk.*

~~~~

"What were you thinking?" Jack ran both fingers through his hair.

I followed him on the sidewalk away from the student center. "What was I thinking?" I asked in a calm-before-the-storm-sort-of-way. I took two steps for every one of his. "Are you kidding me, Mr. There-Will-Be-No-More-Secrets-Between-Us?"
~~~~

He stopped. He rubbed his hands up and down his face making a primal sound that made me back away. We stared at each other for over a minute. Neither of us spoke. Our minds shut off from the other.

"So, Briana?" I finally asked.

He nodded. "She doesn't know."

"Is that why you've been spending so much time with her?" A wad of nerves in my belly tightened into an uncomfortable ball.

He nodded again.

Can you hear her thoughts?

"No." His eyes warmed to mine. *You don't still think I'm interested in her, do you? Surely by now—*

I took a step toward him. Grabbed one of his hands and brought it to my chest, just above my heart. *You've got to start trusting me.*

Ditto. He flattened his hand, his fingers grazing my neck.

"It's not that I don't trust you, Jack." Not exactly.

"Then why did you sneak away last night without telling anyone? Without telling me?"

"I wanted to know the truth, why someone is trying to kill me, and the truth of who I am."

"And? Did Seth answer all your burning questions?" he asked, contempt behind each word.

"I thought you trusted Seth. Thought you wanted *me* to trust Seth."

"Not over me." He pulled my hand. We were walking again. "I knew you had left campus. I couldn't even find a hint of your mind anywhere. It scared me. I was so tempted to report it to the dean, and let the consequences fall."

"Why didn't you?"

"Because I don't know who our friends are here. Your father died trying to protect you from something. I think he knew that the threat had already infiltrated Wellington."

Which was why he was coming to Wellington to move me, I supposed. "You don't trust Dean Fisher?"

"I don't know." *I think we should run.*

I shook my head. *Can't. Too much I still need to know. If the information becomes unbearable, I'll think about it then.*

He stopped again. "Your life is in danger," he said, his voice low. "And I don't know who the threat is."

I squeezed the bridge of my nose. Jack's mind bumped up against the shield I erected.

"What is it?" He reached up and touched my cheek. "Is this about what Seth showed you? Tell me."

Partly.

"Seth should never have taken you to the nursing home. We don't know if you could even heal your grandmother. She's been very sick for so long." *Damn it! He had no right to tell you like that. Especially without me there.*

I stared into his eyes. "That's not all. It's Dani."

"What do you mean?"

I told him how I had found Dani in the throes of a nightmare, and how she had been searching for me with Smoking Man. At least, I thought it was Smoking Man.

"Why didn't you tell me last night? I would have come over."

I cocked my head. "I know you would have."

"You didn't want me to."

I leaned my forehead into his chest. "You can't save me from my friend's dreams, Jack."

"These are not dreams." Jack's voice escalated. His eyes darted around before he continued in a softer voice. "Someone's getting inside your head. Someone like us is using some ability to harm you. And I'm so afraid I won't be able to stop them."

"Someone like us? Briana?"

"No. She knows something's different about her, and that scares her. She's not getting inside your head though. Not with any special power, anyway," he joked. "I almost told her the truth several times. I just couldn't. Not without more information. She's not strong like you. I can't explain it."

I thought about that for a second. Briana and I were friends once upon a time. Something had changed the summer before our sophomore year. She came back to school bitter. She lashed out at me every chance she got. I'd never considered her weak in any way.

"Come on." Jack tugged at me again and led me up the walk toward the athletic center.

I followed him down the hall toward Coach Williams' office. The smell of chlorine reached all the way out into the hallway as we passed the entrance to the pool.

Coach looked up from a laptop when we entered his small office. Familiar images covered the screen. I dropped Jack's hand.

Images of my artwork. Images I'd sent Dad over the years. He had created a website for the art—his way of keeping me "his baby girl." Like I was a kindergartener bringing home that day's craft.

Sometimes I wished I could lose myself in art. My art teacher even encouraged it. But she and I both knew that was not my life's purpose.

How did Coach know about the site? I wiped my sweating palms on my uniform skirt.

"Lexi. Jack," Coach said, flustered. He shut his laptop and stood. A whistle dangled with his Wellington credentials around his neck. "What are you two up to?"

"Hey, Coach," Jack said as if they were long-time friends, which I knew they weren't. "I'm afraid Lexi needs a reminder of what will happen if she leaves campus without permission from her new guardian."

"Lexi, did you leave campus?" He held out a hand to stop me. "Don't answer that. I don't want to know. You will not swim next week if I catch you leaving campus without permission."

Are you serious? You brought me here to be lectured by my coach? Do you truly think I give a flying crap about the swim meet?

I was afraid that's what you would say. Jack closed the door behind him, then turned slowly back to face the coach. "Private Detective Williams, please tell Miss Matthews what else will happen if she were to disobey the rules that have been set forth for her protection."

"I don't understand. Detective?"

A look passed between Coach and Jack, before Coach said, "That's right, Lexi. We tried to keep this quiet, but I always knew the time might come when I'd have to share with you my identity. Especially with your dad gone."

"But you've been here since before I arrived."

"Yes."

"And my best coach ever."

"My credentials as a swimmer are real. I was an NCAA champion swimmer, nine times over, and a certified coach before I..." Coach stopped. Took a breath.

I glanced from Coach to Jack and back to coach. "Before you what?"

"Lexi, no one at this school knows what I'm about to reveal." He crossed his arms and leaned against his desk. "I'm ex-FBI."

"You're an FBI agent?"

"Was. After twelve years in the field, I needed... let's just say, a change of scenery. Your father hired me to look after you. And keep an eye on Wellington."

I raised a brow. "Wellington the person, or Wellington the institution?"

"Is there a difference?" Coach chuckled.

I didn't crack a smile.

"Show her." Jack leaned against the door, crossed his arms.

Show me what?

"Right," Coach clasped his hands together. He was nervous, excited. He approached a cabinet, unlocked it, and pulled out a cuff of some sort.

"What is that?"

"Dean Fisher has authorized me to place this on anyone who decides they simply can't obey the lockdown rules." When I raised a brow, he continued. "This is similar to house arrest bracelets—"

I held up a hand to stop him. An image of Lindsay Lohan popped into my head. "I... I got it." Then, I glared at Jack. "Are we done here?"

A satisfied grin passed over Jack's face.

"Great. Fantastic." I eyed Coach's laptop like it might combust. Then I turned to him, his face expressionless. Part of his FBI training, maybe. "I'm positive I have more questions for you, but it will have to wait. I'm late for class. And quite frankly, I can't look at either of you at the moment."

Jack grimaced. *Don't be mad.*

I placed my hand on the knob. Before I opened the door I thought to Jack, *Don't even think about following me out of here.*

I stormed out, and headed straight to the library computer lab.

TWENTY-FIVE

With the exception of a student worker, I was alone in the computer lab. Everyone else was in class. I pulled up the website, named for the starfish—a site I thought was Dad's and my secret.

A collage of drawings and pictures flashed across the screen. I clicked on the one in the middle. A black and white charcoal of a woman.

"Gram," I whispered. Her eyes stared back at me. I teared up.

It barely looked like her, but I knew the love I felt when I drew it.

I pushed the back button. My dad had apparently added pictures since I last visited. Some I didn't remember sending him. I looked at the last icon. My current work-in-process.

That's strange? How did he get a hold of that?

Almost instantly, Jack responded. *What's strange? Where are you?*

Get out of my head Jack! I closed him off.

I had to learn better control and become more aware of someone slipping into my subconscious. It frightened me to know there were others like Jack and me, and even someone like me who might want to hurt me. Briana might not know her mind was altered, but what about someone else?

The lab worker on the other side of the room giggled as she texted away on her phone.

Wouldn't it be easier to run? Maybe Jack was right.

I gave my head a shake. I couldn't think about that right now.

What was Coach... Detective Williams doing on this website? He'd been watching over me? Did anything in my life make sense anymore?

In addition to the portfolio of my artwork, there was a separate page detailing my swim times. The entire site amounted to an online scrapbook of my activities and hobbies. Evidence of a father's love for a daughter he never saw, maybe.

My stomach twisted and churned. I missed Dad so much. Despite all the secrets.

I clicked on "home" one last time. There were no pictures of me, no personal information. "Why were you so interested in my amateur artwork, Coach?" Maybe he was just clicking through to the swim times. That could be it. Maybe he actually entered the times for Dad. That made sense, too.

Who was I kidding? Nothing made sense.

My pointer hovered over the "x" in the upper right hand corner.

Then, I noticed it. In the sidebar, at the bottom of the screen. A tiny starfish. I ran the pointer over it. There didn't appear to be a link attached to the small icon.

"That's strange," I whispered. Then I remembered some of the computer security tricks Dad taught me over Christmas break one year. I thought of one in particular. Maybe there was a link hidden below this picture after all. I just needed to know the string of key strokes to push before the link would appear.

I stared at the screen for what seemed like hours, not knowing where to begin. I tried "Shift." I tried "Ctrl." I tried "Shift + Ctrl." Nothing.

Since I had missed one class already, it made more sense for me to get to class and think about this later.

~~~~

I entered Advanced Biology II out of breath just as the bell chimed.

The only seat open was directly in front of Jack. After a heavy sigh, I slid into the seat without making eye contact and concentrated hard to shield him from my overactive thoughts and imagination.

I'm sorry. Just those two words from him made my stomach clench.

Mrs. McMillan scribbled the words "Animal Reproduction" on the chalkboard. Snickers erupted around the room.

It's just... I can't protect you when you shut me out like that. What if something had happened to you away from campus? I would have been helpless. You could have been...

I closed my eyes. I could hear the vulnerability in his voice, but he had overstepped. *Who said I need or want you to protect me?*

His fingers grazed the back of my neck. I would never keep up this ironclad shield with him touching me like that. He leaned close, his mouth next to my ear. "It's me who needs to protect you."

Seth said you've been watching me for the past year.

Did he now? Jack pulled his fingers away and I could hear him sit back hard against his chair.

Yes, and I know you're not a stalker, so what—

"Miss Matthews," Mrs. McMillan said over my thoughts.

Shit. I had no idea what she asked.
~~~~

Parthenogenesis, Jack said to my mind.

Seriously? I asked.

Yes, just say it. Parthenogenesis.

"Parthenogenesis?" I answered in more of a question. Okay, maybe this mind thing was handy. I'd thank Jack later when I wasn't so mad at him.

The hour passed, and thankfully, Mrs. McMillan didn't call on me again because I probably would have been distracted then, too. Jack had grown silent.

The bell chimed. I stuffed my notebook inside my bag, and before I could even zip it, Jack grabbed it from me, zipped it, and reached down and wrapped his hand around mine.

He pulled me into the hallway. He was silent as we walked toward our next class.

"Lexi. Jack." I heard our names over the bustle of students behind us. Danielle rushed toward us waving something over her head.

"Have you seen it?" she asked when she reached us, beaming.

"Seen what?" I glanced nervously at Jack.

"The glossies for the art show this weekend?"

Uh-oh. I had totally forgotten.

"What art show?" Jack asked. He took the brochure she offered. "Wellington Boarding School presents its sixth annual Fall Art Gala, featuring the work of Danielle Gray, Barkley Sanders, and Lexi Matthews." He handed the brochure back to Danielle, his eyes never leaving mine. A slow grin twitched at the corners of his lips.

"You didn't tell him?" Danielle asked.

"No, actually, it hadn't come up."

"There's a dance after. I wonder if Barkley has a date yet." She wiggled her brows at me and I couldn't help but laugh.

Just like that, Dani flitted off back where she came from.

"Hey. Can you take me to see Gram today?"

"We don't have permission to leave campus. My father gets back into town today, and he's pretty pissed about the accident last week."

I drilled the heel of my palm into my forehead. "I'm so tired of being controlled. I want to go see my grandmother," I said. "Either you take me or I will find another way."

He yanked me closer. I started to resist, but decided that would not help my cause. "Tomorrow. I'll talk to Father tonight and see what I can do." *Just don't shut me out, okay?*

I make no promises at this point. I'm still mad at you, and I'm tired of so many rules.

Jack frowned. *That's not fair.*

No, it isn't. Nothing about your or my life is fair.

~~~~

Kyle plopped down beside me on the library couch, where I attempted to concentrate on college applications. His woodsy cologne barely covered the remnants of chlorine. "You and DeWeese fighting?"

I kept working. "Fighting?"

"Looked like you were getting pretty intense after biology."

"Did it? No. We're fine."

"You two serious?"

"Serious?" What was this? How could I politely tell him to back off?
~~~~

My phone chimed from the pocket of my fleece jacket.

"You've never dated anyone at Wellington. I'm just surprised, that's all." It wasn't that he seemed jealous, more like he was fishing for information.

"Yes, I guess you could say we're dating." I pulled my phone out and stared at the screen. A text from Marci.

Found Sandra. 106 West Rose Street.

Rose Street? That runs through the middle of UK's campus. I texted back: *What is that? An apartment building?*

I scanned the library with my eyes. "Have you seen Jack?"

"You do have it bad." Kyle chuckled.

"What? No. I just need to go somewhere. And I need a ride."

I didn't see Jack. In fact, I hadn't seen him since classes were over. Which was a good thing. Maybe I could leave and be back before he noticed I was gone.

My phone chimed. *No. University hospital. She is or was a patient there.*

A patient?

Kyle had never been one to worry about rules, and I wasn't sure Jack would take me where I wanted to go. "You in or out?"

"Me?" He pointed his finger into his chest. "You want a ride from me? Did you get permission to leave?"

I really hated lying to my friends. It just wasn't something I did. "If I say 'yes,' will you take me?"

He thought for a solid five seconds. A gleam actually flashed in his eyes. "Let's roll."

~~~~
~~~~

The university hospital was an enormous complex of offices, research labs, a specialized children's hospital, along with several wings of the actual hospital.

"This place has turned into a small city since my grandmother died here a couple of years ago." Kyle looked over his shoulder, switching lanes.

"Your grandmother died here? In this hospital?" I realized I knew very little about Kyle's family. If his grandmother was from the area, his family might live close as well.

"Yeah." He leaned forward and looked up at the tall building in front of us. "Why are we here?"

"I need to visit a friend of my dad's."

"Well, parking is a nightmare. How about I drop you off? That way you can have a head start. I'll park and come find you."

Did I really want Kyle with me when I faced the woman who looked exactly like me twenty-seven years into the future? "Actually, I won't be long. Why don't you grab a coffee at the shop we passed back there?" I thumbed behind me. "I'll text you when I'm ready to be picked up."

"You sure?" He studied me for a second.

"Absolutely." I tried to sound casual. Like this was no big deal.

With that, I jumped out and jogged toward the front entrance. It was definitely better if I did this alone.

Several people congregated, smoking around a bench outside the hospital. The smell reminded me of Smoking Man. An ambulance siren came closer and whizzed past me just as I reached the large revolving door. Once inside, I approached a white-haired lady sitting behind an information desk reading a scraggly-looking paperback.

After finishing the page she was on, she peered at me over her bifocals. "Can I help you?"

"Yes, ma'am," I said, my voice a little shaky. "I'm here to visit a patient. Um... Sandra Whitmeyer."

"Let's see." She clicked her mouse a few times. Typed. Clicked some more. "You family?" she asked without looking at me.

"Yes, ma'am."

A few more clicks and several "hmmms" later, she said, "Just a minute."

She picked up her phone, dialed a number, listened, punched in another number, then hung up.

Strange.

When her eyes found mine again, she smiled and said, "Room 618. Elevators are down the hall on the right."

I edged along the hallway in the direction she pointed. Nurses and doctors in various colors and patterns of scrubs passed me without a glance. The elevator opened and a family rushed out. A small child bumped into me as he ran past. I stepped on, followed by a man in green scrubs, and pressed the number six.

With each floor we passed, the elevator dinged. The man got off on five, and I was alone.

The doors opened on the sixth floor into another bright hallway. To my left, a small waiting area and a series of doors opened to even smaller rooms, and one closed door. Through the window, I saw three people huddled together. Maybe in prayer, but definitely comforting each other.

To my right—a large set of double doors. On the wall beside the doors, gold lettering—Neurology - ICU.

A sign on the doors read, "Ring bell for entrance." Sure enough, a button resembling a doorbell hung to the right of the doors and a card scanner for those with the right credentials.

I approached slowly. My fingers hovered over the button. I didn't know if it was the rumbling deep in the pit of my stomach or the warning bells I imagined inside my head, but I pulled my hand back without ringing the bell.

Was Sandra truly behind this double set of doors? I was struggling to believe that the white-haired woman just sent me straight up to the Neurology ICU, no questions asked other than taking me at my word that I was, in fact, Sandra Whitmeyer's family.

I guessed I could prove it with a DNA sample.

I stared at the door again. What was the worst that could happen? A nurse or doctor could turn me away. Tell me I'm not allowed on this floor unless I'm family. Did I really want to see Sandra? Look into eyes identical to mine? Prove once and for all that I was the freak I thought I was?

Suddenly the door in front of me shook. I jumped back. Looked all around.

I jumped into one of the private rooms like a guilty, crazy person.

The doors opened slowly, the way they do when you hit the handicap button. A couple of nurse-looking people exited and waited for the elevator. Once they were on, I approached the entrance again. The doors were just starting to close.

This was my chance. Did I jump through them? What was I even scared of? I wasn't doing anything wrong. Not really.

I slid through the opening just before the doors closed. On the other side, a hallway of hospital rooms in two directions. A nurse's station to my left. In front of me... Room number 632.

I'd always thought the best way to get where I wanted was to act like I already belonged. So, I walked along the hallway with purpose.

630.

628.

626.

Jack.

I stopped in my tracks, and backed up against a wall. Inside room 624 was Jack. Or a person identical to Jack. I needed to look again to be sure. But I was nearly certain Jack leaned over a bed inside the room.

Slowly, I angled my body toward the room again and was about to lean my head around the corner to peek in when a hand grabbed my shoulder and pulled me backwards.

I gasped, almost letting out a loud shriek. My palm flattened over my heart where I massaged my out-of-control pulse. I gazed helplessly into the eyes of Seth Whitmeyer.

TWENTY-SIX

"What are you doing here?" Seth asked, keeping his voice low.

I stared at him, eyes wide.

"He finally told you."

I shook my head freakishly fast. "Who is that in there? Is it Sandra?"

"Sandra?" Seth asked, confused. "No. That's Addison."

"Addison?"

"Jack promised me he would tell you." He peered around me and inside the room. "Come on." Seth put his hand on my back and led me back the way I'd come.

"Where are you taking me?" I asked, panicked. I could reach out to Jack with my mind, but that would be admitting to having left Wellington. Again. Without permission.

Besides, I wanted to know all the things Jack wouldn't tell me.

Seth flashed the card around his neck in front of a scanner and opened a door. "My office. After you." He gestured with his hand for me to enter.

"You work here?" It all made sense. His mom had said he worked shifts. And he knew so much about Gram and her condition. He was a doctor.

"I'm a neurologist."

His office was small, his mahogany desk cluttered with paper and medical magazines. Very few personal items.

He removed his white lab coat and hung it on a hook on the back of the door. "Have a seat, Lexi."

I sat on the very edge of a leather chair. My right leg shook. "Who's Addison?"

"Addison is the reason Jack finally joined The Program. Addison is the reason he came looking for you."

I sucked in an audible breath. "I don't understand."

"Addison is Anita's eight-year-old daughter."

"Anita? Jack's housekeeper?"

He nodded. "A year-and-a-half ago, Addison and Jack were riding. Something spooked her horse. She was thrown."

"What happened?"

"She broke her collar bone. Suffered some other minor injuries, but she couldn't move. Jack didn't get to her in time. After the horse threw her, it backed up and stepped on her head."

"Oh, God." I covered my mouth with my hand. "Did Jack try to heal her injuries?"

"Of course. And he did. Everything but the brain damage from the horse's misstep. He almost died. Put himself in the hospital—he became dehydrated from throwing up so much after he healed her collar bone and broken ribs."

I picked a speck of lint on the floor and stared at it. My mind raced. Jack had made himself so sick. "Why hasn't he told me?" I said mostly to myself.

"Isn't it obvious?"

"I guess not. Not to me anyway."

"Because he loves you, Lexi, and he's scared. He's scared of losing you. He's scared of what the consequences might be if you were to use your power the way it was meant to be used."

"What do you think the consequences will be?" I asked. Was I seriously wondering if I could use my mind to heal someone's brain? Gram? The little girl lying in that bed for the past year-and-a-half?

Healing either of them went against everything I believed in. It just seemed that using supernatural abilities to heal went against God's plan for the universe—that these abilities were not created by God, but by arrogant scientists. Maybe that was why the consequences existed.

"We won't know until you try. But Jack says you have pretty bad nose bleeds when you use a small part of your power."

"He told you that?"

"He told me that you could bend minds in your favor." Seth grinned. "That must be quite a useful tool."

I nodded.

"Something in your nervousness just now tells me, though, that this mind bending power extends further than I'm aware."

"No," I disagreed. "You make me nervous in general."

He leaned forward against his desk and clasped his hands. "I'm going to be honest with you. You will become a part of The Program sooner or later. Jack convinced me to give you time to come based on your own choice, but eventually, you won't have a choice."

"Are you threatening me?"

His lips curved into a grin. "No, I'm not. I'm finally giving you all of the facts. Eventually, the people who killed your father will be coming for you. Or you'll find the journals that explain everything. Then you'll be begging to be part of The Program."

~~~~

I had three texts and four missed calls when I got back in the car. The three texts and two of the calls were from Jack. The other two calls were from Wellington's main line.

"I'm sorry, Kyle. I hope I didn't get you in trouble."

He shrugged. "I knew what I was getting into. You needed a ride, right?"

I stared out the window. Trees whizzed by on the back road that led to school. What would I tell Jack? That I knew about Addison?

No. I couldn't. Not yet.

"You hungry?" Kyle asked.

"What?" How could he think about food right now? We were going to be in so much trouble when we returned to school.

"Well, there's no way we'll make it back for dinner. I'm stopping for a protein bar and an energy drink." He turned into a gas station with a small country store and parked near to the doors. "Want anything?"

I shook my head.

Kyle shut the door and disappeared into the mini-mart. Something flickered out of the corner of my eye. Kyle's cell phone lay in the seat beside me. A new text lit the screen. I craned my neck to see any signs of Kyle returning. When I didn't, I grabbed his phone and began punching buttons and scrolling through texts.

He had been texting someone by the name of R.W. I scrolled through the texts.

Kyle: We r at UK Hosp. She's not talking. Should I say something?
~~~~

R.W: Don't do or say anything!! Keep ears open. Get her to talk about who she visited. Any mention of journals?

Kyle: No journal talk. Picking her up now.

R.W: Just get back to school.

I darkened the phone's screen just as Kyle turned away from the checkout counter. He pushed through the door with an armful of snacks and a couple of drinks. I struggled to get a couple of deep breaths in before he opened the door and let some of the snacks fall into the seat on top of his phone.

"I got you something anyway."

I took a drink and some of the food from him, giving my hands something to do before Kyle noticed how badly they shook.

After watching the fence line sail past me along the country road for twenty minutes, Kyle finally said, "Who was this friend of your father's that you visited? Someone he worked with?"

"Uh, yeah. A colleague from a long time ago." Too many questions. I wanted to cry.

Kyle's phone sounded. He reached behind his back. He looked at the text, and then over at me.

I stared out the window, counting the light poles. Think, Lexi. Think. Who was R.W.? How did Kyle and this R.W. know about the journals?

"How the hell did he get my cell phone number?" Kyle held his phone up so that he could see it and the road at the same time.

"Who?" I shrugged.

"Jack."

"Text?"

"Yeah. He says that if you're with me, to call him. 'Now!' There's lots of exclamation points."

I scrolled through the names on my phone. What would I say to Jack? Especially with Kyle in the car. Finally, I jabbed at Jack's name and brought the phone to my ear.

"I don't have much time," he said when he picked up. "Father's here. And he's pissed you're not."

"What do you want me to do about it?" I asked. Kyle was back to thumping his hand on the steering wheel. "I have an idea."

"You better think of something, because security was instructed to search Kyle's car as soon as he enters the main gate."

"What, like I'm some sort of fugitive?" This was ridiculous. Why was Jack allowed to leave campus, and I wasn't?

"No, but like I thought your coach made clear earlier, the school takes their lock-downs very seriously. Especially when a student's legal guardian shows up looking for the person he's responsible for and she's not there."

TWENTY-SEVEN

Kyle pulled along the side of the road at the very back of Wellington's property. I jumped out with my backpack. "Go."

"Are you sure about this? I don't care about getting into a little bit of trouble."

"I'm fine. Now go."

I darted toward the shrubbery and searched for the hole Kyle, Danielle, Briana, and I had carved out when we were freshman. We thought it would be a brilliant idea to sneak out of Wellington and go to a party with friends from the public school near Wellington. We've used it a few times since, but the hedges filled back in nicely. Too well, actually.

I followed the path beside the overgrown shrubs, and fearing snakes and ticks, I pushed through the dense greenery.

"Ouch." A branch sliced my shin. Blood stained the area around a tear in my jeans.

A bird fluttered on a branch in front of me, mocking me, I was certain. I ducked under a tree limb and faced yet another obstacle. A tall chain-link fence that appeared electrical.

Fantastic. When did they put this here? And why?

I looked around for something to throw at it. That's what they did in Jurassic Park. Did that only work in the movies? Bending over, I found a small branch and tossed it at the fence.

Nothing.

Next, I stepped closer. My heart pumped fast and hard. I raised my hand. Like a cobra poised to attack, I darted it forward, slapped the metal, and drew back.

Nothing.

Finally, I curled my fingers around the metal of the fence and counted my blessings that I wasn't electrocuted. I leaned my head backwards, studying the height of it, and then I looked down at the flip-flops on my feet.

This was going to hurt. I massaged my right shoulder—the one hurt in the car accident last week. The one Jack had mostly healed. With a deep breath, I climbed.

The climb up wasn't a problem, but my stomach churned acid when I looked down to the other side.

I tossed my bag to the ground, hurled the first leg over the top, then the other.

I moved one foot at a time. A foot slipped, causing me to grasp tighter with my hands. Halfway down, both feet slipped, and I was left dangling, the wire cutting into my palms. I started to turn my head to see how far off the ground I was when two hands eased around my waist.

My body tensed.

"I've got you." Jack sounded irritated, just like I imagined my knight in shining armor should. "Let go."

I did and slid down into his hold. I turned and threw my arms around his neck. "He knows, Jack. I'm so glad you're here."

"Who knows what? What are you talking about?" He smoothed out my hair.

"The journals. Kyle knows." I told Jack about the texts between Kyle and R.W. It seemed everyone was now looking for journals I didn't even know existed until recently. "Do you think my father was killed because of these journals?"

"I don't know."

"Thank you for coming to rescue me, by the way."

"Yeah. Speaking of..." His tone changed from kind to chastising. "You should thank me for not blowing your cover to the dean and my father." He removed my arms and stepped back. "There's a house arrest cuff with your name on it in Coach Williams' desk drawer."

I winced.

"You told me you wouldn't leave campus again."

"No, I didn't. You asked me not to, but I never said I wouldn't. Where were you? I looked for you when I decided to leave. You were nowhere to be found."

Jack cocked his head, considered me. "I told you I'd take you to see your grandmother tomorrow."

It wasn't exactly a lie if he avoided the question all together.

I brushed dirt off my jeans. "Well, I'm fine. Back safe and sound." I glanced down at my leg. "Mostly sound."

"Don't you get it, Lexi? You're reckless. Someone is trying to kill you, and you go off wild and out of control."

"Reckless? I am far from reckless. And I'm completely in control." I tossed my backpack on my good shoulder and started walking away. I made it all of five steps before he grabbed my arm and spun me around. I stared straight into his eyes. They were passionate. Daring and inviting. All I could see, though, was the image of him bowed at that little girl's bedside. My heart shrunk at the thought that I might be capable of helping that defenseless girl. "Don't be mad. Please."

He brushed hair away from my face and tucked it behind my ear. "What am I going to do with you?" He stood so close that a light breeze would slam him into me. The intensity of his blue eyes slowly stripped away the bricks of defense I managed to cement around me.

I slipped my arms around his waist and leaned my head against his chest. I could feel the muscles in his arms relax. How could I tell him that I knew why he wanted me, needed my power? If I didn't have the power to heal that innocent little girl, would he still love me? "There's just so much going on. I miss my dad." I needed Dad here to guide me.

I shivered.

"I know you do. I'm sorry." He leaned in and kissed my forehead. His lips were soft, his touch gentle.

"I think he was trying to tell me everything when he was killed. From a young age, he used to talk to me in riddles. See if I could figure things out. He'd send me coded emails. I'd have to break the code before I could read them. Sometimes, I'd have to go on a scavenger hunt across the internet to find out what my Christmas gift was. And he sent me the most amazing gifts—like these puzzle boxes." I looked up at Jack who had gone silent.

"Puzzle boxes?"

"Yeah, you know. You have to figure out the right piece of wood to move, or remove, in order to get the box to open. The first one he ever sent me had a pewter starfish on top of it." And the last one he sent me was in the shape of a starfish. "With the first one, you had to remove one of the arms before another section could be moved to reveal a key hole." I smiled at the memory. Dad was always so proud when I figured out some of the early boxes.

Some of them even had more than one compartment. That always threw me. "Oh, my gosh!" I gazed up at Jack. "I gotta go." I stood on my tippy toes and kissed his cheek. "Thanks for coming to my rescue, but—"

Jack wrapped his fingers around my arm just above my elbow. "Oh, no you don't."

"I think I figured something out!" I pulled on my arm, but he didn't loosen his grip.

"Figured what out?"

"The last puzzle box that Dad sent me. I only found one compartment. The one with the starfish necklace and key. There must be another." There had to be another clue hidden in what he had sent me.

"Lexi, my parents are waiting in Dean Fisher's office. I told them you were in a study group. We have to go straight there."

~~~~

Cathy DeWeese's back was to us when we entered Dean Fisher's office. "Seth sponsored the entire cost of the art show for tomorrow night?" she asked the dean.

Dr. DeWeese glanced from me to his son. He raised a finger to his lip, silencing his wife.

Cathy turned. "Oh." She opened her arms and walked toward me. "Oh, you poor dear."

I stepped hesitantly into her outstretched arms and turned my head in time to see Jack's eyes roll heavenward. Her bangle bracelets knocked against my shoulder when she released me,
~~~~

holding me at arm's length. "How are you feeling? Still a little shaky?"

Shaky? From the accident? "Um... my shoulder still hurts a little, I guess." I glanced at Jack again. He rubbed a hand over his lips. *Is this woman for real?*

Well, now you know she and I are not related by blood. But she did raise me. He shrugged.

"Have a seat, kids." Dean Fisher gestured toward the chairs on the other side of his desk. "John and I have talked..."

Dr. DeWeese leaned against the desk and faced us. "Neither of you are to leave this campus unless it's with one of us." He pointed back and forth between his wife and himself.

Jack stood. "What? You can't do that."

"We thought you might say that," Cathy said. "But it's been decided." She stared at her son, not blinking once. "You decided to come to this school against my wishes. You get to obey school rules."

"You don't get to make rules for me. I'm already eighteen."

"You're partially right, son," Dr. DeWeese said, his voice calm. "You are eighteen. If you don't want to abide by lame school rules, you can come back home and study there until it's time to leave for college next fall." I think it hurt Dr. DeWeese to utter the word 'lame.' Still, he pulled it off okay.

Cathy's cheeks lifted, like she'd won some small battle. "Son, what's it going to be? Stay at Wellington? Or return home?"

I suddenly felt I was intruding on a family conversation. Jack stood close to his mother, his expression alternating between irritated and humiliated. He turned his head to me.

I lifted a brow. *Don't look at me. If you need to leave Wellington, by all means...*

"I do have a bit of bad news, though, son."

"What bad news?" Jack asked.

"If you'll excuse me..." Dean Fisher held his phone up like he had just received a message. "Unless you need me, I need to check on an issue with preparations for tomorrow night's show."

Without another word, the dean breezed from the room. I turned back to the tension mounting between Jack and his mom.

"It's about Addison, darling. I'm afraid the situation is dire."

I sat up straighter. Dr. DeWeese frowned, and even Cathy's eyes filled with tears.

Jack cast a nervous look at me. "Lexi, can you give me a moment alone with my mother and father?" Then he added, *I'm sorry.*

So much for trust. He didn't want me to hear about Addison. Why was he keeping her from me? Especially if he thought I could heal her.

I stood. "Sure. I need to go... do that thing—"

I am sorry. Meet me at the stables in one hour.

It'll be past curfew. I thought for a second. Could I get out and across campus without being noticed? Would he tell me about Addison then? *I'll be there.* I started toward the door, straining to hear what Cathy said to her son. But heard nothing.

"I'll walk you out dear." Dr. DeWeese followed me.

I exited the dean's office and stood at his secretary's desk. It was late in the evening. The offices were empty except for us.

He clicked the door shut behind us. "How are you really doing, Lexi?"

I shrugged. I missed Dad. "Fine, I guess?" No, that was a lie. "Actually, Dr. DeWeese—"

"Please, call me John."

"Did you find my father's journals in Sicily?"

"No." The disappointment on his face was genuine.

"What did you hope to find in these journals?"

He glanced over his shoulder to the office door behind him. "Jack told me that you now know how you were... created."

I nodded. Why couldn't he just answer the question?

"What Jack didn't tell you, because he didn't know, was that your father didn't know you were implanted in your mother's womb until well after you were born."

"What?" The room started a slow spin. "Dad didn't know?"

"He knew about the clonings and the gene alterations, but your dad thought the embryos had been destroyed, like they were supposed to be. Before they became viable. Then the fire happened, and everyone scattered. Your parents were tricked."

"Tricked? By whom? What do you mean?"

"Your mom went in for a routine in vitro fertilization because she had struggled to conceive. She came out pregnant. With you. Cathy and I have many theories on who was behind making sure the embryos reached hosts."

Hosts? That made me sound like an alien. A parasite.

I walked slowly over to a chair and clung to the arm. My father wasn't directly responsible for the freak that I was? Still, he was very much involved. "What are your theories? You think Sandra was responsible?"

"Maybe. Or the International Intelligence Agency. Maybe Sandra's entire experiment got away from her. She could be mostly innocent in this. No one has talked to her since before the fire. Hell, I hadn't spoken to your father since then."

I squeezed the bridge of my nose.

John continued. "Your dad told me the night of the dinner that he planned to tell you the truth. About everything. But..."

"He was killed."

He nodded.

"Why all the secrets? Why not tell Jack and me the truth sooner?"

"It was too risky. Your dad and I were very much involved with Sandra's wild theories that she could enhance the genetic makeup of certain parts of the brain, and then with proper training, create human beings capable of... well... healing incurable diseases and injuries. We were on board with everything Sandra wanted to do. Until..."

"Until what?"

John rubbed his hand back and forth across his five o'clock shadow. He shifted his weight from one foot to the other. "Until Sandra made a deal with the IIA. Your dad discovered correspondence between Sandra and an IIA agent. He was outraged. She had agreed to sell her research to them. And she secretly copied your dad and me on all correspondence, implicating us."

"But you didn't know what she was doing?" John shook his head. "What happened? What did the IIA do with this information?"

"I don't know. Our labs were destroyed in a fire. Jack had just been born. Everyone went their separate ways in order to protect themselves. Cathy and I vowed to protect Jack at all costs. Your dad kept you hidden from me. From everyone. Not until I saw a picture of a young Sandra Whitmeyer in a newspaper..." John narrowed his gaze at me. "...that was actually you. That's when I started to put things together. That's how I found Wellington."

Deep inside, I knew Dad loved me. He showed me over and over. So why had he kept everything from me? "Why are you telling me all of this now?"

"Your dad wanted you to live a long, healthy life and never have to come face to face with the future laid out before you now. Unfortunately, he also knew that was not the way it would be. That's why he enrolled you here at Wellington, where there were enough people around you who knew the truth and could be trusted at the same time."

"He was planning to move me. Do you know why?"

"No. Who told you that?" he asked, unable to hide his surprise.

I studied his face, a face so similar to Jack's, only older. Mostly the eyes. The same electric blue that made you want to reveal your deepest secrets. However, John's baldness kept me grounded in reality. This was not Jack. Though what he divulged to me made sense with everything I'd learned so far, I barely knew this person in front of me.

I thought of Marci. How scared she was the last time I saw her. "I can't tell you that." He nodded again. He was so different from his wife. A level of understanding passed over his face. "You knew about Jack from the beginning?" I asked.

"Yes and I knew you would turn up sooner or later. I just didn't know where."

I cocked my head. "What do you mean?"

"Well, I knew you'd been created, just like the others. I just didn't know whose child you had become."

I gasped. "What others? What do you mean?" This must be what Marci was talking about. "How many?" My body tensed. How many clones were out there? Did they know? I thought of the person who'd gotten inside my head when I slept.

And of Briana. She didn't know. She couldn't.

"I'm not sure how many survived. And I don't know what the IIA knows." He rubbed his head, very similar to how Jack ran his fingers through his hair. "But your dad figured it out. And he documented everything he knew."

"The journals," I whispered.

John nodded. "That's why finding these journals is so important. The journals contain the information your dad never got the chance to tell me. Including, hopefully, information that will lead to whoever killed him."

"But why kill Dad?" I whispered, mostly to myself. Then realization hit. "Someone doesn't want this information revealed. Maybe Dad had the journals with him."

"The originals. Possibly."

I cocked my head. Stared at the man before me with the same eyes as the boy on the other side of the door.

"Does Jack know all of this?"

"He does now. Unfortunately, what Sandra, your father, and I did all those years ago is who you are now. Only you can decide if you're willing to accept it."

"There are people who would have Jack and me use the powers Sandra gave us."

"They're amazing powers, Lexi. You and Jack have the ability to cure people of things no other person on earth can."

But not without consequences, unfortunately.

John added, "There are also people who would stop at nothing to destroy you and all evidence of your existence. Whoever killed your dad probably thought he... or she... was destroying the original journals and, of course, the information living inside your dad's head would be gone forever."

The information wasn't gone forever. I now knew exactly where Dad had duplicated that information. Could I stay alive long enough to access it?

TWENTY-EIGHT

I raced into my dorm room and tossed my bag on my bed. Dani, Kyle and Bree all looked up from their spots, deep into some sort of study session.

"Oh. Hi," I said, stopping to analyze the three of them.

Dani sat in some strange yoga position, a book on the floor in front of her. Bree leaned against Dani's bed, her legs stretched out in front with a laptop across her thighs. Kyle lay on top of Dani's bed and tossed a Nerf football overhead.

Why couldn't they've studied anywhere else but my room tonight?

If I hadn't seen it with my own eyes earlier that day, I would never have suspected Kyle knew about Dad's journals. Or that he was keeping secrets from us.

"Hi, yourself," Dani said. "Where've you been?"

I shifted from one foot to the other. I just wanted to find the puzzle box and a private spot to access Dad's website. "Um... talking to my new guardians."

Kyle stopped tossing the ball and swung his legs over the side of the bed. "You get in trouble?"

"No, you?" I answered, though being reprimanded for leaving campus should have been the least of my concerns right then.

"Why would either of you get in trouble?" Briana asked.

My body tensed. My eyes pleaded with Kyle. Briana would rat me out for sure, and I'd have an ankle bracelet by nine a.m.

Being lectured was one thing, but having that metal clamped around my leg would not be pleasant.

"Oh, it was nothing. Don't worry that pretty little head." Kyle tickled her ear, then tossed the ball in the air again.

I let out a breath. "I'd love to chat, but you guys look like you're in the middle of a study session. And I really need to do something before curfew."

Briana narrowed her gaze at me, then glanced over her shoulder at Kyle.

Let it go, Briana. Kyle and I are not in trouble. You have studying to do. You better get back to it.

Briana went back to making notes on her computer.

I turned on my heels, reached for a tissue for the inevitable nosebleed, and began sifting through the mess of papers and notebooks on my desk. Underneath the pile, I found the puzzle box dad had sent me.

I opened the compartment I had found previously. Empty. Like I had left it.

The arms of the starfish wouldn't budge. I pushed around different areas of the wood and shook the box. Maybe I was wrong. Maybe there wasn't a second compartment.

"Lexi, honey? What are you doing?" Dani asked.

"Shit!" Briana yelled.

I whirled around. Briana banged on the keys of her computer hard.

"What is it?" Kyle asked.

"The stupid internet is down again."

I walked the three steps to stand over her. "What do you mean? It's been down?"

"Yeah, I've been having trouble with my connection all night. Why can't this stupid school get Wi-Fi in the dorms?" She wiggled the wireless card on the side of her computer.

Kyle sat up. "My phone has no service." He punched around on his iPhone.

I pulled my phone out of my pocket. No service. What was going on?

"I'll catch you guys later." I grabbed my bag and the puzzle box, and blew out of the room.

~~~~

It was ten minutes until ten p.m.—curfew. I had to find Jack.

I pushed open the side door of the dorm. A man in a dark uniform blocked my path.

"Sorry miss. But no one is allowed to leave the dorms to-night."

What the... I backed up a step. "Who are you?" My eyes roamed over the six-foot obstacle in front of me.

He wore a navy uniform, covering his slightly protruding belly. A badge across his right breast read "SECURITY." Around his waist was a utility belt carrying a nightstick, a taser, and a flashlight. A walkie-talkie buzzed on his right hip. His crooked smile creeped me out as he looked down on me.

"Just extra security, miss."

"Curfew isn't for another ten minutes." I made a move to walk around him, but he mirrored my action, continuing to block my path. It was clear I would not get around this buff man twice my size with muscle strength.
~~~~

"I have my orders. No one is to leave the dorm this close to curfew."

Why the need for extra security when Wellington was gated and fenced already? I strained to look around him. I saw no one else. The campus appeared quiet.

Jack? I've got trouble.

Nothing. Where was he? The uneasy feeling started in my legs, weakening me at the knees. I rubbed the spot over my heart where my panic picked up in intensity.

Jack, where are you?

"Look, Mr..." I glanced at his nametag. "Mr. Kakowski, I need to run to the library for a book. I'll be exactly ten minutes. I'll be back before curfew."

"Sorry, miss. You're going to turn around and head right back inside." This time his tone was more severe and quite belittling.

I felt the heat of my anger spread to my sweaty palms. I curled my fingers into fists. *Thank you, Mr. Kakowski, for your dedicated service to this school. I feel so much safer with you here. But you are going to let me pass. You won't try to stop me or find me. And if you remember this for some reason, you will not tell anyone about it because you know you'll be fired and humiliated for allowing a little girl to get past you.*

I skirted around Mr. Kakowski slowly, keeping my body facing him. I backed away, and when he stood at his post once more, staring straight ahead like a British Buckingham Palace guard, I ran.

I jogged along the shadows of the buildings and the trees, making my way toward the stable and blotting my nose as I went. The campus was dark except for path lighting along sidewalks, security lamps in the parking lots off to the distance, and lights from two buildings—the library, which should be closing any minute, and the art building where preparations for the art gala were underway.

Approaching the art building, voices startled me. I backed up into darkness next to the building and watched for the people attached to the voices to appear.

A man and a woman materialized around the corner—Dr. Wellington and Cathy DeWeese.

Strange combination.

Their voices got louder, and my heart beat wildly out of control.

"You'll announce the new rules surrounding The Program tomorrow night? At the gala?" Cathy asked.

"Yes," Dr. Wellington said. "Security is in place. Staff is ready."

"Are the necessary parents or legal guardians on board? Signatures in place?" Dr. Wellington asked.

"All but two." Cathy's lips tightened into a straight line. "But it shouldn't be a problem."

"What about Jack? Is he on board?" Dr. Wellington jiggled the change in his pocket as he walked.

"Jack will be ready by tomorrow night when the announcement is made. He received some bad news tonight. He has no choice but to join our cause."

"Good. And the girl?"

The girl? Me, maybe?

"She'll fall in line."

Fall in line with what?

"Last I checked, she hadn't submitted her application for The Program. How do you know she'll join our new and improved program voluntarily?"

"Because, R.W., she's in love with my son, and she now knows she was created for this. Her father's killing was unexpected, but it will motivate her. In the end, she'll do it for him."

R.W.? Kyle was texting Dr. Wellington?

"Have you had any more contact with the IIA?" Dr. Wellington asked.

"Of course not." Cathy stopped and turned toward Dr. Wellington. "You know you could have saved us all this trouble had you just told us you had Sandra Whitmeyer's replica living right under your nose."

A bone-chilling grin spread across Dr. Wellington's face. "The Program was carefully planned out long before you ever got involved. Timing is everything."

"You think the IIA killed Peter?" Cathy asked.

"I don't know. I wouldn't put it past them. But I just can't figure out why they would want him dead."

~~~~

A cool wind whipped through the barn, stirring up dust and straw. I crouched in a dark corner of an empty stall across from Cherriana.

My mind reeled. Did I hear Cathy right? Was she happy about Dad's death? Did Jack know what kind of controlling, cold woman raised him? Dr. Wellington had known who I was all along? John DeWeese seemed to have my best interests in mind. Did he know who he was married to?
~~~~

Jack, where are you? I buried my face in my hands. Was Cathy involved with the IIA?

I'm here.

I raised my head. Swiped at the tears burning my cheeks.

Back of the barn, he continued. *Where are you?*

I scrambled to my feet, throwing my backpack over my shoulder, and peeked around the stall door. He was right there. I gasped. He turned in a complete circle at the opening to the barn.

I steadied myself against the stall door, causing it to bang into the barn wall. Jack faced me. My feet remained cemented to the dirt floor.

"Hi," he said.

"Where've you been?" I asked. I didn't know whether to blurt out everything that was freaking me out, or give him the chance to explain.

He sucked in a deep breath and released it slowly. "That's a long story. One I probably should share with you."

Cherriana bobbed her head in the stall across from me, nudging me toward Jack. He and I had so much to tell each other. I could see pain and tension in the large "v" between his eyes.

My lip quivered. "Oh, Jack." A sob escaped my mouth. I slammed my hand over my mouth.

Jack dropped the things he held in his hands and closed the distance between us.

Instinctively, I backed away. He stopped, but he was only inches from me. Electricity surged between us.

"What is it?" His hands twitched.

He longed to touch me. I could feel the pulse of electricity between us.

He reached for me, but I leaned further away. It would be so easy to lose myself in him, let him hug my problems away, but his mother... The temperature of my blood rose again. "I think... no, I know... your mother..."

"That woman is not my mother," Jack all but growled through clenched teeth. He looked up to the rafters. When his eyes found mine again, they softened. "Lexi, I am sorry." He ran his hands through his hair. "That woman has pretended to want me to stay away from you, but all along, she knew I would lead her straight to you."

"Why do you say that?"

"It was something Seth told me. He said my mom had a lot to gain from the success of The Program. The way she wants The Program to be run."

"What does that mean?"

"Mom thinks Seth is on her side. That he is ready and willing to teach you and me—"

"And the others," I added.

"Yes, and the others. But the timing had to be right. And Seth has his own motives which I haven't quite figured out completely."

"And that's why you don't trust him?"

Jack nodded. "Not completely, anyway."

"I don't think..." My voice cracked. "I don't think Cathy is very upset that my dad is dead."

Jack's hands clenched into fists. "Your father was going to move you, Lexi. You know that. Probably hide you forever. Cathy DeWeese was not about to let that happen." He said his mother's name like it was venom on his tongue. "I had no idea until now just how important The Program was to her. Cathy is all about control. The Program is her way of controlling us."

"My father's death kept me in place at Wellington. And your parents are my new legal guardians." Something wasn't adding up. Okay, lots of things didn't add up.

He nodded. "And I basically handed you to them on a silver platter. But I didn't know."

"What do you mean? Didn't know what?" Jack was speaking in circles.

"Cathy acted like she didn't want me near you, but in reality, she knew I would find you. I led her straight to you. Father and I both did. She knew because of my father's relationship with Sandra, neither of us would be able to stay away from you."

"She would have found me anyway. Roger Wellington knew who I was. And if she was working with him—"

"Yeah, Father didn't even know until recently that Dr. Wellington was her brother."

Every muscle along my spine tightened. "What? Her brother?" So much didn't make sense. "And who is Kyle to Dr. Wellington?" Jack shrugged. "He calls Dr. Wellington R.W., which is what I heard Cathy call him. You think Kyle might be another clone?"

"It's possible."

I hated with every part of my being that my life had been orchestrated like a marionette. Our DNA and our fathers' pasts threw Jack and me together. Jack needed me to heal that poor little girl in the hospital room. Would he have studied me so long or come to Wellington if it hadn't been for Addison?

Something about the emotion swirling in his eyes drew me toward him. I stepped closer.

He cocked his head. Looked so unsure of himself. "Lexi, please don't hold me or my father responsible for whatever that woman has done."

When I couldn't take the distance between us any longer, I launched myself into his arms. My arms circled his neck. I buried my face into his chest, breathing in the scent of fabric softener. "I'm so scared, Jack. Strange things are happening around here. I don't know who to trust. People close to you. To me. People want something from me that I can't give them. Or they want me dead. And I so want to put all of my trust in you."

He turned his head into the crook of my neck and breathed in. "Shhh. We're going to get through this. I'm going to figure this out." He steadied me with his hands on my hips. "We can't stay here, though. A night watchman will be around any minute. And the curfew—"

"There are armed guards at the entrances of my dorm."

"What?" he asked, surprised. "Come on. We need to find a safer place." After glancing over my shoulder, the length of the barn behind me, he reached down and picked up the things he had dropped. Then grabbing my hand, he pulled me forward.

"What's in the bag?"

"Stuff for you."

"What kind of stuff?"

"Documents for a new identity."

TWENTY-NINE

Passport. Driver's license. High school transcripts. Credit card. Birth certificate. Social security card. Forty-five hundred dollars.

I inventoried the pile of documents and cash in front of me. We sat in the back of a ridiculously-huge SUV, the seats folded down, in the middle of the Wellington parking lot.

It was dark and eerily quiet. The uneven sound of my own breaths added to my nervousness. I raised my head. Jack stared back at me. The whites of his eyes glowed.

"Whose truck is this?" I asked.

"Seth's. He let me borrow it to come back here tonight."

I nodded then reached for the United States passport in front of me. I opened it. Thumbed the pages. Last year's school photo stared back at me. And the name: Sierra Richardson. "I don't know what to say." Was he pushing me away?

"Tomorrow night security will be tight, but enough cars will be going in and out that I think you'll be able to escape. Seth is going to drive you to the bus station in Cincinnati. From there you'll catch a bus to wherever you want to go."

My breathing sped up. "Are you telling me to leave?" I couldn't hide the hurt in my voice.

Did Jack really think I would just run for it? Leave him here? My grandmother? My friends? Turn my back on the fact that Dad was murdered and that I was a human clone? Build a life on more secrets?

He stopped sifting through the pile of documents and placed his hands on either side of my face. "You have to. I would never forgive myself if something happened to you because of me."

"Why the extra security tonight at the dorms?" Not because of the car accident last week, I suspected.

Jack played with the tag of some blanket in the back of Seth's truck.

"Wellington is the new home to The Program."

I cocked my head. "You still haven't told me what that means. Will the students who are eligible and interested in studying cutting edge science and medicine, get to do it here? Isn't that a good thing?"

"Lexi, do you know how many students are currently enrolled in The Program?"

I shook my head. I was told very little about The Program other than I had to apply. It was the precursor to being admitted to the premed program of my choice. I'd been told it was held on the University of Kentucky's campus. I knew Seth was involved. I knew he could teach me about my personal genetic manipulation. Now I also knew Cathy DeWeese was involved.

"Four." He ran both hands through his hair. "Until tomorrow night."

"I don't understand."

"I know. Listen to me. You have to leave. There are too many people who know that you and I were cloned. I have a horrible feeling about all this. Your dad was killed because he was trying to move you. He planned to hide you from them. They need you, Lexi. And if you don't comply with their wants peacefully, they will force you."

"What do you mean, they need me?"

"You can heal diseases and injuries of the brain. That's what you were designed to do."

"No, I can't. I've never done that." I shook my head quickly as I spoke. I thought of my grandmother's brain and of Addison. "But that's why you came here, wasn't it? That's why you found me. That's why you watched me for a year." My voice barely climbed past a whisper.

"Oh, Lexi." He reached for my hand and intertwined his fingers with mine. "I thought... You have no idea how sorry I am. That's why I got all this. I want to make things right." His furrowed brows cast a shadow over his eyes—eyes that were nearly black here in the dark. Anguish passed over his face.

"Your mom said you got bad news tonight. That you'd be on board with The Program once you processed that news." I scooted closer to him and slid my fingers under his chin. I lifted, forcing him to look at me. "Does the bad news have anything to do with Addison?"

Jack's eyes glassed over, but almost as quickly, he blinked the moisture away. "How do you know about her?"

"I saw you with her. At the hospital today." I looked at my watch. 11:17. "I was there. Seth told me about her accident and her injuries." I squeezed his hand tighter. "Why are you telling me to run when you think I could help her? Heal her even?"

He ran his fingers down my face. "I'm scared, Lexi. I've seen your nosebleeds. I've practically felt your headaches each time I've taken your pain away. I know how sick I get when I heal a simple broken arm. I don't want to know what kind of pain and illness you'll suffer after healing something as severe as brain damage. I don't want this for you. Not anymore."

He took a deep breath and continued. "When I first met you, I thought I could convince you that our genetic makeup was a good thing. That we could use what Sandra did to us for good, but I realize now that I'm the naïve one. You have to go. I won't be responsible for forcing you to do something that goes against what you have grown to believe. And I don't want anything happening to you."

Jack's eyes pleaded with me. My heart broke at the prospect of leaving him behind to bear the consequences of Sandra's experiment alone. "Come with me. Please, Jack. I can't do this alone."

He grabbed one of my hands and cradled it in his. "I can't," he whispered. "I promised Cathy."

"What do you mean? You don't owe her anything."

"Yes, I do. They planned to take Addison off life support Sunday unless I agreed to stay here at Wellington. I owe Addison. There has to be another way to heal her."

Cathy DeWeese was a monster. "Then I'll stay, too. I'll do this for you. I'll heal Addison, then we'll both run. Together." What was I saying? Could I do this and live with the consequences? What if I failed and did Addison more harm?

"No!" He ran a hand through his hair. "Don't you get it? I don't want you to stay. You can't heal Addison at the cost of your own life."

"What are you saying?" I didn't understand. "Healing someone might make me sick, but I'll get over it. Like you do."

"I almost died when I healed too much too fast. I refuse to take that chance with you." The anguish on Jack's face about did me in.

"Whether I stay or not, heal or not, is my choice."

"Yes it is," he breathed. "But you'd be making a mistake on both accounts."

"Your mom thinks I'll stay and, in her words, 'fall in line' because..." Heat crept across my face.

"Of me."

Yes, because of you. I wasn't sure Cathy was wrong.

I love hearing your voice inside my head. You and I are connected in a way that we can never share with Cathy or anyone. They would use it against us.

They already are. I leaned my forehead against his.

We stayed there for several minutes. There had to be a way out for both of us.

"Do you have a set of all this?" I gestured to the documents between us.

"Yes. My father made a set for us both."

"Your father?"

"Yes. I don't fully understand it all, but apparently, he had no idea that Cathy was involved with The Program until recently. Your dad brought much of this to light, and he's had his investigator looking into Cathy's background."

Suddenly, a light flashed over us. We jerked our heads, looked out the window in the direction of moving lights. Flashlights.

"Get down," Jack pushed my shoulder. We stretched our legs out and lay flat. Jack handed me the corner of a blanket. "Here, take this."

We shook out the dark-colored blanket, spreading it so that it covered our bodies.

Both of us fought to breathe shallow and remain still. *Nightwatchmen, you think?*

Jack curled his fingers around my hand. *Yes.*

You think they're looking for us?

I don't know. Jack rubbed his thumb back and forth across my hand.

Jack, I'm scared. The guard in front of the dorm freaked me out earlier. All I could think about was getting to you.

Minutes passed. Jack peeked from beneath the blanket. After he sat up, he lifted the blanket off me. "Whoever it was is gone." He lay back down on his side, facing me. He cupped my cheek. "I only want you safe. And happy."

I just want you. I swallowed the lump in my throat.

"How did you find out about Addison?"

"Marci texted me Sandra's last known address. It was at the hospital. I was looking for her when I saw you sitting by Addison's bed. Seth stopped me before I found Sandra."

"I've never met Sandra. Seth is very protective of his sister. He has security in place and receives a text or page anytime someone asks about her."

That explained why Seth found me before I found Sandra at the hospital. Why the precautions? I thought back to my conversation with John DeWeese. How Dad discovered she was involved with the IIA. "Why did your father have documents made for us? Why is he willing to help me?"

"I think he was living in some sort of denial up until he saw your picture. He thought all of this had just gone away. Then he discovered you. When he saw Peter Roslin for the first time in eighteen years, he knew he had to tell me the truth. The whole truth."

I wished someone had thought to tell me the whole truth before now. "So what does he hope will happen now?"

"I think he wants to honor your dad's wishes and send you away from here. He'd like your dad's journals though. He thinks your dad was trying to get the truth out before he was killed."

I sat up suddenly. "Crap, that reminds me. I think I know where the journals might be." I dug in my bag and pulled out the puzzle box. "I think the answer is hidden in here somehow."

I showed Jack how one compartment opened. He took the box, twisted and turned it several times looking for another compartment. Finally, I grabbed the box and slammed it into the sidewall of the vehicle, splitting the wood in several places.

Out fell two small pieces of paper, rolled into tiny cylinders. One with a string of letters, numbers, and symbols—*a password*. The other—keystrokes: Ctrl + Alt + *.

"Does this make sense to you?" Jack asked.

"I think so. But I won't know without a computer." I glanced at Jack. For the first time all night, he didn't look fearful or lost, but more... hopeful.

If I could find Dad's journals, maybe I'd find more information about The Program, Sandra, and why Dad was going to remove me from Wellington before I ever started The Program.

I knew one thing for sure. I would not be controlled by Cathy DeWeese.

"We can't go back to the dorms tonight. We have to assume they think we're there, and not give security any reason to suspect otherwise."

I narrowed my eyes. "So, we're going to sleep... where? Here?" I was suddenly shy.

The corners of his lips lifted in a slight grin. "Yes. Don't get any ideas. I'm a man of virtue."

I giggled.

Just like that, Jack's grin evaporated, and his expression looked more serious. *Thank you.*

For what? I cocked my head.

For laughing in spite of all that I've told you tonight. It helps.

I smiled. *Some really smart guy once told me that if I couldn't laugh through some of this shit, I'd cry.*

"Let's get some sleep," he said.

I nodded, then turned and lay, facing away from Jack. He pulled me closer to his body—my back to his chest—and held me. His palm pressed flat against my stomach. His fingers eased just beneath the hem of my shirt, rubbing bare skin. *I'm really going to miss you.*

I closed my eyes, squeezing them until a single tear leaked out the side.

~~~~

A loud noise startled me awake.

My eyes sprang open. Where was I?

Seth's truck. I lay still. Waiting for the mystery sound to happen again.

Jack had a death grip on my waist. I placed my hand over his. His skin was warm and soft.

Then I heard it again. At first, I thought it was the familiar sound of the flick of a lighter, but this sound was different. It didn't sound nearly as loud as when I was still asleep.

Was I awake now, or was I dreaming?
~~~~

I gently removed Jack's arm and sat up. The windows of the SUV were fogged up. But through the fog I saw a soft glow. And then I didn't.

Then it was there again. Each time I heard a click, I saw orange light. Someone played with what looked like fire outside the window.

Jack's breathing remained constant. I tried to match his even breathing to keep from waking him.

Come on out Lexi. I have something to show you. You need to know the truth.

Truth. I knew that voice. Who was it? Definitely a boy. The window glowed orange again, like something was on fire outside, and I thought of Dad. And the explosion.

Jack rolled over in his sleep. His face was so peaceful there in the dark. I thought of all that he'd brought me last night—the passport, money, all the documents I needed to go to college and fade into a normal college kid's life.

Oh, how I wanted to do exactly that. Escape the messed up life I had here at Wellington and run from whatever Cathy and Dr. Wellington had planned.

I leaned over and kissed him on the cheek. My lips lingered a few seconds while I memorized his scent. *Whatever happens, remember, I did it all for you.*

Grabbing my backpack, I climbed over the seat and out the door.

THIRTY

I followed the figure through the dark, away from the parking lot. He clicked a flashlight on and off, producing the same clicking sound that woke me moments before.

The cool moisture of the morning dew evaporated, lifting with it the smells of grass and pavement. The soft glow of sunshine appeared on the horizon just beyond the administration buildings. It was early. The time of day I usually got up.

But why? I was supposed to be somewhere else. Where?

Why couldn't I see this boy's face? "Hey!" I reached for him, but missed. "Where are we going?" Why was I following him? He promised truth.

We followed the sidewalk around the side of the library and approached a building I knew well. The infirmary. Was I sick? I touched my fingers to my temple. My head didn't hurt. Though my mind seemed a little fuzzy.

I wiggled my fingers in front of my face. My arm wasn't broken.

I stopped walking, considered a broken arm, and thought of Jack.

Jack had fixed my arm.

I raised my head and stared at the figure in front of me. "Come on Lexi. Just a little further. I can answer all of your questions."

"Who are you?"

He tilted his head to one side. "You know who I am. I'm your friend."

Lexi! Where are you? Another voice entered my head.

Jack? I'm in front of the infirmary with... my friend. Jack, I think something's wrong. My stomach tightened. I stared at the figure. His eyes came into focus, then disappeared again. He was supposed to give me truth. That's why I was here.

Lexi, listen to me. Someone's inside your head. You need to wake up. Block them out. Block them out, Lexi. Jack sounded panicked.

Block them out? I can do that. Jack taught me how. I pushed back along the edges of my mind. Reality swirled with my dreams and mixed with my nightmares.

Lexi, can you still hear me? I'm coming.

The figure reached for me. My internal alarm sounded, and a small voice told me not to let him touch me. I jumped back and rubbed my arms from my elbows to my shoulders in a hug. "Who are you?"

"I just want to show you the truth. I know you have a power they want. You could cure your grandmother and help so many others in this world. Take away so much pain on this earth. Wouldn't you like that? Your grandmother would recognize you, and she would no longer feel any pain."

"I'd like that," I whispered.

"Jack wants that, too, Lexi."

"Jack?"

"You and he are a team. Together, you could heal and comfort. You'd live a life of wealth and happily-ever-after."

"I don't care about wealth."

"But you love your grandmother. You don't want to see her hurt, do you?"

"Of course not." Was he threatening me?

"And you love Jack." I nodded. I did love him. "And Jack loves you. He needs you, Lexi. That little girl will die without you. Accept who you are, and you'll be with Jack forever."

"But I don't know if I can help Addison."

"Of course you can. You were created to do so. Jack will try to push you away, but you were made to help people just like Addison and your grandmother. Don't let Jack send you away. He doesn't have that right."

I wanted to help others, didn't I? That's why I wanted to become a doctor.

My gram had suffered from Alzheimer's for the past six years. She'd stopped recognizing me altogether five years ago. Oh, what I would give for even one more conversation with her. To let her know I loved her and that I would live my life to honor her and Dad. To take her pain away.

Would that be wrong? I was so confused. Would that infringe on God's will?

"Lexi!" I felt pressure on both arms. My head bobbled back and forth. Someone shook me, interrupting me from my thoughts. "Lexi, wake up."

The figure disappeared and in his place was Jack. "Jack?"

"It happened again. You were sleepwalking."

I looked around. "But someone was here with me."

"No one was here."

"But..." I stared at the intensity of Jack's blue eyes.

"What did this person say?" Jack's hands continued to rub my arms.

"He said that I needed to accept who I was." I searched Jack's face for the guidance I needed, but he didn't have the answers. Only I could decide what to do next. I knew exactly what that was.

He smoothed the hair on either side of my head. "You said it was a man?"

I tried to picture the figure. "I think so. I thought I recognized the voice and the eyes, but..." I gave my head a little shake. "Everything's so unclear."

Jack gazed intently at me. "You have to go." He reached in the satchel draped across his body and thrust a small bag into my chest, forcing me to take hold. "Take these documents. Keep them close. And tell no one."

"Jack, no. I can't run. And there's no way I'm leaving without telling Danielle."

"You have to. What can I do to make you understand?" He ran his hands through his hair, squeezing his eyes tight. When his eyes returned to me, he spoke in a low, husky voice. "Lexi, someone has already tried to kill you twice. If you refuse to do what they want, they'll try again. And if they succeed..." His voice cracked. He slid his hand around me, settled it into the small of my back, and brought my body flush with his. "I don't know what I'd do if something happened to you." He kissed the top of my head.

"If that's true, how can you push me away?" I thought of the figure's words, *"Don't let Jack send you away."*

He released me, held me at arms' length. "You think I'd put you in danger just to keep you close? That would make me one selfish jerk."

I knew in that moment what I had to do. "What now?" I asked.

He glanced at his watch. "You have practice. You'll only be a few minutes late, but you better hurry."

I raised a brow. "You want me to go to practice?"

"I want you to go about business as usual. Act normal."

"Normal," I repeated, narrowing my gaze. The last person who instructed me to go about my routine died in a car explosion.

"Yes, and I'll see you at the gala tonight."

"Tonight? And that's it?" Dread surged through my voice. "You'll see me at the gala, and then send me on my merry way?"

"This is for your own good, Lexi. I won't let them get to you." He pushed a loose strand of hair behind my ear. "I'll do whatever it takes."

Uninvited tears surfaced. This was what I had wanted, right? To get away from this school. To live a normal life. Become a doctor and help people with the love, kindness and the type of medical care they teach in medical schools.

I didn't want the kind of life Dad had. The kind that played with human life by trial and error. Often error.

Jack's eyes stared into mine, looking for reassurance that I'd do what he proposed.

"I'll see you tonight," I said, deflated.

The back of his hand brushed my cheek. He slid his hand around to the back of my neck and leaned in. He tilted his head. His lips touched mine softly at first then he pressed harder, taking from me like it was his last chance. I felt the effects of the kiss everywhere. A surge of energy started at his touch to my neck and traveled all the way to my toes.

When he released me, he kept eye contact and his lips curled into a slow smile. "We both know Dani will ask, so I'd like to know if you'll be my date tonight?"

A tear streamed down my face. Jack wiped it away with his thumb. I nodded. Anything else and I'd lose the courage to do what I had to do next.

With another quick kiss, Jack turned and walked off toward the boys' dorms. I took off in the direction of the aquatic center.

Before I entered the building, I pulled out my cell phone and called Seth. "It's time I learned how this power of mine works... I'll figure out how to get in and out of Wellington unnoticed. Just come get me."

THIRTY-ONE

"How exactly does the ability work?" I asked.

Gram sat up in her wheelchair knitting by the window. Seth stood by the door while I knelt beside her. She smiled, giving me that look I remembered getting every day after school when I was younger.

I placed a hand on her forearm.

"In theory," Seth began, "you have to be able to imagine the injury or the disease. In this case, the diseased brain."

"Like I did when we were here before."

He nodded. "And you have to know what her brain would look like if it were normal. In simplistic terms, you would use your mind to move and massage the parts of the brain needing healing."

I sat in a chair and leaned my elbows into my knees. "So, basically, I have to have knowledge of the disease, much like that of a doctor." I leaned my face into my hands and rubbed. This was hopeless. I was no doctor.

"Yes and no." Seth moved further into the room and stood closer to me. "You have much of the knowledge that you need. You took the classes. Eventually, you'll go to medical school and know even more. But..."

I lifted my head when his voice trailed off. "Go on."

Across the room, Seth flipped through Gram's chart. "This is not about cutting a person's brain open and doing surgery." He looked up from the chart and focused on me. "You were created for this. You have been given a gift of healing."

His words slid down my back like ice cubes, chilling my very soul. "A gift," I whispered. Could I turn my back on a gift? Wasn't I obligated to learn and appreciate the gifts I'm blessed with in life?

This didn't feel like a gift to me. More like a curse. What if I failed?

Concern etched lines across his forehead as he continued to flip through Gram's chart.

"What is it?" I stood and walked closer.

"Do you know the full extent of your grandmother's health conditions?"

"You mean the Alzheimer's?"

"It's more than that, Lexi."

I raised both brows, urging Seth to continue.

"Your grandmother has an inoperable cancer, and she and your father decided she would not undergo other treatments."

"What?" I grabbed the chart from him, but I had no idea how to read the dang thing. "Why would my father not urge Gram to get the treatment she needed?"

"She has a very specific living will in here. She doesn't want to be treated. Just to be kept comfortable and pain free, if possible."

I backed away from him. Leaned against the wall and bent over at the waist. So even if I wanted to cure Gram, to have her recognize me one last time before I was out of her life forever, I couldn't. "So I won't be able to help her? Not even a little?"

Gram's knitting needle clattered to the floor.

I rushed to her side, picked up her needle and placed it gently in her shaky hand. "I am so sorry, Gram, I didn't know how to help you sooner." If I'd only known. I sucked in an uneven breath.

"We don't know if you even could have helped her, Lexi." Seth's voice startled me. He stood close. "We don't know what you can do. Or at what age your ability would have developed. The fact that I had to show you how to see her brain tells me that you might not be ready yet. Those pills you were taking may take a while longer to wear off. Besides, a condition like Alzheimer's is tricky. There's a lot to consider with a disease like this."

I spoke without looking at Seth. "What about Addison? You don't think I could help her, either?"

"I didn't say that."

"What are you saying?"

"Why are we even talking about this? Aren't you planning to run away tonight?"

I stared at my grandmother's facial features. She was beautiful. Each hard line leading away from her eyes represented a life well-lived. Every laugh line along her lips represented a decade of happy memories.

She had devoted so much of her life to raising me. Made me self-sufficient. Showed me how to help others. How to love.

What did I have to show for it? What would be left of my life after tonight? Another new name. A new high school transcript. Passport. License. A new me.

Would I be different, act different with a new name? Would I regret not helping those I loved? Would I regret leaving Jack behind?

He loved me. I saw it in his eyes the night of our very first date.

I closed my eyes and bowed my head onto the arm of Gram's wheelchair. "Tell me what to do."

"Jack thinks you should leave," Seth answered, though I wasn't asking him. "I can't say as I disagree with him. It's probably for the best."

"Why are you helping me? Jack said you would drive me to the bus station."

"Why wouldn't I?"

"I just don't get it."

"You don't need to." Seth walked to the window. He kept his back to me. "I found Jack for one reason. The same reason I'm glad I found you. To give you the chance to know why you were created and let you choose what you wanted to do with it."

"And you're willing to just let me walk away." Run, more like it. "Will people look for me if I run?"

Seth turned. His eyes bore into mine. "There's no doubt in my mind they'll look for you and find you eventually. You'll need to always be moving. Always running."

I didn't want to hear any more. "Can I have a moment alone with my grandmother before you take me back to Wellington?"

~~~~

I entered the dorm room like a zombie. Danielle was digging through her closet, thrilled to be getting all dolled up for her debut into the art world, even if it was a stupid school gala.

Where'd you go?
~~~~

Jack's voice inside my head sounded nervous. *I had to say goodbye to Gram.*

That's good. I'm glad.

I could almost hear relief in Jack's thoughts. He didn't even ask how I got to the nursing home and back. He probably knew.

Can you meet me before the art showing? he asked. *I want to be alone with you before... Before the dance.*

He wanted to say good-bye. I swallowed hard. I couldn't think about that right now.

"Lexi, are you even listening to me?" Danielle shook two dresses in front of me. "Which one?"

I crossed an arm across my chest and cupped my chin with the opposite hand. The dress on the right was a pale pink dress, strapless, with a pleated skirt. Simple. Elegant. On the left hung a black sheath dress. Tiny rhinestones decorated the straps.

Lexi? Did you hear me?

Yes, sorry. I'll meet you. Where? The stable?

No, on the roof. Twenty minutes.

Okay.

"Is something wrong?" Lexi dropped the dresses to her side. "You hate them both."

"No. Of course not. They're both lovely. One says, 'I'm a sweet high school girl going off to prom with a guy who has one thing on his mind.' The other screams sophistication and 'I'm an artist going to my first art show'."

"Well, that was easy. Basic black it is."

"Oh, honey. There's nothing basic about that gorgeous dress."

"You think so? You like it?" she asked as she slid it over her long, skinny legs—legs I'd donate a kidney for.

I had never heard such a lack of confidence from my roommate. "Of course. It's beautiful. And perfect for you."

"Is the internet back up?" I asked, glancing at my clock. Did I even have time to run to the library?

"Don't know, but Bree left her computer so that I could finish the project we were working on. She's got a card that is working somehow."

"Really? Do you think she'd mind if I looked something up?" Who was I kidding? Of course she'd mind. But this was the first chance I'd gotten to test my theory of the whereabouts of the journals.

The fact that the Wi-Fi was still down was more than a little worrisome. Not to mention the cell towers that seemed to be going in and out of service.

"Yes, but she's not here." Dani lifted the computer from the bed and handed it to me. "Password's SWIM2016."

I lifted a brow. "The next summer Olympics?" Dani nodded. I sat the computer on my desk and booted it up.

Dani leaned into her dresser mirror. "Okay, I think I'm ready. I'll see you there?"

"I'm right behind you. I just gotta check something on the internet." I stood and gave my roommate a tight hug. "I love you like a sister, you know that, right?"

She hugged me back, then held me at arm's length. "Hey. You okay?"

I gave a weak nod. "Yep. Now, go on. Your date's never going to be the same after he sees you."

She gave me one last concerned look, before grabbing a wristlet, big enough for a key and a tube of lipstick.

I turned my attention back to Bree's computer. I brought up the website and stared at the tiny starfish in the bottom right-hand corner. I ran the pointer over the icon verifying there was no underlying link. Then, using the knowledge my dad had taught me, I left the pointer hovering over the starfish and pressed Ctrl + Alt + *.

As I my finger pushed down on the asterisk, the pointer changed to a small hand, indicating a link was, in fact, hidden beneath the small picture. I clicked on it, and suddenly the website of pictures and personal facts disappeared, and in its place appeared a login screen.

I stared at the gray screen. I tried my name and Dad's name every which way along with the password I found inside the puzzle box. Nothing.

I absentmindedly rubbed the charm and the key hanging around my neck. I was certain that the password was correct. It was so difficult to obtain. It had to be right.

But what would Dad choose for a username?

I rubbed the starfish back and forth along my lips. That's when it came to me. My father's personal email address—he only used it for communication with me.

Mylittlestarfish@gmail.com, after the nickname he gave me when I was a little girl.

I typed it into the username field—mylittlestarfish. Then the password.

The screen faded to black in front of me. A moment later, various icons flashed upon the screen—several PDF documents, word documents, and an excel spreadsheet—all labeled.

I didn't have time to look through every document. I pulled up my online email account and emailed each of the documents to myself so that I could pull them up on my phone later.

I double clicked on the PDF titled "Journals 1988-1994"—a six-hundred-twenty-four-page document. I glanced at my watch. I didn't have time. But I had found them. My father's journals that everyone wanted so badly.

Another PDF was titled "Journals 1995-2010". And still another titled "Journals 2011-". The third one had no end date.

An excel spreadsheet titled "Survivors" caught my eye. I double clicked. The columns were labeled: Name, Known aliases, Last known address, Original, Genes manipulated, Known abilities.

What was this? Most of the names were filled in. But many fields for address or known abilities were blank.

I looked up and stared at a picture on a shelf above me of Gram, dad and me from when I first came to Wellington. We'd changed my name. This was supposed to be a safe place for me. Dad always said the name change was to protect me because he participated in controversial medical research, but that wasn't true.

He was hiding me. While searching for others like me. Did he know about Jack?

I scrolled through the names.

There must be over a hundred names.

I found Jack. Last known address: California. Known abilities: General healing, injuries, pain management.

Why were there so many listed here? Including mine, Sarah Alexandra Roslin.

As I scrolled through the list, I began to notice something in common—the last known address for several on the list.

Wellington Boarding School.

Others were blank.

I recognized many of the names. Lower classmen, mostly. Sixth, seventh and some eighth graders.

At the bottom of the spreadsheet was a second tab: Test Group.

That tab brought up the same information as the first, but only seven names were listed: Jack DeWeese, Sarah Roslin, Kyle Jones, Briana Howard and three names I didn't recognize.

I stared at the screen, paralyzed. My heart beat wildly out-of-control. If I didn't get a handle on my breathing soon I would pass out.

Where are you? Jack's thought startled me.

Jack.

I'm waiting.

I closed my mind off from him. Think, Lexi. I closed the spreadsheet. Returned to the main page where I found another icon titled, Letter to Lexi.

Jack, I'm sorry. I'll have to meet you at the gala.

What's wrong?

Nothing. I tried to keep my thoughts controlled. Like nothing was wrong. *I'm just having trouble picking out the right shoes.*

I opened the letter. My hands shook, and my palms turned into a cold, clammy mess. These would be the last words my father had written to me.

Dearest Lexi:

If you are reading this letter, I waited too long to tell you the truth and to get you out of Wellington. I'm sorry. I wanted to explain your creation to you myself. However, I thought it was best to wait until you were of an age to make your own important decisions. I should have trusted you with the truth sooner.

I'm assuming that you know by now that you are the nearly identical clone of Sandra Whitmeyer. I have just gotten back in touch with Dr. John DeWeese, as you know, and I hope that he will help you understand why I did what I did and the reality that you must live with now.

If you are reading this, I am most likely dead. My only regret is that I didn't make you safe sooner. If I am dead, you are in danger. Trust no one completely, Sarah.

Dr. Roger Wellington is the mastermind behind The Program. This "program" is in the early stages of development and was initially designed to teach you about who you are and the talents you were given before you were born. I had hoped to find the others like you before now. At the time I'm writing this letter, there are two other original clones at Wellington with you. Kyle Jones and Briana Howard. And, of course, you now know Jack DeWeese.

Though I never intended for Sandra's experiment to go as far as it did, I can't change the outcome. I have never regretted that you are my daughter. I love you, Sarah. But now, if you are to live the life you were meant to live, you must stand strong and face the facts laid out within this website.

Hidden in this website is my research and all the evidence I have gathered to prove that Sandra Whitmeyer had always intended for the cloned embryos to become actual human beings. She was secretly funded by the International Intelligence Agency, and she planted evidence to incriminate the rest of us in her plan. When the lab went up in flames, so did her plan.

However, evidence shows that the IIA did not stop. Neither did Sandra. Besides the original test group, the IIA continued to clone and genetically alter embryos. You will find more information regarding this in the files. Be careful who you share this information with.

Wellington Boarding School was supposed to be a safe haven for the clones we found over the years. And a school where you could obtain the education you need to go on to college and medical school, but also a school where you could learn the medical knowledge necessary to enhance the powers you were given at birth.

I do not know how long Wellington will be safe for you and the others. That is why I have equipped a safe house for you. The key I sent you is the key to that house. Everything you could need is secure within that house. If you have to run, RUN! You know where this house is.

I'm sorry, Sarah. My hope was to tell you everything by the time you turned eighteen, so that you would be ready to face the reality of your gifts, and with the help of a college education and medical school, you would use your gifts for good.

Your mother and I are very proud of the woman you have become.

Love,

Dad

I stared at the computer screen. The words blurred in front of me. I lost all feeling in my fingers and hands.

Trust no one. A tear fell from one eye, and I shoved it away with one violent swipe of my palm.

A safe house. Where?

And my mother? Dad was in contact with my mother?

"Lexi."

I jumped to my feet, knocking my chair over. Jack stood in the doorway.

"What's wrong?" His voice was low, hesitant.

Trust no one. I studied Jack's face while keeping my thoughts shut completely off from him. I felt his mind knocking on the barrier I erected. I could trust him, couldn't I? I didn't know anymore.

He stepped toward me. "What is it? Why aren't you dressed for the gala?"

"I..." I looked around the room. For what? I had no idea.

Jack glanced at the computer. The letter from Dad was still up on the screen. I quickly punched the "x" at the top of the screen. Closed out of the letter and the website, then closed the laptop.

"What's got you so freaked out?" He closed the distance between us. He placed his hands on either side of my face and tilted my head back to look directly in my eyes. "Whatever it is... just tell me. I can't help you unless I know."

The fear in his eyes sent a chill down my spine. I searched my heart. My eyes darted back and forth between his. My father's words played over and over.

But then I saw it. His eyes softened. What I thought was fear of me knowing the truth was fear for me. "You love me," I whispered.

"Unconditionally. I'll do anything for you. You must know that."

I knew his words were true. He already knew almost everything in the letter from Dad. Jack was willing to sacrifice his life to help me escape. He was willing to sacrifice his own safety in the miniscule hope that he might still save a young girl's life.

Jack lowered his head closer, his lips hovering over mine. His breath warmed against my face. I hungered for his kiss, and when his lips pressed against mine, I felt the familiar tingling in my stomach.

His hand roamed up the back of my shirt. The warmth of his palm pressed against my bare skin, pushing my body against his. I slid my fingers into his hair. Desire erupted between us.

When we were both out of breath, he released me. But only a little. Our heads remained millimeters apart. Our chests rose and fell at a heavy, synchronized rate.

"I love you," I finally said.

"I know." He smiled, but it didn't reach his eyes. "And I love you."

How would I ever say good-bye to him? But how could I possibly stay?

THIRTY-TWO

Jack and I stood in the corner of the school's atrium watching the crowd thicken for the art showing and gala.

His fingers roamed beneath my long hair and massaged the nape of my neck. I wore a long, flowing dress. The fabric formed a "v" in the back, giving Jack plenty of bare skin to touch. His lips grazed my ear as he whispered to me. "I'm not going to stop touching you tonight."

I took in a sharp breath, committing his scent to memory.

The gala was the type of event that drew the school's extensive supporters and trustees for a night of art, cocktails and fun. A silent auction of the art at the end typically raised a ton of money for the school and for the University of Kentucky Children's Hospital, a charity chosen by the students of Wellington.

Seth Whitmeyer sipped punch while speaking with Dean Fisher and Coach Williams across from us.

Oh, what I would give to know what they are talking about.

Jack grazed my neck with his fingers as he brushed my hair to the side. *I'd like to know what you are thinking. I wish I'd never taught you how to shut your thoughts off to me.*

I looked back at him. *We probably would not be standing here like this if you hadn't.*

Good point.

I won't say good-bye to you. I closed my eyes briefly.

You don't have to. It's not good-bye. It's just see ya later. I will find you when it's safe. Jack's hands squeezed my shoulders. *I will always find you.*

You remember the username and password?

Locked up tight inside my head.

I ran my fingers across my lips, remembering the kiss from earlier. After the kiss, I'd shown Jack everything on the site and made him memorize the password.

Dad had thought of everything, all the way down to creating a secured message board inside the website. I assumed he meant to use it eventually to communicate with me, but now, Jack and I would use it.

I thought back to Dad's warning to trust no one. *Do you think Coach Williams was really hired by my dad to protect me?*

The rest of his story checked out, and Father seemed to think so. For now though, we'll leave him on the "do not trust" list.

Though Seth spoke every so often to the dean and to Coach, his eyes never stopped roaming the room. He sipped from his glass again. Then he looked in our direction, his expression severe, before turning toward the door.

"Mommy Dearest is here," Jack said close to my ear. "Her fangs appear to be out."

Cathy entered through the main doors. She was dressed in a bright red, tailored suit with a high collar. I chuckled at the vampire reference.

Dani, Briana, and Kyle approached us, playfully arguing about something.

"This is sooo boring," Danielle said. "We should go see the art, so we can hit the roof once the adults succumb to their adult ways."

"Adult ways?" I raised a brow.

"You know, spiking their punch and shutting us kids out of their stuffy conversations." Danielle smiled. "Besides, I want to see the nude you talked Ms. Waters into featuring."

"How'd you manage a nude, Lexi?" Kyle asked. He hooked his thumbs in his belt loops. "Waters is a major conservative. I heard it was crazy impossible to even get her to allow the models to reveal much skin."

Briana slapped Kyle playfully. "The imagination is an amazing tool." She tilted her head side to side. "I mean... I've seen *you* in a Speedo."

Everyone laughed.

While the others started toward the maze of exhibits, I scrutinized the room again. Something the size of a double bacon cheeseburger sat uneasily in the pit of my stomach.

"Shall we?" Jack stuck out his arm for me. "I'm dying to see the nude everyone's talking about. How *did* you manage to get a nude entered into the exhibit?"

"The mind is a powerful thing, my friend."

Jack raised a fist to his chest. "Oh, you wound me, Miss Matthews. Surely by now we're more than friends."

"Stop. You know we are."

"Let's go see the art."

We walked around the maze of temporary walls filled with art, admiring the many pieces. Jack said his favorite was the charcoal I did of Cherriana. "You're very talented, you know."

"No. I just like to play around. And since I have zero musical talent, Wellington required me to choose some kind of art."

"Her eyes are so sad."

I stared at Cherriana's big brown eyes and remembered the mood I was in when I drew her. "She's somewhat of a caged animal. Literally and metaphorically." In the charcoal, I drew Cherriana running free in the woods where Jack and I had ridden. "I imagined that even though she was the result of mad scientists, trapped inside a body created by man and not by the will of God, she should run free in the world."

Jack stood behind me and wrapped his arms around my waist. "We'll ride together again. I promise."

I swallowed hard and nodded.

We moved on and found the others standing in front of the nude. Dani cupped her hand over her mouth, whispering something to Bree. They both giggled.

It was killing me not to tell Kyle and them both what I knew about The Program. Jack assured me that he would tell them when he was positive it was safe to do so. He thought having me safe on the outside would insure they had a fighting chance to escape Wellington if it became necessary.

Problem was... I wasn't on the outside yet.

The group of us walked to the next painting. Jack kept his promise by holding my hand as we stared at Danielle's dramatic oil painting of two eyes.

Briana sidled up to me. "I think Danielle has a crush?"

"What do you mean?"

"You don't recognize those eyes?" she asked before walking away without telling me who it was.

I stared longer. The eyes were a beautiful color of amber with specks of blue throughout. Almost black eyebrows tilted inward, causing a "v" in the skin between the eyes. The eyes seemed worried. Determined. Yet warm and sad at the same time.

The eyes were definitely familiar to me. But it was an oil painting for crying out loud.

"What do you think?" Dani stood beside me now.

"The painting is superb," I said. "Who's the model?"

"This is the man I'm going to marry."

I smiled. Jack dropped my hand and whispered in my ear, "I'll be right back." My palm turned cold as air hit the skin Jack had been holding tightly.

Dani analyzed her own painting.

"What do you mean marry?" I asked.

"These are the eyes from my dreams." She folded her arms across her chest. I turned back to the eyes. She continued, "Remember the nightmare? The one where I told you I was in the dark, looking for you?"

"You're telling me this is the guy that wanted you to find me?" I stared into the eyes. It hit me. He was from my dream earlier today. He led me to the infirmary.

Was this the same guy from my nightmares?

"Yeah. I've dreamt about him practically every night since then. Never like that first night, though. He's kind in my dreams now. Never leading me in the dark." She stopped and looked at me. "You think I'm crazy, don't you?"

"No, of course not," I whispered.

Briana and Kyle joined us again, each carrying two glasses of punch and offering Dani and me one.

"Thanks." I sipped slowly while I studied Briana and remembered her words. *I think Danielle has a crush.*

If Briana recognized those eyes, and those eyes are the same as from Dani's nightmare… I shifted my stare from Briana to Kyle. *Oh, God. Kyle. He's been right in front of me all this time.*

Did Kyle try to kill me?

I looked around for Jack. The familiar build of panic bubbled up inside my chest.

"Lexi, you okay?" Kyle touched my elbow.

I jerked my head back toward Kyle, who stared at me. A cocktail of emotions passed over his face—curiosity, concern, anxiety. But the desire to kill me?

Behind him, Cathy DeWeese, Roger Wellington and Seth Whitmeyer walked toward us, admiring artwork along the way. Or pretending to, I suspected.

All at once, they turned toward the four of us. Me, Briana, Danielle, and Kyle. Three of us, part of the original test sample.

Kyle moved closer to me. His lips lifted into a nervous smile. "Something wrong, Lexi?" His expression changed, as recognition must have shown in mine. "You know, don't you?" Alarm coated his whispered words. He moved behind me, placing a firm hand on my waist. "Act normal. Don't let them see the fear all over your face or tonight will go very badly."

Again with the 'act normal' stuff. My hands shook. I tucked them into my armpits. *Jack! Where are you? It was Kyle, Jack. Kyle has been inside my head. He tried to kill me.*

I couldn't breathe. I squirmed against Kyle's hand on my waist. I thought my knees might buckle. Jack didn't respond.

Cathy approached. "Hi, Lexi. Loving the art tonight. Your father never mentioned how talented you are." She tapped her compact purse against her lips. "Oh, and honey," she said. Her term of endearment sent a fit of rage coursing through my blood. "Jack had to leave. Something came up with a dear friend of his. He said to let you know."

Shit! Jack wouldn't have left without telling me. Something's wrong.

"Thanks," I said. "Where's Dr. DeWeese tonight?"

"John had an emergency. He had to leave town unexpectedly."

I redirected my gaze toward Seth, who stood behind Cathy and her brother. He lifted his chin and motioned for me to follow him. How was I supposed to do that without anyone noticing?

"May I have your attention, please?" Dean Fisher's voice sounded over the speaker.

Visitors and students made their way out of the maze of art and back into the main room, where Dean Fisher stood at a podium. I glanced toward the door. Seth had his hand on the door handle.

Jack was nowhere. I took a few steps toward Seth, but Kyle was on me. His fingers wrapped around my wrist. "You can't leave." It was a threat. "Not yet."

I looked down at his wrist then up at the arrogance in his eyes.

"As you all know," the dean began, "we have experienced somewhat of a security breach at Wellington recently. But don't worry," he smiled. He raised his hands to the side like he was giving a Presidential speech. "Our students' safety is our number one concern. Which is why—"

"He's convincing, isn't he?" Kyle whispered in my ear. His breath felt hot on my neck.

Panic threatened to paralyze me. I had to get out of there. I had to find Jack.

My backpack, and only source of tissues, was tucked behind a bush near the parking lot, ready for my quick escape later tonight. I looked around for some napkins. If blood began pouring out of my nose now, I was afraid Kyle would know what I was doing. How much did he know?

"Which is why we have implemented our new and improved security system. I must say, I'm pretty proud of it." Dean chuckled, like this was an everyday speech.

Students began to eye each other, whispering nervously.

"First, the outer perimeter of the school is now protected by an electric fence that will keep potential intruders safely on the outside."

"And us on the inside," Briana said under her breath. She didn't seem to notice the death grip Kyle had on my wrist.

"Secondly," Dean continued. "Students will receive new procedures on how and when they may leave the campus based on agreed-upon parameters with parents and guardians of each student."

"Why do I feel we've suddenly been imprisoned?" Dani asked.

"Because we have," Kyle said so that only I could hear. "You knew this was coming, didn't you, Sarah?"

My body tensed at the sound of my birth name. *Jack, where are you?* I slowly turned my head and looked up at Kyle. "How long have you known?"

"Known what? That your father and his friends created us in test tubes, then redesigned our brains with no consideration for the possible consequences?" His fingers had to be leaving impressions in my skin.

"That's not how it happened. It wasn't Dad."

"Shh. Here comes the best part," he whispered.

"And third," the dean announced. "More students at Wellington will be enrolled into The Program and have access to the most innovative learning available to high school students anywhere." He paused. Whispers echoed through the hall. "That's right. The initial year of The Program was a huge success, and now, thanks to the generous donors and boosters of this school..."

Cathy sipped a glass of champagne at the back of the room, then raised her glass, nodding toward Dr. Wellington.

"...The Program has been relocated to Wellington Boarding School."

"I think we've heard enough." Kyle tugged on my arm, pulling me in the direction of the exit.

Seth no longer stood at the doors.

When we were on the other side of the door, I thought tissue or not, I had to get away from Kyle. *Kyle, I want you to let go of my arm right now. You don't want to hurt me.*

He loosened his grip, but his fingers remained wrapped around my forearm pulling me down the sidewalk. "I know you know where your father's journals are. If we have any hope of surviving what those yahoos have planned, you have to show them to me."

Let go of my wrist! Why wasn't my mindspeaking working?

"And if you have any hope of seeing Jack again—"

"You know where he is?" I yanked my arm and actually broke free this time.

He started to grab me again, but stopped. "I know exactly where he is. Right where you and I will be this time tomorrow if they suspect we won't cooperate—on lockdown."

THIRTY-THREE

With a loose grip on my forearm, Kyle led me to the back of the building where the infirmary was housed, but instead of entering the main floor, we descended the stairs to the basement.

I recognized the long, white hallway immediately though I had never been there.

"I dreamt of this place." No, it wasn't a dream, though, was it?

In the back of my mind, a voice told me I should be running in the opposite direction. Nevertheless, if Kyle knew where Jack was, and he was in trouble, I had to find him.

Kyle faced me. "Welcome to The Program."

I forced my feet to move. "Who are you?"

"Don't be dramatic. I'm still your friend. Let's just say you and I have a lot to learn about each other. And I guess we'll get to, now."

"What do you mean... now?"

"The campus has been secured, Lexi. This," he gestured down the hallway, "is our future. We were genetically altered. Cloned for specific purposes. You know all this, right?" He looked at me like I was dense.

"Yes, but I'm just surprised that you do."

"Roger Wellington is my uncle. Sort of."

I thought about that. "Your uncle. And where are your parents?"

"As you can imagine it's complicated."

"Tell me anyway." My voice came out angry. My hands shook at a 7.9 on the Richter scale. I closed them into fists at my side.

"I am a clone of the man who raised me the first ten years of my life. That man was Uncle Roger's brother. He disappeared, and R.W. moved me here. Opened the school."

"How have you kept this a secret from everyone?"

"What?" His voice escalated. "Does it matter?" He reached for my hand, which I hid behind my back.

"You said you knew where Jack was."

Behind us, the door at the top of the stairs opened and closed with a creak. I jerked my head toward the sound of mumbled voices.

"Come on," Kyle whispered. Not having much of a choice, I followed.

He tried the first door on the right. Locked. As was the door across from it.

"No," he protested. "Why are they locked?" He tried them all.

Finally, the last door on the right was unlocked. He pulled me in after him. I entered and turned immediately to peer out the small window of the door to see the owners of the voices we had heard. The room behind me was mostly dark. It smelled funny. Clinical. Sterile.

Kyle stood close to me. At my back. "They'll be looking for you."

"Who? Cathy and Dr. Wellington?" I asked. If Kyle was the person from my dreams—Smoking Man—then he had tried to kill me. Was he leading me to my death now?

"They want the journals."

I whipped around ready to protest when I noticed we weren't alone. I faced three occupied hospital beds. The room extended beyond two other doors that had been locked. Dim lights above the beds illuminated a small portion of the room. Machines were hooked up to two of the people in the beds. The one I faced first was...

"Jack!" I ran to his side. I placed my hand on his cheek. "Can you hear me? What happened to him?"

"He's fine. Just sedated."

"Sedated? Why?"

"To get him away from you, I suppose."

I ran at Kyle and punched him in his chest. "So help me, Kyle, if you don't stop talking in riddles and tell me what is going on..."

"You'll what?" He grabbed both of my arms and easily lifted my body away from him. "You think you have this all figured out, don't you? You thought Jack would get you out of here, and then you'd what? Change your name? Slip into a whole new life?"

"Why do you care? Why not let me go, Kyle? We were friends."

"We still are. Don't you get it? There is no escape from what we are."

"You tried to kill me," I said, surprisingly calm.

His eyes widened. "Kill you? What are you talking about?"

"I didn't recognize you at first, couldn't make out your face. Your voice didn't sound familiar. But this morning, your eyes came into focus." I paused. Kyle's face was completely unreadable. I looked at Jack out of the corner of my eye. He lay motionless. "When I noticed Dani's painting of your eyes, I knew you were the one inside her head the other night, inside my head this morning, and you tried to drown me."

Kyle's eyes widened. "I looked for you by getting inside Dani's head. That is true. I also tried to show you this place this morning." He gestured around the room with his hand. "But Jack showed up and woke you. I even got inside your dream the night you father was killed. I tried to show you this place then and the fact that Jack knew about it. But drown you? Why would I try to kill you?"

I thought back to the dream the night of my father's death. Jack's hand in mine. He'd led me down the long, white hallway. I looked up at Kyle. "You haven't been trying to kill me?"

"Of course not," Kyle said.

"If you're telling me the truth, then someone else is inside my head." Another altered clone? Did I even believe Kyle? I wanted to.

My mind raced through each occasion when someone had been inside my head. It wasn't always inside a dream. Sometimes, I started out fully awake. I was awake when I dove into that pool. I just didn't have control of my own mind and body.

"*If* I'm telling the truth... Lexi, you have to believe me. We're in this together. I dragged you down here for one purpose."

"And what purpose would that be?" I asked, defensively.

"I need you. We need each other." He ran his hand through his hair. "There are consequences to our powers. Sandra has been working on ways to fix that." Kyle glanced past me, over my shoulder.

"Consequences. To entering peoples' dreams?" I couldn't help but wonder if Kyle had another power. Did he know if he did?

"I suffered temporary blindness every time I got inside your dreams."

"And every time you slip inside Dani's dreams?" I asked.

Kyle's face softened. His cheeks drooped at the mention of Dani. "I don't always lose my sight when I'm with her. I'm learning to understand my limits. I'm learning control."

"Kyle, we have to find Dani. We can all get out of here."

"Don't you get it? There is no escape." A distant look passed over him before his focus returned to me. "We can only learn what The Program is meant to teach us. Besides, Dani isn't in trouble. She's not one of us."

Before I could respond, the door opened behind me. I whipped around. It was Seth. His black bow tie hung loose, untied around his neck. "Well, this is convenient." He unbuttoned his sleeves and, one-at-a-time, rolled them up to his elbows.

Kyle sat in a chair beside Jack. Rubbed his hands across his face. He showed no surprise at Seth's entrance.

I looked anxiously at Seth, then at Jack. *Jack! Please wake up.*

"Well, it seems Kyle is one step ahead of me. Did he show you around?"

I studied Seth. Was he here to help me escape? Could I even run and leave my friends to this craziness? There was no way I was leaving Jack like this. His eyelashes didn't even twitch. Not a single movement. Thankfully, I could see the rise and fall of his chest.

"No?" Seth answered his own question. My palms were a sweaty mess. "Well, allow me. This is the new location of The Program. This is where you will learn more about your abilities." Seth stepped closer to me. "Starting tonight."

Tonight?

He gestured with his hand toward the next bed. "Lexi, meet Addison. She's like a sister to your beloved Jack. She's the reason he would never have left with you tonight. The fact that he feels responsible for her predicament... well... just proves how soft he is." Seth seemed to think about that a second.

Addison lay lifeless like Jack. Long, jet-black hair draped across her pillow. She had the most flawless skin I'd ever seen. The machines beside her were lit up like Christmas trees, but remained silent.

Seth continued past Addison to the next bed. "And this is my beloved sister." He leaned down and kissed the infamous Dr. Sandra Whitmeyer on the forehead.

I stared at the third lifeless body. I moved closer. *How was this possible?* I was finally seeing Sandra with my own eyes, but I still couldn't believe what I saw.

It was me, only thirty years into the future. She was lying in a bed with a tube down her throat. "What's wrong with her?" I reached a shaky hand to the end of the bed, steadying myself.

"Coma," Seth said.

"For how long?"

"Can we just get on with this?" Kyle jumped up from his chair and crossed the room.

No reaction registered on Seth's face from Kyle's outburst.

"Get on with what?"

"Lexi," Seth began slowly. "I promised Jack I would help you escape, but that was when my sister was still safely at the UK Hospital. Cathy moved Addison and Sandra late this afternoon. I'm afraid I need you here. You're the only one who can help her."

"Why did Cathy move them?"

Seth's face darkened several shades of red. "Because she could. Because she has control over her brother. And because she wants complete control over me, Jack, and The Program."

The thickness in my chest was back. The crazed look in Seth's eye had me digging the heel of my hand into the spot over my heart. I glanced from Sandra to Addison to Jack, and then I counted the number of steps to the door. I would never make it. Seth and Kyle were both twice my size.

But I was fast. I could come back for Jack.

And Danielle and the others.

"If you're thinking about running, let me assure you there are guards crawling all over this campus, and there is no way you're getting past the electric fence."

I swayed on my feet, suddenly lightheaded. "What do you want from me?" I asked, deflated.

Seth's lips lifted. "That's my girl." He walked over to stand by his sister, glancing over his shoulder at a dark, glass window at the far side of the room. A one-way window, maybe? "Okay, I want you to stand there." He pointed to the opposite side of the bed.

I positioned myself between Sandra and Addison. Kyle backed up against the opposite wall, watching while chewing on a hangnail.

I stared down at the older version of myself and swallowed hard against the urge to vomit. "You want me to heal her," I whispered.

Seth stared at me, but stayed silent. Kyle shifted, appearing uneasy.

"I don't even know what's wrong with her."

"She tried to alter her genetic make-up by injecting stem cells into her own brain."

My mouth fell open.

"Something went wrong." Seth stared down at his sister's face. I tried to imagine the emotion he felt for her. Admiration, maybe. Or did he feel responsible for her? "I think you'll be able to see the damage to her brain."

"Why would I heal her?"

Seth's eyes lifted to meet mine. "Because you have no choice." He looked nervously at the dark window again. "And because she has the knowledge to help all of you with the unintended consequences of your powers."

Did I care about that? I wasn't all that sure we should use these powers to begin with. Especially since I had a super bad feeling about The Program and the intentions of Cathy DeWeese and Dr. Wellington. Dad hadn't mentioned Cathy's involvement.

Just when I thought the situation couldn't get worse, the far door opened, and in walked Cathy and Dr. Wellington. "What's taking so long?" Cathy asked. She glided over to a wall of cabinets, still dressed in a bright red suit.

"Well, Lexi, I guess you have a lot of questions," Dr. Wellington said.

I remained silent, not taking my eyes from Cathy who pulled several items out of a cabinet. She proceeded to place a needle on the end of a syringe, then tipped a small glass bottle upside down. After sticking the needle into the bottle, she extracted the clear liquid.

Dr. Wellington didn't seem to care that I ignored him. Cathy turned and walked toward me.

Don't come any closer, Cathy. I screamed inside my head. Then I thought to Jack. *Wake up!*

Blood immediately began trickling out of my nose. I leaned over and wiped it on Sandra's bed sheet, leaving a disgusting streak of dark red.

"Now, let's see what you can do. We don't have any more time."

What was that supposed to mean? "I guess we're going to skip over the formality of discussing why I no longer think you have my best interests in mind," I said. "You know. As the wife to my legal guardian."

Cathy's lips slowly stretched across her face in a smile that would chill sand in an African desert. "I guess some personality traits did survive the cloning process. You have a smart mouth just like Sandra."

My eyes followed the syringe she waved through the air. "Exactly what do you hope to accomplish tonight? I'm obviously not going anywhere." I gestured toward Dr. Wellington standing guard by one door and Kyle standing at the other.

"Seth says you now understand your power. Tonight, we all get to witness a miracle as you bring Sandra out of her coma."

"I thought you hated Sandra. Why would you have me do this?"

"Because before she slipped into this state, she discovered a way to stop some of the side effects of your... abilities."

"So? What exactly is going on here? What do you hope will come of our *abilities*?"

"You're just as dramatic as Sandra. Always needing to know every last fact before making one single decision." She took a step toward me. "We're not bad people, Lexi. We just want to help you use your gifts... for good."

Somehow, I doubted that. Or maybe Cathy's and my definitions of "gifts" and "good" were different. "If The Program is meant to help and you mean us no harm, then why all the added security? And what's in the syringe?"

Cathy's smile grew. "All in good time. You'll learn everything you need to know, and you'll see that we're actually the good guys."

Are you freaking kidding me with this? I wanted to scream. Instead, I kept my face emotionless and my voice even. "What if I fail?" Did I really want to know the answer to that?

Again, she smiled and a chill moved through me. "Let's not find out." She waved the syringe at Kyle. "Now stand next to her and let's see what she can do."

Kyle approached me with an apology in his eyes.

"Why are you helping her?"

Kyle looked nervously at his uncle and Cathy. "I have to. I have to know what Sandra created me to do. And I need her to take away my blindness."

He made a move.

I held up my hand to stop him. My eyes drifted to where Jack lay, defenseless. "No, I'll do it. Whatever you want." A small part of me died inside.

THIRTY-FOUR

I backed up so I could see all three beds. Seth shifted on his feet. Anticipation flitted across his face. The other three watched Sandra for the slightest change.

I closed my eyes and imagined Sandra's brain. I immediately saw neurotransmitters, neurons and receptors at work. In biology class, we had discussed how the sleep aid Ambien works on our brains—by binding to certain receptors and thereby altering how our brain processes sleep. This had to be how any drug designed to make us sleep or alter our brain activity worked, right?

Except in Sandra's head, electrical impulses fired from neuron to neuron through the chemical synapses. Her brain looked like the Fourth of July. Something was wrong though. Fluid pooled in small quantities in various areas of the brain. It was almost as if her brain activity was no longer communicating with the rest of her body.

I couldn't believe it. I actually saw the spots that needed repair—the tiny holes causing the leaking of cerebral fluid in the brain, thereby causing her state of unconsciousness. What would happen when I healed Sandra Whitmeyer, the mastermind behind an army of cloned healers? Was I destined for imprisonment at Wellington? A life of being forced to play God for the mad scientists who killed my father?

Were Cathy, Dr. Wellington, Seth and Sandra all conspiring with the IIA to control the clones who were just beginning to learn about their abilities? Would I let them control me?

No, thank you.

I could hear Cathy tapping the syringe against her palm. What would she do to me if I failed? Could I live with myself if I succeeded?

I turned my attention to Jack, picturing his brain in my head. It was perfect. Just like a picture from a textbook. Except, by some miracle, I could see a substance binding itself to the receptors of many of the neurotransmitters. Like Ambien, only stronger.

A chill started at the base of my neck and traveled like an avalanche down my spine. I needed this boy lying in that bed. He had become so important to me. A lifeline. What would he tell me to do right now? My stomach clenched.

Think, Lexi.

Next, I pulled up the image of Addison's brain. It wasn't her brain that captured my attention, but the condition of her skull. A large, disfigured circle on the back of it was a different color from the rest of the skull. Like it had been replaced with artificial matter.

Jack. He had healed her other injuries—the skull, maybe—but not the brain. That was what Seth had told me. Addison's brain was nothing like the perfection I had just seen in Jack's. Addison's brain showed two major contusions to the front and right sides.

A huge weight pressed down on my chest. I forced my breathing to be steady and controlled.

"What is she doing? Is it working?" Dr. Wellington asked. The natives were getting restless.

I kept my eyes shut tight. It was decision time. I had seen the brains. I had no idea if I could heal or even help any of them. Or what would happen to me if I did.

"Remember who she's cloned from. Who knows what she's doing," Cathy said with enough sarcasm to practically break my concentration. "It goes against my better judgment to even allow her here."

"She's never tried this. Give her time." Seth was a walking contradiction. One minute he reminded me that I had no choice but help his sister, and in the next, he protected me. Still, I feared what his reaction would be when I failed to bring his sister out of the comatose state—when he no longer needed me.

I blocked them all out and concentrated. If I had any hope of staying alive, I was going to have to give them something they wanted. If I had any hope of escaping, I had to go against the beliefs and values I'd held firmly for most of my life.

Did I have to do it their way? Was there another way? I may have been created with a purpose, but I also had a choice. I would find a way to accept my fate and use it for good. Or I would die trying.

I blocked everything out of my head. All sounds. All smells. All visions. Except for Jack and Addison. More specifically, I brought up their brains like I was viewing them on an X-ray reading machine.

Then I honed in on the many receptors inside Jack's head, all coated with a substance—a drug—designed to make him sleep and block me out. With my mind, I flushed that substance out of his brain, through his body and into his stomach. There, like bad shrimp, it churned until it had to be expelled.

Jack's breathing changed from a slow constant to a more rapid inhale and exhale. Even though I kept my eyes shut, I heard the sound of liquid hitting the bed and the floor in front of him as he projectile-vomited everywhere.

Cathy shrieked.

"Ugh!" Kyle shouted.

Jack gasped for breath. "What the hell?" I suppressed a smile.

The smell hit me, playing with my own gag reflexes.

Tightness began to creep up the back of my neck. A slow fire ignited at the base of my head. I felt woozy. Similar to how I've always felt when I mindspeak, but amplified.

Once again, I shut out everything in the room that didn't matter. If I had any hope of doing what I needed to do, I had to concentrate.

I entered Addison's brain having no idea how to help her. I only knew I had to try. Like Jack's, the receptors inside Addison's brain were coated with a substance that I assumed kept her securely in a coma while the rest of her head injuries slowly healed.

Thinking that Addison might not survive the violent throwing up I had just put Jack through, I decided I would bypass doing anything with the foreign substance keeping Addison safely in sleep.

Instead, I focused on the contusions, massaging the larger one with my mind and willing the indentation to the brain matter outward.

The outer rim of her brain began to transform and smooth over. The contusion had all but disappeared when the throbbing pain behind my eyes worsened.

I swayed. I reached out a hand and steadied myself on the bed beside me. I wasn't sure I could keep going.

"What is going on here? Why is Lexi here, Seth?" Jack's voice broke through my concentration. "Lexi, what are you doing?"

"You can't stop her now," Cathy said. "You'll kill her."

"How can you be sure this won't kill her anyway?"

"A risk we had to take." I heard the frigid temperature of Cathy's words.

I tried again to shut out their voices.

Lexi, can you hear me? You don't have to do this.

I did though. I couldn't stop now. Jack was going to help me escape tonight and leave him here. He never would have asked me to heal this innocent little girl who was like a sister to him.

Now, he wouldn't have to.

When I was nearly certain I wouldn't collapse from the throbbing in my head or the dizziness, I got to work on the second contusion. Though smaller on the surface, it ran deeper. The tissue beneath the surface was a dull gray color. Still, I managed to nurse the injury while fighting the increasing feeling of nausea and blocking out the voices in the room.

Slowly the concave area of the brain pushed out. The tissue gradually took on a healthier color, similar to the perfection of Jack's brain.

The pain behind my eyes grew in intensity. I gripped the sheet on the bed beside me.

"Lexi?" Jack's voice was like a soothing drug.

Skin brushed against my arm. My eyes sprang open. Jack's dark blue eyes were the first things I saw. The room tilted. The walls seemed to close in. I stepped backwards to catch my balance and bumped into a rolling cart. I reached for Jack, but missed him completely as my eyes went fuzzy.

Both hands grabbed at air as I slowly fell backwards. Jack reached for me, his eyes wide. It was too late. I collapsed to the floor.

Jack kneeled beside me. I stared up at him. "What are you feeling? What hurts? Do you feel sick?"

I blinked once. Twice. Too many questions. My head was an exploding inferno. I grabbed on to his soaked shirt and pulled him to me. His ear to my mouth. "I did it," I whispered. "I healed the damage to her brain."

He pulled back. Instead of relief and happiness, his face registered alarm. His eyes were huge. He gripped my shoulders with each hand.

I opened my mouth to say something else, but the words did not come. His face grew fuzzier until the entire room faded to black.

~~~~

My eyes fluttered open. I stared up at a white, tiled ceiling. I turned my head. I was still on the floor.

"Lexi, can you hear me?"

The voice. I recognized it from recent dreams. I placed my palms on the cold floor and pushed myself up. I fully expected to see the faceless Smoking Man. Instead, I saw Kyle. I reminded myself that Kyle was not Smoking Man.

I focused on Kyle's dark brown eyes. Was I dreaming?

Instead of cigarettes, I smelled something worse. I crinkled up my nose, and looked around. A disgusting yellowish-brown
~~~~

substance covered the bed Jack had been lying in and the floor around it.

Dr. Wellington lay sprawled on the floor. Out cold, it appeared. Cathy was lying in a fourth bed beyond Sandra.

"What happened?" I asked Kyle.

"Cathy tried to inject you with something after you didn't heal Sandra, but Jack turned it on her. She'll be out for a while."

"And Dr. Wellington?"

"I punched him."

Jack had Seth in a stranglehold, pushed up against the wall on the other side of the room. "You promised you'd get her out of here." His forearm pressed into Seth's neck.

"I couldn't," Seth choked out. "You of all people know why."

"Jack," Kyle said, "Jack, we have to go. I can't keep this up forever."

"Keep what up?" I asked, confused.

Kyle reached a hand to me. He pulled me to stand. My legs felt funny. Weak and tingly. Like they were asleep.

I pushed my fingers into my thigh and barely felt it.

Jack let Seth go, and Seth just turned and stared at us, rubbing his neck where Jack had been pressing. Surprisingly, he seemed to forgive Jack immediately. "I'll give you as much time as I can, but you need me here on the inside. Cathy and Roger need to trust me."

Jack crossed the room. He reached to brush hair out of my face and tucked the strands behind my ears. "Can she hear me?"

Strange question. Why would he ask that?

"Ask her."

He raised a brow at me. I nodded. My head felt strange. Tingly like my legs.

"She's unconscious," Kyle said. "But I think I can direct her well enough to get us out of here."

"Can you run?"

I shrugged.

"I need you to run. If we have any hope of escaping, you need to run."

Not giving me any more time to deliberate, he grabbed my hand and pulled me through the door. The hallway was long and white, like before. Very much like the first dream I ever had with Jack in it. The night my dad was killed.

We ran together in that dream, too.

This time, Kyle followed close behind.

When we reached the top of the stairs, we took a hard turn to the right toward the parking lot.

"She left her backpack around here somewhere. We need it," Jack said to Kyle.

I turned. No one followed us. Not even Seth.

"It's behind the bush over there," I mumbled and pointed with my finger to where I knew we would find the bag.

Jack looked at me strangely, then at Kyle. "Are you sure she's asleep?"

"Positive. She's not the only one designed to see inside people's brains. She's in a state of non-rapid eye movement, slow-wave sleep."

We jogged toward the bush. The campus seemed too quiet. My peripheral vision was slightly fuzzy.

"Will she do anything you tell her to do right now?"

Kyle didn't answer. They were talking about me like I wasn't even there. So, I was asleep?

Finally, Kyle did answer. "No. I don't think I could get her to hurt herself or others. But I could lead her anywhere I wanted her to go."

"Like the night she jumped into the ice-cold swimming pool and forgot how to swim?" Jack glared at Kyle.

"Jack..." Kyle stood with me while Jack rummaged behind the bush and came back out with my pack. "That wasn't me."

Jack dusted off the backpack and tossed it over his shoulder. "You understand why I'm having trust issues right now. Someone with a similar ability tried to kill her. If not you, then who?"

"I'll do what I can to earn your trust. We need each other. And we'll figure out who's inside her head."

"I'm counting on that."

Jack reached for my hand again. Just as his fingers wrapped around mine, a loud, whirring noise sounded. An alarm. My hands flew to my ears.

Both boys turned toward the noise. "Crap," Jack said. "We have to hurry." He looked at me. "You hear me? I want you to run as fast as you can."

Instead of heading into the parking lot, we took off toward the stables. We ran along the edge of the barn to the far side then darted into the woods behind it, very close to the spot where Jack had found me sneaking back into Wellington after discovering him at Addison's hospital bedside.

I did as I was told and ran. Trees passed by us at rapid speed. I stumbled several times, but Jack steadied me.

Something tugged at the back of my mind. We couldn't go much further, but I didn't know why.

Then I saw it. The electric fence.

I pulled on Jack's hands. "We can't. It's turned on."

"She's right," Kyle said. "I can hear the buzz."

Flashlights darted through the trees behind us. Dogs barked. We were being chased. It felt real, but at the same time, I still thought I might wake up from a nightmare any second.

Jack pulled his phone out of his back pocket. After dialing, he brought the phone to his ear. "We're here." He stared at the fence, into darkness.

Through the shrubbery on the other side, toward the road, I heard the motor of heavy machinery followed by the sound of limbs crackling and small trees crunching. Bright headlights became a spotlight on the three of us, coming straight for us. I gasped.

Jack pulled me further to the right. I looked behind us at the approaching flashlights. The sound of barking dogs rose above the commotion of the tractor.

It reached the fence and plowed right through. Sparks flew as the tractor slammed into and tore down the fence.

Voices erupted behind us. "I see them. Stop!"

"Let's go," Jack said to me. "Watch your step."

Flashlights lit our path by people whose faces remained hidden to me.

"Jack, I'm not sure how much longer I can keep Lexi in this state." Kyle stepped lightly behind us. "I'm starting to lose her. And my vision is getting weaker."

"What do you mean?" Jack's grip tightened around my hand. "What will happen?"

"She'll fall deeper into sleep. Uh..." Kyle hesitated. "She'll just collapse, I guess. And I'll go blind."

"Shit. Why didn't you tell me this?" Jack squeezed my hand. "Look at me, baby. We have to hurry, okay?" I nodded. "Step only on grass and dirt. Avoid the wires. They're live."

I still couldn't see the faces behind the flashlights lighting our path to the other side.

I stepped on grass just like instructed. I swayed slightly. My head started to go a little fuzzy. "Jack?"

He turned to me. "Hang on, Lexi." He steadied me and led me across the wires. "Five more steps."

"I'm losing her," Kyle yelled behind me.

My vision became weaker. My legs went numb. My equilibrium was off. I reached out my free hand, grabbing for air.

"Jack, catch her."

I stuck a leg forward. Leaned closer to the other side. Two more steps. "Jack!" I screamed out. My feet were leaden; my body was falling like a chopped down tree.

I felt a hand on my opposite arm. Jack leaped in front of me, then took me with him. I soared through the air, over the rest of the electrical fence.

We landed with a hard thud on the other side of the fence. Jack's body cushioned my fall. He coughed like the air had been knocked out of him.

I lifted my head briefly. My fingers grazed the outline of his jaw. His lips. His face came in and out of focus. "You're always there to catch me," I whispered just before I drifted away.

THIRTY-FIVE

Voices entered my consciousness in hushed tones.

"She's going to be fine," a female voice said.

"You don't know that." Jack's voice was a bit raspy. "Why won't she wake up?"

"She will. It hasn't been that long."

"It's been almost two days." His voice sounded louder this time.

Two days?

"Why don't you go take a shower? I'll stay with her."

I recognized the voice. It was Georgia. The African-American girl with crazy eye shadow from the bar where Jack's band played. That seemed like a lifetime ago.

"No. I'm not leaving."

I felt a drop of warm moisture land on my hand. Jack sniffled loudly.

"I'm going to help with dinner. Everyone's going to be hungry." There was a long pause. Then, from further away, Georgia said, "Does she know?"

Know what?

Jack must have given her a look because she continued. "Does she know about Fred, Jonas, and me?"

"No. Never really got a chance to tell her."

I heard the sound of footsteps and a door closing. I willed my eyelids up. They were so heavy.

Jack scooped my hand into his. "I should have told you everything the minute I met you. Or when you figured out we were part of the cloning project." The weight of Jack's head pressed down on my hand. "I had so many chances to tell you everything. I thought running would be better for you."

I wiggled the fingers of my other hand. Then I tried my toes. I wanted to reach for Jack, but failed at lifting my hand. I wanted to tell him I forgave him. He was here now.

I would never let him push me away again.

"How can I tell you the rest now? After what you did for me?" *Please wake up.*

I am awake.

Jack lifted his head away from the hand he squeezed and gasped. "Open your eyes."

I'm trying. I can't. I'm so tired.

How are you feeling?

I've been better.

"Why did you do it? Why did you heal Addison?" he practically sobbed.

For you.

Jack sucked in a labored breath and let it out slowly. *I thought you might die.*

Is she okay?

"Seth is working on it," he said. "Hopefully, he'll get her moved before Cathy and others figure out what you did."

What do you mean? If Seth knew what I did, he'd be coming for me.

"Oh, Lexi. If they figure out that you have the powers they hoped you would have, they will stop at nothing to find you. I'm still not even completely sure who "they" is. But since Addison is still in a coma..."

We're safe for now? I didn't believe that for one second.

"I have to go back to Wellington." He laid his head on my chest.

No. I squeezed my eyes tight. Slowly, I was able to lift my hand and place it on his head. I ran my fingers through his hair. *You can't.*

"I was never supposed to leave. But I had to get you out."

My eyes fluttered open and I found his dark blue eyes with mine. I didn't want to argue with him. Not now. Not yet.

"Did I ever tell you my favorite color?" He pressed his lips to my hand.

I shook my head.

"It's the strange, beautiful color of the ocean. A deep, emotional green. The color of your eyes. They change color at times, you know?"

"What color are they right now?" My voice sounded hoarse from no use.

He narrowed his gaze. "The color of a raging sea."

"You're not going back to Wellington."

"Not tonight. But I have to tomorrow."

I pressed my head back, hard into the pillow, and breathed deeply.

Jack pleaded his case. "Cathy will take Addison off the feeding tube and coma-inducing drugs if I don't. Then she'll know. All it takes is one MRI, and they'll know what you did. But if I go back alone..."

"They'll leave her under and not suspect," I finished for him. "As long as you cooperate long enough to get her moved."

"And we'll fake her death and hide her away."

He made it sound so easy for a person to assume a new identity. "Oh, well, yeah. Just pretend to kill her. No big deal. Then it's happily-ever-after. Just like you were hoping for me."

"Don't do that. You know we don't have a choice. They'll force you to heal Sandra... and next time... What you did could have killed you. I won't lose you."

"We do have choices." I could still run. *We* could still run, before Seth comes after me like he promised. Why did Jack not see that Seth would stop at nothing to have me heal his sister, our creator? "You can choose not to shut me out again."

"Can we talk about this later? There's something else I'd rather do now." A sneaky grin crept up on his face.

Because I was too tired to argue right then, I snaked my hand around his neck and brought his head closer. His lips tapped mine, teasing at first. Once. Twice. Then they closed over my lips with a need I had not felt from him before.

When he finally broke away, I pulled back the covers and he crawled in and held me as we both slept.

~~~~

When I woke again, I realized I had no idea where I was. I felt better. Not one-hundred percent, but better. Jack was not in the room.

I slipped out of the bed and made my way across the room. As soon as I opened the door, I heard voices. They got louder as I walked down a hallway toward a light at the end. I was in some sort of modest ranch house.

"You can't be serious," Georgia was yelling. "I, for one, am not setting foot on Wellington's campus. Not after what you've
~~~~

just told me. Have you forgotten the state you brought your girlfriend here in? You really think she'll go back there?"

"No. I don't want her anywhere near that place." Jack spoke with certain finality.

"Oh, but you'd subject your other friends to their freakishly controlling ways? They had an electric fence put around the school, Jack. What kind of non-prison facility does that?"

I padded lightly into the kitchen. Georgia and Kyle turned toward me. Jack opened his mouth to say something, but stopped himself. "Please, don't let me interrupt," I said. "You were telling Georgia how you were planning to keep me away from Wellington." I looked around for something to drink.

Reading my mind, Jack walked to a cabinet and pulled down a glass for me. After fixing me some ice water, he stepped behind me and slid his arms around my waist as he kissed my neck. "How are you feeling?"

"Better." I eyed the others. "So, real names?"

Georgia, Jonas and Fred looked back and forth from each other. Jonas stepped forward. "We're exactly who you think we are. We go by Georgia, Fred, and I'm Jonas. Our real names are dead to us." They were the other three cloned from the original test group. They made up the rest of the seven.

"And I see you've met Kyle." I nodded at him. "Thank you for your part in getting me out of there. Seeing okay?"

"You're welcome and yes, I am now. Glad to see you up and around."

"The only one missing is Briana." I sipped my water and eyed each of them before I turned to Jack. "What's the plan? When do we go get her? And Danielle? And expose Cathy and Dr. Wellington for the monsters they are?"

The others all shifted. Georgia crossed her arms. She looked different without all the dark makeup from the first night I met her. As did Fred without the guyliner.

"It's not that easy." Jack intertwined his fingers with mine and pulled me closer. He stretched an arm around my shoulders and pulled me into a tight hug. "Seth called while you were showering. Cathy wants to make a deal with us."

I tried to pull away, but Jack held on tight. "What kind of deal?" I mumbled into his chest.

"He didn't say, but Seth and Cathy both think that the IIA is behind your father's death. And they think that if the IIA killed Peter, there's nothing stopping them from killing a clone that knows more than he or she should. Especially if they think for one second that someone has evidence to expose them."

I pushed against Jack's chest. This time he let me, but his severe eyes locked onto mine. "Which is why they think we'll seek refuge at Wellington?" And they'd have me right where they had wanted me all along—inside The Program.

Jack nodded.

The IIA did not try to drown me in your pool.

I know. I thought of that. Jack ran his hand through his hair. From the looks of it, he'd done that quite a bit.

I turned and eyed each of them—Kyle, Georgia, Jonas, and Fred. The only one missing from the original seven was Briana. According to Dad's spreadsheet, there were more clones, but they were all younger. There were only seven in the original test group.

Since I didn't believe Briana had tried to kill me the night I went to the bar with Jack... And I didn't think she was capable of drowning me... Someone in this room tried to send me to my grave early. Quite possibly, someone in this room murdered my father.

Jack stepped behind me again and slid his arms around my waist.

Georgia spoke first. "Look, I know you both feel comfortable that Cathy isn't trying to kill us, but come on..."

"She's a controlling freak," Fred said. "If it weren't for Seth, I'd have run long ago."

Jonas laughed. A low rumble vibrated in his throat as he shook his head. "Jack, if you think for one second your mom and dad, not to mention Seth and Sandra Whitmeyer, are going to keep us all safe from the IIA, you've lost your mind. They aren't concerned for our safety."

"We're all tired," Georgia said. "Let's sleep on it. Nothing is going to be decided tonight. Fred, I'm sleeping in your room. You can show Kyle the basement." She turned to us and smiled warmly. "You two can keep my room."

I looked down at my hands, suddenly embarrassed by what that suggested.

Everyone dispersed after that, obviously exhausted and grumpy.

Jack gripped my hand tightly as he led me back down the hallway. He pulled me into the room I had been sleeping in. It was a very nondescript room. Nothing decorated the walls. The only color came from the lavender down comforter on the bed. I was probably the only one who wasn't tired.

Jack turned, dropping my hand, and reached his fingers to brush the sides of my face. "I don't want to make you uncomfortable. I also don't want to leave you alone. Not while someone is getting inside your head."

I nodded, suddenly bashful.

"I'll sleep on the floor. If someone tries to lead you from this room, you'll have to trip over me to get out."

Jack grabbed a pillow off the bed and tossed it on the floor.

I grabbed his arm, stopping him from continuing. He stood close, looked down at me. His warm breath feathered across my face. My knees went weak. "Will you hold me at least until I fall asleep?" I asked.

He grabbed me in a hug and lifted me off my feet. "I will hold you for as long as you'll let me."

"You think we're okay here? You trust those guys out there?"

"I know what you're thinking. You think one of them is inside your head. We don't know that. But that's why I'm sleeping in here."

I wrapped my hand around his neck and into his hair, then leaned down and kissed the spot below his ear. "If I had run, how would you have found me?"

Jack walked me over to the bed and lowered me onto the mattress. He pulled back the covers allowing me to slip in. He crawled in beside me and pulled me close—my back to his chest—and held me. He kissed me softly on my neck and whispered, "I will always find you."

~~~~

Jack slept soundly. Unfortunately, I was not tired after sleeping the past two days. I rolled over in his arms and watched him. I studied the lines of his eyes, his long eyelashes,
~~~~

his nose. Listened to the even rhythm of his breathing. I wanted to run my fingers along the smooth texture of his lips.

The night of the gala did not go as I expected. Even now, I knew deep down something could still separate us if he was to return to Wellington and I didn't.

I couldn't help but wonder what Danielle and Briana knew about what had happened after the gala. It had been a Friday night. Danielle was used to me disappearing for the weekend. But did she know something had happened? That there was more to the extra security around Wellington? I'd text her tomorrow. And tell her what?

After I breathed in the scent of Jack's shampoo one more time, I decided I needed a drink of water or something. I slipped from under Jack's arm, gently replacing the comforter up around his neck. He rolled over and burrowed further into sleep.

The hallway creaked as I walked toward the kitchen of the unfamiliar house. I wondered where everyone else slept. Georgia said she was sleeping in Fred's room. Or was it Jonas'? Maybe the guys were sleeping in the basement.

I entered the kitchen. A small light was on over the stove in an otherwise dark room. Everything seemed calm. Normal. Eerily so. An uncomfortable chill crept across the back of my neck.

I heard the distant sound of music—the faint sound of a guitar or two. I padded slowly over to a door. Mini-blinds hung on a window. I peered through them and saw a small fire on what looked like a patio or deck.

The metal blinds rattled when I turned the knob and pulled. I stepped outside where Fred was playing guitar and singing. Kyle sat in an Adirondack chair, listening.

Jonas simply held his guitar, his arms draped over the instrument.

All three sat around a fire pit. The temperature was chillier than it had been just last week.

In his hand, Jonas held a cigarette. Slowly, he lifted it to his mouth and took a drag. The fire at the end brightened, and I flinched as if a firecracker had exploded in my face.

Kyle looked over at me. "Lex, trouble sleeping?"

I jerked my head toward Kyle, ignored his question, then looked back at Jonas. At the cigarette in his hand.

A slow grin stretched across his face. "Have a seat, Lexi. Join us."

I stepped slowly and deliberately around the fire pit and stood next to Kyle. My heart raced. The breeze carried the stench of cigarette smoke to me, and memories of jumping in the freezing swimming pool flooded back.

After pulling another long drag, Jonas flicked the butt in a high arc to land at my feet. He stood and stepped toward me. After grinding the last of the burning stick into the ground, he looked up at me with a grin that made the tiny hairs on the back of my neck crawl. "I should be more careful. These things can be deadly."

His dark stare seized hold of my body and mind. Sparks from the fire only inches away reflected off of his brown eyes in glints of amber.

Suddenly, I felt his presence inside my head. I could not erect a wall quickly enough. It was as if I was inside a memory. A dream.

I was back inside the girls' locker room at Wellington. Lockers opened and closed. Lights magically shut off. My pulse sped up as I ran into Jack, and pain shot through my arm.

The scenery shifted, and I was running through the grass toward Jack's home and into Jack's arms. I turned, but the figure I ran from had vanished.

"It was you," I whispered, searching his cold eyes. "Were you there?"

The pool. It was so cold. The water covered my head. I floated in darkness. I couldn't breathe. Even now, I tried to inhale and failed.

I fell to the ground, coughing on my hands and knees. I gasped for air.

Jonas held out a hand, and having no control over my own body, I slid my hand into his and allowed him to help me up. He turned me around to face Kyle. Sliding a hand around my waist, he pulled me close, my back to his chest in an intimate hold I was not comfortable with but could not stop.

"Kyle," he said softly. "Stand up and stick your hand in the fire."

I jerked, but Jonas's grip on my body was tight. I tried to speak, but I was somehow silenced.

Kyle stood and walked zombie-like to the fire. I wanted to stop him. Scream out to him. I was powerless. I tried to speak to him with my mind. Nothing. I jerked again and tried to wiggle from Jonas's hold.

"Shhh," Jonas whispered in my ear. "You can't stop it. But you have to see."

A tear leaked slowly out the corner of one of my eyes as Kyle got closer. He lifted an arm and reached his hand slowly toward the flames. His fingers reached through the flames. His face reddened from the heat. Beads of sweat formed along his hairline. But he did not flinch from the burn.

"Kyle, man, what are you doing?" Fred screamed behind us.

Jonas whipped around, taking me with him. "Fred, go back to playing. You did not see Kyle stick his hand in the fire." He turned me again. I watched Kyle in fear. "Kyle, go sit down. Tomorrow, you will share how you clumsily threw a log on the fire and accidentally burned your hand."

Kyle sank back into his chair like nothing had happened.

I thought about the fire alarm at the dorms. How Gram had morphed into Smoking Man, and how the figure had pointed a gun at my face.

I thought about how I had practically drowned. "You want to kill me?"

Jonas released me. I turned and backed away. He lowered his chin, peering down on me. "You will know my intentions when the time is right."

"Did you kill my father?"

A low rumble of laughter rumbled in his throat. Ignoring my question and rocking back on his heels, he said, "You're the key to our future. All I want is to prevent our creators from controlling us—starting with you." Stepping closer, he reached a hand and traced the line of my cheekbone.

I tried to recoil from his touch, but it was futile. Part of my brain was convinced I enjoyed the brush of his fingers. The other part busied itself with constructing barriers to block him out. But his presence was too deeply imbedded. I couldn't even call out to Jack.

"Did you run Jack and me off the road?"

He shook his head. Finally, an answered question. So, I tried again. "Did you kill my father."

"No, Lexi, I did not kill your father."

"But you want to kill me?"

"I want to control you."

A chill moved down my spine as the muscles in my back tightened at his words. "I don't understand. What do you want from me?"

"I want you to go back to bed. Forget that we had this talk tonight." He placed a hand on my waist and pulled me closer, not all that gently. "Tomorrow, you will look at me differently. You'll have a need for me you won't be able to explain."

I tried to push Jonas away with my mind. Then with my hands.

He leaned in close. His breath on my face. His voice next to my ear. "Go back to bed, Lexi. Curl up next to Jack and forget that I'm the one that's inside your head."

~~~~

Jack was warm. I slid between the sheets and curled up against his back.

I had lost so much. But here I was next to the man who kept me safe. *Home.*
~~~~

Jack shifted. He rolled over, facing me. His arm snaked around my waist. His breathing changed; his eyes fluttered open.

"You okay?" he whispered.

I nodded, feebly.

"Can't sleep?"

I hadn't been sleeping, had I? My thoughts were scattered like I had lost time. Maybe I had drifted in and out of consciousness. Confusion clouded my memory of the last hour.

My future seemed so uncertain. *I'm nervous about tomorrow,* I admitted. And something else disturbed the back of my mind, but I couldn't bring it to the front.

Some sort of danger teetered on the edge of comfort and restlessness.

Jack feathered his fingers along my hairline. *Release that worry for now. You're safe.*

Staring into Jack's warm gaze, my body relaxed. My mind followed. Whatever it was that hovered there in my psyche, causing immeasurable anxiety, dissipated.

He leaned in and kissed my forehead, his lips lingering against my skin. *You're home. Wherever I am, you're home.*

ACKNOWLEDGEMENTS

First, thank you, God, for allowing me to wake every day with renewed hope, peace, and purpose.

Second, I want to thank my husband for not laughing at me when I told him I wanted to write a book and for not laughing at me when I told him I wanted to write a second book after I wrote that horrible first book. Mike is my biggest cheerleader and my biggest fan. I thank him for his undying, unwavering support and for encouraging me to pursue my dreams no matter how long it takes. Also, he did most of the work on that killer cover.

I'm grateful to my children for understanding when I sometimes choose an hour of writing over watching a movie or playing Wii.

Thank you, Jessica Patch and Laura Pauling, for reading my manuscript and giving me that honest feedback every writer needs. I don't know if I would have finally published this manuscript if it hadn't been for endless texts of encouragement from Jessica or the numerous back and forth emails and phone calls about formatting and publishing from Laura.

Thank you, Stephanie Lott, for excellent copy editing. Every writer needs editing, and Stephanie's service was money well-spent.

I want to thank the members of my book club who volunteered to read my manuscript for typos and provided me additional encouragement to "Get that book out there already!"

Finally, I'm thankful for the many writers and bloggers who have encouraged me along the way. Without the support of others on this journey, the writing life would be unbearable at times.

ABOUT THE AUTHOR

Heather Sunseri was raised on a tiny farm in one of the smallest towns in thoroughbred horse country near Lexington, Kentucky. After high school, she attended Furman University in Greenville, South Carolina, and later graduated from the University of Kentucky with a degree in accounting. Always torn between a passion for fantasy and a mind for the rational, it only made sense to combine her career in accounting with a novel-writing dream.

Heather now lives in a different small town on the other side of Lexington with her two children and her husband, Mike, the biggest Oregon Duck fan in the universe. When she's not writing or working as a CPA, she spends her time tormenting her daughter's cat, Olivia, and loving on her son's Golden Retriever, Jenny. *MINDSPEAK* is her first published novel.

Heather would like to thank readers for joining her on Lexi's and Jack's journey as they search for purpose and ways to turn unfortunate circumstances into good. She is working feverishly on the next novel in the Mindspeak series. She would love to hear from you. You can connect with her in several ways:

Heather Sunseri
P.O. Box 1264
Versailles, KY 40383

Web site: http://heathersunseri.com
Blog: http://heathersunseri.com/blog/
Email: heather@heathersunseri.com
Facebook: http://www.facebook.com/heathersunseri.writer
Twitter: @HeatherSunseri

And be sure to sign up for **Heather's newsletter – A Piece of My Mind** – at http://heathersunseri.com/newsletter in order to receive the latest news about the Mindspeak series.

Made in the USA
Middletown, DE
20 September 2021

48595908R00236